AF450139

PLAYING IT CLOSE

LONDON LEGENDS RUGBY CLUB

KAT LATHAM

Playing It Close (London Legends #2)

By Kat Latham

Published by Agony and Hope Publishing

Groningen, Netherlands

www.KatLatham.com

Copyright © 2014 Kat Latham

First published 2014

Republished 2021

All rights reserved. No portion of this book may be reproduced in any form without permission from the publisher, except as permitted by U.S. copyright law. For permissions contact:

kat@katlatham.com

This is a work of fiction. Names, characters, places, and incidents either are the products of the author's imagination or are used fictitiously. Any resemblance to actual persons, living or dead, businesses, companies, events, or locales is entirely coincidental.

Cover by Lee Hyat Designs

Cover photograph: copyright © Elovich/Shutterstock

Back cover photograph: copyright © peepo/iStock

Ebook ISBN: 9789083154015

Print ISBN: 9789083154008

For Doodle Bug, who was born when I was 17,000 words away from writing The End. Writing became so much harder when my other option was marveling at you all day long.

And for my parents, who practically shoved me out the door so I could finish this book...and so they could marvel at Doodle Bug all day long. Thank you for all of your support.

ACKNOWLEDGMENTS

I owe thanks, hugs and wine to the following people:

My friends, for answering all of my random questions about British vocabulary. And especially to David, who gave me the phrase "banana hammock."

Arthur Tanner, for answering my many rugby questions.

Johanna Lopez Trimarchi, for describing Venezuelan food to me.

Sarah Oughton, Elise Rome, Moriah Densley and Suzanne Johnson for reading early versions of this story and giving me honest and encouraging feedback.

My awesome editor, Deb Nemeth, whose patient and thorough editing has helped me become a much stronger and more confident writer.

My agent, Laura Bradford, for helping me develop this story.

The readers who gave me such incredible encouragement when my debut novel came out, which gave me the strength I needed to finish writing this book.

My parents, for the countless hours of free babysitting while I worked.

And Tim, who, even though he had deadlines of his own, stayed up late several nights to give me feedback that made this a much stronger story. You will always be my favorite rugby player.

AUTHOR'S NOTE

There are a few words and phrases that might be unfamiliar to readers who don't speak British English.

In the UK, *pants* are underwear. You wear trousers over your pants.

An *aubergine* is an eggplant and *courgettes* are zucchini.

Sarky is British slang for sarcastic.

Something with elastic in it is *elasticated*, not elasticized.

A *leaving do* is a goodbye party, usually thrown by your colleagues on your last day of work (sometimes the night before your last day, which is dangerous when there's alcohol involved and you have to face your colleagues the next day).

The City of London (also known as the City and the Square Mile) is where London's financial services industry has historically been based. The term is also used to refer to the financial services in general, much like Wall Street is both a place and a general term.

When talking about dates, Brits will sometimes use ordinal numbers (e.g. first, second, third, etc.) for both the day and the month. For example, *the first of the third* would be the first day of the third month, or March first.

In British English, collective nouns (i.e. a noun that refers to a group of individuals, such as *family* and *team*) are plural because they're composed of more than one person. That's why you'll see phrases like *my family are* and *England are*—when referring to the England rugby team, not the country—instead of *my family is* and *England is*. I know it looks like a typo if you're not used to it, but it's not.

Brits often refer to *sport* in the singular (*I don't watch much sport*) and *maths* in plural (*I'm great at maths*).

Lastly, Brits don't use the word *gotten* (as in, *I have gotten used to explaining British English*). They use *got* instead.

RUGBY FOR THE UNINITIATED

You should be able to read (and, I hope, enjoy!) this book without knowing anything about rugby. But if you want to find out more about the world's greatest sport, here's a glossary of terms for you.

Rugby union: Over 100 years ago, the sport of rugby split into two types—*rugby union* and *rugby league*—with each developing its own rules and governance. I write about rugby union.

Kit: uniform

Pitch: the playing field

Touch: the out-of-bounds area around the pitch. The *touch line* separates the playing area from the out-of-bounds area.

Kick into touch: to kick a ball out of bounds, a common way of ending a rugby match. The expression *kicking someone into touch* means breaking up with someone.

Try (as in *scored two tries*): the equivalent of a touchdown in American football, only a player has to place the ball on the ground on or behind the try line in order to score. A try is worth five points.

Try line: the equivalent of the start of the end zone in American football (known as the *in-goal area* in rugby).

Backs and *forwards*: Instead of being divided into offense and defense, rugby positions are made up of *forwards* and *backs*. Forwards tend to be bigger and more aggressive, while backs tend to be faster and more skillful—but I would never say that to a forward's face.

Scrum: A scrum is a way of restarting a match. The eight forwards from each team bind together, crouch down and slam into the other team's forwards. They try to push the other team back while fighting for possession of the ball with their feet amid much grunting and sweating.

Front row: This refers to the front row of the scrum, comprising three players—the two props and the hooker (which is a rugby position, not a sex worker). The three players in the front row put their arms around each other's shoulders, crouch and collide against the front row of the opposing team, trying to gain ground by pushing the opposition back while the hooker attempts to "hook" the ball with his feet and push it back to his teammates in the second row.

Second row: This refers to the two players in the second row of the scrum—the locks. They are usually the tallest players on the team...and I mean *really* tall.

Back row: You guessed it. This is the back row of the scrum. It's made of three players: the number 8 (that's the name of the position) and two flankers. So in a scrum, each team binds together in three rows, with three players in the front row, two in the second row and three in the back row.

Fly half: One of the busiest positions on a rugby team, and a key decision-maker on the pitch, the fly half has to excel at passing the ball, running and kicking. This is the position Liam Callaghan plays.

Some of the other rugby positions I mention in this book are *scrum half*, *lock*, *open-side flanker* and *tight-head prop*.

The posts: Just like in American football, there are two metal posts connected by a crossbar at each end of the pitch. The posts are sometimes referred to as *the uprights*. A team can score points by kicking the ball over the crossbar and between the posts—three points for kicking a penalty or a drop goal, two points for a conversion after a team scores a try. Kicking is often the fly half's specialty.

Kick a penalty: When one team has done something naughty, the referee might allow the other team a chance to score three points by kicking the ball through the posts.

Capped for England: playing on your country's national team (in this case England's). If a player has been *capped ten times*, it means he or she has played ten games on the England team.

1

___

Warm seawater sliding over naked skin. That's how Tess wanted to end her second night in Venezuela.

She stood on the moonlit shore and gripped the hem of her T-shirt, battling her misgivings as she scanned the beach. No one. She was completely alone. If she pulled the shirt over her head, no one would see that she'd ditched her bikini top in her room and only wore a pair of frilly pink bikini bottoms. No one would see if she slipped those off too.

Her hand relaxed its grip on the soft cotton before fisting it again and inching it up. *Do it.*

But there could be cameras. She scanned the shore from left to right, then turned to face the beachside hotel and did it again. The moonlight shone brightly—too brightly. The journalists who'd hounded her for eight months wouldn't even need to use their flash if they wanted a decent picture of the Scourge of the City cavorting naked and alone in the Caribbean. How much would the London tabloids pay for a photo like that?

Enough that she might be tempted to send them one herself.

Idiot. You're at a remote eco-lodge halfway around the world. No one here cares or even knows who you are.

Still...

Resolved, Tess let go of the shirt hem and took determined strides toward the water lapping at the shore. She had five more nights here. Plenty of time for the moonlight to die down. She could wait for a cloudy night—if northern Venezuela experienced such things. Tonight she would simply enjoy swimming lazily through the calm water with her T-shirt protecting her dignity.

Although it was past midnight, the sand was still warm from the strong rays it had soaked up throughout the day. The water cooled Tess's sun-kissed skin as it swirled around her knees, her hips, her waist. She brought her hands over her head and dove in, kicking her feet and pulling her arms back in an underwater breaststroke for as long as she could hold her breath.

Freedom. Under here, no one could touch her. Under here, her life was her own.

After ten minutes of paddling around, she swam for the shore and stepped onto the soft sand. A breeze swept over the sea, chilling her skin, and Tess realized she'd forgotten a towel. If she'd stripped her shirt off before getting into the water, she would have had a dry shirt to put on. Now she was half-naked in a translucent white T-shirt. Fabulous.

She shoved her feet into her sandals, crossed her arms over her chest and rushed through the hotel's beach entrance. *Please let everyone be in bed.*

No such luck. As she entered the lobby, the receptionist was handing a man his room key. *Bugger.* She'd have to walk right past them to get to the stairs. Fortunately the lift was right here. She ducked her head and pressed the up arrow, muttering, "Come on, come on."

"We hope you enjoy your stay, Señor Jones," the receptionist said.

"Cheers, Maria."

Come on come on come on! The lift whirred, dinged and opened. *Yes!* Tess hurried into it and hit the button for the third floor a thousand times, like a hyperactive child on a sugar rush—the kind of child she used to be.

A deep voice called out across the lobby. "Hold the lift!"

Oh, hell no. She pressed the door-close button and let out a sigh as it worked its magic—

A foot jammed itself between the closing doors, followed swiftly by a deep-throated "Fucking hell!" when the doors didn't bounce open automatically but clamped together instead.

No! Tess swallowed her cry of defeat as a pair of very big, very masculine hands braced themselves on the edge of one of the doors and pushed. Hard. Like, Superman hard. Within seconds, the man created enough space to squeeze himself and his travelers' backpack through the gap. When he leaped away from the doors as if they might bite him again, Tess had to press herself against the wall to avoid being flattened.

"Are you crazy?" she yelled as the lift's doors bounced closed behind him. Her voice reverberated around the small space, making the thin walls vibrate behind her back. "You could've been killed!"

A niggle of familiarity passed through her at her first glance at him, but then she noticed he was glaring at her hand. She followed his gaze to find she was still pressing the door-close button. Drawing back her arm, she crossed it with the other one over her chest. "Oops. Wrong button."

"Mentalist," he muttered. He pressed the button for the fourth floor and turned his back to her, dropping the weathered blue backpack from his shoulders. The lift shook from its weight.

Holy mother...his shoulders took up nearly half the airspace in the lift. Tess breathed a silent sigh of relief as the lift jerked and started its ascent. Only a few seconds from now, the doors would reopen and this awkward moment would be behind her —literally, since she was getting off on the floor below his and would have to walk away with her wet T-shirt plastered to her skinny arse. He was so much bigger than her. Why the hell had she yelled at him when he first got into the lift?

Impulse-control: never one of her strong points.

Fortunately, he didn't say anything more. She'd caught his accent. British, like her, he'd probably grown up well versed in how to ignore awkward situations.

The lift chugged, its erratic ascent making her imagine it was a bucket being hoisted upward by monkeys working a rope pulley hand-over-hand. She kept her attention on the buttons, counting them as they lit up, as if they were items on a to-do list that she had to get through before she could escape. First floor —done. Second floor—done. Nearly there—

The lift jerked to a hard halt, making her gasp and brace her hand against the faux wooden wall.

"What the hell?" her companion muttered.

The second- and third-floor buttons were both lit, but the doors didn't open. The man banged his fist on them, as though they were a vending machine that had kept hold of his Snickers bar. "Open up."

"Don't think it can hear you," she said.

Mistake. Her sarky comment brought his attention back to her. She could feel it, even though she kept her gaze firmly trained on the opposite wall, not eager to see whether he was ready to throttle or jump her. For several long seconds, she shivered under his silent scrutiny. The water hadn't been as warm as she'd expected. Fine when you were in it, but stepping into the slight breeze had left her covered in goose pimples...and a couple of pointy parts she was desperately trying to cover with her arms, as if he might not have noticed that she'd left her bikini top in her room.

Damn it. One thing she'd learned from working in a male-dominated office was that she had to stand up for herself. She lifted her head to glare up at him, and the niggle of familiarity exploded into awareness.

No way. No *way*.

Liam Callaghan? Liam Callaghan, rugby's all-time leading points scorer? Captain of London Legends and, more recently, of the England squad? Liam bloody Callaghan? Her father would shit a brick when she told him.

She'd leave out the wet T-shirt part, of course.

He was staring at her too. Or, at least, at her hair. She just barely managed to keep from touching it self-consciously. She'd had a lot of funny looks the past couple of days—not surprising since her hair was currently bubblegum pink. After a second in which he seemed fixated on the horror covering the top of her head, Liam Callaghan turned away as if she wasn't worth acknowledging—a posture she'd got used to during her years working in an industry dripping with testos-terone—and banged on the door again, this time shouting for anyone who might be able to hear them. "Hello? We're stuck in here!"

She tried pushing the third-floor button again. And again. Her finger became more frantic as the doors stayed solidly closed.

"Will you stop that?" he snapped. "That'll make it worse. We're probably stuck in here because you jammed the buttons in the first place."

"Wait, are you accusing me of breaking the lift? Me? When you were the one who forced the doors open?"

His eyes went wide in patent disbelief. "Are you having a

laugh? I wouldn't have had to if you'd held the lift like any decent human being would do."

She stuffed down her annoyance. He obviously had a point, though she would quibble with that *decent human being* bit if she weren't half-naked and locked in a lift with a man who made his living knocking seventeen-stone men to the ground. "Look, let's not waste our time arguing about this. How do we get out of here?"

The question was more to herself than him, and she'd already started scanning the doors, walls and ceiling for any indication of what to do in an emergency. No escape hatch in the ceiling, the way there always was in films. Not that she'd know what to do if he did boost her up there. Maybe convince the monkeys to get back to work? No telephone or emergency call button. No security camera.

"Shit. We're fucked."

"Maybe there's a call button," he said, clearly a few mental steps behind her as he peered closer at the panel.

"There isn't. There's nothing. We're well and truly stuck."

He scanned the ceiling and the corners, then ran his hands down the seam of the closed doors. She waited silently for him to catch up with her. "There's nothing. We're stuck."

Echo much? Saying the words aloud would be a bad idea. Another situation she'd learned how to deal with from working with sexist pigs for seven years. Don't antagonize, and try not to respond. They harassed you because they wanted to see you lose your shit. If you didn't, they'd realize it wasn't much fun and stop doing it.

He beat the doors, and the whole lift shook from the pounding. Without thinking, she grabbed his arm to stop him, immediately tugging her hand back when she felt the power in his biceps. She would need three hands to wrap around them.

"Please don't do that. I'd rather be stuck between floors than plummet down to the ground floor."

"The receptionist said she was going home after she checked me in. Maybe she hasn't left yet. Hello! Maria!" He pounded and yelled some more before giving up with a curse. "Fan-bloody-tastic."

They stood in awkward silence for a few tension-filled moments. Her shivers grew more pronounced. The cool dip had felt invigorating after sweltering all day, but now her body registered not only the slight drop in temperature but also the fact that she might be trapped for hours in this lift with a strange man. A frustrated man. A man she didn't know, and she was quite exposed. More than a chill was making her teeth chatter.

"Are you cold?"

"Mmm-hmm." She rubbed her hands up and down her arms as best she could without exposing her breasts. Her shoulders hunched over, both to hide from him and because the more she thought about it the colder she got.

"Are you kidding? It's sweltering in here."

She gave him a look of pure disbelief. "You might not have noticed, but I'm wearing a little less than you."

One corner of his mouth kicked up. He clearly had noticed, and she braced herself for the smarmy comment that would inevitably follow.

Nothing.

He crouched down and unclipped the cover of his ancient blue backpack, then tugged on the drawstring tab that closed the top of the bag. After rummaging for a few seconds, he pulled out a handful of green cotton. "Dry T-shirt?"

Oh, God, yes please. She took it from him with a grateful smile, and he dug into his bag again. "I've got some trousers in here, too, but I think you'd fit your whole body into one of my trouser legs, so they might not be that useful."

He yanked out a pair of shorts and held them up, eyeing her. "Don't fancy the chances of these staying up, either." He dropped them, went back to the bag, held up a pair of gray cotton boxer briefs, his gaze never straying south of her face even though he was squatting level with her girl parts. "How about a pair of my pants? I promise they're clean."

"Thanks for the offer, but I've only just met you. I don't think it would be appropriate to wear your underpants."

"You're right. Much more appropriate for you to stand there wearing nothing but my T-shirt."

With a resigned sigh, she took the briefs from him and said, "Thank you."

"No, thank *you*." He closed his bag, stood and turned his back to her. "Let me know when you're done."

The tiny lift didn't leave much room for maneuver, but she hurriedly stripped off her sodden shirt and dropped it to the floor with a *plop*. She whipped his shirt over her head. The hem fell halfway to her knees, covering her as she wriggled out of her damp bikini bottoms and tugged his pants on. The elasticated waist wasn't small enough to stay where it should, but fortunately it settled around her hips and seemed like it would stay put. She was drowning in clothes now, and he'd kept his back respectfully turned. A dangerous man wouldn't have done that, or even given her his clothes in the first place—right? Her shoulders relaxed. She rolled them around to ease the tension she'd carried from hunching over. "I'm finished."

He faced her again, quickly assessing her outfit. Sticking out a hand, he said, "I'm Liam...uh, Jones."

She kept her brows from rising at his lie, but just barely. "Hello, Liam Jones. I'm Tess. Tess...Crawley."

What the hell. If he was going to make up a name, she might as well, too, so she chose one from her favorite TV period drama. God knew her name had been splashed all over the papers for the better part of a year. She'd come here to escape the legal minefield she'd thrown herself into headfirst, but it had never occurred to her to make up a new identity, which seemed like an oversight now she thought about it. Hadn't she done everything possible to leave her old life behind and become someone new? She'd gone through two hair colors drastically different than her normal boring brown. She'd spent the past two days exploring the jungle treetops instead of the urban jungle she'd been trapped in her whole life. Yet she hadn't considered traveling incognito. Huh. Tess Crawley. What a novelty.

Liam made a sound of pent-up frustration and stretched his arms above his head, his fingertips scraping the low ceiling. He was quite a bit taller than her, probably nearly six feet to her five foot three. Certainly not one of the biggest players, height-wise. In fact, on TV he was dwarfed by some of his teammates. Then again, he towered over others. Funny thing about rugby, how the players had wildly different body types—from twenty-stone goliaths with no necks to garden gnomes who could dart across the pitch...to gods like Liam Callaghan.

But no, he wasn't Liam Callaghan, and she had to remember that. Everyone deserved privacy, especially when they were on holiday—a lesson she'd recently learned the hard way.

He glanced at his watch. "Maria told me the reception desk opens at six. That's less than five hours from now. You don't suppose someone might arrive early and discover the lift's broken?"

"Could do. I'd bet kitchen staff get here fairly early. The breakfast they prepare is amazing. Must take hours of prep."

A growl rumbled and they both glanced at his stomach.

"Hungry?" she asked.

"Yeah. I ate on the plane, but that was hours ago."

"No snacks in your Mary Poppins bag?"

His face lit up and he practically ripped the poor backpack apart. He dumped several rolled-up items of clothing onto the floor before pulling out a plastic container with a triumphant "Ah-ha!"

She grimaced when he popped it open. "What is that?"

"A little something my housekeeper made me for the journey. Can't believe I nearly forgot about them."

"You have a housekeeper?"

A flicker of awareness crossed his face. He seemed to realize he'd given a piece of himself away and evaded the question. "Homemade energy bars. They look a little worse for the journey, but they're great. Lots of oats, sultanas, wheat germ, honey... want one?"

She shook her head. "You lost me at wheat germ."

"Suit yourself." He sat on the floor and rested against the wall. Too tall to stretch his legs out, he kept them bent and spread wide with his backpack in between, invading her space even more. She peeked into the container again. What might've once been bars had been knocked around so much that they now resembled pale, chunky dirt. He scooped up a handful and squished it into a patty before dropping it into his mouth. His eyes closed as he chewed, and the back of his head thunked against the wall. Light gray shadows clung to the skin below his eyes. His wavy blond hair—always famously tousled—stood practically on end. He looked exhausted...and far too big for this lift.

He grabbed another fistful of the crumbled oat concoction and shoved it into his mouth, sighing in satisfaction. She hadn't realized how hungry she was until the smell of honey hit her. Swimming always made her ravenous. Once he'd swallowed, he glanced up at her with sleepy eyes. "Why don't you sit down? We might be here a while. I'm not used to having to look up to talk to women, and I'm getting a crick in my neck."

She slid down the wall, sat with her knees to her chest to help her warm up, and pulled the bottom of his T-shirt over her naked legs. Her tummy rumbled, but before she could steal another peek at his snack he flung his arm out to silently offer it to her.

"Thanks." She tried to be delicate. Her mother had drilled ladylike table manners into her, which made it difficult to find a way to pick up crumbled, sticky oats without feeling like a slob.

Liam shook his head in clear amusement and reached into the plastic container with his whole hand. "Let me help. Open wide."

She opened her mouth.

"Wider than that, Pinkie."

Just to mock him, she opened as wide as she could and tilted her head back, shocked when he dropped a shower of the mix into her mouth. Pieces of something—hopefully whatever the hell wheat germ was—bounced off her chin and rolled onto the canopy she'd made of his T-shirt between her chest and knees. She closed her mouth and chewed, the sweet taste of honey coating her tongue and making her groan.

"Good, huh?"

She nodded, too lost in nirvana to answer with real words. She'd been hungrier than she thought, and the delicious mix hit her sweet spot. Simple but luscious. Satisfying but leaving her hungry for more. More. She needed more. Her head lolled to the side, her mouth opening and receiving another helping. She savored as she chewed, swallowed and let out a throaty sigh, only realizing how embarrassingly sexual the sound was when she opened her eyes and found Liam staring at her with an expression she couldn't decipher. She self-consciously licked her lips for crumbs, and his fern-green eyes homed in on her mouth with an intensity she'd never been on the receiving end of before. It was the way a starving man would look at a steak, or how she would view a bottle of cabernet at the end of a horrendous work week. Desire and need swirling around each other, rubbing up against each other in a seductive dance. Her temperature spiked as he dragged his gaze away from her mouth and met her eyes with a look bordering between fascination and confusion.

He scooped up another handful of his snack and slowly munched on it. "So, uh...tell me about breakfast."

Okay, maybe she'd misinterpreted that look, reading into it what she wanted to see. Or maybe he had a food fetish. She tried to clear the lusty thoughts clouding her mind. "It's a big spread. Lots of tropical fruit, pineapples, mango and even chunks of fresh coconut. But you can also get the local equivalent of a fry-up—beans, scrambled eggs with onions and tomatoes...ooh, and this thing called *cachapa*, which is like a thick pancake made out of corn with melted cheese in it. It's so delicious."

Their stomachs growled in tandem, and he offered her the container of crumbs again. No longer caring if she made a mess, she squished some together and popped the lump into her mouth. "Swimming always makes me hungry and sleepy."

"That why you went in this late at night? Couldn't sleep?"

"No, not that." But how could she explain that she'd made herself a list of ten things to accomplish on this trip, things she'd never done before and had decided her life wouldn't be complete without giving them a go. Skinny-dipping was number one on the list—still unticked.

His voice dropped, his lips curling in a gently teasing smile. "Let me guess. You were sweltering hot and couldn't take it anymore, so you went down to the beach—fully intending to do the decent thing and just dip your toes in the water. Maybe splash around up to your ankles. But then something came over you. Some wicked yearning to be a bit naughty. So you stripped down to your bikini and jumped in...only when you came up for air, you realized your top had magically disappeared."

She bit back a shiver, forcing her brows to rise in mock censure. "That's some imagination you've got there."

"Not really. It happens in a lot of the movies I watch."

"Oh, right. You watch *those* kinds of movies."

He shrugged. "I won't lie. They've been known to catch my attention when I'm staying at a hotel."

"Stay at a lot of hotels?"

He ignored her. "But that's not what happened, is it? Otherwise your shirt would've been damp but not completely soaked."

"You're putting way too much thought into this. Don't strain yourself."

"Hmm...I'm guessing you waited till the middle of the night because you thought everyone would be asleep. You decided to go for a midnight dip in the lagoon. Clearly you've never seen *Jaws*, or you would've realized what a stupid idea that is. But you wanted to go in, all the way in, and you wanted to feel the water all over you."

Her skin flushed, and suddenly the chill left her body, replaced by a heat that percolated just below her surface. How could he know? Was she that easy to read?

Apparently so, because he watched her closely as he continued. "That's definitely it. You wanted to feel that warm water all over your naked body. Or maybe you just intended to go in topless this first time, work up the courage to skinny-dip another time. Break yourself in slowly. So you left your top upstairs because you knew you'd chicken out if you brought it with you."

The way he described the scene was so close to what actually happened that she felt as if he'd been watching her. He obviously hadn't been. The backpack and tired eyes said he'd just checked in. But his keen attention to detail made her breath catch in her throat.

"Only, your shirt's wet, so I'm thinking you chickened out anyway. Convinced yourself that swimming in the dark water at midnight was adventurous enough for tonight, that you'll do the dirty tomorrow night...or maybe the night after. What happened?"

She swallowed, his intense gaze holding her transfixed. "Too much moonlight. Some of the rooms overlook the lagoon. I didn't want anyone to see me. Not when I'm booked in for another five nights."

"So you'll do it on your last night here?"

"Maybe." That was the idea, anyway. She had to. She never let to-do-list items go unticked.

"You know what you need?"

Yeah, she could think of about a thousand things, and in that moment she was convinced he could provide most of them.

"You need a cove. Somewhere with a bit of privacy, hidden from public view."

Sounded reasonable. Why hadn't she thought of that?

"But that's not really safe, is it? What happens if you get a cramp? Or there's an undertow? Who'll watch out for shark fins popping up in the water behind you? Swimming lesson number one—never swim alone."

She closed her eyes, leaned her head against the wall and let his seductive voice wash over her.

"You need a swim buddy, Pinkie. It's a good thing I'm here. I make an excellent partner in crime."

2

*L*iam wasn't here for an easy hookup. He was supposed to be allowing himself time to heal, and his sports psychologist had specifically forbidden casual sex as a route to emotional recovery. After months of ignoring that advice and finding himself at the bottom of a very dark place, Liam had finally decided to follow his therapist's guidance. Time alone, away from all of the distractions of his career—including women—so he could come to terms with his grief.

But then she'd moaned. *Moaned.* Right there, sitting next to him in a space so small he couldn't have lain down in it. Suddenly all he wanted was to get horizontal and release the energy he hadn't known he had left after that bitch of a flight.

She'd fucking moaned—over an energy bar—and that was all it had taken to turn the lift from stifling to sultry. From claustrophobic to intimate.

And her face...he couldn't describe it. The way she'd gone all soft and happy had drawn his attention away from her unfortunate hair and made him picture all the ways he could bring that satisfied look back.

"You're staring at me."

He blinked. "I am?"

"Yeah. It's creeping me out."

He exhaled a quiet laugh. Well, that settled the question of how attracted she might be to him. No wonder—he'd started sweating buckets from the humidity as soon as he'd stepped off the plane. A full day on planes followed by a three-hour car journey to the hotel meant he probably smelled like he'd just stepped off the rugby pitch. When he'd checked in, all he'd wanted was a shower and a beer, possibly together. Fuck, he'd be less sticky if he bathed in lager.

Focusing on the firmly closed lift doors, he said, "Sorry about that. Better now?"

"Yes, thanks."

He offered her the box of energy crumbs again. "Want some more?"

She was quiet for a second, making him think she considered his offer to include more than just energy bars. It did. Finally, she exhaled a sound full of regret. "I shouldn't."

Interesting. He allowed himself to look at her again. "Why not? Are you...committed to other food products?"

"Uh, no. That's not a problem."

"So, you're not into bars and you're more into...girls?"

She laughed. "Couldn't think of a food you could compare women's bits to?"

"Nothing that wouldn't earn me a punch in the face."

She leaned a little closer and whispered as if she were confessing. "I'm definitely partial to bars."

His heartbeat quickened, pounding blood down low in his belly. "Glad to hear it. So if those aren't problems, what's stopping you from tasting more?"

"It's...complicated."

Normally he would've flirted his way to a more favorable answer, but he understood complicated. Fuck, she didn't even know his real name. Somehow, though, that made her reactions to him all the more tempting. Just once he wanted to know what it was like to be with a woman and know she was there because she wanted *him*, not his money, fame or the exposure that came with him.

Most of his career, he'd been surrounded by women who would've found out which hotel he was staying in, jumped in a pool and manipulated their way into the lift with him, exposing everything they had. He didn't have much experience with women who came from the real world.

The fact that Tess was real made her not only more attractive but also more untouchable. He was used to women who knew the rules. Easy relationships with a bit of arm candy—that was what he and they both wanted. He could be the bit of rough who filled out a suit and made a photogenic escort to actresses' premieres. They could be a pleasant diversion from a career that left no time for anything else...not even the family who needed him most.

He tried to push away the thought of what his mother's final days must've been like, but coming to terms with the grief and guilt was why he was here...his therapist's words, not his. He would've said he was here to get the fuck over it, to erase the haunting memory of what his mum had looked like when he'd finally walked into her hospital room.

His gut clenched, drowning his lust. He needed some conversation quick before the ghosts took shape again. *She's been here a few days already. Ask her what there is to do.*

Bang bang bang.

They both sat up straight. "Did you hear that?"

"Yes," she said, rolling to her knees and rapping her knuckles against the doors. *Bang bang bang.* "Hello? Is anyone out there?"

"*Dios mío—sí!* Yes, I am out here. It's Maria from the reception desk. The repairman is working on the problem. He will—"

The doors slid open as smoothly as they should've done ages ago, revealing that they were stuck between floors. A woman in a knee-length skirt bent over to look at them through the gap, a wrinkle marring the smooth skin between her brows. "Are you all right?"

Liam scrambled to his feet and clasped Tess's hand, helping her off her knees. Relief flooded him—God, he *really* needed a cool shower now—and he pulled her against his chest, pressing his lips against her forehead in a loud, grateful, smacking kiss. She laughed and squeezed him in a quick hug before letting go. "Let's get out of here."

The lift was closer to the third floor than the second, but still there was only about a meter gap between the floor and the top of the lift's door. Liam shoved his clothes back in his backpack before he realized that Tess had grabbed Maria's hand and was preparing to hoist herself out. "Whoa, let me lift you."

She gave him a strange look. "I think we've got it."

Tess braced her free hand on the hotel floor and pushed herself upward at the same time Maria pulled. She went up easily, but Liam cupped his hands around her hips, his thumbs braced under her bum cheeks, and gave her an extra boost. Quite a firm bum, considering how small she was. Nothing skinny about it at all, despite his first impression. She twisted in the air and slid onto the floor before swinging her legs around. Lying in the third-floor hallway, she raised one haughty brow at him. "I told you we had it."

"I know. I'm sure you did. That doesn't mean I should just stand here like a muppet, does it?"

She rolled her eyes. "Hand me your backpack."

"That's all right. I've got it," he teased.

"You *are* a muppet."

He laughed as he shoved his bag through the gap and she set it aside, giving him room to climb to freedom. But when she reached out her hand as if she was going to help yank him out, he stopped laughing. "Now you're definitely kidding."

She gave him an enigmatic shrug. "Maybe."

Ignoring her gesture, he pressed his hands flat against the floor and hoisted himself up. For one glorious moment, he lay on the hallway floor and stretched his arms and legs as far as he could. Fourteen hours in planes, three hours in a car and far too long in a tiny lift...he'd started to wonder whether he'd ever be able to move his whole body again.

Maria chattered nervously, explaining that her manager had called her mobile to say that the lift's alarm had gone off. When she'd told him that a guest had just arrived, he'd called the hotel's handyman, who'd driven in from the village and was now working on the control panel downstairs. Liam didn't give a shit about any of it. He craved hours and hours of time spent horizontally, starting now.

"We are so sorry this happened," Maria said. "Please let me know what we can do to make up for it. We can arrange massages for you or give you a free pass to the spa..."

Liam had never found anyone who could massage him as well as Steven, the team's massage therapist, who had biceps and hands bigger than Liam's. And he didn't quite know what happened at spas, but whenever his past girlfriends had gone to one they'd come home with a lot less hair in certain sensitive areas, so that was out. All he wanted was a bed.

Oh, and one other thing. "Can I have a beer? Draft, not canned."

Maria's eyes widened. "Of course! I have the key to the restaurant. I'll bring your beer in a few minutes. How many would you like?"

"Just one." One was an indulgence anyway. He never drank during the season, and in the off-season he held himself to a couple a week. Some of his teammates arrived at pre-season training looking like tubs of lard, and they had to work extra hard to shed the flab they put on. Not him. He worked his arse off to become constantly better, not to regain what he lost through a month of gluttony.

"And you, *señora?*" Maria asked Tess. "What can we do for you?"

Tess was quiet for a moment, and Liam crunched up so he could see her. She stared off into space and had an adorable *oh-the-possibilities* expression that made him wish he'd asked for something different. Something that would give the two of them more time together. Maybe she'd ask for a beer too. They could drink it in his room and reminisce about the time they were stuck in the lift together.

Finally, a sweet smile touched her lips and she turned her attention to Maria. "Could you tell me if there are any coves around here?"

LIAM HELD AN OLD PHOTOGRAPH. His mum—eighteen years old and on a journey to discover herself—stood in front of the Taj Mahal. She shouldered a big, brand-new blue backpack. Liam dropped the photo on the floor, stepped inside and watched the edges blur as he became part of the scene. Women in colorful saris walked past, but he saw only one woman. Barely a woman. His mum's smile transformed her face from pretty to radiant, the way it had his whole life.

"What are you doing here, cariad?" she asked, her Welsh accent stronger than he remembered. Maybe it softened during those five years she spent in London between this trip and his birth.

"I don't know. Looking for you, I guess. Is Dad here?"

She shook her head. "I haven't met him yet. Come back next week when I'm in Udaipur. I'll share a tuk-tuk with him from the station. You can squeeze in with us and watch him win my heart."

She shifted her weight, and he realized the backpack must be heavy. He stepped behind her and slid it off her shoulders, hoisting it over his own. She tried to stop him. "I can carry that."

"I know you can, Mum, but it's easier for me so let me help you."

She grabbed one of the straps and tried to yank it from his shoulders. "Please give it back. I don't want to burden you, cariad bach."

Frustration swept through him. "Cariad is fine, Mum, but I'm not bach *anymore. I'm not little. I can help you. Just let me."*

But she fought harder until she began to fade away, becoming only a shadow and leaving him aching with regret that he'd wasted their final moments by arguing...

LIAM SLEPT THROUGH BREAKFAST. Hell, he slept through lunch too. By the time he woke up, groggy as if he'd been doped-up on pain meds, the sun was already throwing long shadows across the room. He probably wouldn't even have opened his eyes if his stomach hadn't growled so loudly he thought a pack of dogs had broken into his room.

He stretched, yawned and scratched his belly as he stared at the ceiling fan whirring above his head. The stale taste of beer coated his mouth and he needed another shower. The one he'd had last night before he'd collapsed onto the mattress had helped him relax to the point of oblivion. Maybe another one would send him back there.

He rolled over and found a massive fruit basket on the table. It hadn't been there the night before, he was sure of it. The damn thing took up the entire table and overflowed with colorful fruit that made Britain's produce look shriveled and pale. There was a mango the size of a watermelon and a couple of bananas suffering from elephantiasis.

A vague memory prodded him, of his door opening and closing at some point this morning, rousing him to semi-consciousness. A gasp, followed by the rustle of tissue paper had made him think that he should wake up to investigate, but then he'd thought *Fuck it, they can take everything as long as they let me sleep.* Must've been the housekeeper bringing the basket. Hopefully he hadn't shocked her too badly. He'd been too hot through the night to pull the sheets over himself, and definitely too hot to wear any clothes.

He tugged on his pants and flipped open the courtesy folder on his nightstand, searching for the room-service menu. The names of dishes were completely foreign to him. He'd never been to a Venezuelan restaurant before, and if he'd been asked, he probably would've guessed the food would be similar to Brazilian. Lots and lots of meat until a man could hardly walk straight because protein choked his gut. But this menu had a nice variety of meats, vegetables and corn cooked a hundred different ways. He called downstairs and ordered a random selection of five dishes. That ought to cut the hunger at least by half.

While he waited, he took another shower, brushed his teeth and explored his spacious room. One whole wall was windows, and even from his bed he could see the sparkling turquoise Caribbean. On the balcony a hammock was swaying in the breeze. He'd opened the balcony doors last night to get the air circulating, and the sounds of happy chatter and faint instrumental music floated into the room. He stepped onto the balcony and looked out at the lagoon and the crescent-shaped white-sand beach surrounding it on three sides.

A dot of pink caught his attention immediately, as if he'd been looking for her—which, of course, he hadn't been. Being only four floors up, he could see Tess well. She lay on her tummy on a big towel. Or maybe her petite body just made the towel look big. She faced away from the lagoon and was reading a paperback. She wore the bikini she'd had on last night, top included this time.

Maybe she would join him for dinner. He'd come here for time alone, something he never seemed to get. If he wasn't playing rugby then he was fulfilling his duties to his club or to the England team. Press conferences, meetings with coaches and players, charity events, sponsorship obligations... Mark, his sports psychologist, had told him he needed to get away from everything, to have time alone to evaluate how his life had changed in the past six months. Forget reaching the pinnacle of his career by being named England captain for the upcoming Rugby World Cup. Losing his mum with so little warning had rocked him hard, and Mark had said he'd never taken the time to process it.

How the fuck did you process something like that? She was his *mum*. His biggest supporter. His best mate, in many ways. And the way she'd robbed him of an opportunity to say goodbye, or to try to make things better for her at the end...

His throat seized up. He drew in a shaky breath and made up his mind. Alone time was the last thing he wanted.

3

A shadow fell over Tess's book, and she glanced up at the backlit man standing above her. Shading her eyes with one hand, she could just make out his features. Not that she needed to see his face to know who he was. Golden hair covered his calves and thighs, which looked flexed even though he was standing at ease. His body filled out a short-sleeved linen shirt and cotton shorts in a way that dried the spit from her mouth. She'd seen countless photos of him on the rugby pitch, frozen midstride with his left foot firmly planted in the grass and the right drawn back to boot the ball through the posts. His muscular definition had seemed impressive, but nothing compared to the reality.

"Morning," he said.

"Uh, you missed morning by about six hours. What have you been doing today?"

"Sleeping."

She couldn't tell it by looking at him. His eyelids still drooped as though he were fighting off the snooze fairy, and his dark shadows hadn't disappeared. "Sleep well?"

"Like the dead." He dropped to his bum next to her,

stretching his legs out and kicking a bit of sand into her book. She shook it out and sat up, crossing her legs.

"I just ordered dinner. Thought you looked hungry out here. Wanna join me?"

He thought she looked hungry? She knew she was thin, but comments like that weren't necessary. "No, thanks. I gorged myself on wheat germ last night. That'll keep me going for a few days."

His brows drew together. "You *have* eaten since then, right? I mean, you're not...going without food or anything, are you?"

Jesus, first he told her she looked hungry and now he's made it clear she might be starving herself. "It was a joke. I eat plenty. I just have a fast metabolism."

He held up his hands in surrender. "Okay, okay. I just wanted to make sure."

No, it wasn't okay. He'd stomped on her last nerve, one that'd been frayed thin by City boys calling her Titless Tess and, once they'd discovered her blog, Scrawny-Arsed Bitch. "Look, mate, just because I don't resemble the women you typically date doesn't mean I have an eating disorder. I have a fast metabolism, and I do quite a bit of exercise. As for my chest, you'll just have to blame genetics."

His cheeks flushed dark red and he stared at her through too-perceptive eyes. "How do you know what the women I date look like?"

Shite. "Look at you. Educated guess." It was more than that, though. She'd seen pictures. Lots of them. But she waved her hand in the vicinity of his chest to try to give credence to her lie. "I bet you like tall women with shampoo-commercial hair, thighs that could crush coconuts and breasts that could keep the Titanic afloat. Am I right?"

"You got all that just by looking at me?"

"Why are you surprised? Last night you nailed why I didn't

end up skinny-dipping. You're not the only perceptive one around here."

He turned his attention away from her, bracing himself on his elbows and contemplating the water that splashed gently against the shore. After a few moments, he said, "Do you like sport?"

"Some. I play racquetball with friends twice a week, I do Pilates, and I cycle to work every day." Or, she used to, back when she had a job.

"But you don't watch any sport?"

Right...he was trying to figure out if she'd recognized him. Should she 'fess up or keep the lies going? Honestly, she would never see him again after Sunday, so what did it really matter? Even though he'd annoyed her a few minutes ago, he'd made her laugh last night. She hadn't laughed in a hell of a long time. If she told the truth, he might back away. Or he might feel like he had the right to dig in to her own reasons for being here.

Neither of those options was acceptable to her. She'd been at this resort a couple of days and had spoken to almost no one apart from the staff. She'd eaten alone, surrounded by kissy-kissy couples and families. She'd gone on excursions—diving around a couple of sunken boats, exploring the cloud forest in the nearby national park—but people seemed uncomfortable around her, as if being a single woman on holiday by herself might be terminal and they didn't know what to say to comfort her.

"No, I don't watch much sport." *Liar, liar pants on fire.* She was no die-hard supporter. She and her father did, however, have season tickets to London Legends, so she'd seen Liam play live at least a dozen times every season for the last five years. Plus the fifty-odd times he'd been capped for England, games she'd watched from the comfort of her couch. That didn't count as being a die-hard supporter, right?

"What would you say is your favorite sport?"

"If you held a gun to my head, I'd have to say football." That, at least, was true. You really would have to put a gun to her head to make her say such a thing. The choice between football and rugby said so much about where a person had grown up and in what circumstances. She'd been raised in a lovely house in North London. Her parents had post-graduate degrees and made it clear that university was not a choice. It was simply expected—as was a career where she exercised her brain. Not to sound too snobby about it, but she preferred rugby crowds to football crowds and avoided pubs when big football matches were on.

"Football? Really?" His voice was tinged with distaste. "Who do you support?"

"I grew up in Islington. Who do you think?" One of the nation's biggest clubs played within walking distance from her parents' front door. Another reason she grew up disliking the sport. Mornings after matches, she used to have to hose the vomit off the pavement out front. "How about you?"

"Me? Oh, I'm a Liverpool supporter."

"Really?"

"Yeah. Big, big football supporter. Love it. Can't get enough."

She hid her smile by biting her lower lip. "Well then. Something we have in common."

"Yep." Finally he faced her again. "I'm sorry about earlier. I don't know exactly what I said to offend you, but I wasn't making a comment on your body."

Surprise stiffened her spine. "What do you mean?"

"I can't even remember what I said, but you took it the wrong way...or maybe I said it the wrong way. Either way, I wasn't trying to say that you're...lacking in some way. You're not."

Blood rushed through her, bringing tingles of sensation to every bit of her body. "I'm not lacking. Thank you."

"Shit. It wasn't an insult."

"I didn't take it as one. I mean it. Thank you."

He jerked his head in a nod. "Anyway, I ordered room service a while ago. It's probably there now. I might've been a bit greedy when I ordered, so I wondered if you would join me, help me do it justice."

"That would be great. I've worked up an appetite, what with all this reading and sunbathing. It's exhausting, you know."

"I don't, actually. Can't imagine anything more boring than lying around baking myself. I've been too lazy today. Need to get out and do something tomorrow. Any suggestions?"

"The spa didn't tempt you?"

He grimaced. "I'm not really interested in sitting in a hot tub with a bunch of strangers and wondering if any of them are farting and passing it off as bubbles."

She burst out laughing as she stood and shook out her towel. "Oh my God. Who the hell have you shared a hot tub with before? What kind of people would do that?"

He didn't answer, but his face said everything. Rugby players. They would do that.

"Maybe I had your girlfriends all wrong. Do you go for the beefy, hairy types with digestion problems?"

Finally he cracked a smile, and it was as if a ray of radiant light beamed down on her from heaven. "No. Actually, I'm partial to mouthy women who can put me in my place."

She bent to shove her towel in her bag, praying he couldn't see her face. It was sure to betray the bizarre, pathetic hope that welled up before she smothered it. "Well, if I see any of those around here, I'll be sure to let you know."

THE HAMMOCK on Liam's balcony rocked Tess in a hypnotic back-and-forth motion. Her eyes were closed and her arms stretched over her head. Her belly was full of food and *tizana,* a fruity drink like a nonalcoholic Spanish sangria. Who would've thought she could relax so deeply without the aid of alcohol?

Beside her, Liam let out a deep, satisfied sigh that told her he'd relaxed too. Turning her head slightly, she opened her eyes and watched him. He'd kicked back in a sling chair with his bare feet perched high on the post that her hammock was tied to. One of his feet pushed the end of her hammock, keeping the gentle rhythm going.

"This is the life," he murmured.

Interesting, coming from a man many would consider to be living *the life.* What was he doing here on his own? She could understand needing a holiday and traveling incognito, but why not bring along one of the actresses or swimsuit models he was frequently photographed with? Why spend time with *her* instead?

"I can hear you thinking, Tess. It's stressing me out."

She grinned and turned her face toward the moonlit beach, where a couple lay on the sand kissing. "Sorry. I have a busy brain. It's difficult to switch off."

He grunted, his foot never changing the rhythm he rocked her with. At some point she should think about getting out of this hammock and going back to her room. She'd thought he might make a move, but throughout dinner he'd never gone beyond mildly flirtatious.

"Tonight the night?"

She blinked and swiveled toward him, nearly dumping herself out of the hammock. "Pardon?"

He sat up and grabbed the rope holding the hammock up, steadying it so she didn't fall out. A suggestive smile touched the corners of his lips. "The night you go in the water starkers."

Ahh. Skinny-dipping. "Still too light out. And look." She

motioned toward the beach, where a couple were making out on the shore. "Three would be a crowd."

He straightened and peered over her toward the sand. "I see what you mean."

The faint sounds of muffled giggles and splashing water drifted over them. Tess watched Liam's face as he took in the scene below. His brows rose at a feminine squeal. "Yeah. You can see everything from up here."

Unable to help herself, she glanced down at the couple. The now-topless woman laughed as she ran through the shallows, her wet breasts bouncing and practically glowing in the moonlight while the man chased her. When he reached her, his hands went straight for her tits and he covered her neck in open-mouthed kisses.

"I really don't need to see this." Tess swung her legs over the hammock's edge and stood.

Liam tore his gaze from the beach, but his attention seemed to catch on her legs. He let it glide lazily up her body, spreading heat like a laser beam everywhere it landed. When he spoke again, his voice had gone gruff. "It's a good thing you didn't do the deed last night. I would've hated to miss it."

Tess swallowed. She had nothing—*nothing*—to compare to the woman down on the beach, but Liam hadn't sounded like he was mocking her. He'd sounded genuinely interested in seeing her naked.

Adrenaline pumped through her. She surreptitiously wiped her aching palms over the bum of her shorts. Maybe she should test the waters a little herself. Gathering her nerve, she said, "I should go..."

But she let the end fade out on an unspoken *unless...*hoping he might fill in the gap.

He stood next to her, towering in a way that should've been

intimidating but instead set her hormones into a tizzy. "All right."

All right? Seriously? Damn. That toss of the dice hadn't paid off. She shoved her hands in the pockets of her shorts. "Um, if you let me know how much dinner was, I'll pay you back."

His brows drew together. "Don't be ridiculous. I was going to eat anyway."

And there went her excuse to see him tomorrow. "Okay. Well...cheers." Suddenly desperate to leave before things became more awkward, Tess stepped into his room and headed for the door.

She'd just opened it when he called after her. "Tess?"

Trying to smother the hope that leapt inside her, she turned. "Yes?"

"Do you have plans for tomorrow?"

She should make something up, pretend to consult her agenda at the very least. She shook her head.

"I saw a brochure for hiking in the cloud forest. Come with me?"

The eco-lodge sat at the edge of a national park and was surrounded on most sides by mountains. Tess had already gone on an excursion into the cloud forest. It'd been stunning, but with only a few more days here she hadn't expected to do the same thing twice. "Okay. Meet you in the lobby at nine?"

Way to play hard to get.

Liam leaned against the balcony door, the shadow over his face keeping her from interpreting his thoughts. "Sleep tight."

Tess let the door close quietly behind her, her busy mind flying out of control, certain of only one thing: she wouldn't get much sleep tonight.

. . .

TESS WENT through the list of items she needed in her daypack one last time, just to be sure. Swimsuit—*tick*. Sunscreen—*tick*. Sun hat—*tick*.

Going into the cloud forest twice hadn't been part of her plan, but miss the opportunity to spend the day with Liam Callaghan, who turned out to be not just a sporting legend but also funny and flirtatious? Not a chance. If she did, she'd be ignoring the number one item on her most cherished list—her Ways To Change My Life list: *Grab hold of the good times.*

That list only had a couple of items ticked so far. *Travel somewhere exotic at least once a year.* Okay, she shouldn't have ticked that one off because hopefully she had a lot of years left. But she'd done it this year. She was here now.

Dye my hair blue. She'd done that, hoping for a classy dark blue, the kind that women with jet-black hair sometimes go for, which made alabaster skin look amazing. Sadly, she hadn't started out with jet-black hair, and putting blue on brown had looked a mess. So she'd gone to a funky student salon in Soho and told them she wanted to try a different color. A drastic change. Now she had a separate list: Mistakes I'll Never Make Again. Number one: *Tell a student hairdresser you want a drastic change.*

So her hair had been bleached and turned bright pink, which did nothing for her skin, especially when she'd been spending time in the sun building up an English tan: medium pink all over. Her skin would soon match her hair if she weren't careful.

Hence the SPF 50 sunscreen.

Ready to go, she swung the pack onto her back and was nearly out the door when the phone rang. The hotel phone, next to her bed. She'd kept her mobile off and hadn't booted up her laptop since she'd arrived. Only three people knew her room number: Liam, the receptionist, and her cousin Charlie, who owned an eco-travel company and had booked her onto this trip.

Please be Liam.

She closed her door and rushed to the phone, sitting on the edge of the mattress as she picked it up.

"Hey, Tessy. I didn't wake you up, did I?"

Damn. Charlie. "Not at all. I was just on my way out, in fact."

"Oh? What're you doing today?"

"Going up into the cloud forest."

"Ah, it's brilliant. You'll love it."

She didn't reveal she'd been there the other day.

"That was one of the things that sold me on having a contract with Casa del Sol in the first place. Let me know what you think. In fact, I want to know all about how they're treating you. Obviously they knew who I was when I went there, so they kissed my arse for a week."

"You want me to spy for you?"

"No, not at all!" He paused. "Okay, maybe a little. Think of it more like a secret shopper situation. Aaand...can you keep an eye out for a special guest?"

Tess braced herself. "Special guest?"

"Apparently Liam Callaghan booked a holiday through us. He should be at the hotel now, but he's traveling incognito so you might not recognize him."

Right. Like a man with Liam's charisma and build could blend in among mortals. "What do you want me to do with him if I see him?"

"For God's sake, *nothing.* Leave the man alone and let him have a peaceful holiday. But if you happen to notice him having a good time, let me know. I might approach his agent later about doing some low-level promo for us—you know, give us a quote or something."

Tess's hand tightened around the phone. Poor man probably

couldn't go anywhere without people wanting a piece of him. She would've felt guilty about inserting herself into his holiday, except *he'd* been the one to seek her out for dinner yesterday, and he'd invited her on his excursion today. She understood Charlie had a business to run, and what he asked of her was hardly unethical. Still, passing on information about Liam didn't sit right with her. "Is that why you called, Charlie?"

His silence stretched over the line until a headache burrowed behind her eyes. "It's not, is it?"

"'Fraid not. Aunt Jean's trying to get hold of you. She's sent you a few emails and you haven't responded."

"I'm on holiday."

"I know that, Tessy. But you really need to talk to her."

"Did she tell you why? Does she just need me to check in, or...?"

"I think it's an *or* situation. I'm really sorry."

She groaned and collapsed back into the fluffy pillows. "All right. I'll check my email. Thanks for the heads-up."

"No worries. I know this'll sound daft, but try to relax. Enjoy yourself while you're there."

His statement didn't need to be finished. *Enjoy yourself while you're there because you'll come back to the same shit storm you left behind.*

She hung up and booted up her computer. Glancing at the bedside clock, she willed the browser to open quickly. She was supposed to meet Liam in the lobby in two minutes and despised being late. Her email finally opened to reveal she'd received over a hundred new messages since she'd arrived. She probably should've checked her email at least once, but she'd wanted to completely escape. Most of them were from journalists who'd somehow found out her personal email address, but around a dozen were from her aunt Jean, who'd been acting as her legal counsel since her blog had sparked the biggest-ever inquiry into working practices in London's financial services industry. Tess had spent weeks giving testimony in front of a law lord, Lord Justice Tarrington, and his team of experts about the things she'd experienced while working for one of the country's largest investment banks.

Jean's last few emails had been marked *Urgent*. Tess's breath caught in her throat when she saw Jean's latest email, sent thirty minutes ago. The subject line had clearly been written to get her attention, and fucking hell, did it ever.

Come home now. You've been counter-accused of sexual harassment.

4

*P*atience was a virtue Liam was well familiar with. The young pups on his team often thanked him for it when they fucked up during their debut match and he merely patted them on the back and said, "Stay calm, mate. You'll get it next time." The women he dated usually appreciated it—particularly in bed—until they began to picture his ring on their finger and realized his patience extended far beyond theirs.

He glanced at his watch again and leaned back in the lobby armchair, his foot swinging back and forth in annoyance. He wasn't good at sitting around and waiting for something to happen. A teeny tiny part of him was guiltily relieved he'd been spared the experience of parking himself next to his mum's deathbed while she passed away. What torture it would've been to know what was going to happen, yet be unable to do anything to help and have no fucking clue when it would all be over.

What an arsehole he was.

He jumped up and stalked across the lobby for a third time. The receptionist saw him coming and picked up the phone, already knowing he would ask her to dial Room 317 again. A few seconds later she hung up. "Her phone's still busy, *señor*."

He pressed his lips together to bite back his curse. Tess's phone had been bloody engaged for the past ten minutes. If she wasn't down here in another five, he was jumping into the van without her.

And spending the day alone. Again.

Jesus, he was sick of his own company. The past two days, she'd been the only person he'd talked to—really talked to—and those few hours had soothed the beast inside that'd been snarling at him for six months.

One last glance at his watch. Two more minutes, then—

The squeak of hiking boots against Spanish tile made him spin around.

"Liam, I'm so sorry I'm late."

She looked harried and more than a little worried. Shite, he hadn't considered that maybe she'd had an emergency. "Everything okay?"

"Yeah. Fine. I just...slept through my alarm."

His brows drew together. Who'd she been on the phone with for so long? She'd said she wasn't in a relationship. Was that true?

"Thanks for waiting. I've wanted to see the cloud forest ever since I got here. Shall we go?"

He nodded slowly, still trying to work her out. She was hiding something—but, then again, so was he, so why push it? "I'm ready. The driver's waiting in the car park."

She beamed, and he was struck in the gut with an invisible fist. She hadn't smiled like that since he'd met her. With her pink hair falling in soft layers around her face and a glimmer in her eye, she really did look like a pixie. He couldn't hold back his chuckle. "Let's go, Pinkie."

"I ignored the first time you said it, since we were stuck in a lift together and I thought it was easier than having a go at you, but I really don't like that nickname," she admonished as they crossed the lobby toward the door, each carrying a small day pack.

"No? What would you prefer?"

"Tess."

"That's not a nickname. That's your name."

"Actually, it's not, but I'm not telling you my full name."

"Why not?"

"Too embarrassing."

He cocked his brow. "Really? You know you've just encouraged me to dig now, right?"

"Go ahead. You'll never figure it out. It's too strange."

He laughed as he held the door open for her. "So I couldn't just look at your passport?"

"You could, but you'd have to figure out the combination to my hotel safe in order to find it."

"Hmm...I have resources at my disposal, you know. Shouldn't be too hard for me to figure out."

She skipped down the veranda steps in front of him and started down the path toward the car park, drawing his gaze to her tight little body hidden under khaki hiking trousers and the way she moved. As if she were lighter than air or walking on bubbles. He'd often been written up in the sports press for his ability to dance around the opposition, but at five-eleven and nearly fifteen stone, he hadn't felt light since he'd started hitting the gym when he was fourteen.

Suddenly, she turned and called back to him. "Resources, eh? What are you, a detective?"

Shite. He shouldn't have taken them down that conversational rabbit hole. "Not a detective."

She gave him a thoughtful look. "A billionaire playboy tycoon?"

He laughed. "What?"

"Hey, you're not the only one who likes a little fantasy in life.

Mine just comes in the form of novels instead of films. Too bad you're not Greek. They make the best tycoons."

"Right. The Greeks are doing really well, financially."

"Fantasy, remember?" She reached the van before he did and slid open the side door. Tony the driver rushed around from the driver's side to help, but she'd already climbed in and settled on the bench seat in the middle, leaving Liam with a quandary. He could sit in the front seat, so Tony didn't feel like a taxi driver. He could sit in the far back row, so he could stretch out. Or he could squeeze into the seat next to Tess, making it obvious that he didn't want to separate from her.

Fuck it. He didn't want to separate from her, so why not sit next to her?

He stepped into the vehicle and tossed both of their day packs into the back, making room for himself. She gave him a look of surprise when he sat down, taking up most of the two-seater space. His shoulders brushed against hers. She didn't have much room with him next to her, so he tried to give her more by resting his arm across the back of the seat, right behind her.

"Are you going to pretend to yawn and grope me next?"

"Pinkie, you need to start seeing some real men if that's what you think I'm doing here."

"I won't argue with that," she grumbled as she clipped her seat belt. "Except for the *Pinkie* part."

"How about Pixie? That any better?"

"Hell no!"

Her vehemence made him pull back. "All right. Jesus, I didn't mean to offend you."

A thunder cloud passed over her face and he started pulling together the threads of their conversations. Last night she'd been annoyed when he'd asked whether she was eating okay. Pixie was apparently an insult, though he certainly hadn't meant it as one. Was she sensitive about her size? She was small, but as far as he could tell perfectly formed. Quite appealingly formed, as a matter of fact. "No Pinkie and no Pixie. Just Tess."

"Yes, just Tess," she agreed.

Tony climbed into the driver's seat and twisted around to see them. "Nice to see you again, Señorita Tess. You enjoyed our trip to the forest so much you wanted to go again?"

A slow smile spread over Liam's face as a blush colonized hers.

"Mmm." Her lips were pressed together so tightly it was a wonder any noise made it out at all.

"So you've been up there before, have you?"

The old van sputtered to life, and the seats vibrated as Tony shifted into reverse and backed out. She leaned over to whisper conspiratorially beneath the van's loud rumblings, but she wouldn't look him in the eyes. "Don't say anything, but I think he's got me confused with someone else."

"Uh huh. With that other pink-haired woman who's staying at the hotel?"

"Exactly. Wait—are we the only ones going on this excursion?"

"We are."

She finally looked at him, clearly bemused—and he didn't blame her. The hotel had originally told him they kept excursions to a minimum of five people in order to save on fuel emissions. He'd managed to convince them otherwise by donating an obscene sum to a carbon offsetting scheme. His turn to whisper a confession, only—unlike Tess's—his admission was true. "Hope you don't mind. I asked for a private trip."

"Just...just the two of us?"

"Uh-huh. I heard there's a waterfall and a small natural pool just off one of the trails. Since Maria said she didn't know of any private coves around the lagoon, I thought you might like to explore the waterfall with me."

Her throat flexed in an audible swallow, and she stayed silent for several seconds. The longer she stared out the window, the more he feared he might've crossed the line from playful flirting to creepy stranger. He was just about to apologize when she leveled him with a determined look.

"Only if you'll promise to join me."

Anticipation pumped through Liam, the way it always did when he heard he'd been selected to play in a big match. Even after all these years of representing his country and playing in top teams, the thrill never lessened. Strange that the thought of stripping down with Tess had the same effect.

Tess's hand lay on her thigh, limp and relaxed except for the thumb that beat out a soundless rhythm against her leg. Reaching out, Liam slid his hand under hers. The difference in size wasn't too remarkable. She might look small compared to him, compared to the women he usually spent time with, but she was hardly tiny. Just...compact. But powerful. The muscles in her hands were surprisingly well developed. She'd said she played racquetball and cycled to work. It explained the strength he felt in her, the long, toned muscles of her thighs, which he'd struggled to avoid staring at too blatantly last night when she'd lounged in his hammock wearing shorts and a tank top with the straps of that damned ruffled pink bikini showing.

With his free hand, he stroked the thin skin covering her tendons. Soft. For some reason, he slipped his fingers between hers so they curled around her. Holding hands. Not something he often did. Most of his relationships were of the "I recognize you. Wanna fuck?" variety. Just a pleasant diversion, a way to blow off steam and—if he was honest—an invitation to a glitzy world that most rugby players never got to see. Film premieres. BAFTA after-parties. London Fashion Week piss-ups.

But it all got boring after a while. It'd got boring a while ago, but he'd been too slow to realize it.

Now he was in Venezuela, a country he'd never considered visiting before his sports psychologist had recommended an exotic eco-holiday away from his real life. And he met someone he'd never expected to. He'd found himself contemplating her secrets, wanting to ask her questions but holding back because he wasn't ready to reveal his own. She would be leaving in a few days, but they both lived in London. Maybe this needn't be a one-time thing. Maybe she wouldn't mind too much when he confessed he wasn't who he'd said he was.

Tess gave his hand a squeeze. "You okay?"

"Yeah. Course. Why?"

"I don't know. I offered to strip down and you didn't show much reaction."

Didn't show much reaction? He was holding her bloody hand. Somehow it seemed more intimate to him than anything else he could've done. What did she want—for him to growl like an animal and start licking her as Tony watched in the rearview mirror? But something in her eyes gripped him. Resignation? Nerves? As if there was even a chance he might reject her idea of them skinny-dipping together. Whatever it was, the vulnerability gutted him.

He laid her hand on his thigh and pulled her against his side. She slotted under his arm perfectly but held herself stiff. Leaning down, he nuzzled her ear and kept his voice quiet so Tony wouldn't overhear. "I'd love to go skinny-dipping with you. It's been plaguing me since you ran into the lift in your transparent shirt."

She inched closer and whispered, "What has been?"

"The thought of you, naked and wet. I've tried not to dwell on it, but every time I close my eyes I see you splashing around, pushing your hair off your face as you stand under a waterfall.

Diving into the water with not a stitch of clothing covering you."

She tilted her head back so she could look him in the eyes. Her tongue touched her lips, and they moved as if she were testing out words she wasn't sure she wanted to say. He helped her along by rubbing the pad of his thumb over them. She swallowed hard. "Is this another of those movies you've seen?"

"No, Tess. This is all inspired by you. No one else."

Finally her body relaxed against him, and they leaned against each other for the rest of the drive.

THE CLOUD FOREST lived up to its name. The first time she'd hiked along these trails, she'd felt like she was on the set of *Jurassic Park*. Ferns bigger than her lined the narrow dirt path, and ancient trees unlike any of their more cultivated cousins in England stretched overhead, forming a canopy to block out all but a few rays of sun. Mist swirled around their feet. Up here, the weather was cooler than down below, but the humidity was off the charts.

Tony stayed with the van in the car park at the base of the trail. He gave Tess and Liam a packed lunch and pointed them toward a trail she hadn't been on the other day. "It's a more difficult path, so we don't take groups on it unless they're all in good shape. It should be very quiet today. You'll hike for a couple of hours along a stream and then come to a waterfall. Nice place to stop for lunch."

Yeah, lunch and some nekkid time with Liam Callaghan. God, the thought of it almost made her nervous enough to throw up. She'd been naked with men before, of course, but she'd also seen their disappointment in her lack of certain physical attributes. Though most of them hid it well, she'd have to be blind not to have noticed the resignation when she stripped off her padded bra and revealed that even her modest cleavage was an illusion.

But when she'd confessed that to her sister, Gwen had said, "Are you kidding? Don't you think men feel the same about themselves? They're probably just as worried about the first time you see their beer bellies or the unimpressive size of their dicks. I mean, it's hardly like you're sleeping with athletes."

Except that thought stopped being comforting when she was on the verge of sleeping with an athlete. Or, if not sleeping with him, then at least getting naked with him.

They hiked for nearly two hours, chatting about meaningless things. He seemed relaxed, happy to point out bird species he'd read about when he was a boy in London and had gone through a brief involvement in a local Young Ornithologists club. He also quizzed her about football—her favorite players, who she thought would win the league this season—as if he wanted to be sure she really was a footie supporter. She hated to sound like a stereotypical girl, but her football knowledge was completely limited to which players looked hottest in underwear adverts, so she mostly bemoaned the fact that David Beckham had retired.

They reached the pool as hunger pangs began clawing at her energy levels. They nearly walked past it, since it was hidden by a ring of trees, ferns and other junglelike bushes. Liam spotted the tiny break in the brush, a small path that had been created by people—and probably animals—pushing through the undergrowth to get to the water. With a sly glance at her, he grabbed her hand and led her to the pool, holding back tree branches so they didn't slap her in the face.

When they broke through, Tess's breath caught. A waterfall about twice Liam's height rumbled at one end of the pool. The water from the stream above flowed over a rock shelf, creating what looked like a hidden room behind the waterfall. The pool was filled with clear water, revealing pebbles in the shallows and turning a deeper blue in the middle. Several large flat rocks ringed the pool, perfect for drying off or snoozing even if there wasn't enough direct sunlight for tanning.

Perfect for sexy times.

"I don't know about you, but I'm starving." Liam let go of her hand and crunched over the stony ground to the biggest rock. He dropped his backpack, pulled their packed lunches out and glanced back at her with a raised brow. "Coming?"

God, she hoped so. In every way possible. She climbed up on the rock, sitting cross-legged next to him and taking her sandwich with a smile and a mumbled thanks.

She hadn't told him, but today would be her last day here. She'd booked a flight out of Caracas in the morning, which meant she would have to leave the lodge before sunrise. She'd run away from her problems, and apparently that'd just made them worse. Thanks to her no-longer-anonymous tell-all blog, she'd lost her professional reputation and her job. She'd sparked a legal inquiry that had embroiled her in a process she'd never wanted to be part of. She'd been called a feminist hero and a gutless bitch, when all she'd wanted was a way of relieving the overwhelming stress of her job. Having given her testimony, she'd thought she was in the eye of the hurricane. Turns out her former employer thought it the ideal time to strike back and release the email she'd stupidly sent a senior staff member, criticizing his bedroom performance. *Fuckers.*

They ate in silence, both content to listen to the forest's sounds as they reenergized. The river tumbling over the ledge and onto the pool. The water babbling as it left the pool behind them and carried on its journey down the mountain. The screech of a howler monkey somewhere in the tree branches behind them. The rustle of bushes made by a small creature— hopefully a frog, not a snake.

So different from the noises Tess had been surrounded by her whole life. Horns honking. Brakes squealing as a Tube train pulled into a station. Cyclists shouting at taxi drivers, and taxi drivers cursing back at cyclists. The forest's noises acted as a balm to ease the nagging stress that had eaten away at her nerves and her stomach lining for years.

Liam balled up the wax paper his sandwich had been wrapped in and shoved it into the paper bag. Stretching his arms overhead, he lowered himself onto his back and closed his eyes, a slight smile touching his lips. One of his hands reached out and found her lower back, insinuating under the hem of her shirt to skim her skin with a touch as light as butterfly wings. She shivered with anticipation. Such a simple touch, yet nothing about the feelings it provoked was simple.

"This is paradise." He let out a deep yogic sigh, as if the forest had helped him release toxins that had plagued him too. "I wish I could stay here forever."

Her brows drew together. She'd only known him a couple of days, but that was long enough to see he was exhausted and preoccupied with something other than having a holiday. What could have knocked him back so hard? The upcoming World Cup, which England was hosting? The normal stress of a season, or was it something more? She wished she could stick around long enough to find out.

His fingers set up a rhythmic back-and-forth stroke, following the path of her waistband from hip to hip. She shoved their rubbish into her backpack and drew her knees under her chin, content to allow herself to be mesmerized by his touch and the wild sounds creating a tranquil den around them. Her feet ached from the hike, which hadn't been *too* diffi-cult but had been steep and required a lot of climbing. Her feet felt swollen, sweaty and constricted. She tugged at the knots of her laces, loosening them until she could slip her boots and socks off. A quiet moan escaped when she wriggled her toes. Freedom.

Liam chuckled behind her, and she glanced over her shoulder. "What?"

His eyes stayed closed, but his grin had grown. "I was just lying here thinking I'd found Eden, and then I heard Eve moan. Seemed like perfect timing."

Waves of energy rolled through her from his fingertips stroking back and forth, back and forth, back and forth. She took a risk and lay down on her side next to him, inside the arc of his arm but just far enough that she could pretend it wasn't an intimate gesture if he rejected her. He didn't. He drew her closer, cuddling her against his side with her head and one arm propped on his broad chest. His breathing evened out, his lips softening as he seemed to fall asleep.

"You look exhausted," she whispered.

"Been having weird dreams," he mumbled, as if he was only half conscious.

She brushed her fingers over his cheekbone, just below the shadowy skin under his eye. "Nightmares?"

He was quiet for a second. Then he turned his head slightly to the side, snuggling deeper into her touch. "Dreams about my mum."

She stilled, shocked to get such a personal answer. "Your mum?"

His eyelids opened to narrow slits, and the pain she saw behind them nearly made her heart stop. "She died in February."

Tess's breath fled her lungs. "I'm so sorry."

The tip of his tongue touched his lower lip, his brows drawing together. He searched her face for some answer. After several moments, seeming to find whatever he was looking for, he said, "I think I've dreamed about her every night since.

They're so vivid, like she's right here with me...or I'm there with her."

"Where?" *Heaven? Hell?*

"Everywhere. She was quite a storyteller. When I was growing up, she told me lots of stories about her life. How she met my dad, how she felt on their wedding day and the day I was born... Now I keep dreaming that I'm part of those experiences, only she knows I'm there. She can see me, talk to me." He drew in a deep breath, his chest rising beneath her. "And we always end up fighting."

"Fighting how?"

"Arguing over...stupid things. We're both so stubborn, neither of us can give in, and then she just fades away and I wake up knowing I've wasted whatever time I had with her."

Tess cupped his cheek and he leaned into her touch, closing his eyes as if his confessions had exhausted him further. Gratitude welled up that he would share such personal things. "Liam?"

"Hmm?"

"You were very close to her, weren't you?"

He nodded.

"Then you didn't waste the time you had with her. It sounds like you cherished her, and I'm sure she cherished you." Who wouldn't?

He pulled her hand over his mouth, kissing the sensitive center of her palm and nuzzling her. Heart swelling painfully, Tess slid her hand out from under his and replaced it with her mouth, trying to tell him everything with her kiss. His mouth opened, his fingers sliding through her hair, holding her close as his lips slanted under hers. When his tongue touched hers, she was lost.

His free arm wrapped around her back, clasping her hip so he could drag her lower body to lie on top of his. He hugged her so close she rode every breath, every ripple that passed through him. His shivers of delight became hers. The sights and sounds of paradise disappeared until all that was left was him, hard and getting harder under her.

When she pulled back to catch her breath, he buried his face in her neck. His voice was low, gruff, as he said, "I don't know about you, but I'm ready for a swim."

"So soon after eating?" *Nice one, nervous ninny.*

He gave her an assessing look, then glanced at the pool. "I don't think it's that deep. But if you want, I'll test it out and let you know."

Tess rolled off him and watched as he stood and dusted off his bum. Never taking his eyes from her, he crossed his arms in front of his stomach and whisked his T-shirt over his head. Her mouth went utterly dry at the sight of his chiseled chest and abs. Jesus, the man had better breasts than she did. So bloody unfair.

She'd seen him topless before. In fact, her sister gave her a London Legends calendar every year, which featured twelve players lounging around the changing room in various states of undress. Last year, Mr. July here had been starkers. She'd really hated that strategically placed rugby ball he'd held.

Being confronted with his body in person, though, was a joy she'd never imagined she would have. His muscles bunched up as he bent to undo his laces. Within seconds he'd dropped everything except his tight knit boxers, which were at her eye level since she was sitting at his feet. His arousal strained against the front.

He hooked his thumbs in the waistband and cocked a brow at her in question. "I did bring swimming trunks, if you'd rather I put them on."

Waving her hand as if she'd seen it all before, she attempted a blasé voice. "Please, don't feel inhibited by me."

One corner of his lips kicked up and he swept his pants

down, stepping out of them without looking away from her. *Don't look, don't look.*

She looked. Swallowed hard. Her body clenched with longing.

Water splashed against her burning hot face, shaking her from her trance. He'd jumped in feet-first and was now swimming toward the waterfall, his tight back, biceps and bum working with each stroke. When he got to the middle, he trod water and faced her. "Coming in?"

Oh yes. Before she could second-guess herself, she jumped up and whipped off her shirt and hiking trousers. She'd worn her bikini under her clothes, but that was coming off. Now.

Liam's body moved gently from side to side as his legs scissored underwater to keep him afloat, but he watched her with unwavering interest. *This is Liam Callaghan. He's been with some of the hottest women in the world. Remember that Brazilian model— whatshername? She only has one name. Whatever it was, you don't look like her. You're Titless Tess.*

Yeah, and? She was the one here right now, and he'd found this spot for *her,* so she could fulfill one of her trip's goals. She just had to work up the bollocks to follow through. Squaring her shoulders, she reached behind her neck and yanked on the tie holding her top together. The cups fell toward her waist, and a breeze tickled her breasts as she shifted to untie the string around her ribs.

"Jesus." Liam's reverent utterance floated across the water to her. The tip of his tongue touched his bottom lip, and his eyes narrowed in concentration. "More. Please," he croaked.

Confidence swept through her. He wanted this. *She* wanted this. She had no idea how her world had collided with his, but she wasn't going to ask questions of a gift horse. No, she was going to turn her back on it instead—momentarily, so she could tease him a little as she wriggled out of her knickers.

His groan reached her across the water, and she slowly stood up again, tossing him a sexy smile over her naked shoulder.

"Tess, I don't mean to be rude, but if you don't get over here right now I'm going to have to take matters into my own hands."

She broke eye contact long enough to step carefully off the boulder into the water—because nothing would kill the mood faster than her losing her balance and belly-flopping in front of him. The cool water came to her knees, and she took a few steps across smooth stones before lowering herself until the water lapped at her neck. Ooh, yes. She was Eve. The original woman, at one with nature. Keeping her movements slow, she pushed her hands out and swept them back, lost in the sensuous flow of water over her heated skin. She came within a meter of Liam before kicking swiftly away and twisting to do the backstroke toward the waterfall, exposing her body to the elements and to his gaze.

She wanted him. But more than anything, she wanted exactly what she had right here, right now. To float. To see the trees stretching far overhead. To hear the waterfall growing louder. To know that, for the next few hours, her life was completely her own. She owed nobody any explanations, didn't have to lay her motives bare for the world to examine, or do anything other than whatever the hell she wanted to do.

And she wanted to do Liam Callaghan.

She swam to the waterfall and dunked herself under. The water beat against her shoulders, knocking out any remaining tension like a brutal massage. Finding her balance, she stood and arched her back, pushing her wet hair off her face. Something big blocked the sunlight and she smiled, cupping a hand over her eyes to keep the water from streaming into them as she looked up at Liam.

He slowly brought a thumb to her cheek, sweeping it across her skin before leaning down to capture her lips with his—

except...no, he didn't kiss her. He let his lips whisper over her jaw, nuzzled the sensitive underside and found the hollow behind her ear. His hand settled on the curve of her lower back that he'd explored earlier and pulled her flush against him. Skin to skin. Flesh to flesh. Her breasts pressed against the arch of muscle below his lower ribs. Her thighs between his. Her belly against his erection.

"If I can't call you Pixie," he murmured in her ear, "can I call you Nymph?"

Nymph. A sensual, alluring siren. "Oh, yeah," she sighed. "I'll be your nymph."

She slid her fingers through his hair and twisted until she found his mouth, pressing against him as she kissed him with all the passion she'd never had a chance to indulge. The strong bands of his arms tightened around her and he held her so close she couldn't tell where she ended and he began. She opened her mouth, inviting him in. He wasted no time accepting her invitation, kissing her over and over until she had to pull back to fill her lungs with much-needed air—only to nearly drown herself with a mouthful of waterfall.

He patted her back as she sputtered, but instead of teasing or letting her lack of grace ruin the moment, he walked her backward until her bare bum hit a wall of slick rock. She caught her breath and glanced around. Now they were hidden behind the falls in a tiny cavern, protected by the out-jutting rock above them and the curtain of water behind Liam. He rested his forehead against hers, one hand still rubbing between her shoulder blades. "Okay?"

"I think the water gave me amnesia."

"You want me to remind you what we were doing?"

"Yes, please."

His lips were curved when they met hers again. He braced his hands under her bum, lifting her until his erection slotted perfectly between her spread legs. God, he felt so hard all over, yet one of his arms protected her back from scratching against the cliff as he rocked against her. "Oh, God," she moaned, "please tell me you brought a condom."

He paused only long enough to settle her on her feet before diving away. Even through the roar of the waterfall, she heard the urgent splash he kicked up as he swam swiftly to their rock. Moments later he parted the wall of water and stepped into their private room, condom packet gripped in his front teeth.

She laughed. "You were pretty sure of yourself, were you?"

"Just hopeful."

The water here came up to his thighs, leaving most of his beautiful body bare to her sight. She sighed. "It's not fair."

"What's not?" He ripped open the packet, then looked around for somewhere to put it. "Shit. I didn't think about this. I'm not littering Eden with condom packets."

She tilted her head. "Plural?"

At least he had the good grace to look sheepish. "I was *very* hopeful."

She laughed and shook her head as she took the foil from him. "Suit up, Poseidon. I'll hold this till we get back to our rock."

"Poseidon, huh?" He rolled the condom down his thick length and then lifted her again, finding exactly the spot that'd driven her wild moments earlier. "Does that mean you're impressed with the size of my trident?"

Her laugh turned into a moan as he rocked into her. Her head rested against the wall, and she tilted her hips to give him a better angle. A few pumps and he'd slid home, his pelvis grinding against her sweet spot. "Oh my God. Your trident is magical. Keep it right...*there*."

He didn't listen. Her sea god set up a rhythm that made her vision swim and her inner ears roar with the lust pumping through her. She cried out as his fingers found her clit, pulling her lips tight around it so every stroke did double duty, rubbing her from the inside and out. She tightened her legs around his waist and drove her hips against his, riding him until her orgasm crashed over her, through her, liquefying her. All she could do was collapse against him and hold on while he thrust a few more powerful times before groaning his release against her neck.

They held each other for countless silent heartbeats, uneager to let reality return. When he finally disengaged, Tess let her jelly legs slide over his hips and into the water again, but she tightened her grip around his neck. How could she let go? He'd helped her feel something she never had before: completely, utterly desirable. Like a woman who could drive a man mad with desire. Playful yet sensual.

Like a nymph.

He nuzzled her temple and held her close. "You okay?"

"Mmm-hmm." Finally she let her arms relax, and he slowly lowered her into the water again. But he still held on with one arm. Good thing too. She would've collapsed in an embarrassing sloppy heap without his support.

He stroked her, and they both watched his hand roam over her breasts, lazily circling her nipple before journeying farther south to tangle in the dark hair over her sensitized mons. "So..." he said, "you're not a natural pinkhead."

His meaning took a moment to sink in, but when it did she laughed so hard the sound bounced off the rock and vibrated around them. When she caught her breath again, she kissed his pec, grateful that they wouldn't have an awkward post-coital moment. "Sorry to disappoint. Maybe I should've dyed the hair down there to hide the evidence."

He cringed. "I don't know much about genital grooming, but I'm fairly sure it's a bad idea to put chemicals down there." He leaned into her and gave her a gentle kiss before pulling back and looking at her with a teasing glint. "Besides, I like you just the way you are...Nymph."

A COOL BREEZE drifted over Liam's skin and sunlight glowed through his closed eyelids, prodding him awake from a deep slumber. He stretched, his muscles thanking him for a day of activity after one spent on planes and another lazing in bed. *Activity*—that might describe yesterday's hike, but it didn't even come close to summing up the afternoon of earthly delights he'd shared with Tess.

And not just *earthly* delights. When they'd started their hike yesterday, he hadn't intended to develop terminal chattiness and tell her all about his mum.

Well, not *all* about her...but enough to ease some of the tension that had been squeezing the life out of him. Last night was the first night he could remember sleeping a dreamless sleep. Good thing, because a ghostly visit from his mum would've been a real mood-killer.

Reaching across the bed, he searched for Tess. When his hand touched nothing but cool sheets, he reluctantly opened his eyes and blinked a few times to get rid of the blurry sleepiness. He was alone in the bed. He glanced toward the bathroom, but the door was open and he didn't hear the shower running.

Then a dreamlike memory came back to him. Tess leaning over him at some point in the night, her hand wrapped around his biceps as she kissed his shoulder and whispered, "I have to go. Thank you for everything."

He'd thought it was a dream, and even at the time he'd felt a twinge of discomfort at whatever part of his ego had conjured up a lover thanking him for services rendered. Or maybe she'd thanked him for the dinner he'd bought when they'd returned to the hotel, which they'd eaten on his balcony again before curling up together and kissing in his hammock.

Or maybe it was for the shell necklace he'd got her in a village Tony had stopped at on their way down the mountain. Several women there had been selling items they'd made, and he'd told Tess that every nymph needed some shells.

"I think you've got nymphs confused with mermaids," she'd teased.

He'd looped the necklace over her head and let it slide through his hands. It was long and could've been looped twice, but instead he let it fall between her breasts and hang nearly to her belly button. "No, I haven't. Mermaids cover themselves up and have fish tails. Vastly overrated. I much prefer nymphs."

She'd worn the necklace and nothing else when she'd put those womanly legs to good use and ridden him hard later in the night.

The solar-powered clock next to the bed said it was ten, so he shouldn't have been too surprised to wake up alone. In fact, part of him was grateful for it, since it would give him time to think. He should confess to her today, tell her who he really was. He had nearly a week left in Venezuela, but she was leaving in a few days and the thought of sticking around without her lost its shine. He wanted more time with her, and those days would only pass quickly if he knew he could see her again when he got back to London.

He had no idea what the hell had happened, but a gut feeling told him that this wasn't a short-term affair. He wanted to explore whether they could have something more significant, something that lasted beyond their time in paradise.

He picked up the hotel phone and dialed her room number, ready to insert himself into whatever plans she had for the day.

*Ring...ring...ring...*Nothing.

Shoving himself upright, he hung up and took another look

around the room. A folded piece of paper on the desk caught his eye. He kicked the sheet off, unmindful of the fact he was naked and walking in front of the open balcony door, and picked up the note. A woman's writing stared up at him before his vision went blurry with disbelief.

I have to go back to London. It was a pleasure getting to know you, Liam Jones. I'll remember our time here always. —T

What the fuck? She'd *left* him? *Really* left him, not just gone back to her room for a shower and a change of clothes? His jaw went slack with shock.

Maybe he could still catch her. He bolted across the room to the phone and waited impatiently for the receptionist to pick up. "Can you tell me if Tess Crawley has checked out?"

There was a pause and the light clack of computer keys before the receptionist said, "I'm sorry, *señor,* but we don't have a guest named Tess Crawley."

An empty place opened in his chest, the same bleak powerlessness he'd been punched with when he'd realized how badly his mum had lied to him. Tess had lied too? About something as simple as her name? Why?

Unable to take time to examine his own hypocrisy in feeling angry over that, he asked the receptionist, "Are you sure? The guest in Room 317?"

More clacking keys. "Oh, yes. Countess Chambers. Yes, she checked out very early this morning, and Tony drove her to the airport."

He hung up and collapsed onto the bed, countless questions attacking him at once. Had she known about this all day yesterday? She'd had to—she'd been with him all day and night and couldn't have rebooked her flight without him knowing it. She'd lied about her name? Why? He understood his own reasons, of course, but why would a woman who wasn't in the public eye take on a new identity?

Jesus—had she recognized him? Had she known who he was all along? She'd written *Liam Jones* on her Dear John letter. Was that a joke? Was she laughing at him? Using him the way other women had but, worse, pretending she wasn't?

Then her name hit him. She was a bloody *countess?*

5

Tonight I was at my desk, getting my things together to go home, when P. perched his scrawny arse on the edge of my desk and smirked down at me. "So, you fucked the boss, huh?"

I felt sick—with myself, with him, with M. for blabbing about it. I thought I could ignore P. and leave, but he touched my neck with his clammy fingers. I jerked away from him, and my bag fell to the floor. When I bent over to pick it up, he said in this smarmy voice, "While you're down there, love…"

"Fuck off," I snapped, but it just made him laugh.

"I like feisty women. Rawr!" He clawed the air. "Do something for me, though. I heard you're bushy. Make sure you shave it for me. Women with pubes…" He shuddered with revulsion. "Revolting."

—Sexists in the City blog

"Ms. Chambers, please read your email dated the first of the third last year."

Tess shuffled through the sheaf of papers stacked on the desk in front of her until she found the email she'd sent on March first. A humiliated heat swept over her neck and face as she reacquainted herself with its content. It was worse than she'd remembered.

The courtroom was silent, and she sat alone at a desk facing Lord Justice Tarrington and the team of experts and ministers he'd assembled. Nine against one. Somehow the odds didn't seem fair.

"Ms. Chambers, I assume your hearing hasn't been affected by your new hairstyle?"

Arsehole. She'd quite liked Tarrington when her former employers had been the targets of his caustic wit. She'd planned to dye her hair back to its original brown before appearing in court, but a flight delay in Caracas meant she missed her connection in Miami, and that meant Aunt Jean had had to meet her at Heathrow with a gray pantsuit and spring for them to take a black cab straight to the Royal Courts of Justice. If only she'd checked her damn email earlier.

But then you wouldn't have had waterfall time.

She cleared her throat. "No, it hasn't been. All right, my email dated March first last year."

"Read aloud, please, whom the email is addressed to, as you don't use his proper name in the salutation."

Tess's jaw hardened. "It's addressed to Michael Mulligan at Dartford Bank."

"Thank you. Now read the content of the email."

Tess faced the inquiry panel, but she felt the stares of her parents and sister boring into her back. They probably thought they were propping her up, but she wished like hell they'd skipped coming today. "'*You fucking bastard.*'" She glanced up at Tarrington. "That's how I start my email, sir."

His mouth quirked upward. "Yes, thank you for clarifying to our friends in the press that you were addressing your former colleague—not me—that way. Continue."

"'*You have some nerve calling me Titless Tess when you're the owner of the stubbiest, most flaccid dick I've ever had the misfortune to encounter.'"* Oh, God. *"'If I'd wanted to eat a mushroom, I would've gone truffling.'"* Jesus, please strike my dad deaf. *"'The only good thing I can say of our night together is that you lasted no more than three seconds. Bravo, you arse-faced lying bastard.'"*

The worst part was that she hadn't even been clever. The second worst part was that her mother's horrified gasp echoed in the otherwise silent courtroom.

Tess laid the paper down before she strangled it. Fucking hell, Sunday lunch was going to be excruciating.

Tarrington let her words settle for several long seconds before responding. "And please tell us the email address you sent it from."

"T dot Chambers at Dartford Bank dot com."

"Your work email address, correct?"

"Yes."

"And the device you sent it from was...?"

"My work BlackBerry."

He raised his brows. "Yet you publicly accused several of your colleagues of sexual harassment on your blog, correct?"

"Yes, that's correct." If someone would only give her a shovel, she'd happily dig her own grave right here. "I was sexually harassed at work, and I snapped and wrote an email I'm not at all proud of. In fact, I'm horrified by it."

"Are you horrified only because it's become public?"

Tess's memory transported her back to that day, just a few hours after she'd done the walk—or, cycle—of shame to work after drinking too much and going home with one of the senior managers. She'd prayed no one had noticed that she wore the same clothes, but apparently the dead giveaway had been when Michael blatantly told their colleagues he'd fucked her. He'd said a few other things, too, and by lunchtime she'd discovered her new nickname was Titless Tess. She'd fumed, had a few drinks after work and fired off this appalling email without stopping to think, feeling instantly relieved of the burning bile that had choked her all day.

Was she only horrified because she'd been found out and was now being whipped for being a hypocrite? *You better believe it.* "I do regret that this email has been released. It wasn't my intention at the time to publicly shame anyone, the way I was publicly shamed. I had intended that my thoughts would only be expressed privately, but since my former employer's legal team decided to share my email, then I will confirm that I meant every word. I swore to be honest here today, so I have to admit that I have never had such a disappointing sexual encounter in all my life."

Suck that, Michael Mulligan.

There were a few snorts of amusement from the observers crowding the seats behind her. She'd lay money that none of the laughter came from anyone with the surname Chambers.

Tarrington and his crew couldn't ask her much after that. They'd probably scheduled several hours of grilling in order to get her to the all-time low she'd taken them to directly, but why prolong her own torture?

After a shocked pause, Lord Justice Tarrington twisted the knife a little deeper. "Let me confirm that you feel no remorse over writing this email."

"Oh, I'm remorseful all right. I'm full of remorse—and quite a bit of shame and humiliation." She propped her elbows on the table and leaned forward. "Look, I have never intended to portray myself as a cowering victim here. In fact, if you read my blog carefully, you will see that my biggest regret comes from not having the courage to stand up and say 'This is wrong' earlier. *That* is what I regret most." She paused. "That, and sleeping with Michael Mulligan in the first place. Huge mistake."

Several people chuckled behind her, but a choking sound in the row directly behind her made her even more aware of what she was doing to her parents. As she kamikazed her remaining self-respect and her chances of any career that didn't involve doing a price check on tampons, she realized that she actually *had* lied to the Tarrington inquiry. Her biggest shame wasn't her own cowardly behavior at work or sleeping with Michael. It was the fact that she'd just publicly humiliated her family with her behavior.

Tarrington dismissed her and announced a short recess. Tess tried to leave the courtroom as quickly as she could, but she couldn't rush past her parents and Gwen. Her dad stared at an invisible spot on the floor, probably thinking about how much easier his life would be if that speck of dirt was his eldest daughter. Her mum stood with her arms folded across her ample bosom, eyes narrowed and mouth firmly pressed into what Tess had always considered the ruler of her disappointment. The thinner her lips, the bigger trouble Tess would be in. Today, her mother had swallowed them.

And Gwen—sweet, supportive, optimistic Gwen—tried to keep an encouraging face, but even she was fighting a cringe.

"How'd I do?" Tess joked, trying to ease the tension.

Silence. If they hadn't been in central London, she'd have heard crickets. Tess let out a deep sigh. "Yeah, that's what I thought. I'm really sorry."

Her father dropped his head back to contemplate the ceiling, his jaw working hard to contain his obvious anger. Her mum had less self-control. "Why did you do it, Tess? Why did you send such a reprehensible letter?"

Because I was drunk didn't seem like the kind of answer that would assuage her mother. "I wasn't thinking straight."

Mum's nostrils flared. "I'd have thought you'd learned your

lesson in the sixth form. Really, Tess, that kind of retribution never works out for you."

Ah, yes, the sixth form. When she'd sought revenge against a boy who'd made Gwen cry, and her father had had to beg the headmaster not to throw her out of school. Humiliation swept over her. "I swear, Mum, I'll never do anything like this again. I'll walk the straight and narrow, stay off the internet and away from the public eye, and avoid getting entangled with colleagues." *Should I ever get a job again.* "I never, ever want to put you through something like this again. I'm so sorry."

Her mother's lips eased slightly, and Gwen slipped her arm through Tess's. "Why don't we go celebrate the fact that you don't have to give any more evidence? Who's ready for lunch?"

When they stepped out the front door of the Royal Courts of Justice, several journalists shoved microphones in her face. "Ms. Chambers! Ms. Chambers! Did you ever have sex inside your office with Michael Mulligan? How many of your colleagues did you sleep with? Just how unimpressive *was* he in the sack?"

Tess bit down hard on her tongue. Her mother, however, had no such patience. She gave the reporters a bollocking until they backed away like a pack of beaten dogs, mumbling apologies for asking such impertinent questions. As her family acted like a human shield and swept her away, she swallowed the fear that always plagued her in the aftermath of her disasters. One day, they would finally get fed up and abandon her. One day, she would wake up and find herself all alone.

6

Liam clutched a rugby ball and jogged down the center of the pitch, pretending to run at full tilt as a gaggle of eight-year-olds gave chase. Their high-pitched squeals of delight made him laugh. They were so young the boys and girls sounded exactly the same. When one of them got close enough to tag the back of his leg, he tumbled to the grass with an exaggerated cry.

Just as he would during a real match, he laid the ball behind him on the green grass, away from the opposition, so one of his teammates could grab it and keep running for the try line.

"Where's my team? I need my team!" he yelled, trying not to eat too much dirt as the munchkins tackled him from all sides. Clearly they hadn't yet been taught that they needed to stay on their feet in the ruck.

Finally someone came to his rescue. The ball was snatched from his hands, and he peeked through the tangle of skinny arms and legs to watch his most senior player, Ash Trenton, jog a couple of meters before lobbing it to Liam's best mate, Spencer Bailey. More kids ran after Bailey Boy, but the weight of young bodies on Liam's back didn't change. A knobby knee jammed into the cartilage of his nose, making his eyes water as he pushed it gently aside.

"Hey. Kids." He wriggled to get their attention, but that just made them giggle harder. Great, now he was a vibrating jungle gym. "Go after Bailey. He's got the ball."

A bit of the weight lifted and a couple kids ran away, but others clung on. There was nothing for it, so he did his Incredible Hulk impersonation. With a roar, he scrambled to his feet and kids tumbled off all around him, laughing hard as they landed on their arses. He raised his arms and a child clung to each of his biceps, hanging in the air and grinning at him. One was a pale, bespectacled ginger boy who seemed to be the runt of his class. The other was a dark-skinned girl in a sparkly headscarf with her two front teeth missing.

Liam roared again and spun in a slow circle. The hangers-on tightened their grips, throwing back their heads and grinning at the sky as their feet flew outward and they became part of his human helicopter.

Finally, a whistle blew and Liam lowered the kids to the ground.

"Match is over!" shouted Chloë, the Legends' community liaison, from the touchline. "Legends, you did fairly well, but Bethnal Green Primary won by three points."

Liam and his team did their best to look sheepish as the kids jumped and shouted all around them. It was hard to keep a smile off his face, seeing kids from a neighborhood that wouldn't normally be populated with rugby supporters enjoy the sport. Once Chloë gave them permission, the kids rushed to their kitbags and pulled out stuff for the team to sign. Only a couple had official Legends shirts, several had illegal knockoffs, but most had nothing but paper. One scrawny girl with overly big Harry Potter specs brought him a folder, which she opened to display a maths exam with *7/10—Excellent improve-*

ment, Brita! scrawled across the top in bright green ink. Brita blushed as she shoved the test toward Liam and asked in a voice so quiet he had to stoop close, "Could you sign that for me?"

"Your exam?" He glanced at her teacher, who stood behind her beaming as Brita nodded. He balanced the folder on his knee and signed. "Do you like maths?"

Brita's blush deepened, her shoulders hunching up as if she wanted to disappear. Or, more likely, as if she couldn't admit her loathing for the subject in front of her teacher. Liam leaned in and whispered, "I hated maths. Least favorite subject ever. Well done for getting seven right. You must've worked hard."

Brita's smile stretched across her face. "Hours and hours."

"Good on ya. That's the kind of commitment you need to get better at things you don't find easy." Handing her folder back, he winked at her teacher, a stylish woman in her fifties. She blushed too. "And always mind your teacher. Here you are. Good luck."

Brita ran off and found another player to sign her prize. Ten minutes later, after Chloë had corralled the tykes and escorted them off the Legends' practice pitch, Liam and his teammates gathered in the team's meeting room for one last session before their first friendly of the pre-season. When the head coach finished up his analysis of the opposition's strengths and weaknesses and announced a few last-minute changes due to injuries, he nodded to Liam, signaling that it was time to wrap up.

Liam leaned forward in his seat, resting his elbows on his knees. The team turned toward him, and he looked at each one of them. No matter how many seasons he had the privilege of captaining his team, he didn't think he'd ever get used to this: the massive responsibility of leading a group of men he admired the hell out of. Each time he dug down to find words to inspire them, he secretly feared it wouldn't be enough. Nothing he said would be enough.

"Last season was great, lads," he started, "but we're about to embark on something even bigger. Our greatest season ever. With the World Cup starting next month, the world will be watching all of us—whether we're chosen to represent our county or not, and no matter what country you play for." He took in the expressions on his teammates' faces. They came from as far away as Samoa, Tonga and South Africa to play for London Legends. Most of them were world-class and had little doubt of being selected to play for their home countries, but several would start this season fighting to prove themselves on the pitch so they had a chance. "A month from now, some of us may face each other as enemies on the battlefield. But today, and tomorrow, and every day that we put on our green-and-whites, we are a team. We are champions. We are *Legends*."

The team roared, a ferocious noise that matched the feral faces surrounding him—faces marred by bones and cartilage that'd been beaten into submission from years of playing a brutal sport. They stood and huddled while their coach reminded them when to arrive at the stadium in the morning. Liam spent several more minutes with each of the coaches going over details before he could finally grab his kitbag and leave. Just as he was heading out the door, though, eager to kick his feet up, the CEO huffed and puffed down the hallway. "Cally! Wait a minute. I need to talk to you."

Liam bit back a groan. Never a good thing when Frank Swan needed a word. If it was about something unimportant, he'd get one of the lower-level managers to ask. A conversation with Frank usually meant Liam having to glad-hand some corporate giant Frank wanted to get into the team's bed, Liam's least favorite part of being the face of the team. But he waited anyway.

Of course he waited. He'd sever an artery and bleed green and white for his team. "What's wrong, Swanny?"

"Come to my office a minute." Frank wrapped his beefy arm around Liam's shoulder—a reminder to Liam that he would need to work extra hard to keep in shape after he retired. Frank had never been at the top of the game, but he'd been close enough until he'd blown out his knee and decided to get an MBA. Apparently all that sitting on his arse had jellified his muscles.

Frank steered him toward the lift, but when he caught Liam glancing at his watch, he changed direction and shoved open a meeting room door. "Won't take long. Why don't we chat in here instead?"

"Sure." *Shit,* he was going to be late...again. He'd promised to pick Samantha up at Heathrow. They'd met a couple of weeks ago, when she'd been in London shooting scenes for a film. She'd had to catch a flight to L.A. a few hours after they'd met, but she'd phoned him last night to say that she would be in London for the weekend and was desperate to see him. *Desperate* sounded a little too...well, *desperate* to Liam. But he liked her well enough, they seemed to have decent chemistry—not that they'd tested it out much yet—and he needed to get a certain lying pixie out of his head. Plus, he'd promised to be there. He despised failing people, but surely she'd understand why he was a little late, especially when he described how sweat was running rivers down Frank's ruddy cheeks.

He took a seat at the round meeting table and Frank hefted himself into a chair across from him. Folding his hands on the table, Frank stared at him with a grave expression. "We have a problem. A major problem."

Fuck. Liam didn't bother cataloging the possibilities. He could always count on Frank being candid with him.

"Have you seen the news today?"

"No. Been a bit busy." Ten hours of intense training, interviews with the press, team meetings and messing about with the kids didn't leave much time for TV.

"Well, Sharecore has gone into receivership. They're fucked."

Liam jerked back in his seat. "They what?"

"They're so far in debt the bank's administrators have stepped in. They're breaking agreements left, right and center."

"Where does that leave us?"

"We're either left, right or center, but who the fuck cares? They're breaking their sponsorship agreement. Our corporate funding for the season just sprayed the porcelain bowl."

A sharp pain throbbed behind Liam's eye. Although much of the club's funding came from ticket sales, they relied on sponsors like Sharecore to provide a steady, reliable stream of income. Without it, they'd struggle to pay back-office staff salaries, utilities and a whole host of other bills. Finance wasn't an area Liam normally got involved with, but management did like to trot him out whenever they needed to schmooze a sponsor, and his contract included getting involved in their events to promote the partnerships. "What about our other sponsors? Can any of them step up?"

Frank's face screwed up into a grimace. "Most of them have said no, but a couple are still checking. I only got a call from Sharecore's CEO last night—right as I was cuddling up with the wife. Fucker said he wanted to tell me in person but hadn't done it sooner for fear it would hit the papers before they could make an official announcement, as if I couldn't be trusted to keep my yap shut. I've been here since six this morning calling everyone I know to see if they want to become our principal sponsor, but so far I only have one lead. And here's where I need your help."

Liam perked up. "Anything."

"I've arranged a dinner with their CEO. He made it clear that this is a lot of money for them, so he needs to be sure they'll get enough publicity out of it." Frank grinned, showing off the extensive dental work he'd had to replace a few knocked-out teeth. "You're our best asset in these situations, Cally. I need you to kiss their arses so hard your nose is imprinted on their cheeks for weeks."

"Absolutely. I'll be there. When is it?"

"Tonight. Seven sharp. Julie can give you directions."

Liam checked his watch, even as his gut tightened with sickening disappointment. He would have barely enough time to get to Heathrow and back, maybe not even enough time to drop Samantha at her hotel. He cringed as he imagined what her reaction would be to finding herself abandoned on the first night of her visit. What would be worse—doing that or calling a car service to meet her at the airport in the first place? Either way, she wouldn't be happy. "I don't suppose we can push the dinner back a couple hours?"

Frank hooted with laughter. "If you saw how far I had to bend over just to plant this idea in their minds, you'd never ask that. Look, I know it's shitty timing, but I'm begging you here. Finding a new principal sponsor weeks before the regular season starts is bad enough. Redoing half the promo we've got lined up once we sign the agreement is what really has me cacking my pants. We need this. We need you."

Liam bit back his groan of frustration and capitulated with a terse nod. "Have Julie text me the details. I've got a few things to take care of, so I'll meet you at the restaurant."

"Good man." Frank stood, walked around the table and clasped Liam's shoulder. "Remember, charm the pants off them tonight. They need to know we can do more than just provide eighty minutes of entertainment every weekend. We can help them sell themselves to our adoring fans, but first you need to sell *them* on *us*."

Frank led him out of the meeting room and toward the front

door. Inside the training ground, Liam belonged two hundred percent to Legends. Once outside, he would have to figure out how to handle tonight without hurting Samantha. Having her own career, she would hopefully understand that his time was devoted to his team—one of the benefits of sticking to women whose careers demanded as much as his. Still, he constantly walked a tightrope of not making it insultingly obvious when a woman was little more than a pleasant diversion.

Legends were his priority, no question. He hated letting someone down when he made plans with them, but tonight he really didn't have a choice.

When Liam reached the front door, Frank slapped a plastic envelope against his stomach. "Here. Take these and study them as much as you can. It's everything we know about the company."

Liam popped the flap open and reached inside. "Who are they?"

"An eco-travel company. They arrange adventures in exotic places, all designed to benefit local economies somehow. Sounds pretty good. I might look into taking the family on one of their trips, if we end up signing them."

The skin on Liam's neck prickled, his short hairs bristling. As Liam drew the papers out, Frank continued, "They're called Kijani Adventures. I think it's Swahili or something. We're having dinner with their CEO, Charlie Chambers."

Chambers? Suddenly, thoughts of Samantha dissolved, replaced by the pink-haired pixie who'd cracked him wide open and left him bruised and battered.

7

———

oday the guys in the office played their usual game of Snog, Fuck or Kill. J. stood on his desk and waved his arms about like a sweaty ape, shouting for attention. "Snog, fuck or kill?" he yelled, holding up a picture. Usually it's of a celeb, a client or one of the unfortunate women in HR, and I bite my tongue as the men debate whether a woman's too fat/thin/ugly to be allowed to live. Today, though, a weird silence fell over the office, and I turned to see J. sneering in my direction as he held up a photo of me wearing face paint at our teambuilding paintballing session. Then the chants started. "Kill, kill, kill..."

—Sexists in the City *blog*

THE SHRILL SHOUTS of her former colleagues morphed into the ring of a phone as consciousness gradually wormed its way through Tess's sleepy brain. The sun threw sharp rays over her bed, and agony arced through her head.

She fumbled for the mobile vibrating on her bedside table, accidently knocking over the wine bottle that'd helped her fall asleep last night. Fortunately, it was empty. Or perhaps that was unfortunate, since its emptiness was the reason her head was about to split wide open. She felt like mythical Zeus, whose head hurt so badly he had to crack it open with an axe. Unlike Zeus, though, the goddess of wisdom probably wouldn't emerge from her head. The goddess of all hangovers, more like.

She hit a button to answer the phone and collapsed back into the pillows, covering her eyes with her arm. "Hello?"

"Tessy? You all right?"

"Hiya, Charlie. Yeah, I'm fine." Not a lie, as long as *fine* could be defined as *drinking oneself to sleep...alone.*

"You sure? You sound all croaky."

She muffled a groan as she forced herself to sit up straighter. If she wasn't careful, word would get back to her mum that she was still asleep at—what time?—shit, 2 p.m. on a weekday, and she'd find herself fending off an overbearing visit and tankards of chicken noodle soup—or worse, an intervention. "I'm fine, promise. Is everything okay? Are you calling from work?"

Work—that thing she desperately needed to get or she'd slip further into a depression from feeling so bloody useless.

"I'm great, love. I was just calling to see how your job hunt's going."

"Yeah, wonderful. Companies are falling all over themselves to hire me. Everyone loves a colleague-shagging whistleblower."

"Good. I was hoping you hadn't found anything yet. I have an opportunity for you. Actually, it's more an opportunity for *me*, and I need your help."

Tess's jaw went slack. She tried to swallow, but her mouth was full of fuzzy dryness. "A...a job?"

"Yep. If you want it, it's yours, but I need you to come to my office, like, *now*. Sorry for the short notice. Are you free?"

She leaped out of bed and nearly collapsed from an exploding head. Biting back a yelp, she sat on the edge of her mattress and dug her fingers into her temples. She bought herself a few moments to recover from the vertigo by saying, "Hold on, let me check my diary."

After taking deep breaths to settle her stomach, she replied, "Yeah, I'm free. I can be there in about forty-five minutes. Is that okay?"

"Perfect. Cheers, Tessy."

She hung up and stumbled into the bathroom, where she turned on the sink and cupped her hands under the tap to capture a few palmfuls of water to rehydrate herself. After a quick shower, she could walk nearly upright to her closet.

AFTER SEVEN YEARS of working in the City, Tess was accustomed to wearing a suit to work, but when she arrived at Kijani Adventures' office in a converted factory in Shoreditch, she realized her clothes made her stick out like...well, like a suit among a bunch of hipsters.

She should've known. With Charlie at the helm, the travel agency was bound to be different. He greeted her in the lobby of the large brick building they shared with several start-up tech companies seemingly staffed by teenagers. A receptionist sat to her left while much of the open-plan lobby was filled with bouncy balls and table football. On a square of AstroTurf in the corner, garden chairs were occupied by several creative types who sipped energy drinks while brainstorming.

Perhaps she should've kept her pink hair. At least then she would've had a shot at blending in with the zoo of ultra-cool trendies. Instead, she was a brunette with a bob wearing the most outrageous suit she could find in her closet—one with pinstripes.

She'd been thrown off balance even before she'd entered the building. On the wall outside, passersby could still make out the old factory's name painted in large block letters sometime in the last century: Jones's Fabric Dyes.

Jones—Liam's fake name. For the millionth time since she'd abandoned his warm embrace and debated whether to wake him or just leave a note, she tried to push him from her mind. Charlie was offering her a new start, and she wouldn't spend her first day at work moping because the building made her feel like she was wrapped up in Liam all over again.

"Tessy!" Charlie's voice boomed across the open lobby. She finished signing her name at the reception desk and greeted him with a smile and hug. He wrapped his arms around her. "How's my favorite uptight cousin?"

"Ready to whip these slackers into shape. Do their bosses know they're lounging around playing table football?"

He laughed. "They *are* the bosses...but not of Kijani. I'll introduce you to them later. They're working on some really cool apps. You're looking at the next Google."

"They can't be the bosses," she whispered as Charlie led her past the group. "They're fourteen. Look—they can't even shave yet."

"Don't need to be hairy to be a tech genius. Come on, let's go up to our office and I'll show you around."

He gave her the grand tour of their fifth-floor office, which didn't last long since Kijani only had forty full-time staff in London. The rest worked remotely in cities around the world. Charlie introduced her as *my cousin Tess, who might help us out with an exciting new project.* She tried not to let her eagerness bubble over into an embarrassing display of emotion. Truthfully, she'd take the position even if the exciting new project was scrubbing toilets. She needed a job. Not for the money—she still had plenty saved from her years of managing multi-million pound accounts. But for the sense of purpose. She'd lost her reason for waking up in the morning, and that could never be a good thing.

Plus, the vibe she got from Kijani was so exciting and different to the corporate environment she was used to. One wall of their office space was covered with a world map that had pins stuck in about twenty countries, including Venezuela. The rest of the wall space was a gallery devoted to National Geographic-like framed posters, some of which she recognized. Charlie's photos from his travels around the world.

"Are all these yours?" she asked, taking a closer look at one with several smiling African women, their necks elongated by colorful beaded necklaces.

"Yep. That's my most recent. I don't think I've shown you my Kenya photos yet, have I?"

She shook her head.

"Those women are from the Turkana tribe in the north, near the border with South Sudan. Those beads are their wealth, their dowry, so the more they have, the richer they are."

Tess had always been jealous of Charlie's travels. He was a few years older, and while she was still in school he'd skipped university in favor of traveling the world without taking a single flight. He'd spent three years backpacking through Europe, Africa and Asia while she'd studied her arse off to get three As and an A-star in her A-level exams. Her head had been filled with maths, business, finance and—just for the fun of it—international politics, while he'd filled his camera lens with stories. She'd gone straight into university while he'd horrified his family by coming home and declaring that he would start his own travel company without having any sort of education to fall back on.

But he'd done it. And he'd clearly made a success of it. At a time when traditional travel agencies were closing their doors, he'd found ways of staying relevant and vibrant. Tess tried not to see that as a reflection of the differences between the two of them.

When he'd finished introducing her to everyone, he led her through the small kitchen to a meeting room that would seat eight comfortably. The company's only meeting room was a far cry from the boardrooms she was used to. It even had large blue rubber balls like one would find in a Pilates classroom.

"I know you're wearing trousers today, but I wouldn't sit on one of those in a pencil skirt," Charlie said.

"Thanks, I'm familiar enough with them not to try. I'm just not used to seeing them in the corporate world."

Charlie shivered and closed the door behind them. "Okay, first rule of Kijani. The C-word is banned."

Thank God, Tess thought before realizing he must not have been referring to the four-letter C-word her former colleagues had batted around as if it were no more offensive than the words *coffee* or *cat.* "Wait—*corporate?*"

He made gagging noises. She would've thought they were a joke except his face turned a strange shade of gray. "Seriously, Tessy. Stop. I'm allergic."

She laughed and sat in one of the regular chairs. "Okay, that's the first rule of Kijani. Is the second rule that I can't talk about Kijani?"

"Absolutely not. You can talk about her all you want."

She rolled her eyes. "Men and their feminizing of objects they love."

Drawing his brows together, he gave her a concerned look. "Was that sexist? I didn't mean to be sexist."

And this was why she loved Charlie. He was the most sensitive man she knew. He could always read her moods, could be relied on to keep a secret and gave fantastic advice when it came to facial cleansing products. The world needed more metrosexual men.

She reached across the table and patted his hand. "I think you're okay. Go on, then. Tell me about Kijani and what you want me to do."

He talked for ages. His company was his baby, but the man didn't have a finance-oriented bone in his body. He was the creative driver behind the company's success, but he'd also been born with some sort of gene that helped him identify the perfect staff members to fill key positions. He explained that as Kijani was rapidly expanding, he felt the need to bring on a new project manager. Sounded perfect to Tess, even if he hadn't given her details of what the project would be. *Any* job sounded perfect right now. She desperately needed to get out of the house and find something to do that made her proud of herself. Being able to guzzle a bottle of wine all by herself wasn't that thing.

"Anyway," Charlie said, "we have a new promo opportunity that just cropped up today. I'm really excited about it, and I think it'll help us reach an audience we sometimes struggle with—middle-aged family men with disposable income who want to do something exciting. But it's a big commitment—not just financially but time-wise as well. And I need someone with a brain like yours to help me suss it out and determine if it's the best thing for us."

"A brilliant brain, you mean?"

"An evil money-making brain. A capitalist brain. A brain that thrives on finding the easiest way of bilking people out of their paychecks."

Tess pretended offense. "Is that what you think I do?"

"Not anymore. Now you could work for the good guys—a small, thriving business that's at the heart of the global community. Mostly—at first—I need you to be a number-cruncher, but I thought that might be offensive."

"Charlie, I will crunch any number you need me to. Tell me more about this opportunity."

"Well," he said, a grin turning up his lips, "you know how I told you a certain rugger bugger was at the hotel in Venezuela the same time you were?"

No. Oh mother of God, no.

"His team have just lost their biggest sponsor. I'd contacted them earlier this year about possibly doing some promo work with them this season, and they called this morning to see if we're interested in doing something bigger. Something really exciting." He leaned forward, his face lighting up like it had on Christmas twenty years ago when he'd been given his first point-and-shoot camera. "Tessy, I want to sponsor London Legends."

Tess bit the inside of her cheeks so hard she tasted blood. *Fucking hell.*

SEVERAL STREETS away from the restaurant, Liam threw his car into park and whipped his mobile out of his trouser pocket so he could tap out a message to Frank to explain his tardiness. *Traffic. No parking near restaurant. Be there in 5. Need an extra seat— brought a guest.*

That guest leaned over and nuzzled him behind the ear. He tried not to pull away from the uncomfortable wetness of her tongue.

"Tell me again how committed you are to this dinner," Samantha murmured before taking his earlobe between her teeth.

"Very. Sorry, Samantha. I know it's not an ideal start to your visit."

"Call me Sam." Her hand snaked up his thigh. "And I bet I could change your mind..."

"Bet you can't." The sultry promise in her voice irked him

instead of arousing him. He removed her hand from just below his groin and put it back in her own lap before lifting his hips so he could slide the mobile back into his pocket. She pouted, so he leaned over and gave her a quick kiss. "I really am sorry."

"You'll make it up to me later tonight, though, right?"

He didn't say anything, and her patience snapped.

"Liam." She must've seen the answer on his face. "You have to be kidding me."

"I can't help it that you flew in the night before a match, Sam. I have to get to bed early."

She exhaled so hard she wilted against the car seat. "You're fucking joking." She jackknifed up again and twisted to face him across the center console. "The whole twelve hours I was stuck on that plane, all I could think about was what I wanted to do to that big, hot body of yours when I landed. I was going to fuck you every which way to heaven. I had to jerk myself off in the airplane bathroom *twice*—do you know how difficult that is for a woman? But I was desperate and so eager to see you, and now... now you want me to come to some fucking boring business dinner without any payoff?"

The funny thing was that she'd made a name for herself playing virginal teenager characters in family-friendly films, and she'd struggled to break that image. If only the Hollywood producers could hear her now.

"Sam, you have no idea how badly I want you to do those things to my big, hot body." Except the thrill of that fantasy had worn off the second he'd heard Tess's surname today. Truthfully, he hadn't been all that interested when Samantha had contacted him yesterday, but he wasn't going to say no, either.

"Liam, this is my first night in London and I have a shitload of energy to work off."

"I'm sorry, but I have commitments."

"I don't give a shit about your commitments—"

He gathered together all of his patience. "Well, I do. So you can join us for dinner, or you can take a cab back to the hotel. Alone. Make up your mind quickly. I have to go."

At some point in all of his so-called relationships he found himself having to lay down the law, though usually not this early on. He hadn't lied when he'd told Tess that he was attracted to mouthy women who could put him in his place, but he also wasn't afraid to let them know when the place they tried to shove him into didn't fit.

"Fine." Her voice had turned pouty, as if she thought that excused her from having to say *sorry*. Not that he cared to hear it. In fact, that was part of his problem. He just didn't care enough about most of the women he was with to be upset when the relationship fractured under pressure.

What about Tess?

Yeah, well, she'd been the big exception in more ways than one, hadn't she? And look how that'd turned out for him.

Samantha capitulated with a sigh. "I'll come with you. I'm only here for a few days, and I won't be back until the premiere just before Christmas. Let's make the most of it."

He nodded and reached for his door handle. For the first several years of his career, women had been one of the greatest perks. Now he just felt...empty.

They got out of the car, and he'd just locked it when his mobile buzzed with an incoming message from Frank. *Just got here. Hope your guest is female. Charlie brought his wife.*

A dark premonition snaked up Liam's spine, making the short hairs on the back of his neck stand to attention. He tried to brush it aside as he wrapped his arm around Samantha's waist. She kept up an endless stream of chatter about her film while they walked to the swank Shoreditch restaurant, but his mind was full of the pink-haired pixie and what her relationship might be to his dinner companion. She had to be related somehow. Kijani Adventures had booked him into the hotel in Venezuela. It would be too coincidental for a Countess Chambers to be there without having any sort of relationship with the travel company. Charlie Chambers was the CEO of a successful business. Probably an older man. Maybe Tess's father?

He hoped not. He really didn't want to meet Tess's parents—especially if they were aristocrats. *He'd better not expect me to bow.*

Liam pushed open the restaurant's door and let go of Samantha long enough for her to precede him into the dining room. Her hips rolled confidently as she struck a pose to the side of the door and waited for him to join her, as if they were pausing on their way down a red carpet. Most of the diners turned to stare, not so much at him as at her. He didn't blame them. He'd been struck dumb the first time he'd seen her freckled face, long locks of golden hair and, well, her tits. Mostly her tits. Her body was a thing of wonder, and right now it was shrink-wrapped in a snug green dress that she'd probably worn because it was one of his team colors.

Or maybe she hadn't. Maybe that was his ego talking.

Liam scanned the room and found Frank sitting with his back to the door in a dimly lit corner, a man sitting opposite him. Grabbing Samantha's hand, Liam headed for the table. The man noticed them and waved in their direction. Frank turned around—and that was the first moment Liam noticed the woman sitting next to the waver. She'd been hidden by Swanny's big body. His gaze was drawn to the top of her head, since she was bent over rooting through her bag for something. She was dressed demurely enough that she didn't reveal anything that would grab his attention. But she had a presence he couldn't ignore, as if she were a red-hot flame and he was a helpless moth moving across the restaurant to get to her.

Then the man leaned down to whisper in her ear and her head shot up, and...

"Fucking *hell*."

Samantha stopped, and only then did Liam realize he had too. "What? What's wrong?"

"Fucking. Hell." He'd used up all his breath in his first curse. The second was practically airless. The sight of her gutted him, leaving him floundering like a fish yanked onto a trawler's deck.

Samantha gave a nervous laugh and glanced around the restaurant. The three at the table had stood to shake their hands even though they were still several steps away—and hopefully out of earshot.

Charlie brought his wife. Hot, furious blood pumped through Liam, replacing his initial shock with a more familiar sensation, the one he got just before a big match against an old foe. God help her because he was ready for battle.

He stroked the small of Samantha's back as they crossed the rest of the room. When they reached the trio, he held out his hand to the man. "Hello. Liam Callaghan."

"Charlie Chambers, CEO and founder of Kijani Adventures. A pleasure to meet you, Liam."

Charlie Chambers was young. Mid-thirties, tops. Lanky with artfully tousled blond hair. He wore a powder-blue blazer over a white vest. God in heaven, Tess was married to a hipster. A hipster earl. The man wore a scarf in August, for fuck's sake. No wonder she'd lied about her name.

Charlie's smile grew as he glanced significantly toward Liam's side.

Oh. Right. "This is my...friend, Samantha Hughes."

Charlie stuck out his hand and shook Sam's. "Samantha Hughes. What an honor."

Her smile lit the dim restaurant. Seriously, the whiteness of her American teeth was blinding. Clearly not a tea drinker. "Very nice to meet you too, Mr. Chambers."

He laughed and, before Liam could point out that she

should probably call him *Lord Chambers* or *Your lordship* or something equally ridiculous, said, "Please call me Charlie."

The two of them shared a moment that Liam would've had to have been brain dead to miss. Apparently he wasn't the only one who'd noticed. Tess cleared her throat, wiped her palm down the side of her pinstriped trouser suit and reached across the table. "And I'm Tess...Chambers. Nice to meet you."

She shook Samantha's hand then turned to Liam. Her hand was still extended, her expression begging him for something. Secrecy? Understanding? He couldn't tell. Once he figured it out, he'd be sure not to give it to her.

He took his time taking her hand, making her wait for it. Her hand was freezing and clammy compared to his. Thank God his fury had got his blood pumping again. He was on fire. Had she known he would be here? If so, she hadn't composed herself particularly well. Her face was pale, her lips looked half-chewed and her eyes were full of pleading. He'd never slept with a married woman before, and Hide the Affair from the Husband wasn't a game he was willing to play.

He held her hand longer than was polite. He didn't make pleasantries. She dropped the handshake like a hot potato.

Frank jostled him, reaching in front of him in his eagerness to shake Samantha's hand. He pumped it up and down so hard Liam half expected water to shoot out of her mouth. "Miss Hughes. Lovely to meet you. Lovely. Lovely." He shoved his chair back. "Here, why don't you sit here next to Mrs. Chambers? You two ladies can chat while we gents get down to business."

Tess's eyes narrowed, her head tilting as though she wasn't sure she heard correctly and she needed the words to bounce around her skull some more before she could be sure. Frank didn't seem to notice, but Liam did, especially since Charlie's arm snaked around her shoulders like a restraint in case she pounced.

"Isn't this a wonderful little place?" Samantha asked the table as she lowered herself gracefully into her seat and scooted forward. "So quaint. That's what I love about London. It's so full of tiny little quaint places like this."

Liam took his seat next to her, across from Tess. For a few moments, Swanny and Tess's fucking husband made small talk as a waiter brought menus and took their drinks order. Tess pretended to focus on what the other two men were saying, but her attention was so obviously split between Liam and Samantha that she needn't have bothered. Her eyes flicked in his direction, and whatever she saw discomfited her enough to make her swallow so hard he could see the muscles of her slender throat working.

He stayed silent, merely crossing his arms, leaning back in his chair and waiting. Making her wait. Playing a mental game not unlike the one he played every weekend against opponents much bigger than her—hell, much bigger than *him*.

When the waiter brought a glass of water for Liam and a bottle of red wine for the other four to split, Liam waited until they all had full glasses and then held up his glass. "I know we haven't agreed anything yet, but I'd like to start us off by proposing a toast."

Charlie Chambers grinned. "Excellent idea. Thank you."

The man wouldn't be grateful in a second. "I'd like to propose a toast to fidelity."

The table fell silent. Liam glanced at the other two men long enough to catch the confusion on their faces.

"Fidelity?" Swanny asked.

"Yes. It's important in partnerships, wouldn't you say, Charlie?"

"Of—of course. You have to be able to trust your partners."

"Exactly. And that's what a sponsorship agreement is, in a

way. We trust that you can fulfill your financial obligations, and you trust that we can get you the exposure you need."

Charlie cleared his throat. "Well, I'd say there's a little more to it than that. We can't just trust each other. We have to examine the details, make sure we're signing a contract based on facts and figures, not just trust. Isn't that right, Tess?"

"Yes. Absolutely right." The corners of her mouth had turned down, and Liam was annoyed that he knew that meant she was disappointed—and even more annoyed that he cared.

"Excellent point, Charlie," he said. "You should always carefully vet your partners before jumping into bed with them, so to speak. Never know what they might be hiding."

Swanny shifted his girth anxiously in the seat next to Liam's, knocking against Liam's shoulder. "Is there a point to this, Liam? I don't want to speak for the others, but I'd like to start enjoying this wine and the company of these fine people."

Liam lifted his glass higher. "To fidelity."

"To fidelity," Samantha and the other two men chimed. Tess simply stared at him and put her glass down without taking a sip.

"Now," Swanny said, "let's take a few moments to look at this menu before we get down to business."

Liam skimmed the single-page menu twice before noticing a problem. He flipped it over, but the back was blank.

"Something wrong?" Tess asked.

God, her voice made every muscle in his body tighten. She'd gone all husky, just as she had after they'd spent the afternoon laughing and moaning under the waterfall.

"I think part of my menu's missing."

"No," Charlie piped up, "that's it. It's not a particularly varied menu, but I can vouch for the fact that it's all delicious."

"Are you sure?" This couldn't be the whole menu. There was no meat on it.

Charlie chuckled, the fucker. "I'm sure. It's a raw-foods restaurant. I hope you don't mind. I'm a vegan, and I try to eat raw as often as possible. I thought it might be a novelty for you."

Samantha gasped with delight. "Oh! That's excellent! I love eating raw too. It's wonderful for detoxing, isn't it?"

"I couldn't agree more." Charlie's grin grew broader.

Swanny's laugh was so hearty and fake it made Liam cringe in embarrassment for the man. "That *does* sound novel, doesn't it, Cally? Well I, for one, am really looking forward to it. A new experience. I always say...um...stay open to new experiences. They're...the spice of life."

Liam put the menu down. Not only no meat, but nothing *cooked*? Fan-bloody-tastic. He was going to starve the night before a match. And, to make matters worse, Tess was married to a bloody *vegan*. Liam had gone out with one of them once. By the end of the relationship, he'd figured she'd probably become a vegan just to make his life hell. It had worked.

When the waiter arrived, Liam waited for everyone else to order before randomly pointing to six dishes. The waiter paused in writing them down. "Uh, sir, three of those are mains. Are you sure—"

"Yes." Apparently he would be eating his weight in sundried tomatoes and raw mushrooms tonight. Hopefully that wouldn't have any ill effects on his digestive system tomorrow.

Once the waiter had disappeared, Swanny leaned forward and clasped his hands on the table. "Let's get down to brass tacks. We're honored that Kijani Adventures is considering sponsoring London Legends. My promotional team and I did some brainstorming today, and I'd love to share with you some of our ideas about how the deal could benefit you."

He reached into his briefcase as Charlie eagerly looked on. Samantha seemed to grow bored as soon as the topic switched to something she wasn't involved in. Mesmerized by her wine, she held the stem and gently swirled it around until the liquid danced around the rim. And Tess...Tess gave her full attention to her husband and Swanny.

So many questions sprang to his mind that he didn't know which he wanted addressed first. She looked totally different than she had in their paradise. She had brown hair now, and, judging by how well it matched her complexion and chocolaty brown eyes, he'd guess she came by it naturally. The older Liam got, the more attracted he was to *natural.* But he would never get the natural Tess. Charlie did.

Her hair wasn't the only part of her that'd been tamed. Her suit was dark and boring. Gone was his nymph, replaced by a London businesswoman. The fury eked from Liam's body, leaving a deep, dank emptiness worse than the one he'd gone to Venezuela to try to escape. Even after all the lies he'd uncovered, he still wanted Tess. What the hell did that say about him?

Shake it off, mate. Don't let her see your weakness.

Her. *She* was his weakness.

The waiter appeared and slid several plates of food onto the table. Liam had three starters, but they were so small and dainty they should've been classified as nibbles. "I might have to order more food," he muttered.

Swanny elbowed him in the ribs, making him look up in time to catch Tess trying to hide her grin behind her wineglass.

Was she laughing at him? What—because he didn't fit in to this frou-frou Mecca for turf-munchers? His face must've betrayed some of his turbulent emotions because she sat up straighter and set her wineglass down.

"How's yours, Mrs. Chambers?" he asked. "Or, sorry, should I call you Lady Chambers? Or Her Ladyship?"

She blinked. "I—what?"

"I've never been very good at knowing how to address the aristocracy. I wouldn't want to offend you."

Her husband glanced between them as Frank tugged at his collar like it was choking him. Charlie was the first to pipe up. "Aristocracy? What're you talking about?"

A bad feeling settled over Liam, as if he were plunging toward Earth and suddenly couldn't remember whether he'd strapped his parachute on. "You *are* Countess Chambers, aren't you?"

Tess's chest rose and fell with quick breaths. A flush spread up her neck and overcame her face.

Charlie gestured between them. "Have you...have you two met before?"

Tess didn't even give him the courtesy of answering. Instead she tilted her head and arched a brow at Liam, as if to say "You started this, arsehole—go ahead and finish it."

Maybe she wasn't thinking *arsehole*. Did countesses think like that?

Liam cut a bite of his garden-on-a-plate. "We stayed at the same hotel in Venezuela last month. The staff all treated her like royalty, so I asked who she was. *Countess Chambers,* I was told."

"Liam, stop." Tess's face was carefully blank, but she couldn't hide the anger in her eyes any more than he could stop himself.

Charlie nudged her, a big dopey grin on his perfectly groomed, probably moisturized face. "You told me you hadn't seen him there." Turning to Liam, he asked, "How did you find it? Was the lodge acceptable? Did they explain to you how they've set up collectives so the staff are all co-owners? Or did they show you the way they recycle rainwater so it's used three times over in various ways throughout the lodge?"

"It was a lovely hotel. I have to say, your company's services were surprising. I never expected such...hospitality from a tour operator before." *Your wife gave me the most amazing blowjob of my life, and that's saying something, mate.*

Charlie didn't seem to pick up on the subtext, but Tess did.

"Liam, that's enough. I'm not a countess. You've grasped the wrong end of the stick."

"I guess that's happened to me quite a bit recently, hasn't it?"

Fuck. And now he'd revealed more than he'd intended to. Shrugging, he took a bite. "Anyway, it was a nice enough holiday. Not my best, but definitely top twenty."

Frank coughed. "Liam—"

But Charlie interrupted. "No, that's okay. I'm always eager to know how we can improve. Tell me—what would've made your holiday better?"

Not waking up alone. He stared at Tess, the baffled hurt he'd felt when he read her note swiftly returning. He'd spent the rest of his week in Venezuela obsessing about signs he might've missed, things he could have been doing with Tess instead of on his own, when he should've been focusing on healing from his grief.

Tess shook her head almost imperceptibly, her eyes pleading as she whispered, "Please, stop. You're just—"

"Companionship, Charlie. It would've been better if you'd provided me with some companionship. Without it, my holiday was—" he cut a glance at Tess, "—utterly forgettable."

8

Forgettable? Tess had been trying to stop him before he made a fool out of himself, but now the bastard was on his own.

And, judging by the aghast expressions on his girlfriend's and his CEO's faces, he was as alone as alone could be. "Liam... mate..." Mr. Swan's nervous chuckle turned into a choking cough until he picked up his wineglass and swilled it down in one.

Charlie seethed next to her. "Are you saying you expected your hotel room to come equipped with a prostitute?"

Liam blinked, seeming to come awake as if doused by a bucketful of frigid water. "Wait, what?"

"I'm sure that wasn't what he intended," Mr. Swan said so emphatically that it was obvious that was *exactly* what he thought Liam had intended.

"No—"

"Why don't you explain it to me, then?" Charlie took the cloth serviette off his lap and tossed it onto the table. He leaned back and waited. Poor man wouldn't be used to that kind of talk.

Tess, sadly, was. She'd launched her blog after a dozen of the most successful traders had been given a special Christmas bonus: a trip to an exclusive ski resort in Austria where they were entertained by prostitutes all weekend. Their manager had written it off as a hospitality expense. Based on job performance, Tess should've been on that trip. She hadn't been invited—not that she would've wanted to be. The whole thing was disgusting and insulting, and she would be sick if it turned out she'd started to fall for someone just like the scum dogs she used to work with.

"I—" Liam leveled her with another stare. His jaw hardened, and she realized in a blaze of understanding that he hadn't been referring to a prostitute. He'd been referring to her...but in the same terms as a prostitute.

Her chair scraped against the floor, piercing her eardrums as she pushed it back. "If you'll excuse me a moment."

She walked around the corner to the toilet, Liam's gaze burning her back. She shoved the toilet door open, walked straight to the sink and gripped the edge, letting her head drop forward as disgust crept up the back of her spine.

Forgettable. He'd called her forgettable. Of course, he was a professional athlete. His girlfriends—like tonight's reality-check, Samantha Hughes—had a lot more in the way of personal assets than she did, if one looked only at their outward appearances. Maybe their inward appearances too. For all Tess knew, Samantha was a lovely person who devoted her free time to feeding orphans and saving abused circus animals. Maybe Tess really did pale in comparison.

If that was the case, she'd hate to see how eager Liam was in the sack with his usual lovers, because he'd been incredibly thorough with her.

The door clicked open, and Tess drew in a deep breath, ready to pretend that she was okay in front of a stranger. But when she lifted her head, Charlie's concerned eyes met hers in the mirror.

"What're you doing in the ladies' loo?"

"Making sure you're okay. Tessy—"

She pretended nonchalance and washed her hands.

"Tessy, did something happen between the two of you?"

She smiled and told the story that she was going to have to start forcing herself to believe. "No. Nothing."

His lips compressed as if he didn't quite believe her but wasn't willing to push her. "What do you think we should do about the sponsorship, then?"

Run away as fast as we can. But this was Charlie's business, and he'd saved her by giving her a job. He trusted her to do the best for his company, and she would never sell him short. "I think I need to see what they're proposing. After that, I can give you a better answer."

He nodded thoughtfully. "All right, then. If you're sure you're okay?"

"Of course. Come on, Charlie, it would take a lot more than a crude comment from some oversexed jock to get me worked up." Sleeping with him, though—that'd do it. "Now leave so I can wee, please."

"Uh, you just washed your hands."

Ah. So she had. She shrugged. "You know women. We like to be extra clean."

"WHAT THE *FUCK* are you playing at, Cally?"

Liam took a sip of his water and tried to ignore the twin glares coming from either side of him. His throat was so parched he could barely speak. What the hell had he just said? He never meant to insinuate that he'd wanted his holiday company to supply him with prozzies, but obviously that's how it had come across.

He'd never been that guy. Some of his teammates? Yes. Him? Never. Sure, he'd enjoyed his share of easy, random hookups, but he'd never paid for it. Well, not in cash. Some of his girlfriends had got expensive gifts out of him, but that was different, right? They'd had a relationship...of sorts.

He answered Frank honestly. "I don't know. I'm not playing at anything." Turning to Samantha, he squeezed her knee in apology. "I'm sorry, Sam. I shouldn't have said that."

Her nostrils flared a bit. "It was just gross, Liam."

Shame burned his face. "I know. Sorry. I didn't mean to embarrass you."

She shrugged. "You embarrassed yourself a lot more than me. *I'm* not the one who asked for hookers."

Frank shoved at his shoulder so Liam would look at him. "I thought I was clear with you this afternoon. We need these people a hell of a lot more than they need us. All the risk is on their side. We're trying to get them to sign over hundreds of thousands of pounds to keep the club running—dosh that no one seems to have right now. And you go and tell them... Jesus, what the hell is wrong with you tonight? This isn't you."

No, it wasn't. He knew how to behave in public. His mum would have smacked the back of his head right now if she'd heard him speak that way. "I'm sorry. I'm having an off night. I'll apologize."

"You'd better. Look, Charlie's on his way back to the table. Make it right."

The other man wouldn't look at him when he sat down. His face was grim, and Liam knew he'd gone into the ladies' to make sure Tess was okay. Judging by Charlie's expression, she wasn't, and didn't that just make Liam feel like the world's biggest shite?

Leaning across the table, Liam said, "Charlie, I'm sorry.

What I said earlier...I didn't mean it the way it sounded. Not at all. I just—" He searched for a way of explaining that wouldn't reveal his affair with Tess. He found nothing. "I don't have any excuses. I'm just sorry."

Charlie's eyes stayed narrowed, but at least he looked at Liam now. "I'll be honest with you. I don't want someone representing my company who would expect those kinds of services —or even engage in them. I know you wouldn't be signing on to promote us directly, but you are a representative of your team, and I came here tonight in the hope that your team would help represent *us*. I don't really care what you do in your free time, but if you were ever caught in a situation like the one you described—and on one of our holidays, to boot—I would drop our sponsorship deal so fast you wouldn't even have tied off the condom yet. Is that clear?"

Shame filled Liam's gut. "Perfectly. And I would expect no less."

"We're a family-friendly company, and that's one of the things that attract me to rugby, of all sports. I haven't been to many matches myself, but I know from talking with my uncle that most teams create a family-friendly viewing environment. He always took his kids to matches as they were growing up, even before rugby became a professional sport, and he assured me that the risk of scandal was fairly low, as far as professional athletes are concerned. I'll need your assurance that that's the case."

"My players may not always be angels, Charlie, but they are professionals." What killed him was the fact that since he became Legends captain, he'd constantly drilled into his teammates the need to be professional both on and off the pitch. No women in the hotels. No cheating on wives. No badmouthing the opposition or referees. Yet here he was, having to defend his own honor in a mess of his own making. He'd embarrassed himself and had only himself to blame.

"Good," Charlie continued. "I've always said that my company is a family, and that's more true than ever now that Tess has joined us. I expect her to be treated with respect."

Liam blinked. "She works for you?"

"She might be. She's the one examining the proposal and contract and advising me on whether this sponsorship deal makes sense."

Fucking hell. They were dead. "I didn't realize that. I thought she was just here as your wife. I hope she can see beyond my momentary lapse in judgment."

Charlie choked on his wine. When he finished sputtering, he said incredulously, "Tess? My wife?" He laughed so hard people around the restaurant stared at them.

"She's...she's not your wife?" Swanny asked—and thank God, too, because Liam couldn't have got the words out.

"No! She's my cousin. God, the thought of it..." Charlie shuddered.

Liam was going to be sick. Tess wasn't married. She was here as a professional, the same as he was supposed to be. And if today was her first day with the company, she'd likely had as little warning of the coming collision as he'd had.

He was such a dick.

"If you'll excuse me, I need the gents'." He stood and dropped his cloth napkin onto his chair. He strode around the corner and stood outside the ladies' loo for as long as he could handle until he decided she wasn't coming out. Another woman did, though, and he said, "Excuse me, is there a woman with brown hair in there?"

"Uh, yes, there is."

"Is she okay?"

"Well, she seems quite upset."

Fuck. "Is she the only one in there?"

The woman nodded and he thanked her.

Then he shored himself up before breaching the girl cave that men never dared enter.

Tess was bracing her hands against the sink muttering to herself, but when the door shut behind him she flipped on the tap and pumped soap into her hands without looking up. "Charlie, I told you I'm okay."

He didn't say anything. When the woman had said Tess was upset, he'd expected messy tears or other dramatics. That was the kind of upset he was used to. But Tess looked caught between anger and shock, as though someone had drowned her kitten. "Are you sure you're okay?"

She spun around. "What are you doing in here?"

"I wanted to apologize."

Her mouth opened and closed a few times before she finally clamped it shut and glared at him.

He gathered up his pride and his courage and dug deep to be the man he knew he had to be. "I shouldn't have said what I did. I didn't mean it like that. Seeing you here tonight threw me completely off, and my brain sort of stopped communicating with my mouth. I'm sorry."

Her gaze settled somewhere around his clavicle—the only bone he'd broken twice in his career. Feeling her accusing stare there brought back the searing pain until his whole chest throbbed. He needed her to understand he wasn't the man he'd come across as tonight.

She finally wet her bottom lip and said, "What exactly did you mean, then?"

Shite, he should've known that she wouldn't make this easy. "I went to Venezuela to be alone and try to figure some things out. Meeting you was...unexpected."

She closed her eyes as if she couldn't bear to look at him. "Unexpected but forgettable."

He took a step closer, but she must've heard because she backed up into the wall. He stopped, not wishing to push where he wasn't wanted. How could he explain, though, without opening himself completely up, making himself vulnerable to every weapon she had in her arsenal? If he'd learned anything, it was that he didn't know her at all, but he could give her this reassurance in all honesty. "It wasn't forgettable."

More than that, he couldn't admit. Not without understanding it better himself.

She drew in a deep breath and let it out slowly, her shoulders relaxing somewhat. "I'm not a countess."

"Why did the receptionist tell me you were?"

"Because sadly, that's my name."

It took him a minute to figure out what she meant. "Your parents named you Countess?"

She nodded. "Sick, isn't it? That's why I go by Tess."

"What the hell were they thinking?"

"I assume they had aspirations I could never fulfill. Look, Liam, I didn't really want to be here tonight, but I had no idea that you'd be invited to join this meeting. If I'd known, I would've..." She paused. "I don't know. I guess there's no way I could've got out of it. But maybe I could've warned you somehow."

The fact that she would've known how to contact him reminded him that he wasn't entirely at fault here. "I told you my name was Liam Jones. When did you figure out who I really am?"

She swallowed hard. "Before you told me your name was Liam Jones."

Reality punched him in the vulnerable spot just below his ribs. "You knew the whole time?"

She nodded.

Fuck. Everything he'd thought he'd had during those two days—anonymity, a lover who enjoyed spending time with him because of who he was instead of what he did, the opportunity to figure out who the hell he was away from his career and his obligations—none of it was real. It vanished in a puff of smoke. He was struck nearly dumb, and the only thing he could think to ask was even dumber. "Are you really a football supporter?"

She grimaced. "I hate football."

With most women, he would take this as a sign of extremely good taste. It was the last thing he'd wanted to hear from her, though.

"I asked you before, and I need to know the truth now, Tess. Do you watch any sport?"

Her whole body proclaimed her guilt, from the way her shoulders hunched to the drop of her gaze to the floor. "Yes."

"Which sport?"

"I mainly watch rugby."

He tried to keep from cringing. "Who do you support?"

She groaned and swiped a hand over her face. "Does it really matter?"

"Yes." It mattered more than he cared to admit. "Who do you support?"

She whispered, "Legends."

"Have you been to any of our matches?"

Her face screwed up in a rueful expression. "I'm a season ticket holder."

Fucking hell. He was shocked at how hard the sense of betrayal hit him. He'd been delusional in Venezuela, but the blinders cleared from his eyes now. God, how he wanted to tell her exactly what he thought. *I hope fucking a sporting superstar matched your perviest fantasies. I hope you brought home some great stories to tell your friends. I hope you didn't sell any information about me to the tabloids. And if you did, I hope you kept in mind the water was fucking freezing.*

But he couldn't do any of that. Not without risking his team's financial well-being. So he practiced what he preached to his teammates and put on his professional cloak of armor. "Then you'll know we can offer your company a good deal. Our stadium's packed every game day, and we always strive to keep our supporters satisfied."

If only he'd known last month that that's exactly what he'd been doing.

TESS LEFT THE LOO FIRST, eager to get back to the table before Mr. Swan decided that he too needed to visit her in the toilet. When she reached the table, Charlie lifted his brows as if to ask "All right?"

She gave him a tiny nod as she sat and laid the serviette on her lap, but inside she was a mess. Why had Liam placed such emphasis on whether she'd recognized him? When they'd first met, she hadn't thought anything of the pretense. He had clearly wanted privacy, and she'd thought the polite thing was to give it to him.

Should she have confessed at some point during their two days together? Truthfully, when he'd told her he'd found paradise at their watering hole, she had thought she'd discovered the same thing. The weeks since her return had been an ulcer in her life, churning up a burning pain like nothing else. Thanks to the inquiry, she had little pride left to lose. Those two days with Liam had been Eden.

She should've realized that her knowledge of his identity would destroy paradise.

She'd somehow hurt him by lying, possibly more so than by leaving before he woke up. Obviously it hadn't taken him long to get over that, considering the bombshell sitting next to her signing an autograph for the guests at the next table.

The scrape of his chair told her he'd returned. He'd composed himself to the point that she couldn't see anything other than polite interest.

Mr. Swan laid some colorful papers on the table and glanced around, as though he were checking whether anyone else wanted to start a conversation he played no part in. "I hate to interrupt food with business talk, but as that's why we're here…"

"By all means," Charlie said.

The next half hour was filled with chat about what the club offered their sponsors and what they asked for in return. Mr. Swan showed them examples of previous sponsors' promotional activities, and Charlie chipped in with several excited questions. She watched him with what she feared was a dopey smile of pride on her face. She'd always known her favorite cousin was great at his job, but she'd never been able to see him in action before. For the first time in a long while, she felt the green shoots of hope pushing up through all the fertilizer that had choked her in the past few years.

Charlie asked her several questions, and she drew out her tablet to make calculations. He wanted Kijani Adventures' name and logo on the players' shirts, and Mr. Swan had the nerve to say, "I'm afraid the team kit for this year has already been ordered and delivered. It'll cost extra to put your logo on the shirts now."

No stranger to men trying to take advantage, Tess lifted one of her brows and gave him her don't-fuck-with-me look. "Whose logo is on the shirts now, Mr. Swan?"

"Please, call me Frank." He obviously thought to distract her with friendliness. Fine, she could be friendly and make sure her cousin didn't get taken for a ride.

"Thank you, Frank. Whose logo is on the shirts now?"

He tugged at his tie, a sign she'd already decided meant he was uncomfortable. He'd had reason to do it a lot throughout dinner. "Well, they have Sharecore's logo."

"So I assume you meant that it will cost *you* extra, as you'll have to replace those shirts anyway."

He swallowed hard. "Yes. Of course that's what I meant."

Out of the corner of her eye, she caught Liam's slight grin, but it disappeared quickly—perhaps because the waiter showed up with the mains, and Liam's three servings didn't look like enough to feed her, much less him. How on earth did Charlie survive on this? Most of it was tasty enough, but even Tess would have to stop for a kebab on her way home.

Eager to start building bridges, she whispered across the table to Liam as the other two discussed logo ratios and pixel sizes and Samantha chatted with the waiter about how brilliant her new film was. "How is it?"

"All together it makes for a great starter."

"Maybe your housekeeper can make you something when you get home."

Oops. Wrong thing to say. His face darkened, and she couldn't figure out why. Was it the reminder of their time in the lift? Of him feeding her crumbled oats and asking her if she was committed to other food products?

"She doesn't live with me full time. She works one day a week and sometimes leaves me nice treats, that's all. I cook for myself."

"You're doing better than me, then. I can't cook. I usually get takeaways."

"You survive on takeaways?" Liam made a show of gazing down her body, and she knew exactly what he saw. Scrawniness.

She straightened her shoulders, as if that might bulk her up. "Mostly. That and energy bars. Anything you only have to unwrap in order to eat."

He shook his head. "It's criminal to do that to your body. You do all that exercise, yet you fuel yourself with rubbish? At least this food's healthy, even if I can't find the protein."

Charlie's voice interrupted. "Tess, what do you think of that?"

She jerked her attention back to the two men, who were staring at her expectantly. "Sorry, think about what?"

Charlie waved at the brochures and spreadsheets Frank had explained earlier. "The sponsorship deal, for starters."

"You want my decision now? Don't you think it would be better if we went away and discussed it?"

Frank leaned in. "I really hate to push, but because of the situation we're in we don't have much time. We need to move swiftly. If you decide this isn't for you, then we'll need to start over first thing tomorrow morning. I understand it's a big decision to take—"

"In that case, you'll understand why it's important for us to run all the figures. I'm sure you wouldn't want another sponsor who has to back out because they can't afford the agreement."

Frank backed off and cleared his throat. "Too right. Just tell me what you need from me in order to make your decision, and it's yours."

Before she could say that she'd like to have until lunchtime tomorrow to check all the figures, Charlie squeezed her hand. "Look at the numbers now, Tessy. In fact—" he shoved her untouched plate of food toward Liam and replaced it with a set of spreadsheets and graphs, "I know you're just going to stop for a kebab on the way home anyway, so why don't you concentrate on these instead?"

She sighed. This wasn't the first dinner when a boss had demanded she work instead of eat. She was used to caving in to unreasonable demands. Charlie's demand—delivered in such a hopeful manner by someone she would walk over coals for—seemed neither unreasonable nor demanding.

Liam chimed in, glaring at Charlie. "Tess, if you're hungry, you should eat."

"It's all right, Liam. Charlie's right. The starter will keep me going until I can get to a takeaway." She turned her attention to earning her pay, making notations and doing as much research as she could to verify that Frank's figures were correct. She'd developed an innate ability to block out noise when she concentrated, so the conversation floated around her without weaseling through her thoughts. But when someone slid a plate of raw cacao cake under her nose, she crashed back to earth. She could always break her concentration for chocolate.

"We ordered you dessert," Charlie said, and for the first time she noticed that he, Samantha and Frank both had chocolaty confections while Liam was munching on a plate of fresh fruit.

"Thanks."

"So..." Frank gave her an expectant look as he tucked in to his dessert. "What do you think?"

She turned to Charlie. "Can we talk privately?"

He nodded toward the ladies' loos. "In our office?"

She laughed. "How about just outside our office?"

He led the way around the corner, and Tess laid her tablet on a side table that held a massive flower arrangement. She expanded a couple of spreadsheets. "Here are the figures your finance director sent me. These three lines show your projected growth over the next five years depending on whether the economy grows, stays shitty or tanks even further." She tapped on the screen again. "And this spreadsheet shows the ROI on your current marketing efforts. What's the first thing you see?"

He scanned the columns. "We're spending a shitload on magazine advertising, and it's not paying off."

"Exactly. Now, you managed to survive the last financial

crisis, and you're weathering the storm right now. According to your projected growth, you should be okay unless the economy goes completely tits-up, but if that happens then we're all fucked anyway. Still, I'd recommend not doing anything drastic right now, so..."

His shoulders slumped. "So we can't do it."

"Actually, I think you can."

He looked at her with such eagerness that she wanted to laugh even as she cautioned him. "There are always risks involved in something like this, Charlie."

"I know."

"And there's no guaranteed return. In fact, it could prove quite costly."

"I know, Tess. But—"

She laid her hand on his forearm. "But, all in all, I can see why it appeals to you. If you offset some of it by cutting back on your magazine advertising—and perhaps thinking about bringing all of this digital work that you're outsourcing in-house —then it's a risk I think you can afford."

The muscles around his mouth and eyes softened. "Really?"

"I don't see it being a crippling financial burden, so if you think it's a good promotional opportunity, then go for it."

He looped an arm around her neck and squeezed her tightly before planting a noisy kiss on her cheek. "Thanks for the analysis, Tessy, and for doing it so quickly. I knew being related to a swot would come in handy for me one day. And you'll help me manage the deal?"

"Well, really you should have your lawyers be involved in the contract."

"No, I mean, the things Frank and I were discussing while you were checking the figures. You'll do it? I really think you'd be perfect for it, Tessy. I need you to do this for me. I wouldn't trust anyone else with a deal like this."

God, she would take any job going, and here he was practically begging her when she should be the one pleading for a chance? She let out a deep breath. "Anything for you, Charlie. You know that."

He led her back to the table, where the sight of Samantha snuggled up against Liam punched Tess in the stomach all over again. She smoothed her suit jacket over her ribs, trying to cover up how wrong and right it felt to see Liam with a beauty like Samantha.

Charlie pulled out her chair before sitting. "We'll do it."

Frank and Liam let out audible sighs of relief, their shoulders relaxing.

"And Tess has agreed to help us manage the partnership," Charlie continued.

Tess glanced around the table, taking in the triumphant expressions Frank and Charlie wore...and the glower on Liam's face.

What the hell had she just promised to do?

9

Last week a couple of the other traders duct-taped S. to her chair, rolled her to the lift and pressed the sixteen buttons between us and the ground floor. Apparently when she arrived there, someone else pressed all twenty-five buttons, sending her up to the top. After T. finally took pity on her and pulled her out, she had a spectacular meltdown and quit.

M. told me to call the recruiters. He only had two criteria for me to pass on to the head hunter: "No birds, no queers."

—Sexists in the City *blog*

"YOU WANT ME TO DO WHAT?" Tess sat at the table in Kijani's meeting room and stared up at Charlie with horror, but the look he returned was confused.

"We talked about this last night at dinner. You agreed to help."

"I thought I was agreeing to help manage the financial transaction, not become a cheerleader."

Charlie perched his bum on the edge of the desk next to

Tess. "I would never ask you to become a cheerleader. Only to get the crowd going a little so we're more than just a logo on a shirt they buy."

Tess groaned and dropped her chin to her chest. "You've got to be having a laugh. Tell me you're having a laugh."

"Not at all. Don't you see? It's brilliant. We can offer something unique to the fans, something most other sponsors never could. What could Sharecore have given away?"

"Stock options."

"Right. I'm sure they would've done that, Tessy. Especially considering they're worthless now. We have something even better, something that'll get the crowd excited about us. At each Legends home match, we'll give away a long weekend at one of our most popular UK or Western Europe destinations. People love a free getaway. And they'll be so excited about it, that when our web address flashes on the big screen they'll get online and see we offer exotic foreign holidays without the guilt. It's perfect."

Tess had to agree that she would definitely check out the website if she thought a free trip was on offer. But that wasn't her problem. "You don't need me to do that. You can do it. Or—" she glanced through the meeting room window at the open-plan office before waving at no one in particular, "—or any of these people. Or the announcer. There's a man who stands on the pitch during halftime and introduces whatever entertainment they've got on. Get him to do it."

Charlie shook his head. "If the announcer does it, then we're missing an opportunity to connect the crowd with us. We're just another faceless company giving shit away. I don't want that. I want them to have warm, pleasant feelings when they hear our name. I want them to feel like we're a family so they trust us to take care of their family when they're on safari in Botswana."

"Okay, fine. But that still begs the question *why me?*"

He ticked the reasons off on his fingers. "Because you're young, you're cute, you're professional and everyone else in this office knows fuck-all about rugby. Plus, you're desperate for work and therefore easy for me to exploit."

Tess opened her mouth to argue that most of the people in the room could be considered young, cute professionals, but she couldn't argue with the last two bits.

"This is more than just walking onto the pitch at halftime and getting the crowd excited about possibly winning a trip to Skye or Brittany. It's about creating a relationship. Frank explained that we get several perks for sponsoring the club, like our own hospitality box where we can entertain clients. But since we don't really have traditional clients, I might find a way of giving that away as an incentive for booking a holiday with us. Whatever we do with it, we need a host who can talk to people in the language they speak. You know rugby, you know Legends and you'll know all about our holidays by the time we start doing this, so you'll be able to make that connection with people."

Tess squeezed her eyes shut, momentarily despising Charlie and his mustard-colored skinny jeans. "That's all? You'll pay me to show up at home matches to play hostess and go onto the pitch at halftime?"

"Well, there will be a few other things involved—"

"Such as?"

"I'm not sure yet. Everything's still up for discussion. But I'll let you know." He grabbed her clenched fist and gave it a squeeze. "I don't want to force you to do anything you're not comfortable with. I know the other night was...tense...and I'm not sure what happened."

"Nothing happened."

"If you say so. I got the impression that when you two met in Venezuela, you didn't exactly hit it off."

"It's no biggie. We were on a hike together. But that's it." That so wasn't it.

"If that's the answer you're sticking to, I'll take it for now. But if there's something bigger going on that I'm not aware of, just say the word and I'll find someone else." He raised his brows and tilted his head down, like he was peering at her seriously over an imaginary pair of spectacles. "In fact, you should know that I have a strict no-fraternization clause in my employment contract."

"Does that mean what I think it means?"

"If you think it means that you can't fuck around with anyone related to your work, then yes."

Tess pinched her lips together in an effort to control the annoyed words that wanted to burst free. Charlie knew her too well to let the matter lie.

"I'm not saying that because of your recent past. I'm saying it because of mine."

The penny dropped with a clang. Before Charlie came back from his travels and started Kijani, he'd briefly lived in Ghana and run a guest house with a local woman. They'd married, but he'd returned to London without a wife and without a share in that business. Charlie had never confided the details to her, but Tess's career obviously hadn't been the only one destroyed by sex with a colleague.

Pushing her misgivings aside, she patted his knee. "You don't have to worry about that. And of course I'll do what you need me to. I'm happy to take the position."

"Thanks. And I know I'm asking you to give up some of your weekends to do this, so I'm more than happy for you to take time off in lieu during the week. Just let me know when you won't be here so I can plan around it."

"Charlie, you don't have to do that. I'm used to working ridiculous hours."

"I know you are, sweet cheeks, but your former employers were dicks, and they could throw money at you to make it somewhat worth your while. I don't have those kinds of resources, and I'm not a dick. So take time off when you've worked on a weekend, or I'm going to start feeling really guilty."

"Instead you're making me feel really guilty about wanting to say no to your evil scheme?"

He smiled. "First day and you've already figured out my management technique. I knew you were brilliant."

He had just turned away to go back to his desk when Kijani's administrator, Georgie, sauntered through the meeting room door with a swish of her round hips and handed him a bundle of envelopes. "Today's post."

"Thanks, Georgie," he said, but she ignored him and walked away. Attitude and style. Georgie had them in such abundance that Tess had a momentary dream of rubbing against her in the vain hope they were contagious. If Georgie had been alive in the fifties, she would've made it as a pin-up. Marilyn Monroe with a Lancashire accent. And the way Georgie dressed and moved proved that she knew it.

Aware she was staring, Tess turned her attention back to her cousin and caught him staring, too, the post all but forgotten. She lowered her voice so no one else could hear. "Rumbled."

He jerked from his daze. "What?"

"You've been rumbled. Don't try to deny it. I caught you staring."

"I don't know what you mean. She works for me."

"And?"

"And what?"

"She works for you, and you want to get in her pants."

He looked affronted.

"I'm not blaming you. If I had any leanings in that direction, I would too. She's stunning."

"She's my administrator. That's all." He pretended to ignore her by flipping through the envelopes.

"Has something happened between you two?"

"Of course not! I'm her boss. You of all people should know it wouldn't be appropriate."

There it was. Would people ever forget the way she'd fucked up by...well, fucking Michael? "You're right. It's completely unethical, if it's one-sided. But if it's mutual—Oh! Georgie would be a natural at getting involved with the team. Think about it—I bet the men would love her."

"Georgie knows less than fuck-all about rugby."

"So? Lots of men see ignorance as an attractive quality in a woman. Look at her. They won't care if she's talking to them about rugby, Madagascar or puppies. They'll just want her to keep talking."

He glared at her. "I'm not running that kind of business, Tess. And I'm surprised at you, drawing conclusions based on how a woman looks."

"I didn't—"

But he lifted a disbelieving brow, as if to say "Rumbled."

Shame overcame her. How could she have done that after so many years of being the victim of the same line of thinking, only more crudely expressed? "Sorry, Charlie."

He flicked an envelope into her lap. "I was going to try to find a way to sweeten you up before dropping this on you, but you've pissed me right off. Hope you don't have plans for Saturday."

"I'm going to the London double header with Dad. Why?" She grabbed the envelope and turned it over, the Legends logo stamped in green ink across the front.

"Good. You can surprise him with these tickets. They're for the hospitality suite at Twickenham. You'll need to be there at least half an hour before kickoff." He walked away, calling over his shoulder, "And please don't wear a suit. You're representing the Kijani team now. We dress down for rugby matches."

Saturday lunchtime Tess stood with her father outside England's national rugby stadium, Twickenham. For years, the London double header had been their annual father-daughter date. Her mum and Gwen had never shown any interest in rugby, so it'd been one thing that Tess and her dad could bond over. No matter what Tess had going on at work or which academic conferences her dad might've wanted to go to, they set aside this Saturday for the opening of the rugby season, when the four London-based teams played each other in two matches in front of sell-out crowds.

Supporters, decked out in the kits of the four teams, streamed through the regular entrances around the stadium. Where Tess and her dad stood, they could hear music pumping inside and from the live bands playing in the lot where fans gathered to drink and eat fried foods. The smell of Cornish pasties and hamburgers wafted their way from the food vans nearest them, making Tess's stomach rumble. Frank —or, more probably, his P.A.—had sent a letter with their tickets telling her that there would be a spread for sponsors in their hospitality box, so Tess had decided to hold out until she got inside to eat. Her dad hadn't had the willpower. He'd downed a portion of fish and chips, calling it an *amuse bouche.* He did like to eat when he was nervous. Beside her, he bounced from foot to foot, like a four-year-old with a bladder infection.

"Dad, don't take this the wrong way, but do you need a wee?"

He rolled his eyes. "I think we're still a few years off before you need to worry about asking me things like that."

"Would you mind not dancing around, then? You're making me nervous."

He looked at her in shock. "Nervous? You? I've seen you tear grown men apart, littl'un. Men with money, power. How can you be nervous about meeting rugby players?"

Not players, plural. Just one.

But her dad didn't know that, of course. He threw his arm around her shoulder and drew her into his side before giving what she thought of as his republican speech. It was the same one he'd delivered when she was six and had been chosen to hand a bouquet of flowers to the queen, when Her Maj officially opened a new wing at her school. "Remember, sweetheart, we are all equals. Everyone who acts honorably deserves your respect, but no one deserves it simply for the job they do."

"Then why are you shaking, Dad?"

For a moment, his nervous trembling stopped, as if his big, logical brain finally overpowered his body's natural reactions to meeting the team he'd supported for years. "Good question. You're right—I shouldn't be nervous either. They're just men."

Well, one of them seemed a bit more than that to her, but she wasn't going to tell her dad that.

A woman about Tess's age speed-walked over to them, a clipboard in her hands and a headset over one ear. Her power suit and green silky top made Tess feel underdressed in her jeans and Legends rugby shirt. *Damn it. I knew I should've worn a suit.* At least the woman's smile was welcoming. "Are you Dr. and Ms. Chambers from Kijani Adventures?"

"Yes." Tess held out her hand. "I'm Tess, and this is my father, Ben."

"Ruth Higgins. I work in the Legends' press office. Lovely to meet you both. Tess, I'll be your main contact, so I'll meet you before every match, escort you to the pitch just before halftime and at the end of matches, and just generally be on hand to answer any questions you or your guests may have. Do you have any for me so far?"

Tess shook her head. "Don't think so."

"Excellent! Let's go in, then, and I'll introduce you to the team."

Tess shoved her hands in the pockets of her jeans and straightened her shoulders. She needed about six feet of courage. Unfortunately she only found about five feet and change. "Are you sure? They're probably busy preparing for the match."

Ruth waved off her protest. "They are, but our captain told me to make sure he knew when you arrived."

"Liam said that?" Tess's voice had gone all high-pitched, so she cleared her throat. "I mean, did he?"

"He did. After all, you're our very special guests today."

Special. Tess managed to keep from snorting. If there was one thing she certainly wasn't to Liam, it was special. But that brief wounded look he'd given her in the ladies' loo came back to her, making her wonder if she could've been, had she treated him differently.

LIAM WAS HUDDLED in the corner of the changing room with the backs coach going over last-minute changes when the door opened. Normally he would've ignored any intrusions as he concentrated on all the details he needed to absorb before the match, but this time something told him to look up. It was the same something that had drawn him to the top of Tess's head in the raw foods restaurant before he'd even known it was her.

This time, it was her front that drew his attention. Or, rather,

her calm, serious face as she followed Ruth into the room—and the Legends jersey she wore. The logos marked the shirt as being several seasons out of date, as did the faded green horizontal stripes and the way the fabric looked soft from years of washings. Now he had no doubt she'd been supporting the team for some time.

He glanced around quickly to see what states of undress she might've caught the team in. They always arrived wearing their matching tracksuits, and their clean kit hung in doorless cubbies around the room with their numbers facing outward, making an excellent backdrop for the TV journalists who shot their opening remarks here before the team arrived. However, once the team clambered off the bus, this room became a chaotic hive of activity as every player prepared in his own way. At least one of his teammates had a ritual that included dressing as slowly as possible and doing a range of stretches between putting on each item of clothing. Tess did not need to see Shaggy—the Samoan tight-head prop—bent over in a down-dog yoga pose wearing only his green socks.

Fortunately, Shaggy seemed to have passed that stage of his ritual. At least he was wearing his pants, though they were tight, white and cut high on the thigh.

Liam stood to welcome Tess and the man she was with, his duty as team captain. Perhaps it wasn't written into his contract, but this was his team and making introductions was part of his role. He'd told himself he would treat her just like any other sponsor, which is why he'd asked Ruth to bring her down before the match. He just hadn't expected the sight of her to stir up the adrenaline that he tried to keep a tight rein on until just before a match started. Adrenaline—that had to explain the waves of electrifying sensation flowing through him at the sight of her, right?

Ruth beamed as he approached the trio. "Dr. and Ms. Chambers, I'd like to introduce you to the Legends captain, Liam Callaghan."

Another Chambers man? This one resembled Tess even less than the first one. He towered well over Liam—probably about six-five—and looked like he enjoyed his food, if his barrel belly was anything to go by. This time, though, Liam wouldn't make the same stupid assumption he'd made before. "Dr. Chambers, pleasure to meet you, sir. I take it you're related to Tess and Charlie?"

The older man shook his hand in a strong, enthusiastic grip. "Please, call me Ben. And indeed I am. I'm Tess's proud papa and Charlie's uncle. It's a pleasure to meet you."

Meeting Tess's father...Fuck. "The pleasure's all mine, sir. Ms. Chambers, lovely to see you again."

And, surprisingly, that wasn't a complete lie. She gave him a tight-lipped smile and a polite greeting, as if apologetic for having put him in this situation when she knew it was awkward. Ever since their dinner the other night, he hadn't been able to get her out of his head. One night he'd even dreamed about her, something that never happened. Oh, he'd dreamed of women before, but they were always anonymous, faceless. Tess had been all too real, sultry, wet and naked under a waterfall—but it hadn't been exactly the same waterfall they'd made their own in Venezuela. He hadn't recognized it, but, then again, he hadn't been so focused on the location as he had been on making her groan and tremble.

Think of something else, mate—anything else. The last thing he needed was for his shorts to get tight. They were short enough that they didn't leave much to the imagination.

Turning his attention back to Tess's father, he said, "You look like you might've played rugby in your day, sir."

Clearly chuffed at the observation, Ben puffed out his chest. "I had a fairly distinguished career. I was a front row for the

Middlesex Under 16s, and then I hit my growth spurt. I was a lock at Oxford when I was doing my undergrad in the seventies. You might've heard of me," he said with mock seriousness. "I had the distinction of being the only forward to score a drop goal during my first season. Sadly, I'd got turned around, so I kicked it through the posts we were trying to defend. Even worse, I'd just met Tess's mum a few weeks before, and I'd invited her to come watch me play. Fortunately, she knew nothing about rugby, so she assumed I'd done something magnificent."

Liam laughed. "There are some benefits to being with someone who knows nothing about the sport. Let me introduce you to the team." He called the two locks over first. "Little John Sheldon and Shorty Dunston, I'd like you to meet our newest sponsor. This is Tess Chambers from Kijani Adventures and her father, Ben. Sounds like he might be ready to step into either of your shoes, so I'd watch myself if I were you."

Little John—all six-foot-nine of him—and Shorty—so called because he was two inches shorter than Little John—listened to Ben recount his gloryless days with good humor and even asked for kicking pointers, a skill locks weren't known for. They were huge men—the height of professional basketball players but twice as wide and usually half as fast—whose main function on the pitch was to apply brute force, not athletic finesse.

Liam listened to the three but couldn't stop himself from glancing at Tess. She came up to the middle of her father's chest, if that. Her mother must be built like a Chihuahua because Tess certainly hadn't inherited any of her father's genes—at least, none of the ones that determined physical characteristics.

She laughed along with the men, looking more relaxed as she joined their conversation. "Never trust a lock to do a fly half's job."

The locks reared back in surprise as she not only took the

piss out of her father—and of them—but revealed a smidgen of rugby knowledge. The reminder that she'd lied about recognizing him and about being a rugby supporter put Liam's back teeth on edge. Something on his face must've given him away, because her smile slowly froze before disappearing.

Liam cleared his throat. "I'll just introduce you around to the other lads."

He performed the duty on auto-pilot, but inside his blood pressure ratcheted up as Tess found something to compliment each player on. She seemed to know every man's biggest accomplishment and congratulated the cubs on having been selected to play without him needing to point out that this was their first season with the team. Yet another sign that she was not only a rugby fan but had followed the team for a long time.

While her father tripped over his tongue a few times when meeting some of the players, Tess stayed cool...until the trio reached the most legendary of Legends, scrum half Ash Trenton. Ash was the man whose shoes Liam was trying to fill. Since Ash was thirty-four, everyone knew he'd be retiring soon even though he'd yet to announce a date. Seeing a need for succession planning, their Legends coach had named Liam captain last year, a move Ash said he was happy about but must've been tough for the man who'd held the reins for eight years, building the club into one of the country's best.

Liam performed the introductions, waiting to hear how Tess would address the great man himself, but Ben never gave her a chance. He thrust his hand out, pumped Ash's up and down vigorously, and gushed, "It's a great honor, isn't it, Tessy? We've watched you for years, and meeting you in person—I'm speechless."

Clearly he wasn't, though, because he plowed on, nudging his daughter's shoulder so hard she teetered into Liam's side and he had to steady her by grabbing her arm just above her elbow. "Did you ever think you'd meet Mr. April?"

Tess's triceps flexed under Liam's palm. "Dad..."

But the man went on, mindless of the flush crossing Tess's cheeks. "My daughter here bought your calendar last year. You know, the one where you lads got your kit off and held onto your balls—rugby balls, I mean. I think it's been April in her kitchen ever since."

Ash flashed Tess a wicked smile and said something Liam couldn't hear for the blood rushing in his ears. She'd had fucking *Ash Trenton's* naked photo up? He dropped his hand as if her skin had scalded him. Judging by the heat pouring off her face, he was just in time too. She closed her eyes in obvious mortification, and Ruth stepped in to whisk the visitors off to the hospitality suite. As they reached the door, Tess glanced over her shoulder, her troubled gaze meeting his, and he shook his head. *Don't say a word. I don't want to know.*

Ash fucking Trenton. Bad enough Liam was constantly compared to the man by sports pundits. Worse that he'd thought he'd found someone he could be Just Liam with only to discover she'd known him all along. But now he'd have the sickening doubt about whether she'd pictured Ash fucking Trenton while she'd slept with him.

And yet, he *still* had to professionally seduce the only woman who'd ever left him a Dear John letter. Fucking hell.

The trio was out the door and halfway down the hall by the time he realized he needed to sort something else out.

"Ruth!" he yelled.

The group stopped, and Ruth hurried back when he beckoned her. Dropping his voice, he said, "I need you to do me a favor."

. . .

Plates piled high with a variety of meaty, messy food from the gourmet buffet, Tess and her dad settled into their seats in the hospitality suite. Dozens of corporate types milled around, networking and boasting the way Tess used to have to do. She'd never felt entirely comfortable in the role, but being an outsider and watching sycophants practically bend over double to lick their clients' arses made her feel ill. She shuddered, glad she was well shot of that career.

"I didn't embarrass you, did I, littl'un?"

"Not at all, Dad." No, *embarrass* didn't begin to cover it. Humiliate? Still not strong enough. Destroy? Maybe.

Having anyone's idol know that she'd kept a calendar with his nearly naked picture up in her kitchen was humbling. But much worse, Liam had looked completely disgusted by her when she'd left. How could she ever face him again?

"Sometimes I get Tourette's and I can't help the things I say. Your mum would have a go at me if she knew what I said to that man. I'm really sorry."

She took a deep yogic breath—in through her nose and out her mouth to a count of ten—before feeling calm enough to respond. "Hey, what're fathers for if they can't provide their children with stories about how embarrassing they are, right?"

He made a noncommittal sound that let Tess know he felt too awful to joke.

"It's all right, Dad. Really. Make it up to me by enjoying the match. Look at these views. We'll probably never get to see something like this again." The room was long, with one wall entirely built of windows overlooking the halfway line. The players jogged onto the pitch amid flares, and the crowd surged to its feet to applaud the start of another season.

"Tess?"

She turned and found Ruth holding out a paper bag printed

with the Legends logo and a photo of Liam flying through the air to score a try. "A little gift from our captain."

Stomach knotting at the words, Tess thanked her and took the bag. She peered inside and pulled out two brand-new plastic-wrapped Legends jerseys. Dumbfounded, she handed the XXL to her father and ripped open the XS. This season's kit, complete with the Kijani Adventures logo printed across the chest.

Smoothing the bag over her knee, unwilling to crumple Liam's determined face or throw him away, she felt something else in the bag. She drew out a note card with a hastily scrawled message.

T—

You can't wear our kit from 2005. It's embarrassing.

—LC

She mumbled her excuses to her father as she headed for the ladies' to change her top. Hope bloomed in her chest that maybe, possibly she was forgiven for deceiving him.

But that look of disgust he'd given her remained too strong a memory for her to believe it.

When she returned to the hospitality suite, her dad was twisted in his seat, watching out for her. Too far away to be heard unless he shouted, he raised his arm and jabbed a finger in the direction of the tandoori chicken kebabs laid out on a table Tess was about to pass.

How many? Tess mouthed.

He held up four fingers, scrunched his face up like he was reconsidering, then added his thumb. Jesus, five more kebabs on top of everything they'd already eaten? The man was a candidate for a coronary. Not that she was arguing from a position of strength when it came to diets, but at least she made sure to burn some of the grease off every day.

Her dad faced the pitch as the players warmed up, and Tess

grabbed another plate, piling it high with kebabs. What the hell —she might as well add a couple for herself while she was there.

"I see you still eat like shit."

The voice hit her just a second after the cloying cologne did, and the combined effect made the hairs on her neck stand on end. Forcing every muscle in her face to relax so she gave nothing away—not even one iota of the molten revulsion in her gut—she turned toward the man who was directly responsible for her having to cut her time in Venezuela short. "Michael."

I see you still smell like shit. Once upon a time, she wouldn't have hesitated to stoop to his puny emotional level. But giving up tit-for-tat insults was high on her list of ways to live a happier life. She could defend herself by being the better person...and with Michael Mulligan, that shouldn't be difficult.

He smirked and made a show of looking her up and down, taking in the still-creased Legends shirt before he smoothed his hand along his suit lapel. The only sign he was at a rugby match was the yellow-and-black tie, the colors of one of Legends' cross-town rivals where her old employer had corporate season tickets for entertaining clients. "Must be nice to come to one of these events and dress down. Unemployment clearly has its benefits." He gave her a mock thoughtful look. "What *is* unemployment benefit these days? About eighty quid a week?"

"At least it's an honest living, and I don't have to deal with twats all day," she said. *Whoops.* So much for rising above. She gave him a smile she clearly didn't mean and tried to step around him, but he grabbed her elbow, jerking her hard enough that the kebabs tumbled to the floor.

"Listen to me, you scrawny-arsed bitch. You've made all of us look like dicks. Don't think for one second that we'll forget that. I still know things..."

"Please, Michael, you didn't need *me* to make you look like a dick. And we both know you shot your wad when you handed over my email to the lawyers. You have nothing else on me that I need to worry about."

"Really? We'll see. I can make life very unpleasant for you, little girl."

"Oh, I know you can. You did for years, so why should it be any different now?" She pulled her elbow free and calmly refilled her plate with only five kebabs for her dad, since she'd just lost her appetite. Nodding toward the ones on the floor, she said, "I'll let you tidy those up. I know how at home you are snuffling around in the dirt. Excuse me."

She returned to her seat and handed the food to her father, then squeezed her clenched hands between her knees to keep him from seeing how they shook. She pretended to focus on the match, but her mind betrayed her, setting up a slideshow of her career lowlights.

Michael had interviewed her when she'd applied for a graduate placement at the investment bank straight after uni. He became what was known in the industry as her rabbi, not technically her boss but someone higher in the corporate food chain and rising fast. He'd seemed eager to bring her up with him, even—she suspected—twisting a few arms when a lucrative new position opened among the traders...a position most women wouldn't have applied for because they knew their chances were hopeless. She'd been determined to prove herself, not by out-bloking the blokes but by working her arse off and showing that she was just as capable as anyone else.

Michael had been one of the few men she worked with who saved his inappropriate remarks for the pub. Or, at least, she'd thought he had. It was one of the characteristics that had made him grow more attractive to her over the first couple of years they worked together. His confidence came with only a moderate amount of cockiness, and he'd treated her the same as the other traders...until the night they both got too drunk at a colleague's leaving do and she went home with him.

By Monday lunchtime, she'd begun hearing whisperings and tried to convince herself that the smirks were her imagination. Then she overheard Michael telling her team leader that he'd fucked Titless Tess, and her professional world had collapsed. The nickname stuck. The smirks and smarmy comments never disappeared. Colleagues openly asked if she'd succeeded in making big deals by sucking clients off. *We know it's not by titty-fucking them,* one had joked in a staff meeting.

On principle, she refused to quit. She'd already started blogging at that point, but now rage infused her writing and some of her posts were picked up by the City's daily newspaper. Other women wrote in with similar stories, and her one bad decision snowballed until the national media caught wind of scandal and the politicians began making noises about gender equality in the workplace. Someone uncovered her identity, and after that it wasn't difficult for the papers to expose the real-life characters she'd written about.

If only Tess had confined her writing to her blog. If only she hadn't fired off that angry, drunken email mocking the pathetic size of his cock and generally proving herself to be little better than he was.

She was sick of being in the public eye. She'd humiliated herself and her family—who'd stuck by her even as the darker side of her character was exposed to the world. The greed. The pettiness. The sexual insults.

With her eyes on the match starting down below, she sought out Liam. She'd understood his desire for privacy in Venezuela, but his public role was so much different to hers. He was beloved by the nation and even exalted by his rivals. He was a golden boy who could do no wrong. She was either a feminist freedom-fighter or a hideous bitter bitch, depending on the cartoon and the newspaper.

She wanted to be anonymous again. The first step to achieving that was to stay away from scandal. The second step was to never, ever let anything compromise her professionalism again—and Charlie was right that that meant avoiding relationships with anyone remotely involved in her work.

Good thing Liam had made his disgust in her clear. Otherwise, she might've been tempted to follow him down a path to her own destruction.

10

The morning of Legends' first home match, Tess took advantage of the quiet roads and sunshine and cycled from Stoke Newington to their stadium in Stratford, East London.

Charlie still hadn't figured out how best to use the extra tickets Kijani got as part of their match-day sponsorship deal, so when Tess met her father she kept her fingers crossed that he wouldn't have any opportunities to humiliate her today of all days—her first time walking onto the pitch to give away a trip.

"Hi, Dad." She kissed him on the cheek and leaned into his brief bear hug.

"Morning, Tessy. Ready for a pie and a pint?"

"Always." She walked with him to their favorite food van and ordered two steak-and-ale pies while her dad sought out one of the men wandering through the growing crowd with a backpack full of beer from the local Legends brewery. Tess's chest filled with pride over her team's traditions. They'd started over eighty years ago, when young men working at Legends brewery had decided to form a team at the weekends. Men's rugby had only gone professional in the nineties, but for decades before that it was played purely for love of the sport.

After they ate, Tess excused herself to change in the toilets. She'd brought proper clothes in a small backpack, so she stripped off her cycling gear, gave herself a quick wash in the sinks so she felt a bit fresher, and pulled on her brand new shirt, smoothing it down and checking herself out in the mirror. Seeing the name of Charlie's company printed across her chest made her smile. He had done well for himself, and now she was here to help him do even better.

Even if that meant seeing Liam again.

And Ash Trenton.

Oy.

Ruth met Tess and her father at the stadium entrance and showed them how to use their special electronic passes to buzz themselves through the security doors, then led them up several flights of stairs. The sell-out crowd of fifteen thousand thinned as most supporters found their seats on lower levels. When they'd reached the top floor, Ruth motioned toward another closed door and Tess buzzed them in. They entered a long room containing several buffet tables set up with food, glorious food. And a fully stocked bar.

"I'll come get you when the game clock says there's five minutes left before the half," Ruth explained. "I'll introduce you to Gerry—he's the on-pitch announcer—and from that point on you really just have to do what he says. He's been doing this since before God was born, so you'll be in excellent hands. Any questions?"

"Just why did I eat that pie?" Tess joked, taking in the assortment of nibbles, curries and mini pork pies that didn't look as if they'd been microwaved. And a table of healthy salads, which she ignored.

Ruth laughed. "You'll know better for next time. Now—I

have to dash, but here's my mobile number if you need me for anything, anything at all during the match." She handed Tess a card. "I'll see you soon."

Tess's father had already disappeared and was chatting with the barman, who was pulling a couple of pints. Tess wandered over. "No more for me, Dad. One was enough. I'm working, remember?"

"You sure you don't need some Dutch courage?"

"Positive." Already, the pie and nerves were making her stomach ache, and the last thing she needed was to stumble onto the pitch half-cut and take control of a microphone.

Just like at Twickenham, the room was full of corporate types. They'd dressed down for the occasion, but Tess could still smell them a mile away. Not difficult, since they tended to like bathing in strong cologne. Around the room, men laughed too heartily or talked too loudly on their mobiles. She shuddered. As hard as she'd fought to keep her career, she was through with it now. The money had been fantastic, but it certainly hadn't been worth it. Not when it meant sacrificing her pride, her self-respect and her ability to be a decent human being. Thank God Charlie had given her this chance, even if it was currently making a mess of her stomach.

She and her dad took their seats, and he buzzed with boyish excitement next to her. "Look at this, Tessy. We're right over the halfway line."

Tess let herself get lost in the spectacle surrounding the start of the match. Once, while on a business trip to New York, she'd gone to an American football game. Fighter jets had flown over and members of the special forces had parachuted into the middle of the stadium while fireworks went off and the crowd roared. She'd been astounded—and a little bit frightened. Nothing like that happened at rugger matches. Every Legends match started the same way. Around forty children from local rugby clubs—each wearing a Legends jersey and waving a flag—formed two parallel lines facing each other. A woman tried to corral the children so their lines were fairly straight, and she coached them to raise their flags at her signal. The announcer—Gerry—stood on the pitch and read out happy-birthdays to several kids in attendance. He announced last-minute changes for both sides, then the opposing team ran onto the pitch to polite handclaps and cheers from their section of supporters.

"And now, ladies and gentlemen, please welcome...your London Legends!" Finally, the big moment. The Legends players jogged out of the tunnel and through the gauntlet of local children, who went crazy with their flags while smoke machines sprayed green and white smoke on either side of them.

Liam led the line of players, setting a leisurely pace because he held the hands of two small children. This was a tradition that choked her up every time. Sometimes they were the kids of season ticket holders or people important to the club. Other times, they were children the team met through local charities they were involved with. Always, they beamed with pride at being the team's mascot for the day.

"Our mascots today are five-year-old Stephanie and her big brother Lucas from the Smile Children's Club in Stratford. Please give them a big hand, ladies and gentlemen!"

Tess watched the big screen so she could see their expressions. Little Stephanie had Down's Syndrome. She and her brother grinned at Liam as he led them to the center of the pitch, crouched down to their height and pointed toward the touchline, probably at their parents or someone from their charity. They waved with such excitement that Tess and her dad laughed. Liam put his arms around their little shoulders and drew them close so a photographer could snap their picture together, then he said one last thing to them before Ruth led them off the pitch. He smiled, but by the time he jogged over to his team, his face was in game mode.

Tess's dad leaned into her side. "Do you remember when you were the mascot?"

"Vaguely. Mostly I remember being confused about what was going on because Mum had come to the match too, and that never happened. Then you were telling me to hold this giant stranger's hand and to mind whatever he told me, and that never happened either."

He laughed. "The look on your face in that photo they took. Priceless. You were so serious, even then."

"I was trying to figure out if they expected me to play."

Shaking his head in obvious amusement, her dad said, "I remember that season. They'd have done better if they *had* asked you to play."

As she'd promised, with five minutes still to play in the half Ruth came for Tess and led her down the stairs to part of the stadium she'd never been to before. Under the stands, they passed the changing rooms and walked through the tunnel Tess had seen the team line up in many times, but only on TV. The crowd's cheers grew stronger, echoing off the tunnel walls. They met Gerry at the mouth of the tunnel, and Ruth introduced Tess to the man who was just as legendary as any of the players, the man who'd been getting the crowd excited for as long as Tess could remember.

He shook her hand, his brows drawing down in confusion. "I know you, don't I?"

Oh, shite. Here was something she hadn't considered. Her face and name had been all over the news for weeks during the inquiry. Her breath caught in her throat as she realized she was about to walk onto a pitch surrounded by thousands of people who would know exactly who she was and everything she'd gone through in the past year. Even if they hadn't followed the inquiry closely, they would still associate her with it. What if they booed her?

Worse, what if Charlie's whole plan flopped because his company's name became associated with her own disgrace? He'd paid a hell of a lot for this promo, and he'd entrusted her to represent him well. Her mottled history could cost him dearly.

She tried to brush off Gerry's recognition. "You must have an amazing memory. We met about twenty-three years ago when I was a mascot."

He grinned, obviously knowing that wasn't where he recognized her from but willing to play along anyway. "Ah, that's it! You're taller now, but I definitely see the resemblance." Lowering his voice, he asked, "You're not one of the ones who wet themselves before going on, are you?"

"N-no."

"Thank God for that. We'll have no problems today, then. Right. Here's what'll happen."

He explained that the teams would run off the pitch in a moment, and then there would be five minutes where kids from local rugby clubs played touch rugby. After that, he would escort Tess out to the center of the pitch, introduce her as one of their sponsors and let her take over. "Any questions?"

"Just one," she said. "When you introduce me, could you just call me Tess from Kijani Adventures?"

"Of course." He made a note on his clipboard. "All right, Tess from Kijani Adventures. That was the whistle. Step to the side now. You don't want to be mown down by this lot of beasts."

No kidding. She barely had time to flatten herself against the wall before the first players from the opposition jogged past her, leaving a puff of sweaty air in their wake. The cement beneath her feet trembled as they ran past.

And there was Liam, leading his team off the pitch as he'd led them on forty minutes ago. He was already looking at her by the time she found him. His tight shirt clung to his damp skin, defining every muscle. His short white shorts and long, thick thighs were stained with mud, blood and grass, evidence of a hard-fought match. As he passed, he glanced down at her chest and gave her a little smug smile that made her girl parts clench. Why was he checking out her chest? Was it her Legends jersey— or a not-so-subtle reminder that he'd seen beneath her shirt? Either way, the effect was the same. She was off-kilter, palm pressed against the cool concrete of the tunnel wall as she watched him disappear around the corner to the changing room.

God, how could she still want him so badly? Their time together in Venezuela had been magical, like a break from reality, but everything that had happened since had simply reminded her that she didn't belong in his world. If she'd had any question, watching her dining companions' faces as Samantha Hughes described the nude scene she'd just shot would have answered it.

Tess glanced down at her chest. *You, my dears, would never inspire that kind of attention, I'm sorry to say.*

Maybe it was time to fix that. Maybe it was time to explore item number five on her ways-to-change-my-life list. The pink hair hadn't worked out for her, but maybe more drastic measures would.

"Tess? It's time."

She tore herself from daydreams of having a decent rack and followed Gerry out to the middle of the pitch. The little kids who'd been playing touch rugby were all packing up their equipment and following their coaches off.

"And now, ladies and gentlemen, we have a special treat for you. Our newest sponsor, Kijani Adventures, offers guilt-free holidays for families, couples and intrepid explorers," Gerry read from a card into his hand-held mic. "Whether you're looking for a tailor-made luxury holiday at an eco-lodge that's committed to doing more good than harm, or you're eager to wander off the beaten track, Kijani Adventures is the tour company for you. At all of our home matches this season, the lovely Tess from Kijani Adventures will join me to give away a weekend break to one of our lucky supporters. Tess, why don't you tell us what you're giving away today and how we'll choose a winner?"

Gerry handed Tess the mic. Her fingers tingled with adrenaline as she took in the thousands of faces surrounding her. At least they were far away. During the inquiry, crowds of journalists and photographers had followed her in and out of the courtroom, pushing so close she'd been in danger of passing out from lack of oxygen.

"Thank you, Gerry." Her voice boomed through the speakers, so she moderated it. "Um, thank you. That's right—today we have an extra-special getaway for you. Four nights in a French villa, just a few steps from the Mediterranean. The villa grows all of its own food and produces its own solar energy, and we'll even throw in tickets for the train, so you don't need to pollute the air with a short-haul flight. I'll randomly draw a seat number, and that person just has to kick a penalty to claim the prize. Ready, everyone?"

Ready or not, Tess was part of the Legends team now.

That made Liam her captain—and completely off-limits.

"AND TODAY's Man of the Match is…Liam Callaghan!"

The announcer's voice made the tiniest dent in Liam's concentration. Less than a minute left in the match and he was squirting water in his mouth, while medics attended one of Exeter's players who'd been knocked out and swallowed his tongue. The match would resume shortly, with Legends two points down and deep into Exeter's territory.

Medics helped the Exeter player walk off the pitch while his replacement ran on to try to earn a few seconds of glory. The two teams took their positions. The forwards from each team gripped each other, bending down on the referee's command, and then slammed their shoulders into the opposing side, each side trying to drive the other back with pure physical power while using their feet to gain possession of the ball. Liam and the other backs spread out across the pitch, but the play was obvious. With barely any time remaining in the game, Liam's right boot was their only shot at winning.

Yes. Legends gained control. With a titanic shove, they shunted the Exeter pack off the ball. Their number 8 scooped it up and charged infield, shaking off a handful of would-be tacklers before finally being brought to ground in front of the posts. In a second or two, with characteristic precision, Ash fizzed the ball directly into Liam's waiting hands. Liam let muscle memory do the rest, drop-kicking the ball right between the posts.

Legends 24, Exeter 23.

Victory. Adrenaline flooded him, a different quality than the kind that kept him revved up during the match. Euphoria. Endorphins. No better feeling than winning a match. Nothing came close.

Waterfall.

Okay, maybe one thing had come close. He'd tried to forget that she would be here today, but the thought had been damn near impossible to push from his mind. When he'd run off the pitch at halftime, he'd known where she was standing without even having to look. So why had he looked?

Probably the same reason he played rugby. Sometimes the pain was worth the rush. And seeing Tess in his shirt? A bigger rush than he'd expected.

Liam shook hands with the Exeter players and jogged over to the side of the pitch, where Ruth stood in the press area. Lavinia, a journalist from one of the sports networks, waited for him, but when he got closer he found Tess right next to her, gripping a bottle of champagne as if she were trying to strangle it. Damn it. She was too cute in that Legends jersey, looking all nervous and unsure of herself. He knew secrets about her no one else would ever suspect, considering her conservative hairstyle and buttoned-up posture. He'd struggled to scrub those secrets from his memory ever since he'd discovered she would be part of his working life.

"Great match, Liam," Lavinia said with a big smile. She said it without raising the mic, so they must not be on-air yet.

"Cheers, Vinnie. Tough one."

She held up a finger. "Say no more till we're on." With a glance at her cameraman, she nodded at something that came through her earpiece, then turned to him again. "Ready?"

"Ready."

She positioned herself to face the camera and put on her broadcasting voice. "That's right, Robin. I'm here with Liam Callaghan, Legends captain and today's Man of the Match. Congratulations, Liam."

"Thank you, Lavinia." He put an extra dose of charm behind the words, inordinately pleased at how Tess's nostrils flared. If she gripped that champagne bottle any tighter, it would shatter. Her hands had a good strong grip—he knew that from experience.

"You were down by twelve at the half. What did you say to the lads to get them to come out fighting?"

He'd been doing this for so long he didn't need to use even half his brain to answer. He used the free half to watch Tess. She stared at his chest, his abs, the players behind him. Anyone else would think she was bored, but he knew better. He knew she was a fan, so he made a facetious comment that only a die-hard Legends fan would get and watched her try to hide her smile.

When he first discovered her lies, he'd been furious. He'd slept with his fair share of groupies before he'd been named captain, but he'd always known that was what he was doing. With Tess, he'd thought he'd found something more, so her lie became a cutting betrayal, a deception that left him feeling like a fool. But now...now the shock had worn off, but judging by his sleepless nights, the lust hadn't.

Lavinia wrapped up the interview. "Congratulations again, Liam Callaghan, Man of the Match."

She nodded toward Tess, who seemed stuck inside her own head, or maybe mesmerized by his chest. He cleared his throat, holding his hand out, but she just blinked and looked at him blankly until Lavinia nudged her with her elbow.

"Oh! Sorry." Tess grimaced and handed him the champagne bottle.

Lavinia let her mic drop to her side. "Liam, always a pleasure."

"Pleasure's all mine, Vinnie." He grinned at her and stepped away so she could get back to work. As he passed Tess, he snagged the sleeve of her shirt between his thumb and forefinger, dragging her with him. She stumbled a little, but righted herself quickly and walked alongside him off the pitch.

"How was your first match as a sponsor?"

She started, as if she was surprised he was talking to her. He was a little surprised himself. "Uh, it was quite good. Very good, I mean. Well done on winning. Great drop goal there at the end."

He acknowledged her with a small nod. "Must be fairly diffi-cult, having to remember to hand the Man of the Match his champagne at the end of the interview."

"Well, you know, it *is* a major responsibility. That's why

Charlie entrusted me with it. I can always be counted on to tackle the really important projects."

"Is that a hint of frustration I hear?"

"Perceptive. Anyway, I didn't think you were speaking to me. Not when we're alone, anyway."

They approached the sideline, where the team celebrated. He leaned down close so only she would hear him. "No choice. It's my job."

That stopped her dead in her tracks, leaving him free to jog to his team and celebrate with them. Victory suddenly felt hollow, though, after seeing the flash of hurt he'd inflicted. He hadn't felt like this big of a dick since...well, since the night he'd humiliated her at the raw foods restaurant. She'd brought out the best in him in Venezuela. Now she seemed to be bringing out the worst.

She lied to you.

But somehow the words had lost the power they'd had when he first found out.

You lied too, mate.

And that didn't seem to matter, either. He wanted her. No point in denying it, even though he just had, telling her that the only reason he was speaking to her was because he was obliged to do so.

She was his sponsor. Like it or not, they worked together now. He needed to get himself under control before he did something he couldn't recover from.

11

————

"How'd it go on Saturday?"

Charlie perched against the edge of Tess's desk, cradling a package wrapped in plain white paper that was leaking white liquid.

"Uh, fine. Yeah. Crowd got really excited when I told them about the special code for ten percent off their next holiday booking. Lots of them seemed to get out their phones, but that might've just been because it was halftime. I don't know if any of them did anything about it."

Charlie rocked a little, his legs bouncing with excitement. "Our web traffic spiked four hundred percent, Tessy. Ten people booked overseas holidays with that code by Saturday night and a few more yesterday. I'm hoping several more are talking it over with their families and will pull the trigger sometime this week. It's working. It's really working."

"That's fantastic. I'm so pleased. But, um, your package is dripping."

He glanced down in horror at his crotch, then at the thing he held. "Oh! The falafel. Here, I bought this for your lunch." He cleared a space on her desk and set it down. "I'll get you some kitchen roll for the mess. They put a lot of yogurt dressing in it. And I ordered extra peppers on the side so you can burn a hole through whatever's left of your stomach lining."

She tore into the bag and revealed an overstuffed falafel in pita sandwich. The delightful smells of grease, coriander and pickles hit her. This must be what manna smelled like to the Israelites. "Oh, you beauty! To what do I owe this honor?"

"Well, I really appreciate what you've done for us so far. I hope you're enjoying the matches. What's the hospitality box like? I'm picturing free booze, massages…"

She nodded and tucked in to the food, taking a huge bite. Lebanese spices exploded over her tongue. The peppers burned and the yogurt cooled while the fried balls of ground chickpeas added just the right crunch. "Mmm, it's great. God, this is delishhis."

Charlie held up a hand. "That's all right. Don't try to talk while you eat. Just listen to me for a second."

Uh-oh. Her I-need-a-favor meter went *ding*. She swallowed and took another big bite, certain she was about to be put off her lunch by whatever he said.

"I need a favor."

"Reeeally?" she murmured. "Quelle surprise."

"Xander was supposed to go to this Legends promo shoot we've got lined up, but he's got norovirus and can't get off the toilet."

Grimacing, Tess dropped her falafel onto its bag. "Aaand I'm done. Cheers for that."

"Sorry. Anyway, I need you to go in his place to make sure it's the kind of promo we want."

"Are you kidding? Charlie, he's the art director. What the hell do I know about art?" She ticked items off on her fingers. "I know it's kept in museums. I know I avoid museums because they're boring. And I know that the lowest-ever mark I received in school was in my art class. Xander can't do simple addition, and I don't know shit about art. What on God's green earth could I possibly be Xander's substitute for?"

"Legends are doing their calendar photo shoot tomorrow. I've convinced them to go with an exotic holiday theme this year, since we're sponsoring the calendar. Our logo will be all over it, so I need someone there to make sure it's tasteful."

Good thing she'd put the falafel down or she would've choked. "Tasteful? You're not talking about their annual naked calendar, are you?"

"That's the one."

"Let me get this straight. You want me to go to a naked photo shoot and ensure it's tastefully done?"

"That's about it, yes."

She rolled her eyes. "And I thought investment bankers expected miracles."

TESS COULDN'T RESIST LOOKING ONLINE for Liam's previous calendar shots. Purely for professional reasons, obviously. Still, not wanting to risk her job by typing *Liam Callaghan naked* into her work computer, she used her personal phone—and good thing, because dozens of photos popped onto her screen showing Liam in various states of undress. Liam standing on the pitch looking totally unconcerned after his shorts had been ripped off in a tackle. Liam lying on his side smiling down at the topless Brazilian model he'd been linked to briefly. Liam laughing with his teammates in a changing room as a photographer captured his bare arse in black and white. The only thing Tess knew about art: if a photo was shot in black and white then it was art, not porn.

And God, *art* didn't even begin to describe the perfection of

Liam Callaghan. *Porn,* however, did describe the visions cavorting in her head.

She perused the photos far longer than was strictly necessary, putting off the moment when she had to face him in reality. When she couldn't delay any longer, she changed into her spandex cycling gear, got on her bike and began the trek from Shoreditch to Stratford. Lusty hormones surged through her, and she fought them off by pushing harder. The air was humid and warm, and she began sweating almost immediately. Her bum came off the seat, and her legs pumped till they burned, but the images wouldn't fade away. Liam straddling a bench press, while she supervised and gave opinions on whether the rugby ball he clutched provided a proper amount of coverage. Liam—

Hoooonk! The blast of a lorry's horn yanked her out of her daydream, and she jerked her bicycle away from the noise as the huge truck shot past her. Her front tire hit a pothole. She somersaulted over the handlebars, miraculously managing to land on her feet while her riderless bike rode off into the sunset—or, into the traffic, where a black cab bulldozed it.

"Fuck," she whispered, taking in the mangled remains. Cars swerved, drivers honked and a couple of cyclists shouted at her as they rode past.

"Fuuuck!" she screamed until she was probably blue. Her hands clenched into fists and she bent over to squeeze every bit of air from her lungs. Needing to kick something, she looked around and only found objects made of cement and metal, so she stomped her foot instead. As soon as there was a break in traffic, she ran into the street and dragged her bike back. It'd been a gift to herself, bought with the shut-up-and-go-away money her bank had given her when she'd threatened to sue for wrongful termination. Now, as the front tire stuck out at an unnatural angle and cried with a metal-on-metal squeak as it rotated, she felt as though she were carrying a comrade's body back from the trenches.

She laid it on the pavement and crouched next to it, touching it gently as she examined all its parts. Maybe an expert could fix it.

She was a mile from the stadium. She would give her bike every chance at survival. Hoisting it over her shoulder, she staggered a little. When she'd found her balance, she set out on the long, slow trek.

Twenty minutes later, she arrived ready for a fight instead of feeling mellowed from the ride. Damn Liam anyway. He was speaking to her because it was his job? Arsehole. She'd apologized for pretending not to know him, even though she hadn't done anything very terrible.

Okay, so disappearing in the middle of the night and leaving him only a note hadn't been her most stellar move. She'd have felt used and filthy if he'd done that to her. But he'd been the one to lie about his name first. She'd just gone along with it. What was she supposed to do, say "No you're not—you're Liam Callaghan, rugby union's leading points-scorer"?

After locking up her bike, she shoved open the glass door, her small backpack gluing her sweaty top to her skin. *God, if you're listening,* please *don't let him see me like this.* She walked to the reception desk, grateful for the burst of air conditioning. "I'm Tess Chambers from Kijani Adventures. I'm here for the photo shoot."

The woman smiled and pushed a sign-in sheet toward her. "Welcome, Ms. Chambers. If you could just fill that in for me, I'll get you a visitor's badge."

Tess thanked her and took the badge, looking down at her tight cycling shirt and shorts. Dirt streaked her calves, and she tried to wipe it off with the bottom of her shoe. Didn't work. "Is there somewhere I can change?"

"Of course. The ladies' is just outside the room where they're doing the photo shoot today. Down that hallway, then the first right down another corridor. It's at the end. You can't miss it."

"Thank you."

Tess shifted her backpack, catching an unpleasant whiff of herself that she hoped wouldn't reach the beautifully poised receptionist. Thank God she'd brought a small towel so she could wash herself in the sinks. She hadn't expected it to be so muggy out today. Just what she needed was to show up hot, sweaty and bothered.

She speed-walked toward the photo-shoot room, vaguely noting the meeting rooms with their high-tech gear inside. Just as she approached the loo, the double doors in front of her banged open and an angry man with flushed cheeks and a massive camera around his neck rushed out. "Are you the woman from the sponsor?"

"Y-yes." Was she in trouble already?

"You're late. You should've been here a half hour ago."

"What?" She looked at her chunky watch. "No, I'm here with two minutes to spare."

"You've the wrong time, then. Get in here. We need to start. I don't have all day. C'mon, now!" *Snap snap snap* went his fingers in her face.

And *snap* went her patience. She grabbed his hand and shoved it away. Keeping her voice über-calm, she said, "I take it you're the photographer. I'm sorry for the mix-up. If you ever snap in my face again, I will rip off each of your fingers. Slowly. Got it?"

He blinked down from a height several inches above her.

"I'm not joking. I've had enough of men pushing me around. You can either talk to me like one professional to another, or you can try to take pictures with bloody stumps. Your choice."

His Adam's apple bobbed. "We're running behind schedule.

Come in. We need you to approve the final set design before we get started."

Some of Tess's adrenaline ebbed, replaced by a wicked euphoria. She wasn't naturally the type to intimidate or threaten people, and—having worked with plenty of people who were—she'd never wanted to be that type, either. But maybe shocking people was a good thing every now and then.

She stepped around the photographer and entered the spacious room. It had been separated into different areas with varying backdrops—surprisingly realistic backdrops. These weren't the ugly paper backdrops that she'd had her school photos taken in front of. No, these actually looked like real places. In one corner, a jungle. In another, sand and palm trees and a green screen that presumably would complete the beach scene with a fake ocean. In another...a waterfall. Yes, a real, flowing waterfall.

No wonder the man was annoyed. It looked like he and his assistants had been here for ages setting up.

"Well?" he asked. "What do you think?"

She nodded slowly, as if assessing it with an artistic eye. "I suppose it'll do. Now, what do you need from me?"

"Just your signature here that you're happy with the scenes. And if you could stick around, we might be short-handed today. Something seems to be going around. I'm Andre, by the way."

She shook his hand. "Tess. And it's norovirus."

The man dropped her hand as if she'd said *plague*. "You don't have it, do you?"

"I wouldn't be here if I had it. Anyway, I need to get changed." The sooner she got out of here, the better. God only knew where the players were, and she didn't need them to see her in her skin-tight cycling outfit, covered in mud, sweat and grime, and smelling—well, like them.

"Not yet. I assume you're familiar with the calendar concepts?"

"You assume incorrectly."

"Let me fill you in." He seemed thrilled with her ignorance, perhaps because it gave him a chance to show off his brilliance. "It's quite simple, really. We'll have two different versions of the calendar."

"Two? Who needs two calendars?" Come to think of it, who needed one anymore? Didn't most people keep their diaries electronically? Her sister bought her the team's calendar as a joke every Christmas, while Tess always bought Gwen a calendar with kittens wearing ridiculous outfits that no self-respecting feline would be caught dead in. They both knew the calendars were just decoration for their kitchens.

"We have the traditional calendar," the photographer continued, "which will show each of the men indulging their inner beasts in these wild surroundings."

Okay, Tess *had* to be there when he told the team to indulge their inner beasts. She had no idea which players had been chosen for this calendar, but most of them seemed to have a good-enough sense of humor that instructions like that would lead to antics she wanted to witness.

"In years past, the men have either been in their pants or naked with a prop to maintain some of their dignity. This year, though, we have sexy costumes for them, depending on the scene they'll be part of. Then we'll have the digital version of the calendar."

Tess's attention caught. "Digital?"

"Yes. I'll explain more about that later." He sniffed the air. "For now, we're about ready to start, and you may wish to... freshen up."

As if he could really smell her. This side of the building

whiffed of men's sweat and aftershave. Still, she did need to change before Liam—

"Chambers? What the hell are you doing here?"

Oh, bugger. She should've known. After all, Liam was famed for his timing. He strode out of what she assumed was a changing room, several players following behind him in varying states of undress.

Good Lord...*very* good Lord. Liam wore a towel slung about his waist that covered him nearly to his knees, but it parted as he walked, giving her a flash of muscular thigh with every stride. She'd seen underneath that towel. She'd touched and tasted underneath that towel. Okay, maybe not *that* towel specifically, but the memory was enough to set her heartbeat to thundering and make her lower belly twitch in anticipation.

"Tess?" His voice sounded somewhat more amused this time, as if he knew the direction her mind had wandered. Probably not difficult to guess, since she suddenly realized she was staring just below his waist and chewing on the corner of her lower lip. She let her lip slide free and forced herself to look him in the eyes. "Last minute change of plans. A colleague was supposed to be here but he's ill, so you get me."

His mouth curled grimly at the words. "Great. Welcome. You know what we're doing today, right?"

"Mmm-hmm." Nearly naked photos. Tastefully done. Without her jumping him. Yes, she would become the ringmaster at the circus of impossibility today.

Andre clapped his hands and whistled for attention. "Let's get started, boys. Gather round and I'll explain how the morning will go."

Tess leaned over and hissed, "No no no no. I need to change my clothes."

"No time for that now. I told you I needed your help. We only have two hours to get all the photos we need before the team starts their training. Besides, you look…" He gave her a critical glance. "Anyway, we don't have time."

Damn it. Not only did she wear an outfit that revealed every curve she didn't have, but she was surrounded by men in front of whom she needed to maintain a professional persona. After seven years of being the odd one out, she'd learned to mask her discomfort by maintaining a cool image. She had a no-wrinkle suit folded in her backpack for just this purpose.

"When's the first break?" she asked Andre.

He glared at her. "No breaks. We work hard. We don't take breaks." He shifted his attention to Little John. "You. We'll do you first. In the jungle, I think. You look like a wild man."

That sparked good-natured ribbing from his teammates and provoked a hint of a proud smile from the giant lock.

"Beth will give you a costume and show you what to do."

A woman who'd been messing about with a light meter beckoned him over, and he dropped his towel along the way, completely unconcerned about his total nudity. Beth, Andre and Tess sucked in their breath.

Liam cleared his throat softly in Tess's ear. "Problem?"

The heat of his body warmed her back, making his presence impossible to ignore as she tried to convince herself to look away from the man tugging on a tiny Tarzan loincloth. Tess kept her voice low, hoping the threads of conversation around her would keep her words from traveling too far afield and reaching any of the other players' ears. "He's the most…uh, *proportionate* man I've ever seen."

Even though she couldn't see Liam behind her, she got the feeling he rolled his eyes. "You think that's impressive," he bragged, "you should see…"

He stopped, as if just remembering that she *had* seen, and done far more than that besides.

A conversational crossroads. She could make a joke and risk

offending him. This would be her default choice. Or she could be honest with him. Probably the wrong option, but since when had that ever stopped her? Besides, she was sick of the lies that had settled between them and was willing to take a gamble on a little honesty. "I have seen, Liam. And I can't stop seeing. You're burned into my memory in a file marked *Perfection*."

He exhaled slowly, his hot breath hitting the top of her head. "Jesus. Don't say things like that when I'm wearing a towel."

She twisted to face him, curiosity suddenly overtaking pride. "Are you wearing anything under there?"

"You'll find out soon enough."

She studied the rest of the team. Little John now had a short leopard-print sarong wrapped around his waist, while most of the other men waited either in towels or in their pants. A couple wore bikini-style swimming costumes that left little to the imagination. Was Liam wearing a pair of those?

She gave him an assessing glance. "Let me guess. Banana hammock?"

He pulled a face, momentarily taken aback before a teasing grin beat his surprise. "You should know better than anyone that I couldn't fit my trident into a pair of Speedos."

"I think you'd look good in them." What the hell was she doing, opening herself up for humiliation like this, making it clear that she'd thoroughly enjoyed him and his body when he'd left her in no doubt that he was angry and willing to use those memories to hurt her?

His face turned serious, and he let his gaze rove so slowly down her body that she remembered what she was wearing—an outfit just as embarrassingly revealing as Speedos. Andre's attention had turned away from her, and she could've taken this opportunity to change instead of baiting Liam. But he held her rapt, just as he had through most of their conversations—and all of their shagging.

When he finally spoke, his voice was a caress across her overheated skin. "Perfection, huh?"

Time for a joke, Tess. Smash his ego to save yours. But she couldn't. Somehow she couldn't bring herself to make the kind of cutting remark he'd delivered on the pitch a few days ago. More fool her. "Yeah. Perfection."

She couldn't stand the possibility of him slicing her down, humiliating her when she had to spend the next couple of hours with a roomful of rugby players who dropped towel with no warning. Before he could respond, she bent over and grabbed her backpack off the floor.

"Excuse me. I have to get changed."

She'd only taken a step when he grabbed her elbow, sending sparks of awareness straight up her arm to her heart.

"Tess..."

She waited, breath held until black spots danced across her vision.

"Changing room's empty, if you want to have a quick shower. I'll stand outside the door and make sure no one comes in."

Fab. She should probably be grateful for his thoughtfulness, but really, did he have to make it obvious he'd noticed how gross she was just after she told him his body was perfection?

"Great. Thanks. Appreciate it." Flat words, delivered with all the enthusiasm she could muster...which was none.

Who would've thought that her former career gambling on the performance of financial markets was safer than working for a travel agent?

LIAM STOOD in front of the changing room door and battled the urge to rake both hands through his hair, giving it a good tug in the hopes it might ease some of his frustration. Not wanting the team to see how their sponsor affected him, he kept his hands at his sides, only his fingers moving with involuntary twitches from the nerves Tess set alight every time he saw her.

Damn it. He'd told himself to stay distant, since he couldn't stay away, but she'd shattered him with one word. *Perfection.*

He was used to people fawning over his body. He'd even been told it was perfect before. It was a nice side benefit of the career. But Tess hadn't fawned—not today and not in Venezuela. Somehow her one-word description meant more than any gushing praise that had been heaped on him by women in the past.

Tess wasn't perfection. If he'd been asked two months ago to build his perfect woman, Tess wouldn't be it. Why couldn't he stop thinking about her? Images of her leaning backward while the waterfall pummeled her from above kept him awake at night. His hands still felt the imprint of her tight arse from when he'd held her up so he could thrust harder. He was haunted by the memory of the slick heat of her body pulsing around his as he took advantage of how sensitive her nipples were. He couldn't take a shower anymore without needing to take care of himself.

More than that, though, he craved the feeling of relief he'd experienced when he'd talked to her. The lightening of his burdens and the simple, sweet comfort he'd found in her arms. He hadn't dreamed of his mum once since talking to Tess. Instead, his sleep was disturbed by the erotic visions his mind conjured up of Tess.

And now she was in the changing room—*his* changing room —probably thinking about their waterfall as she washed London's mud off herself. And she...well, she thought his body was perfection. She was hardly acting coy.

A simultaneous high-pitched scream and a masculine shout of "Fuck me! What the hell?" shattered Liam's mental wandering. He shoved through the door of the changing room and found Ash, completely bare-arse naked, facing the showers with a hand shielding his eyes.

Liam sprinted over, barely hearing several teammates clambering into the room behind him to see what was wrong.

Jesus Christ. He skidded to a halt on the wet tile floor, throwing his arms out to brace himself against a wall when he caught his first look of Tess in the shower. She was bent over, trying to cover herself with what appeared to be a tea towel as water rained down on her curved back and steam billowed around her. She glared at him. "You're supposed to be guarding the door!"

Fucking hell. He was a dead man. "There's a second door." The one that led to the hallway. The one Ash would've used when he arrived.

The words sounded lame to him, and she clearly agreed, bending over farther in a vain attempt to cover more of herself. She glanced behind him and cursed. A dozen of his teammates had gathered behind him to stare at her in wonder.

"Everyone out! Move it. Back to the shoot."

The herd moved slowly, as if the ones at the back were reluctant to go when they'd barely been able to see anything. "Line sprints for anyone who's still here by the time I reach two. One..."

They hustled. Ash was the only one who stayed put, one hand covering his package and the other covering his eyes.

"Mate, turn around," Liam told his most senior player, the man who'd been a mentor to him ever since he'd joined the team at sixteen.

Ash did as he was told, bracing both hands on his hips now. "Who the fuck is she?" he muttered while Tess fumbled to turn off the showerhead.

"Our sponsor. Kijani Adventures. You met her at the double header."

Ash's body stiffened, awareness apparently hitting him at the same time it hit Liam. A slow, dirty smile spread over Ash's face. "The one who kept my picture up all year?"

"My dad was exaggerating!" Tess flung her arms out in frustration but quickly covered herself again before Liam could appreciate the glory of her wet, naked body. "Liam, please..."

He slapped Ash's shoulder. "Grab a towel and get to the shoot. And do me a favor? Make sure it doesn't fall behind schedule. I may be a few minutes, and we don't have any time to spare today."

Ash nodded, already striding toward his kit bag. "Sure thing, skipper."

Liam waited until he was out the door before daring to face Tess again. "I'm sorry. He'd called to say he was having car trouble and was going to be about an hour late. I didn't expect him this early."

Tess shivered but at least she was standing upright again, one arm wrapped around her breasts and the other holding her tiny towel just below her waist to hide secrets he'd already discovered.

He hurried to the bin of clean towels, yanked a couple out and brought them to her. Draping one across her shoulders, he gave in to the urge to rub and squeeze her arms and upper back, as if he were helping to dry them instead of relearning the feel of her. She pulled away and tugged the towel around herself.

"I can't believe the whole Legends team saw me naked," she groaned.

"Not the whole team."

"Right. Only the twelve selected for this year's calendar."

"And no coaching staff or management. Be grateful for that. At least one of them is a heart attack waiting to happen. The sight of you naked could've killed him."

Her eyes narrowed, as if she weren't sure that was a compliment, so he leaned down as he ran his hand down to the small of her back. "One word, Tess," he whispered. "Nymph."

Her nostrils flared. "Liam..."

He couldn't help himself any longer. He had to touch her. His thumb traced the sensitive skin of her neck to her strong jaw. She sucked in air, tensing as she pulled the corners of the towel tighter around herself. He captured the lobe of her ear between his teeth, holding her gently and flicking it once with the tip of his tongue. She gasped, one hand letting go of the towel to brace against his chest. Or to push him away?

He would never know. A throat cleared behind him. He instantly let her go and spun around, shielding her from Ash's gaze...which was trained on the ceiling anyway. Smart man.

"Photographer says he needs you both. Apparently there's a problem."

There sure as hell was. Liam was hard as a goal post, wearing nothing but a towel he would have to lose in a second to have his photo taken. He had no problem being starkers in front of his team. Erect was another matter. Plus, the woman who tempted him more than she should stood naked and shivering behind him. Oh yeah, and she was his team's sponsor—someone he and the team had to maintain a professional relationship with—which was difficult to do when they'd all seen her naked.

Problem didn't cover it.

"Be out in a second, mate."

Ash left him alone with Tess, who now stood shivering under the showerheads with the towel tucked safely around herself. "Tess, we need to talk."

She cut him with a sharp look. "Because it's your job?"

Regret for his hasty, face-saving words swept over him. "No. Because—" He stumbled. *Because I barely know you but for some reason I miss you? Because we can't keep hurting each other? Because we want each other and I can't remember why we shouldn't satisfy ourselves?*

She gave up on him and pushed past. "Would you mind leaving while I dress? Or perhaps there's a stall with a locking door around here, since you make such a shit bodyguard?"

That's right, nymph. Come out swinging. "The toilets are around the corner, but you might not want to go into the stalls. I'll go out there and make sure no one else comes in. Change quickly, though."

She was clearly in no mood to listen to him now, and if he couldn't even figure out why they needed to talk then what would he actually say? He'd get her on her own later, when he'd had more time to think about his approach. Tactics. Strategy. That's what he needed here.

He walked into the next room, gestured behind him and bellowed, "No one goes in there."

Most of the team smirked. The photographer and his assistant didn't even look up, too busy snapping photos of Spencer Bailey lounging on the beach in the tightest, shortest shorts Liam had ever seen. Bailey-boy was used to this shit, and he ignored ribbing from the team as several of them gathered round the edge of the scene shouting out encouragement like, "Work it, baby!" and "Bailey, when did you start shaving your bollocks?" Bailey-boy scratched his cheek with two fingers, subtly flipping them the V without breaking concentration.

His face and body were on billboards across the city flogging anything from pants to sports drinks to spectacles that he didn't need in real life. Not that Liam could blame him. With his wife Caitlyn about to burst with a baby, and the fact that most rugby careers ended when a player reached his early thirties if he wasn't seriously injured or deselected before, Liam didn't begrudge anyone making their money while they could.

Liam approached the photographer to find out about the

problem before Tess came out. He stood quietly, hands on hips, waiting for the man to reach a stopping point. A few seconds later, the photographer finally lowered his camera and gave a full-body shuddering sigh as though he'd just orgasmed. "Aaand I'm spent. Mr. Bailey, that was a true pleasure. You have the kind of face a camera loves."

Liam couldn't help it. "Cameras love hideous mugs?"

The photographer glared at him, obviously not catching Spencer's confident chuckle as he wiped baby oil off his skin with a towel the assistant handed him. Andre said, "No. Cameras love faces with interesting features. Noses that aren't perfectly straight. Teeth that are just a little crooked. Ears that aren't exactly symmetrical."

Now Liam laughed as Spencer gave a glare that had made grown men wet themselves in the past. "What the hell does that mean?"

Slapping his best mate's shoulder, Liam said, "It means you're a gargoyle. Good thing American women go for an English accent or Caitlyn would never have looked at you twice."

"Caitlyn thinks I'm beautiful."

"And it would be rude of me to question her obviously questionable taste. Now, when's it my turn to pose? I'm afraid the camera won't love me as much, seeing as my face is perfect. But I hope you can live with the disappointment."

"I've done everyone else, so you're next. We're doing you in the waterfall." The photographer winked at him. "I want water streaming down all those muscles of yours."

The team laughed, and Ash joked, "Make sure you push his face behind the water so no one can see it."

Liam rolled his eyes. "Why do you think this calendar's so popular, mate? Need I remind you that sales skyrocketed the first year I was included?"

Everyone groaned. Little John said, "No need to remind us. You tell us that every year."

Pointing at the big man, Liam raised a brow in a mock stern face. "And they fell the first year you were in it, so I'd keep my trap shut if I were you. You're just here to make up the numbers."

Little John grinned, his ego just as impressive as parts farther south.

"Anyway," Liam said to the photographer, "I heard there was a problem."

The man nodded toward the corner of the room, where a bikini-clad woman was watching the team. Holy shit. When had she arrived? Normally if there was a half-naked woman in a room, she grabbed Liam's attention straight off. He had a homing device for exposed female skin, but he hadn't even noticed this one...or her incredible attributes.

"Only one of the three models showed up for the digital calendar," the photographer explained. "We wanted one per backdrop. We can make do by having Lucy here pose for two different shots, but it'll look strange if we use the same model for all three shots. We only have a few minutes, and we have to find another female model to pose with you men." He raised his brows and glanced not-so-subtly toward the changing room.

Tess. No, she would gut him before she did anything like this. But apparently the photographer's mind was working in a similar direction because he said, "We don't have much choice."

Liam gestured helplessly toward the man's assistant.

"Anna can't do it. I need her to help me during the shoot. Besides, she's always refused to have her photo taken. She prefers to be behind the camera."

Liam's shoulders slumped. Across the room, Tess emerged from the changing room looking prim and buttoned-up in a gray trouser suit, jacket included even though the room was stuffy. From a distance, he could easily mistake her outfit for a coat of armor. "I can't ask her. It wouldn't be appropriate. I mean, look at her."

He meant that she was a woman who was obviously uncomfortable exposing herself. He'd figured that out quickly enough in Venezuela and been grateful when she'd decided to shed her clothes and share herself with him. But the photographer clearly misunderstood because his voice sounded resigned when he said, "I know, but she's our only option. Besides, we'll be rubbing her face out, so that doesn't matter. We just need to get her to agree."

Anger arced through Liam. "What do you mean, her face doesn't matter?"

"N-nothing. Just that she doesn't need to look like a professional model. We simply need a female body. The rest we can take care of in the editing suite."

Liam bit the inside of his cheek, trying to give the man the benefit of the doubt. "And if she says no?"

The photographer grimaced. "We won't have enough variety for customers to choose from, and you'll risk raising a lot less money. It's up to you."

Liam exhaled. These calendars—and their special digital version—would be sold to fundraise for the charity Spencer's wife Caitlyn worked for, one that helped women after disasters like earthquakes and hurricanes. Over the last year, she'd convinced him to do ridiculous things to support their harder-to-fund projects. Two months ago, he'd spent an hour in a vat with snakes slithering around him while people pledged money to keep him in there longer. The least he could do was try to convince Tess to help out by stripping off. She was less scary than snakes...by a small margin.

"Fine. I'll ask. But if anyone sees her lunging for me, do me a favor and step in. She may be little, but she's fucking strong."

12

The boys took me out for my birthday last night. After a few rounds at the pub, we stumbled into a table-dancing club around the corner from the office. Not my idea. Never my idea, but I've been here before. It's hard to say no when my strategy for keeping my job is to blend in as much as possible. I tried to pretend I was having a good time, mostly because if the boys see me squirm then they know they've got to me. I won't give them the satisfaction.

But soon after we'd arrived, X. disappeared and returned with "Sugar." (I don't think I need to make her anonymous, as I doubt that's the name on her birth certificate.) She leaned down and whispered (in what I guess was supposed to be a seductive voice but just made me think she'll have lung cancer soon if she doesn't cut back on the fags), "So you like a bit of minge, do you?"

She was bent over rubbing hers in my face before I could figure out what the fuck she was talking about. The boys just about pissed themselves.

One of them looked at me, pointed at Sugar and said, "Happy birthday, T. Now you can finally have a pair of tits."

—Sexists in the City *blog*

. . .

THE HALF-NAKED WOMAN was the first thing Tess saw when she left the changing room. Difficult to miss in a room full of rugby players, most of whom were about three times the woman's width, even if some weren't that much taller than her. A couple of the players were talking to her—or, more accurately, they were talking to the breasts practically falling out of her red bikini top.

Tess tugged the bottom hem of her jacket, straightening her shoulders. Thank God the men would be distracted. They'd probably already forgotten they'd seen her mostly naked now they had this bounty in front of them.

Most of the action seemed to be taking place around the waterfall. Catcalls and whistles rang out, so Tess crossed the room to see who was the center of attention. Stuck behind several of the taller players—and, really, even the shortest among them would block her vision—she raised up on her tiptoes but still couldn't see anything. Shorty Dunston, one of the massive second-rows, did a double-take when he noticed her next to him and he stepped aside, tapping the shoulder of the player in front of him so he'd also make room for her. She was about to protest, but Shorty laid his hand on her back and gently guided her through the crowd. He had to lean down quite a way to give her a wink and murmur, "Turnabout is fair play, love."

What did he mean by that?

She didn't have to wonder long.

Ho-ly…Liam stood in water up to his ankles in a paddle pool surrounded by large, real-looking rocks. He wore not a stitch of clothing. Bent at the hips, he hiked up a skimpy swimming costume, shaking his naked arse to entertain his teammates, who started to hum a stripping tune. Tess pressed her hand against her mouth to suppress her amusement.

Damn but Liam had a beautiful body. The way he was bent over hid his most sensitive parts but left the rest of him exposed to her gaze. Muscles rippled over his back and arms, bunching and narrowing down to his waist. His bum was tighter than tight before flaring into the most powerful part of his body: his legs. He led the league in points scored, and he'd racked up most of those points by kicking the ball through the posts from angles and distances that were impossible for most players to hit unless they had God and a stiff breeze on their side. She'd watched those legs work for years, could mimic the stance he adopted whether he was kicking a leisurely penalty or dropping a hasty goal with the opposition rushing toward him. Those legs were the secret of his success, and when he'd pulled the ridiculously short, tight shorts all the way up to his hip bones, she was glad to see they left even more of his legs bare than his rugby shorts did.

She didn't notice she was standing next to Ash Trenton until he called out, "Anyone else getting an erection?"

Kind of.

Decently covered, Liam straightened and turned to face the team, his gaze immediately colliding with hers. One corner of his lips tipped up, as if he knew exactly how her body burned at the mere sight of him—possibly because the heat in her cheeks gave her away. Thank God she'd gone back to being a brunette or her face would probably match her pink hair right now. Her jacket felt suddenly too tight, and she wanted to flip open her buttons, undo her shirt and flap some air beneath it to cool her skin and help her breathe again.

"All right, we don't have all day," Andre said. "Mr. Callaghan, walk under the waterfall and dunk your head back, slowly. Just a bit at a time. Thaaat's it."

Tess's breath caught in her throat. He leaned back, teasing himself with the water as his back arched and his chest tilted forward. She felt the pose as if she'd made it herself—which she had, when she'd first reached their Venezuelan waterfall. She recognized the natural sensuality of it and remembered the cool water streaming over her shoulders and between her breasts, down her belly and legs, just as the water sluiced along Liam's muscles now.

Was this a show just for her? Was he cruelly teasing by adopting her pose? Or was it so instinctive when one met a waterfall that neither of them could help it?

"Excellent! Excellent! Now look this way and let the water fall over your shoulders." Andre moved around just enough that he partially blocked Tess's view. Liam did as he was told, looking toward Andre—

No. Looking toward her. He raised his hands to his hair, threading his fingers through it so his arms and chest flexed to form great mountains and valleys for the water to run through. He never broke eye contact, leaving her in no doubt whom he posed for. His motives for posing remained unclear to her though.

Torture. That had to be it. He was torturing her.

Her breath came more quickly as the photo shoot progressed. She tried to get control of herself, but she refused to concede the point. He might know how much he affected her, but that didn't mean she would admit defeat by walking away. If he wanted to put himself on show for her, she would damn well enjoy it.

At some point, Ash nudged her and said something, but it might as well have been her own ears under water for all she heard. His voice was just noise. Liam caught the one-sided conversation, though, his eyelids narrowing as he shot a glare in Ash's direction.

"Yes! That's it! Let's see that smoldering sensuality. You are a beast. A beast!"

Tess laughed with Ash as if they shared a wonderful joke. She was more than willing to mete out some torture of her own.

Liam didn't let her get away with it for long, though. He hooked his thumbs into the waist of his swimming costume and applied just enough downward pressure to reveal the indentations that swept over his hipbones to the line of golden hair that trailed from his belly button to his groin. Tess's laughter dried in her throat. She'd kissed her way down that trail and discovered the wonders that hid at the end of it. God, she wanted to do that again.

The session lasted minutes, but it could've been hours. Every second stretched into oblivion. When Andre dropped the camera to dangle around his neck and shook out his neck and arms as if he were between rounds in a boxing match, the spell was broken.

"Right!" Andre faced the men. "That's enough for the individual shots. I just need the three men and two women who'll be taking part in the digital version to stick around. The rest of you are free to go."

Most of the players made their way toward the changing room, slapping each other on the backs and laughing as they ripped the piss out of each other's performances. Ash stayed by her side while Liam toweled off. The woman in the bikini left her two admirers and strode across the room with a confidence Tess would never feel in a bikini. Tess concentrated on Liam as he dried off. Why not? She would never get to see this much of him again, so she might as well take advantage of the opportunity.

A few seconds later, Liam stepped out of the paddle pool and stood next to Andre, considering her with a gleam she didn't understand...until she glanced around and was hit by a startling realization. Liam, Ash and Matt Ogden, a reserve player, made one, two, three men. The bikini model made one woman...

She sucked in a breath and spun around to escape the group, but Liam caught up with her quickly, pulling her to a halt with a strong hand wrapped around her elbow. She shook him off with a ferocious glare. "Andre mentioned two women taking part in the digital version. I only see one."

He grimaced. "Yeah, well, I see two."

She swore so loudly the others gave her admiring looks. "You've got to be kidding me," she hissed. "Have you taken a hard knock to the head recently?"

"Afraid not. Look, Tess, we need you."

"When hell freezes over."

"Please."

Adrenaline surged through her as her fight-or-flight instinct kicked in. "Need me to what? I see one man dressed as a porno Tarzan and two wearing bathing costumes that're so tight I can count their pubic hairs. Then I see a woman with a bikini that might as well have been painted on for all the coverage it gives. Fucking hell, I can tell from five meters away that she's cold. What exactly is this digital version and what do you need me for? Bear in mind, if you dare to suggest I do anything other than hold your towels while you preen for the camera, the answer will be a resounding *sod off*."

He bit one side of his lower lip, and she couldn't tell if it was to hold back his amusement or because he was considering a strategy to win. He always made this face as he lined up the ball for a penalty, glancing several times between the ball balancing on the ground and the uprights he aimed for before he finally took a couple of long, fast strides and booted the ball right on target.

She pitied that ball. When his hand gentled on her upper arm, she had a terrible feeling she would soon know what it was like to be airborne, thanks to the strength of Liam's determination.

"Last year our charity calendar didn't make as much as it had in the past," he started, his voice husky as if he knew the seductive effect it had on her. He'd talked her out of her clothes once with that voice. Twice, actually—first at the waterfall and then in his hotel room. Apparently he thought he could do it again. "This year we decided to do something different. Along with our traditional calendar, we're making something for our website. Three of us are supposed to pose with women in these exotic backdrops. The models' faces will be rubbed out and women will be able to go online and pay a pound to upload their own photo, as if they're posing with us."

"Like those cutouts you see at funfairs?"

"Exactly. Great idea, huh?"

It was. She could see her sister uploading a photo of Tess's face and printing it off as joke for her. Of course, her sister still thought she was infatuated with Ash Trenton, so she'd probably pick the wrong man.

"This year all the proceeds are going to IDEA, the women's charity. Have you heard of them?"

"Of course." They were all over the news whenever a disaster struck.

"Last year, Spencer Bailey married one of their aid workers. She came to give us a presentation a few weeks ago, showing us a video of some of the families they've helped. Kijani Adventures is underwriting all the costs of the production of the calendar and the digital version, which means that everything will be profit. It'll all go to help women and girls get better healthcare when they're living in—" he shook his head as if he couldn't find the right words, "—absolute fucking squalor. I can't describe it. I wish I could show you that video."

"Let me get this straight. You want me to get my kit off and be photographed for the good of womankind? I'm pretty sure I've heard of this before. It was called—" She snapped her fingers as though searching for the word. "Oh, yes. Bullshit."

He gave her a hard look. "That's rich coming from a woman who can afford clothes in the first place."

"Low blow." But his argument started to have an effect. She exhaled through her nose, feeling like a bull that smelled defeat at the hands of a tenacious bullfighter. "You want me to be one of these models?"

"I don't just want you to be one. I *need* you to be one. The women need you to be one."

She scoffed. "I'm not that altruistic."

His brows rose in surprise.

"I'd be more than happy to give you a generous donation, but I've never stripped for charity before and I don't intend to start now."

"You don't have to strip."

She laughed and gestured toward the model posing with Matt Ogden on the beach. The woman had her breasts plastered flat against his chest as he held her close with one arm wrapped around her back and the other gripping a rugby ball beneath her bum. "Right. I don't need to strip because you often find women in business suits in the jungle."

"Okay, so you wouldn't be in your suit. But you wouldn't be naked, either. I wouldn't ask that of you."

She shot him a disbelieving look.

"I wouldn't." His voice dropped a notch past seductive. "Not in front of other people, anyway."

She suppressed the shivers that wanted to rack her body, but just barely. Time to be honest with him because that was probably the only way to explain why she couldn't do what he was asking. "Look, Liam, you might not know this, but all year I've had my dignity stripped away—no pun intended. Hell, make that the last seven years. Layer after layer. I'm just now getting it back."

Venezuela had been the first step in that direction. Come to think of it, stripping off with him had been the biggest step, but admitting that wouldn't help her cause now.

His face fell, his eyes closing momentarily as if her words made him feel like hell. "I'm really sorry to hear that. Truly sorry. I'm not here trying to be one more person who takes away your dignity. If you say no, I'll take that as your final answer. Let me just say this. No one has to know that it's you. The whole point is that your face will be cut out. Your name doesn't have to appear anywhere. I'll tell everyone else to go away, and you can pose with just me. Andre and his assistant will be the only ones in the room. It'll take fifteen minutes, and you'll be doing something to help make life a little better for other women who're struggling to hold on to their dignity. Think about it at least. Please."

She closed her eyes to block him out. She'd been completely incapable of saying no to him in Venezuela. The main reason she'd left in the middle of the night without waking him was because she'd been in danger of shirking her legal responsibilities for a few more hours in his arms. Shit. Shit shit *shit*.

"Right! All finished with you, Mr. Ogden. Who's my next victim?" Andre cradled his camera over his gut and glanced expectantly between them.

Standing on his own in a Tarzan costume next to the jungle, Ash called out, "What do you say, Tess? Will you be my Jane?"

Liam bristled beside her. A year ago, she would've passed out at the thought of the great Ash Trenton asking to be photographed with her, but now there was no question whose arms she wanted to be caught up in.

Before she could crush Ash's dreams—or, more likely, make him feel relieved that she wouldn't take him up on his polite offer—Andre cleared his throat and took a couple of scraps of leopard-print fabric from his assistant. "We, uh...we brought a costume, but it was custom made for someone with—" he eyed her flat chest with a grimace, "—different proportions. I'm afraid we'd have to do a lot of pinning and padding for it to hold up."

Brilliant. Just what she needed today. Add that to the near-death cycling experience then having a whole rugby team watch her struggle to cover her bits. Now a reminder that those bits were nothing to get worked up about. "I'm not doing this," she muttered to Liam.

He squeezed her arm. "Not with Trenton, you're not. Mate," he said to Ash, "you pose with...uh..."

"Lucy," the model said.

"You pose with Lucy. Tess and I will go last."

"With what costume?" Tess asked.

He nudged her arm so she would face him. Sliding his hand up to her shoulder, he hooked his thumb under the neckline of her shirt and jacket, pulling it aside to expose her bra strap. "You're wearing a bra and, I assume, pants?"

"Of course."

"Perfect."

She raised a disbelieving brow. "You want me to be photographed in my bra and pants?"

His wicked grin made her belly clench, liquid heat spreading through her lower body. "More than you could know."

She capitulated with a sigh. "Why would a woman wear her underwear in a waterfall?"

"You're right. Much more likely she'd be naked. Fully naked. Jaybird naked. But our website's family friendly, so even if you beg me I'll have to insist you stay covered."

Andre took a few steps closer. "Yes, the bra and pants idea has merit. At least we know they fit. And it won't be too difficult for us to make them look like a bathing cozzie. So you'll do it?"

Flippin' heck. Liam's bare naked chest and tight shorts didn't leave her much in the way of brain cells for decision-making. She wished she could say she was doing this for charitable reasons, but the heat he transferred from his hand to her shoulder made her temperature rise to the point where it destroyed her sense of self-preservation. She was the proverbial frog, jumping into a nice warm pot of water and never noticing she was in trouble until it cranked up to a full boil.

"I'll do it. For the women." What a load of bollocks. Self-loathing ate at her when Liam squeezed her shoulder and dropped his hand.

"Excellent. Andre, why don't you take your snaps of Ash and Lucy? I'll go see if the changing room's empty yet so Tess can get changed."

He strode away before she could tell him not to bother. After all, if everyone was going to see her in her bra and pants, who cared where she took her suit off?

Before Andre could get back to work though, Tess whispered, "Hey, can I ask you a question?"

"Of course."

"What else can you fix in editing?"

His brows drew together. "What do you mean?"

She had one specific question but didn't want to come right out with it. "Could you, for example, make me a blonde?"

He hesitated. "I could, but I don't think that would suit your skin coloring. Besides, Lucy's a blonde, so it works better that you're a brunette."

"Mmm-hmm. And what about...increasing the size of some of my attributes?"

His brows shot up. "Would you want me to do that?"

"I'm not necessarily saying that a bustier version of me needs to make it into the final version. But it might be interesting to see myself as, say, a C-cup?"

He chuckled. "Considering the size of your frame, a C-cup would be a bit drastic, I think. You'd look like a porn star. But I could make you a good round B-cup, if you like."

She stuck out her hand and they shook on it. "Done. Pleasure doing business with you."

"Pleasure's all mine. I'll send you the photos as soon as I have them."

THIS WAS, quite probably, the worst idea he'd ever had.

All right, it wasn't originally his idea anyway. Why the hell had he agreed to it?

Because you wanted her in your arms again, mate, and you saw your opportunity.

Unfortunately, that meant he was now in old-fashioned skin-tight swim trunks, standing in a pool of water that was a poor substitute for their private waterfall, waiting for Tess to come out of the changing room wearing hardly anything so he could pretend to make love with her while a photographer snapped photos.

He hoped to hell Andre could edit out erections.

Everyone else had left, so only Andre, his assistant Anna and Liam waited for Tess. Andre fiddled with his camera, Anna checked lighting for the millionth time, and Liam struggled to come up with a game plan for coping with the burst of lust he knew would hit as soon as he saw Tess again.

Remember when your collarbone snapped? Or the time you dislocated your elbow? That hurt like fuck. Think about that.

He was mentally transferring the pain from his groin to his elbow when his phone beeped from the kit bag he'd stashed against the wall. Since it might take Tess a couple minutes to undress, he jogged over to the bag and took his phone out. The screen showed a text from Samantha: *What R u wearing?*

Damn. He glanced down at himself. She wouldn't believe it if he told her. Not that he planned to tell her, anyway. He hadn't expected to hear from her again. When he dropped her at the hotel, he'd apologized for giving her such a rubbish evening. She'd invited him up, but he'd turned her down. She'd pursed her lips, flared her nostrils and slammed his car door as she left. They hadn't had any contact since.

What should he do now? Respond with a brush-off? Ignore her text? He didn't want to hurt her feelings, but he wasn't interested in pursuing anything with her.

Sorry, Sam. Busy.

His phone stayed silent for at least a minute, and relief settled across his tense shoulders. The changing room door clicked open behind him, so he stashed his phone and turned to face his fate.

Tess walked out with a towel wrapped around herself. Light blue bra straps emerged from the top of the towel. He focused on his breathing, keeping it deep and even. Would her bra be that sheer fabric that made a woman's skin look shimmery but didn't hide a thing? God, he hoped not. He loved that fabric, and he was battling an erection as it was.

She approached the pool, exhaled deeply and asked Andre, "Ready?"

"Just about." He adjusted one more thing on his lens, took a few snaps of the empty waterfall, checked them and said, "Ready."

"Let's get this over with." Tess dropped her towel, stepped into the paddle pool and strode toward the waterfall as if she was determined to kick its arse...giving him a fantastic view of *her* arse as she passed him.

"Huh," Andre muttered. "This is a lot better than I thought it would be."

Liam shot him a glare, and the photographer wisely refocused his attention on his lens.

Jesus, he was an idiot for talking her into this. The flex and sway of her athletic bum cheeks as she pushed through the water made blood rush to his cock. He couldn't tell about her bra from behind, but her panties were lace. Light blue lace, cut like a little boy's underwear except they rode high on her cheeks, not quite covering them. What a thing to hide under a suit. If he'd had any idea women did that, he'd have gone into business instead of rugby.

She turned around before she was close enough to the waterfall to get wet. "Well? Where do you want me?"

Anywhere. Everywhere. Wherever you'll let me take you, that's where I want you.

Dislocated elbow. Hurt like fuck. He shook his head clear.

"Mr. Callaghan, would you sweep her passionately into your arms? I want her hair to stay dry, so make sure you don't get her too wet."

A blush spread across Tess's chest, and Liam grinned. Thank God he wasn't the only one suffering here. Now that she'd turned, he could see her bra wasn't sheer. It wasn't even lace, except for the straps that stretched across her ribs. It was well padded, pushing her breasts up and together like an offering for his lips. When he reached her, he wrapped his arm around her waist, yanking her against him until she gasped.

"Passionate enough for you?" he asked Andre.

"Mmm...you're a wild man. Wild! Play with her hair. That's right. Run your fingers through it as she tips her head back. Yes! Look at her just like that. Like she's the sexiest woman you've ever seen and you want to eat her alive."

Fucking hell, he'd thought he'd managed to hide that look from his face. With Tess's compact body pressed against him from hips to toes, her back arched to thrust her gorgeous little breasts toward him and her head cradled in his hand, he went from semi- to fully interested in four seconds flat. Her eyes widened a little. Obviously it wasn't something he could hide from her.

Then her eyes narrowed. She ran her hands up his biceps, squeezing his shoulders before looping her arms around his neck. Wriggling her hips just enough to rub against his erection, she gave him a satisfied smile when he bit back a groan.

"I think you might've been injured in your last match, Liam," she whispered.

"Oh yeah?"

"Mmm-hmm. You're swollen." She arched further back as if to shake her hair out, but the move was clearly orchestrated so she could tip her hips, sliding the smooth skin of her lower belly against his aching cock.

Two could play this game. He pulled her upper body flush against his so he could nibble her neck. She shuddered, tilting her head as her fingers grabbed hold of his hair and tugged.

"What're we doing here, Liam?" she murmured in his ear.

"I don't know about you, Chambers, but I'm raising money for a very important charity."

"Mmm...me too."

"You're so selfless."

"So are you. It's one of the things I remember most about you. You're such a...giver." She released the last word on a moan as his hand cupped the bare lower curve of her arse cheek and pulled her in tighter.

"Tess?"

"Yeah?"

"I could easily forget there's a photographer taking pictures."

She stiffened in his arms. "Oh. Right."

Giving her bottom a pat, he said, "But he'll be leaving soon, and we need to talk, my little nymph."

But the steel had returned to her spine, and no amount of coaxing from Andre could get her to relax again.

"Well," the photographer said, "I think I got what I needed."

Tess pulled out of Liam's embrace, leaving him disappointed

that whatever spell she'd briefly been under had disappeared. She stepped away but stopped when he touched her arm. "Tess..."

"I need to get dressed and get back to work, Liam."

"Just tell me one thing. Why did you agree to do this?"

She cocked a brow and subjected him to a slow up-and-down that must've told her his interest hadn't faded. It wouldn't until she was dressed and out of his sight. Maybe not even then.

She cleared her throat. "Because I had to. It's my job."

She was stepping out of the pool before he recognized the words he'd carelessly thrown at her last weekend. A slow smile stretched his lips. When he'd said that, he'd been just as full of bullshit as she was now.

She stooped to pick up her towel and wrapped it around her chest as she chatted with Andre. Liam was right behind her as the photographer got out a piece of paper and wrote down her email address, saying, "I'll send you your special version as soon as I can."

"What special version?" Liam asked.

Tess adjusted her towel and wouldn't meet his eyes. "It's nothing. I have to go. Thank you again, Andre."

As she hurried away toward the changing room, he focused on the photographer. "What special version?"

Andre fiddled with his equipment, also not looking at him. "I just meant I'd send her a copy. That's all."

Liam's eyes narrowed at the whiff of shit. He didn't like secrets. Despised them, in fact—especially when he was the one left in the dark. This was his team, his project, and...and fuck, it really had nothing to do with that. He just hated not knowing what was going on. He could either try to get the answer out of the photographer or Tess, and since he had several other things to say to a certain nymph anyway, he might as well add this to the list.

Tess had hardly been gone a few minutes before she walked out of the changing room in her suit, mobile phone in her hand.

"Tess! Wait for me."

She waved goodbye without glancing up from her phone. "Can't. Charlie emailed and asked me to meet with your press team while I'm here, and then I have to drag my bike to the bus and argue with the driver till he lets me on. Gotta go."

Then she pushed through the door and disappeared. Cursing, he ran after her, giving the receptionist an awkward wave as he shot past her desk in his arse-tight swimming costume. He caught Tess just as she made it to the lift, where she jabbed the call button repeatedly.

"Careful," he said. "You don't want to get stuck again."

She rolled her eyes but kept her lips firmly clamped shut. Clearly the subtle approach wasn't working for him, so he ran his fingertips down the arm of her suit, wishing he could touch bare skin instead. Her head tilted slightly forward, and he could tell she followed the action from the corner of her vision. "Tess, I'm through fucking around. There's something between us that's not going away. We need to talk about it before it becomes a bigger issue than it already is."

"Do we?"

He skimmed the backs of his fingers down her neck, making her shiver. "You know we do. Not here, though."

"Where?"

He didn't have to think hard. She'd been invading his space for weeks now. The season had only just started, and he knew it would be a long time before he got used to running past her when he left the pitch at halftime or accepting the customary champagne bottle from her whenever he was named Man of the Match. He would have to work hard to keep his focus. If she was going to invade his space, then he would invade hers—in any way she let him.

"Your place. Dinner. Tomorrow night."

"What if I have plans?"

"Then I'll come over tonight instead."

"No." She pushed him back enough to look him in the eyes. Hers were filled with longing and trepidation, making his heart pound with anticipation when he recognized the very same feelings that plagued him now. "Tomorrow works for me. Seven o'clock. Don't be late."

13

Tess pulled out all the stops for Liam's visit. She even braved a visit to the supermarket—a real supermarket, not the convenience store where she usually picked up her milk and white bread on her way home from a takeaway.

Just because she ate like a slob didn't mean she couldn't entertain a guest...she hoped. Most of her guests didn't have food standards, but Liam had seemed particular about what he ate in Venezuela and the raw foods restaurant. Not that she wanted to impress him. Really. He was just coming over to talk, and he was right—for the sake of the partnership, they did need to come to terms with whatever was going on between them.

That didn't mean she should serve him lamb shish from one of the local Turkish takeaways, though. No, she would do this right. So after stopping off at the supermarket, she bought an apron that had been hanging in the window of a designer boutique on Church Street. It had a print of Rosie the Riveter flexing her biceps and saying, "Cook your own damn dinner." It was probably meant as a feminist assertion that Mama shouldn't be expected to put food on the table both financially and physically, but tonight Tess needed the motivation to cook her own damn dinner.

She'd been tempted by the high-end ready meals at the supermarket. Surely she could put an organic-beef lasagna in the oven, serve it without Liam seeing the plastic tray and bluff her way through a description of how she'd prepared the béchamel sauce. Then she realized she wasn't even sure how to pronounce béchamel, so Liam would doubtless know she'd read it off a label.

Jamie Oliver was good for situations like this one, right? Her sister Gwen had given her one of his cookbooks years ago in an effort to nudge her toward culinary self-sufficiency. Where was that book? Tess perused her bookshelves and cupboards. She finally remembered having found a use for it—propping up a broken sofa leg that she'd always meant to get fixed but had never got around to.

Flipping through it, she discovered a critical oversight on her part. She should've chosen her recipe and *then* gone to the supermarket for ingredients. She'd gone about this ass-backward. Instead, she'd bought a load of random things without any clue how she would throw them together into an edible meal, racking up a food bill of over a hundred pounds in the process.

Nice work, idiot.

Rosie gave her a stern glare. *Cook your own damn dinner.*

I will, you smug witch.

She flipped through the book. Pasta. Anyone could do pasta, right? And Liam was an athlete. Didn't they live off pasta?

She chose a recipe and dug through her bags of ingredients. Hmm...apparently she only needed four things for the sauce, but she was missing the garlic. It had never occurred to her to buy garlic.

Or pasta.

Damn it. Time to phone a friend. She texted her sister asking her to phone back when she was on a break. Five minutes later, Gwen rang.

"Don't ask questions," Tess said, "but I need help."

"I'm sorry, is this Tessy? You sound like her, but the words coming out of your mouth confuse me."

"Ha ha. I have a guest coming over and I need to cook for...her."

Gwen was quiet for a beat. "Her?"

"I told you, no questions." Tess pressed her palm against the woodpecker pounding away at the inside of her forehead. "You know what? Never mind. I'll call for delivery."

"Wait! Don't do that. I'll help you. Does your guest have any dietary requirements?"

"Oh, shit. I forgot to ask."

"Okay, well, let's assume that *she* would've told you."

Damn sisters.

"I'm guessing you want something easy."

Tess rolled her eyes. "How do you do it, Holmes?"

"You want my help or not?"

With a sigh, Tess admitted the inevitable. "Yes."

"All right, then. What do you have in the house?"

She rooted around in her bags. "Uh, a rainbow of vegetables, three...no, four kinds of cheese, a couple kinds of fish, some steaks..."

"Okay, stop. Did you rob a supermarket?"

"No, they robbed me! I can't believe how expensive steak is. This is why I stick to kebabs."

"Right. Like you're hurting for dosh."

And there was one of the sore points between her and Gwen. While working in the City, Tess had made enough money to buy her own home and take lovely holidays. Gwen had taken a worthier path in life, becoming an underpaid, overworked casualty nurse.

"Okay, did you buy any carbohydrates?"

Tess dumped the contents of one bag onto the counter. "Does couscous count?"

"I was hoping you'd say that. Grab a pen and paper. I'm about to save your sorry arse."

Tess's shoulders relaxed. "Cheers, Gwenny."

"Don't thank me. The thought of you cooking steak for anyone is terrifying. I'm doing it to save your guest from hugging the porcelain throne all night. I don't want to see you both in Casualty later."

"His intestines thank you, I'm sure."

"I *knew* it! You are spilling your guts to me later, my friend."

"Damn you," Tess joked. "Fine, but if you say anything—anything—to Mum or Dad, I won't tell you a thing."

"Even better. All the goss, just for me. Now boil some water. You can do that, can't you?"

Tess flipped her sister the V, even though she wouldn't be able to see the gesture from three miles away.

"Tessy, put those fingers away and fill your kettle."

"How did you know?"

"You're my older little sister. I know everything."

Tess smiled. *Older little sister.* They'd figured out as children how to confound the nosy adults who couldn't hide their curiosity and exclaimed *Sisters! But you look nothing alike!*

Of course we don't, Tess once replied. *She's my younger big sister.* The opacity of the comment left people even more confused but it also made them question their own intelligence so they never asked follow-up questions.

"Tessy, I don't hear that kettle boiling. You do realize I have to hang up as soon as someone comes in bleeding, right?"

"Sorry, hon. Boiling it now."

"Good. Now, I know you're more familiar with vegetables when they're covered in gloop, but can you identify any of the vegetables you bought?"

"You're really enjoying this, aren't you?"

"You have no idea."

LIAM DOUBLE-CHECKED the address against the one on the slip of paper Tess had given him before she'd beaten a hasty retreat yesterday. Confused, he stepped back and stared up at the elegant Georgian townhouse in the center of a crescent that backed onto a large park. The area was leafy and secluded even though it was just around the corner from a popular street lined with expensive boutiques and niche restaurants. A few minutes away lay a grottier part of Stoke Newington—the part he'd assumed she lived in because he remembered her comments about eating takeaways...and because he couldn't imagine that she could afford something better. For one thing, who would live off takeaways if they didn't have to? For another, London was the kind of city where the average person struggled to afford a decent life. Liam had saved for years to afford a down payment on his flat in Limehouse. He'd lived in shitholes until he'd been capped several times for England and had signed a few sponsorship deals.

But Tess's place looked posher than his. How could she afford this working for a travel agency?

She must have flatmates. Or—Liam's finger paused over the doorbell as horror hit him—maybe she lived with her parents. It wouldn't be *that* unusual for Londoners of their generation.

He cringed and pressed the buzzer. He should've thought this through. Granted, he'd met her father at Twickenham, but he was *not* ready to meet the parents in any other sense.

The lock clicked on the other side of the door, then it swung open. Tess, rumpled and a little sweaty, collapsed against the wall and blew out a breath. "You're early."

"You only told me not to be late. You didn't say anything about early."

She rolled her eyes and stepped aside so he could enter.

"Difficult day?" he asked.

"Like you wouldn't believe. I was nearly beaten by an aubergine, but I've triumphed."

"An aubergine? You don't mean to tell me you've cooked something?"

"What did you expect? I invited you over for dinner—"

"Technically I invited myself."

She waved away his words. "Still. I couldn't give you a take-away curry, could I?" She paused. "Could I?"

"No, you couldn't. But nice try." He leaned down and pressed a kiss against her soft, flushed cheek, letting himself linger a moment too long before he held out a bottle. "I brought some champagne."

Taking it from his hands, she gave it a funny look. "Is this the same champagne I gave you at the match last weekend?"

"Maybe. I have shitloads of the stuff. I can usually only get rid of it at Christmastime or when I'm invited round to friends' for dinner."

She smirked. "Must be tough being one of the world's best rugger buggers."

"What do you mean 'one of'?"

"I mean 'one of.' Have you forgotten David Finchley? I'm sure you haven't. He handed you your arse when you toured Australia a couple of years ago. And don't get me started on the All Blacks."

Jesus, she knew her rugby. For the first time since he'd figured out she not only recognized him in Venezuela but was actually a fan, the thought didn't fill him with sickening disappointment. Still, it was unsettling. He hadn't slept with fans or groupies in years, preferring not to shit where he ate, so to speak. But Tess...she didn't fall into the groupie category. She just seemed to genuinely love the same sport he did.

If he'd known that from the beginning, things might've been different. He wouldn't have convinced himself that she'd slept with *him* instead of his status. But since she'd started off hiding her passion for the sport, he was left with the nagging doubt that her attraction to him stemmed from being star-struck or, worse, a feeling that she was adding a Legends experience to her collection. Buy season tickets? *Tick.* Get the official shirt? *Tick.* Fuck the captain? *Triple tick.*

"Anyway, come in. Dinner's nearly ready...I think." She led him down a long, narrow hall past a staircase that went up at least two stories, then past an open door on the right. He glanced in and promptly braced himself in the doorway.

"Fuck me," he breathed.

"Pardon?"

He shook his head, unable to speak as he walked further into the living room. He ignored the two comfy-looking sofas and the armchairs, focusing instead on the object they faced. "Your TV. It's massive."

The flat screen took up most of one wall. Speakers sat on the built-in bookshelves and were mounted in the corners where the walls met the ceiling. One of the bookshelves was entirely dominated by DVDs. This was no living room. It was a home cinema. "You watch a lot of films?"

She shrugged. "A fair amount. Mostly I have this for watching matches."

His brows shot up as his stomach dropped. "Rugby?"

"And tennis," she said almost defensively. "The occasional big athletics meet."

"But no football?"

She gave a mock shudder. "I prefer sports played by professionals, not overpaid prima donnas."

"Thank God. You had me worried in Venezuela. Football's more like theater with all that playacting, throwing themselves down on the grass pretending to be injured when no one's touched them." He crossed to her DVD collection and discovered several that lined his own shelves. Pulling out a highlights video of England's last tour of South Africa, he glanced at her over his shoulder. "Please tell me you don't watch this on repeat every night."

"I'm not obsessive, Liam. My sister got that for me. Besides, that was hardly your best tour. I think the producers struggled to find enough footage to fill ninety minutes. It's mostly you boys messing about in the changing room, which is usually a sign that there weren't enough highlights on the pitch."

He slid the DVD case back into its slot between *Rocky* and *Heathers.* "We *were* a bit rubbish," he muttered. It'd been his first time captaining England, and the pressure had got to him.

"Can I get you anything to drink?" Tess asked from the doorway. She held up the bottle. "Glass of bubbly?"

"I don't drink during the season. Just water's fine." He followed her down the hallway to a bright kitchen and dining room. Although it seemed to be one big room, the dining area must've been added on to the original house because it stuck out into the garden and was surrounded by glass, like a conservatory. The late summer sun cast yellow beams of light against the walls and wooden floor. A small desk in the corner was covered with papers, letters and a laptop, but otherwise the place was immaculate. "This is a beautiful house. How long have you lived here?"

"I bought it four years ago, but it needed some work so I only moved in about three years ago."

She didn't live with her parents, then. Tension eased from Liam's shoulders, and he sat on a bar stool on the opposite side of the kitchen counter from Tess, who filled a glass with water from a bottle in the fridge. "Want anything in the water?"

"What, like lemon?"

"Yeah, or I have some powders that'll give it flavor. Raspberry? Strawberry?"

He grimaced. "The more I hear about your diet, the more I'm appalled. Do you eat anything natural?"

"I will tonight, thanks to you." She didn't sound pleased at the prospect. Pouring a glass of water for herself and adding a heaping teaspoon of something pink, she said, "I'm going to come clean here. I'm not much of a cook. My goal for tonight is to avoid poisoning us both."

"You're not serving anything raw, are you?"

"Not if I've turned the oven on correctly."

"Good. I'm fine with anything as long as you don't grate a bunch of courgettes and tell me it's pasta."

"At least that's one thing we can agree on."

He thought they'd found a few things they could agree on. Firstly, their mutual love for the world's greatest sport. Secondly, his lackluster performance during his first England captaincy, which he preferred not to dwell on. Even if he didn't want to admit it, his worries about her being a fan eased somewhat when she'd been honest with him. She'd never gushed over him, and he was grateful for that—though he wouldn't mind if she stroked his ego just a little bit.

She opened the oven door and steam poured out, blowing tendrils of her hair away from her cheeks, which turned pinker from the heat. A second later, a delicious smell hit him. "What's that?"

"Cod and roasted vegetables. I thought it would be safest if I stuck with food I'm used to eating, even if the cod I eat's usually battered and fried." She closed the door and gave him a concerned look. "Does it smell okay?"

"It smells amazing."

Her shoulders eased down. "Good. I wasn't sure how long to give it."

"Open the oven again."

She did, and he leaned across the counter to look inside.

"I'd give it at least another five minutes, until the veggies stick to the pan a little."

"You can cook?"

"Of course. I've lived on my own for a long time. If I didn't cook, I'd starve."

She grimaced. "Is there anything you can't do?"

Get you out of my mind. There. He'd admitted it, even if only to himself. He couldn't get her out of his mind, and that was the reason he was here. He'd been prepared to bravely swallow whatever shit food she put in front of him in pursuit of getting answers to all the questions she'd left him with when she'd abandoned him in Venezuela.

He stood and walked around the counter. Laying his hands on her shoulders, he let his thumbs stroke the hollows above her collarbones. Her eyelids grew heavy, and she tilted her head to one side, as if he was slowly melting her, and her neck no longer had the strength to support her.

Brushing the underside of her jaw, he stepped closer and gazed down into her lovely brown eyes. "Tess?"

"Hmm?"

"I enjoyed yesterday morning."

She gave him a funny little smile. "You enjoy getting your kit off in front of your team?"

He chuckled. "I never need much encouragement to get my

kit off. But I meant I enjoyed being in the water with you. It brought back good memories."

Her smile faded. Disappointed, he stroked her lower lip with his thumb, trying to bring her smile back.

"What's wrong, Chambers? They weren't good memories for you?"

She sighed and shook her head. "They were some of my favorite memories."

"Then why the sad face?"

"Because..." The hesitation just about killed him. "Because I feel awful about how I left you. I should've had more courage than that, and I'm sorry. I...I didn't think. I made assumptions, and I'm afraid they were wrong, and I might've hurt your pride in the process. I never meant to do that."

There was so much he wanted to unpack from that little speech that he didn't know where to begin. He dove right in to the part he suspected might hurt the worst. "What assumptions did you make?"

He stood so close he could hear her swallow as well as see her throat move. "That since you were a professional rugby player, you'd be grateful that I left without a fuss. That you'd probably expect it. That you'd do it to me, if we'd ended up in my room that night."

"You basically assumed I'm a slut."

She jerked, but he kept his hands gentle, not letting her pull away. "I—I don't think..."

He saw the moment she came to terms with the fact he was right. Her head dropped forward, chin against her chest, and she looked like a chastised little girl. He tugged her closer until her forehead rested against his chest. "It's not an unfair assumption, Tess. You just happened to meet me during a time when I wasn't inclined to be slutty."

Her hands rose, hesitated midair, then settled on his hips,

her touch shooting endorphins though him. He slid his fingers into her slightly sweaty hair and pressed a kiss to the crown of her head.

"What were you inclined to be, then?"

He thought about it for several seconds before finding his answer. "Whoever I am away from the rugby pitch, I guess."

Tilting her head back, she considered him with a probing look that made him wish he could snatch the words back. "And who's that?"

That was the million-pound question, but he wasn't ready to admit he didn't know. Shit, why was he doing this? He'd wanted to find out why she'd left him, not bare his own soul. "And who were you trying to be, little Tess?"

"What do you mean?"

"Come on. Pink hair. Skinny-dipping. I've seen you in your real habitat now. You're too comfortable in suits for them to be a new personality you're trying on. Wet T-shirts on the other hand —" he grinned at her scowl, "—*that* was something new for you. You went to Venezuela to try on a different you. A wilder you. How was the fit?"

She pulled away and leaned against the counter. "I think I could get used to the fit, but it didn't come naturally to me. I spent so many years working in an environment that's both conservative and out of control. I never wanted to be either of those things, so I've tried to live my life somewhere in the middle. But it all fell apart about six months ago. I thought maybe it was time for a change, time to see if there was someone else I'd squished down inside me who was ready to come out."

Her words pinged through Liam's mind, hitting so many familiar emotions that he felt like a human pinball machine. He'd searched for balance throughout his career, but he'd been a Legend nearly as long as he could remember and it had dominated his life. He'd played for the Under 16s while he was still in school, then left school at sixteen to join the academy. From the time he was ten, everything in his life had been geared toward a rugby career. His parents had been proud but had tried to encourage his interest in other things, other people, and they'd mostly failed. His mum's death had finally shaken him from a life that that had become self-absorbed—so much so that his own mum hadn't been able to depend on him being by her side when she'd needed him most.

Like Tess, he was ready to find out whether there was someone else he was supposed to be. Something had happened to her around the same time his mum died, and now he realized they had another thing in common: they'd gone to Venezuela to discover themselves and had discovered each other instead.

He had to know more about what she'd gone through. "Why did it all fall apart six months ago?"

Her jaw worked, as if she fought with her reply. She finally sucked in a huge gust of air and let it slowly out. "I was fired."

"From?"

"I worked in the City trading derivatives."

"You were a trader?"

She nodded.

"What'd you do, lose millions for your bank?" His confusion grew as she shook her head. "How'd you lose your job, then?"

"Blogging."

His face went slack. "Blogging?"

"'Fraid so. The atmosphere at work was…" She paused. "I have to think about how to phrase this so I don't end up in court again. It was fraught with misogyny."

"Honey, I'd be the last person to unleash lawyers on you. Just tell me what happened."

She glanced at the clock, then turned away to open the oven. Donning a spotless pair of white oven mitts, she slid the roasting tin out and set it on the cooker. "This look okay?"

"Perfect." His chest ached with the need to find out more, but she clearly wouldn't be rushed. If she needed a little space before spilling her guts, he would give it to her. "Put me to work, Chambers. What can I do?"

"Take some plates out of that cupboard while I get the cod and veggies out. I made some couscous, hummus and tzatziki earlier. You can take them to the table. I'll just pop the pita into the toaster and be right over."

He did the heavy lifting, taking everything to the table. He couldn't help but be impressed by what she'd made, considering her admitted lack of kitchen skills. "Are you sure you haven't done this before?"

"Wait till you taste it before you start complimenting me. I'm pretty sure I put too much lemon in the hummus and not enough in the tzatziki."

She brought toasted pita triangles to the table on a side plate and set it between them. They sat and she served him in silence while he tried not to jump all over her for more information. When she finally spoke, her voice was so carefully casual that he almost thought she'd changed the subject. "Have you heard of the Tarrington inquiry?"

He searched his memory. "Not that I can recall. Why?"

"Don't watch the news much?"

"Watch it all the time, but I'm guessing you don't mean the sports news. If I can avoid politics, I do."

"You're probably a much happier person for it. Anyway, I'm one of the key witnesses."

His brows shot up. "In a judicial inquiry? What the hell happened?"

She scooped couscous onto her plate. "I wrote an anonymous blog about some of the things I heard around the office. Needless to say, my employers weren't impressed. They fired me, so I got angry and took them to an employment tribunal. They settled out of court, but by that point it was all over the news and other women came forward with similar stories. Then the politicians got involved. It's been messy and humiliating and I wish I could go back in time and quietly quit before it all went to hell."

She suddenly put down her fork and knife, folded her hands primly on the table and lifted her eyes to meet his. "That's why I left you. I'd thought my part in the inquiry was over and I could get on with living my life, but I was recalled to the stand. I had to come home."

"And you couldn't tell me this?"

She hesitated. "I could've. Maybe I should've. But I acted like a chickenshit instead. That day, Liam...it was so perfect. Being with you, nothing could've been better for me. It was like a fantasy come to life. And I didn't want to pop that bubble by bringing reality into it. I wanted to leave the memory intact so I'd have something sweet and sexy and romantic to cling to when real life got too real."

His jaw clenched. She didn't know it, but she'd just nailed every single one of his sore points. "I was a fantasy?"

"Better than a fantasy. You were a perfect reality."

"You knew who I was the whole time."

"Y-yes."

"Was part of the fantasy the fact you were sleeping with the England and Legends captain?"

Her lips softened like she would say something, but nothing came out.

"It's all right if you admit it. I just need to know." It wasn't all right, but it was like an infected wound that he couldn't keep from scratching. The suspicion had grown itchier over the month, and he was ready to douse it in kerosene if that would only ease the annoyance for a little while.

To her credit, she didn't break eye contact. She chewed her

bottom lip as if she were just as conflicted as he. Finally, she said, "I don't know. Maybe."

Kerosene burned. He bit the inside of his cheek and slowly nodded as he digested her admission.

"I can tell you this, Liam. I've never built up an image in my head of what you men must be like away from the pitch. I'm not one of those fans who worships the players or sticks around the stadium afterward for a chance to have a pint with you. I admire the way you play. You're obviously incredibly talented and hard-working. But—until I met you in person—you didn't occupy much of my head space once I left the stadium."

"So I was just a form of entertainment for you."

She cringed. "Before we met, yes. I'm sorry. That sounds horrible now."

Actually, it sounded promising to him. "And once we met?"

"You made me laugh. And you gave me your clothes instead of making me feel awkward or vulnerable about being barely decent in a lift with you. Plus, you're not bad to look at."

"I'm no Ash Trenton."

Her gaze flicked to the side. When he followed it, he found a small rubbish bin next to her desk. A piece of crumpled glossy paper lay on top. "Fucking hell. That's not what I think it is, is it?"

He got up before she could answer and yanked the paper out, smoothing it on the desk. Ash lounged on a bench press like a pasha, naked except for the rugby ball lying on his lap, and smirked up at him. "I can't believe you've held onto this. I'd almost prefer you to be a football fan."

"Liam, you're right—you're no Ash Trenton. You're much better. I look at that picture and I question my own sanity. Besides, it was just a joke between me and my sister, me keeping it up for so long."

A sudden, terrible thought hit him. "That's not what your

'special version' of yesterday's photo shoot is about, is it? Andre's not going to Photoshop Trenton's head on my body?"

Her jaw dropped and she slowly shook her head. "Damn. I wish I'd thought of that. Do you have his phone number?"

Her teasing tone called him a fool, and he considered her carefully. Strangely enough, the fact she hadn't tried to lie about whether being a fan had played a role in being with him made him feel better—but that was tempered by the fact she'd kept this photo. "When we met, you knew I was lying about who I was, and you let me believe I was anonymous. You even went so far as to pretend you like football."

"Yeah, that was the hardest part of the charade."

He smiled before taming his amusement. "I don't know why, but it meant something to me that I could just be myself around you. It was important to me."

She stood and walked slowly toward him. When she reached the desk, she tilted her head back to look at him, but she didn't touch him. "I think I understand."

"You do?"

She nodded. "It was similar for me. I got a taste of fame—or infamy—during the worst parts of the inquiry. All I wanted to do was get away somewhere that I wouldn't be recognized or hounded. The fact that I didn't exist for you before we met was an aphrodisiac. I can imagine it would be even more so for you. I'm sorry I couldn't give you that in reality."

"No, you can't give that to me. But maybe we have a second chance."

One of her brows arched. "You—you want..."

"You, mostly. I want you. But I also want to know that you see who I really am, not whatever image you might've built up in your imagination based on seeing me in the news."

She pulled in a deep breath, and she let it out slowly, dragging out the torture as he waited for a response. "I can't do that, Liam. I can't get involved with a colleague. I'm sorry."

He leaned closer. It only took a few millimeters for her to be backed against the desk with nowhere to look but at him. "I'm not your colleague. We're not employed by the same people."

"But we still have to work together. I can't—"

"I can't, either. I can't keep seeing you at matches and events without wanting you. I need to do something about this, Tess. It's distracting me, and right now I need to be completely on top of my game."

"You need to get me out of your system or not see me at all, is that it?"

He shook his head. "It doesn't work like that. Sleeping with you won't get you out of my system. It won't make you *less* attractive to me. If you turn out to be a stark-raving psycho, *that* will make you less attractive to me. I want...I want to figure out what's going on between us, and I don't think talking about it will be enough."

She was quiet so long he'd started to work out his exit strategy by the time she finally said, "I'd like to get to know you better."

He grinned, a stupid gust of relief blowing through him. Eager to touch her, he leaned down, closed his eyes...and felt her finger push against his lips. He stilled and opened his eyes.

"I want to make sure you know who I am too. I come with plenty of baggage. And I don't want you to have any doubt about why I'm sleeping with you when—if—I finally do."

"If?" Fucking *if*?

"We made a lot of assumptions about each other in the beginning. Let's not make that mistake again. The next time we're in bed together, I want to know we're both there because we can't keep our hands off each other, not because we're unhappy with ourselves."

Fucking hell, this wasn't what he'd pictured at all. "Let's not be hasty, sweetheart."

"Exactly. Let's not be hasty. We have to work together all season, and we both take our commitments to our jobs seriously. It could ruin mine if anyone finds out we've been together. I don't want to risk us rushing into something and having it all fall apart in a way that affects the partnership. I can't go through the humiliation of torpedoing my own career all over again, especially when it's my cousin's company we're talking about. Getting involved with you is a risk for me, Liam, and it's not a risk I want to jump into."

His gut sank. "What are you saying?"

"I'm saying let's not rush this. We've already had sex, and we know how good it is."

"Good? Try mind-blowing."

A huge smile spread across her lips. "Yeah, mind-blowing. So let's see if we fit together in other ways."

He groaned, scrubbing a hand over his face. "You want us to avoid doing the one thing we know we're good at together?"

She hesitated, and hope flared that there might be room for negotiation. "Not really. But I think it might be for the best in the long run."

"I can't believe I'm even considering agreeing to this," he muttered. His first lesson in discovering who he was away from the rugby pitch: either a very patient man or a complete sucker.

But then Tess pinched the corner of the calendar photo and tugged it away from him. She flipped a switch on a small shredder sitting on the desk and fed it Ash's photo, flaring a perverse happiness inside him. Maybe some things were worth being a sucker for.

He ran his open palm up her arm to her shoulder, her neck, her cheek, loving the way she leaned into his touch. "What are you worried about?"

She nibbled her lower lip for a second. "My job. We have to work together, Liam. The Tarrington inquiry has dragged me through the mud and exposed things about my life that were humiliating enough to experience alone, much less having them bandied about in the press. I just want to be really cautious."

"You don't want anyone to know about us—is that it?"

"That's partly it. It's definitely a requirement."

"I'm fine with that." More than fine. All of his relationships had been in the public eye. Whatever was happening with Tess, it was different and he wanted to treat it that way, needed to keep it private until he could figure out what it was.

"And if things don't work out between us, I don't want to have to watch you play every weekend and be involved in your career. It's difficult enough after Venezuela, but if we give this a real chance now and discover we just don't work—"

He pressed his lips to her mouth, silencing her except for the breathy moan she made when his tongue touched hers. Holding her close, he put all his powers of persuasion into the kiss, invading and retreating, murmuring encouragement as she refused to let him back away, following him, lifting onto her toes so she could get closer and press her advantage. He loved it when a woman showed him what she wanted, and Tess clearly wanted *him* even if she had qualms about taking him.

He broke away, their lips making a gentle smacking sound. They both breathed heavily, wrapped around each other because they couldn't get close enough. Leaning his forehead against hers, he whispered, "Starting next week, my life will be all about the World Cup. I won't be playing for Legends, so you won't see me around. We won't be working together. I won't even be living in my own flat most of the time. I'll pretty much be sequestered at a hotel across town. No women allowed at the hotel. Not even Twitter to distract me. I'll have fuck-all free time, but if I get even two seconds for myself I want to spend them with you."

She tipped her head back and captured his lips, sliding her hand into the hair at his temple to hold him still while she kissed him. When she pulled away, she took a deep mouthful of air and plunged them both into the unknown with one breathy word. "Deal."

14

*T*ess found herself suddenly airborne, thanks to two large palms cupping her bum and lifting her off her feet. Liam strode through her kitchen and down the hall, kissing her until she lost track of where they were. She had just enough brain power left to cling to his neck and say, "Dinner?"

"It'll keep." His mouth settled over hers again, maintaining contact as he murmured, "Bedroom?"

"Upstairs."

He broke the kiss as he trotted with her up the stairs. Wrapping her legs around his waist so he wouldn't drop her, she pressed her lips against the sensitive skin under his ear. He groaned as he made it to the landing. "Which door?"

"Up one more flight."

He cursed. "Why do you have such a big house?"

She didn't have the breath to answer. It'd been a status symbol at the time she'd bought it. What single woman needed three guest rooms? But she'd fallen in love with the place, and— not needing a dick extension—she couldn't care less about owning a sports car like most of her male colleagues, so why not buy the house?

Liam made it to the second floor and practically jogged into her bedroom. Setting her on her feet next to the bed, he whipped his shirt off and started flicking open the buttons of her shirt before she had a chance to gain her equilibrium. Head swimming from the rush upstairs, the fact she would get to sleep with him again and her fear that doing so would lead to her downfall all over, she sat heavily on the edge of the mattress and pressed her forehead against his abs, waiting for reality to return.

His fingers left her buttons, sweeping through her hair and cradling the back of her head without trying to budge her. "Tess, you all right?"

"Yeah." Perfectly, perfectly perfect. She kissed his navel, trailing her fingertips lightly across the muscles of his tight abs and down to the waistband of his khaki trousers. "More than okay."

She popped the button open and slid his zip down with infinite slowness. Their first time together had been impatient and fast, an explosion of desire and longing. Their second and third times had been more leisurely, giving them time to explore each other's bodies and discover their most sensitive parts. Liam had one right here, right where his skin stretched between his groin and his hip bones. She ran her tongue along it, eager to explore it again.

Pushing his trousers and boxer briefs down, she liberated his erection. It popped out, as obviously eager for playtime as she was.

He groaned. "God, baby, yes. Take your shirt off before you do that."

He didn't give her a chance to obey before yanking at the placket of her shirt. The last few buttons pinged as they bounced off the hardwood floor. Jerking the shirt down her arms, he left it gathered at her wrists, trapping her arms behind her. She tried to pull free, but he tipped her head back and gazed down at her with lust-filled eyes. "Only your mouth this time. No hands."

She smiled, braced herself with her hands on the mattress behind her and arched her back to thrust her breasts out. Closing her eyes and letting her head fall back, she said, "This bra unhooks in the front."

Needing no other explanation, he found the clasp and flipped it open. The cups fell to the sides, and he shoved the straps down to the shirt holding her wrists hostage. His fingertips swirled around her nipples, and she sucked in a shuddering breath from the jolt of pure pleasure. Her nipples tightened into hard darts. They were big—something she'd always been self-conscious about since they didn't resemble the cute little buds often portrayed in novels and porn. Proportionately, they took up too much of her breast, unlike the nipples on the strippers at the clubs she used to go to after work.

But Liam didn't seem to notice any of that. If he did, he didn't mention it. She opened her eyes to watch him toe off his shoes and socks, kick his trousers and pants across the room and stare at her breasts as he knelt on the mattress with his knees either side of her hips. Still arched back, she started to lean forward to take his cock in her mouth, but he stopped her by cradling her cheek. "Wait."

He wrapped his free hand around the base of his cock and rubbed the tip against her nipple. She gasped, the erotic sight and feel of him almost too much. A bead of fluid came out of his tip, and he painted her nipple with it. She bit her lip and tried to keep from moaning as he moved to her other breast, stroking the sensitive underside with his entire length.

"Oh, God," he groaned. "You feel so good. So smooth and soft."

Her breasts had never been the subject of this kind of attention before. Men tended to pay them lip-service, so to speak, before moving on to other parts. Liam seemed to draw genuine pleasure from playing with them, and his sensuous, erotic movements ratcheted up her desire.

When his hand fell away from her face, she knew what he wanted and was eager to oblige. She surged forward and drew the tip of his cock between her lips, sucking gently and pulling back until he slid out with an audible pop. His breathing grew ragged above her, and she didn't make him wait long before she took him back into her mouth, this time sucking him down as far as she could go. He held the back of her head gently, not forcing or demanding or even guiding her actions. It seemed like he just needed something to help him balance. She tugged at him, swept her tongue around him, sucked harder as he grew in her mouth.

She could stay here all day, but he gently pulled her away and stood up. His arm swept around her back, lifting her to her feet so he could yank her shirt off completely. Arms free, she hooked them around his neck, opening her mouth as he kissed her and worked at removing her trousers. When she was finally naked, he clasped her bum cheeks and dropped her back onto the bed, his erection sliding right over her swollen clit. She let out a shuddering, laughing groan as he tilted his hips and did it again.

"God, Tess, you're so hot. I need you. I need you now."

Even though he hadn't asked anything, she knew from his tone that he sought permission to finish things quickly. She was so ready. She flung her arm to the side, hitting her nightstand and fumbling until she could yank open the drawer and pull out a box of condoms. She dumped whatever remained of the box onto the bed next to them. He ripped one open with his teeth, rolled it on and spread her legs. Hunched over so they could both watch their bodies join, he nudged her clit with the tip of his penis.

Her head dropped to the pillow, back arching as she sought him with her hips. She needed him badly, needed the fullness and completion he offered, and she wasn't too proud to beg for it. "Please, Liam. Now."

He didn't make them wait any longer. Surging his hips forward once, twice, again, he planted himself fully inside her. His body stroked hers from the inside out. His thumb found her clit, putting just the right amount of pressure on the skin above it to drive her crazy. Lowering himself so he could keep up the pressure, he rubbed his whole body against hers, capturing her moans with his mouth as he pumped over and over and over.

She wrapped her legs around his waist, pulling her knees up as high as they could go so he thrust deeper with each stroke. He murmured unintelligible encouragement against her lips between kisses. God, she'd missed him, hadn't realized how much until he'd shown up tonight and let her know he wanted to explore whatever they could be. Their separation had left her feeling empty, yearning, and the knowledge that he wanted her so badly cranked up the desperation she felt to let him fill her. To forget everything and everyone who'd gone before, to shuck every fear of what could happen tomorrow and live in this moment. She clung to him, pumping her own hips in time with his, squeezing her inner muscles to his groaning delight, needing to stroke and stoke his desire as he did the same to her until they both exploded into oblivion.

He collapsed on top of her, breathing hard in her ear as her jellified legs slid away from his hips and flopped against the mattress. A thin sheen of sweat slicked their bodies, enhancing every movement as aftershocks rippled through them. His heart pounded against her breast. When she could move again, she nudged his jaw with her nose, feeling as cuddly and sinuous as a puppy.

Neither of them spoke for several minutes, both trying to

hang on to every second of pleasure. Liam softly stroked her, sending shivers along her arms, her ribs, her hips, her thighs. She tightened around him and he shuddered, teasing her with tiny circular motions of his hips.

"Liam?"

"Hmm?"

"I'm glad I talked myself out of waiting."

He made a breathy sound of amusement, tickling her ear. Sliding one big hand beneath her bum, he rolled so she sprawled on top of him. She crossed her arms on his chest and rested her chin on the backs of her hands while he lazily stroked her anywhere he could reach.

A satisfied smile firmly planted on his face, he said, "It's like I tell my team. You have to get the basics right before you can do anything else, and to get the basics right you have to practice them over and over again. You and me, Tess—we do the basics very right."

15

$\mathcal{E}$ngland went rugby mad. Normally, rugby fans were keenly aware that they supported a minority sport, with rugby matches rarely making the news unless they were a cup final or something freakish happened.

But with England hosting the World Cup for the first time in decades, the country threw their support behind their team and, as captain of the host nation, Liam was a wanted man by every reporter for thousands of miles.

It made keeping their relationship a secret very difficult, particularly since, with the Tarrington inquiry wrapping up soon, Tess found herself called to give interviews at all hours.

But Tess and Liam were determined not to let their relationship go public. They both had too much to lose. Liam couldn't let anything distract him during the most important weeks of his career. England were starting out in what most sports journalists were already calling the pool of death and would have to beat some of the world's best teams just to make it out of the group stages. Liam refused to be the host captain whose team crashed out before the tournament really got going. And any relationship with Tess was likely to spark a scandal, considering her love life had been put under a microscope during the worst parts of the inquiry.

Despite the fact that he wouldn't have a day off until the group stages were over, they still managed to communicate. Liam sent her a text every night before bed, some sweet—*Don't worry about the inquiry. It'll all be over soon*—some blowing off steam—*Jenkins is the biggest twat in the world. Who did he have to fuck to get a referee's whistle?*—and some flirty—*What're you wearing under that suit today, nymph?*

Ten days after they'd first agreed to explore whatever was between them, Liam had a rare evening off, a night he could spend in his own home, so he invited her over. She changed out of her suit and into a blue sundress she'd bought for Venezuela. She wouldn't be able to wear it much longer, since autumn had arrived in London, but she wanted to hold on to as much of her summertime memory as she could. She shivered under her cardie as she jogged up a few stairs and buzzed his flat.

His deep voice over the intercom filled her with anticipation. "Come up."

She took the lift to the top floor and waited for him to open his door. When he did, the violent bruise under his eye made her gasp. "What happened?"

"Brutal training session today. Don't want to talk about it." He clasped her elbow and drew her into the flat. As soon as he closed the door, he pushed her gently against it and held her there with a full-body press, his hands cradling her jaw as he captured her lips. She dropped her handbag and opened her mouth to his, so eager and seeking. She slid her tongue along his as he clasped her hands and lifted them above her head.

He groaned, tilting his head to get more of her. "I need you, Tess. Ten days is too long."

She made an incoherent noise but wriggled her body to get her point across. She needed him too. It'd been an age since they'd been in each other's arms, and she couldn't stand the separation any longer. She needed relief, relief from the legal battles she'd fought and relief from the fears and guilt she'd faced, blatantly lying to her cousin and risking her job.

Liam shifted to hold both of her hands in one of his, keeping them aloft so she was stretched tall. His free hand wandered down her body, flicking over one of her tight nipples on his way to find the hem of her skirt. He worked his hand under it, sliding up her thigh as need throbbed between her legs. He didn't tease her long, making straight for the spot where she ached for him. Slipping his fingers under the elastic of her panties, he stroked her swollen lips as he kept up his deep, seductive kiss. She groaned, trapped by him and desperate to move but unable to do more than rock her hips a little.

"I've thought about you all day," he groaned. "About you, right here. About this." He jammed a knee between her thighs to keep them open and pulled his fingers from her long enough to unzip. "Keep your arms in the air."

He let go and pulled a condom from his pocket, rolling it down his thick length. Ignoring his order, she wrapped her arms around his neck as he yanked at her underwear. A ripping sound was followed by a feeling of liberty from her bonds. "Are you going to destroy an item of my clothing every time we're together?" she murmured against his lips.

"Mmm...probably, until you learn to wear things that give me easy access to you." He lifted her, thrusting hard when her legs wrapped around him. Her head whacked against the door as months of frustrations welled inside her, gathering in one spot low in her belly that Liam hit with each stroke. Her back slapped against the door, but she barely noticed because his thumb was rubbing her just the way she loved, his pelvis keeping up a hard pressure and his cock filling her.

The ball of desperation grew, spinning and burning in her

lower belly as his thrusts became more frantic. "Harder," she panted. She needed him to keep hitting that spot, needed the forcefulness of his body to explode the frustrations that had gathered inside her with no outlet for so long.

He grunted almost-incoherent words right next to her ear. "Tess...fuck...love..."

That did it. Her body splintered into a thousand pieces, throbbing and pulsing around him, trying to draw him deeper than he could ever possibly be. He groaned and thrust one last hard time, his fingers biting into her bum so hard he would leave bruises, but she didn't care.

She was skewered. Open and vulnerable. Completely spent and yet desperate for more.

He collapsed against her, the weight of his body pinning her against the door as one of his hands fell away from her bum. His head lolled against hers, his body shivering with tiny quakes. Tess squeezed her arms around his neck, half fearful that she would collapse to the floor and half fearful that he would pull away too soon. But as one minute bled into another and he didn't move, except for his breath evening out into a steady, deep rhythm, she nudged him and whispered. "You haven't fallen asleep, have you?"

His chuckle warmed the side of her neck. "My stamina's better than that."

"Mine's not," she confessed, battling a bone-deep lethargy. The imminent wrapping-up of her life's biggest trial, coupled with the best sex she'd ever had, had left her limp. "I might need a bit of a lie-down before dinner."

Speaking of dinner...a scent reached her from the kitchen, tickling her nose with an acrid warning. "Uh, Liam? Is something burning?"

He jerked back with a curse, quickly lowering her to her feet before pulling away and shuffling into the open kitchen, his movements impeded by the trousers and pants he'd shoved just below his bum in his desperation to get at her. She bit back her laughter at the sight of his bare arse jogging toward the oven. Her laughter died when he bent to open the oven door and took a cloud of smoke to the face. Coughing, he waved it away, and she rushed to grab a tea towel, waving it up and down like a fan to disperse the smoke.

He grabbed an oven mitt and pulled out a dish filled with charcoal lumps.

"What was it?" she asked.

"Lemon chicken." He sounded crushed. "I wanted to make something nice for you."

Her heart gave an unexpected leap. No one—other than her parents and Gwen—had ever cooked for her before. She'd been taken to Michelin-starred restaurants and served the most intricate, delectable foods, but no man had ever invited her to his house and gone to the trouble of cooking for her.

"It looks delicious," she said, only realizing how ridiculous that sounded when he turned a disbelieving look her way. "Maybe we can salvage some of it?"

"You don't want to eat burned bits, Tess. They're carcinogenic."

She blinked, somehow surprised that a big, tough rugby player who'd quit school at sixteen would know a word like *carcinogenic*. Guilt followed swiftly after. Just because he wasn't formally educated didn't mean he wasn't smart. As captain of the country's national team, he had to be sharp as knives, and she'd do well not to make any assumptions about him.

He slid the dish into the sink, tidied himself and tugged his trousers up. Scrubbing a hand over his face, he grimaced. "I have some more chicken, but it's frozen and will take a while to thaw. How hungry are you?"

Closing the distance in a few steps, she ran her hand up his body from his taut belly, up between his pecs to the curls at the base of his neck. Pulling him down toward her, she murmured, "Food can wait. Why don't you come have a lie-down with me?"

LIAM LAY with his arms wrapped around Tess's naked body, cuddling her from behind on his couch. He'd managed to make love to her, cook more chicken, watch one of the World Cup matches between two teams that weren't in his group, and make love to her again. She hadn't complained that their third bout was a rushed affair at halftime. In fact, when the teams had jogged back onto the pitch on his muted TV, she'd grown more frantic as if she was trying to hurry them both to orgasm before the real action started.

Sex with a rugby fan. Who would've thought it could make him smile this much?

The match ended up being an upset, with Japan beating Wales. Liam loved an underdog coming out on top—as long as the teams he captained were the underdogs.

As they watched the post-match interviews, Tess stroked his forearm and pulled him tighter around her. For the past forty minutes, she hadn't spoken other than to shout encouragement at the Japanese team and curse the referee, so she took him by surprise when she asked, "How does a boy with a name like Liam Callaghan end up playing for England?"

He smiled and kissed her bare shoulder. "My dad was Irish and my mum was Welsh, but I grew up in London. I could've qualified for Ireland or Wales, but why do that when I've always supported England?"

"You supported them because you grew up here?"

"Partly. But also because supporting Ireland or Wales would've been like choosing one of my parents over the other.

They were both into their rugby, and I guess I didn't want to upset the balance."

She shifted a little, turning her head in an effort to look at him. "Were, past tense? Your dad's gone too?"

He nuzzled the side of her face, trying to come across as affectionate while holding her still. "He died when I was twenty-two. His diet was even worse than yours, if you can believe it. He smoked and had a fatal heart attack when he was only fifty."

"Wow. So young."

"Mmm." His dad's death had been sudden yet inevitable, considering how he'd treated his body. He'd looked perfectly fit and healthy from the outside, but inside he'd decayed faster than a man his age should've.

"And your mum passed away earlier this year?"

He pulled her closer, not wanting to give her space to turn around and see him. "Mmm-hmm. Cancer."

"Oh, Liam." She shifted, but he tightened his arm until she seemed to get the message. He could only talk about this if they weren't facing each other. If she couldn't see the confusion that would probably never leave him. The shock that would never wear off. She whispered, "I'm so sorry. That must be so hard."

He didn't say anything. *Hard* didn't even begin to cover it, especially considering the way his mum had died and the guilt that had pressed on him heavier than being at the bottom of a pile of a half-dozen players. Talking to Tess on the rock next to their waterfall had released some of it. Opening up again might help more, but he wasn't ready to trust her that far yet.

Several heartbeats passed before she broke the silence. "You said you didn't want to choose one of their sides over the other. Did they argue a lot?"

Surprise hit him. "My parents? No. Well, occasionally, but mostly they were disgustingly affectionate with each other." A memory floated back at him, one he hadn't thought of in years, and he allowed himself a small grin. "I vaguely remember being really young—maybe five or six?—and hearing them wagering on the outcome of an Ireland-Wales match. It had something to do with what one of them would do in bed, and when I asked what they were talking about they both went all awkward. Mum finally said the loser would have to make their bed, and I got excited and asked if I could play. I had to choose a different team to support, though, so I chose England. Wales ended up winning the tournament, and Mum gloated as Dad and I made our beds. I have no idea what else he had to do, but I do remember him smiling a lot considering his team had lost."

Tess laughed softly. "It's too bad you and I support the same team. That could be a lot of fun."

"You could always bet against me."

"I know better than that."

He pushed himself up and put a little pressure on her shoulder until she lay flat under him. Her pelvis cradled his and their legs tangled, but he kept the weight of his upper body off her so he didn't smother her. Brushing a strand of hair away from her face, he said, "I could make it fun for you to lose."

"Likewise, Cally." She batted her eyelashes, making him laugh.

"All right, what would it take for you to bet against me?"

"Against you? There's nothing you could offer me to tempt me to take that bet. Against England? There are several teams that could beat you. I'd have excellent odds if I wagered on almost any of the Southern Hemisphere teams. But I don't want you to lose, even if it means you'll cater to my every naughty desire and indulge my most shameful fantasies."

One of his brows shot up. "Care to tell me about those?"

"Maybe one day."

"Hmm..." He kissed along her collarbone while one hand

stroked the skin over her sternum. He'd discovered how sensitive she was here—all around her breasts, actually. She seemed to enjoy having her chest petted and played with even more than having him go down on her. He kept his touch light and teasing, and she shifted restlessly under him. "I helped you fulfill one fantasy in Venezuela. Tell me about another one and let's see what I can do about it."

She stretched her arms over her head, her breasts rising and seeking his attention. He tugged one nipple between his lips just long enough to tease her before letting it pop out again. She groaned. "Please."

"Nope. Not until I hear about another fantasy."

Grimacing, she admitted, "My fantasies have always been a little boring. I don't want to get your hopes up. I'm not talking a threesome or anything. I mean, seriously, skinny-dipping was the most daring one I could come up with at the time."

"Yeah, I was bored stiff when we were skinny-dipping together," he drawled and pressed his lips to the smooth skin where her neck met her shoulder. "Stiff as a board."

She closed her eyes and breathed softly as he kissed and stroked and licked around her nipples without ever touching them. With a shudder of pleasure, she finally moaned, "I want to be tied up."

He paused. "Tied up?"

Swallowing hard, she kept her eyes squeezed shut and her wrists crossed above her head, as if imagining she was already bound. "Not with a rope or something abrasive like that. I don't want to do a kidnapping role play or anything. But I want to be tied up...and maybe blindfolded."

"You want to give up control." Despite having gone three rounds in as many hours, his cock swelled, aching at the mental image of her at his mercy.

"Yes. Just for a little while, I want to give up control."

He jumped off the couch and lifted her against his chest, striding to his bedroom.

"What're you doing?"

"What do you think? You can't tell me something like that and expect me to just lie there and say, 'That's nice, dear. Fancy a cuppa?'"

A strange mix of fear and anticipation crossed her face. "You're actually going to do it? Now?"

He shifted her in his arms so he didn't knock her head against the door jamb, cradling her closer against his chest before settling her on his bed. "Tie you up? Oh, yeah. Why? When did you think I'd do it?"

She gulped. "I thought we were talking about making bets on the World Cup, so at the end of the tournament..."

"You think I can wait that long?"

He bent down to kiss her, but she lifted her foot to his belly and held him off. "I think you're going to have to. You see, I really want England to win, and if you're this eager to tie me up and have your wicked way with me, then maybe tempting the captain with sexual favors will increase the chances of victory."

He glared at her. "I'm going to win no matter what."

"Good. I'm glad to hear it because I've just decided you only get to tie me up if you do. If any other team wins..." she shrugged, somehow managing to look like a coy yet severe schoolmistress, "...then you will really disappoint me."

16

*L*iam lowered himself carefully into the ice bath across from Bailey Boy, wincing as the cold seeped into his aching muscles. Every bit of him throbbed, including his brain as he'd crammed it with plays, strategies and the weaknesses of the French team they were due to play that weekend, but Spencer gave him no time to decompress as he broke the silence.

"This is brutal."

Liam grunted.

"Tell me again why wives can't stay with us at the hotel?"

Liam simply raised a brow.

"Yeah, I know. Distraction. Team bonding." Spencer let his head fall back against the edge of the bath. "I miss my wife."

A pang of longing bounced through Liam's chest. He missed Tess. But since he couldn't reveal anything about her to Spencer, he joked, "I miss your wife too."

"Dick." Bailey-Boy straightened up. "Wait. That's great."

"Huh?"

Leaning forward as if carried there by the momentum of a sudden great idea, Spencer said, "I think she's going slightly mad. She told me she's too big to sleep. I'm not around and Granddad's been hovering over her for the last two weeks. We've got tomorrow night off. You need to come over for dinner."

"No way. Isn't she due to pop anytime?" The last time he'd seen Spencer's wife, she'd been massively pregnant...and that had been several weeks ago.

"In two weeks. Come on, mate. She needs a distraction from wondering whether every twinge is the start of labor. She needs a night to relax and enjoy herself with an old friend. You're coming over. End of." Spencer gave him a hard look. "Unless you have more important plans than making my pregnant wife happy."

Fucking hell. What could he say to that, especially when he wasn't allowed to admit he had another woman he was hell-bent on making happy. "Dinner. Only dinner. I need an early night tomorrow."

An early night, but not early to sleep.

He texted Tess as soon as he could, telling her he wouldn't be free for dinner. She replied almost immediately, saying he should let her know when he was on his way home and she would come over. As he slipped his mobile into his pocket, he couldn't help but feel a little confused. Things with Tess were easy. Too easy. He'd never experienced a relationship that was so lacking in drama. They simply enjoyed being with each other—and only each other. No red carpets, no rugby club fundraisers. Fuck, not even dinner in a restaurant. Was this what relationships away from the spotlight were like? Because he could certainly get used to it.

Spencer and Caitlyn's flat in Wapping was only a fifteen-minute walk from Liam's in Limehouse, but he did a bit of shopping before he went. When he arrived carrying a box of specialty chocolates from a boutique in Spitalfields, Caitlyn waddled toward him and gave him a huge hug.

Emphasis on huge. She'd always been curvy, but now she defied the laws of physics. She shouldn't be able to stand up without toppling forward—but he was too smart to say that out loud. Her bump was so big he had to lean way over to wrap his arms around her and kiss her cheek. "How's my favorite mum-to-be?"

"Better now that you're here," she said, eyeing the box of truffles.

"Me or my chocolates?" he teased.

"I think you mean *my* chocolates. Thanks, Liam." She took them from him and walked into the living room, ripping the box open before she made it to the couch, which she plopped onto with an *oomph*.

Spencer's granddad, Philip, stood with the help of a cane, and Liam couldn't hide his frown. He and Spencer had known each other for a decade and been best mates most of that time. Philip was like a grandfather to him, and seeing his body growing weaker hit a sensitive spot. "When did you get the stick, old man?"

"Oh, a couple of weeks ago. I strained my knee in my tango class, and the doctors want me to be extra cautious when I walk so I don't fall." Philip waved it in the air, as if to demonstrate he didn't really need it. "You know how it is."

Yeah, he did. He'd been injured enough times to suspect when doctors were being overly careful.

Caitlyn popped a truffle into her mouth and moaned, a sound so provocative Liam chuckled. "Ohmygawd." She held a hand over her mouth as she closed her eyes and settled back into the couch. "I've been trying to avoid chocolate for the baby's sake, but this is amazing."

She dug into the box and took another one out before offering it to him and Philip. They both declined, sharing a look of amusement over her ecstasy. "Mmm..."

Spencer popped out of the kitchen holding a small glass of lager and three waters. "You're not going into labor, are you?"

"Not until I finish this box." She dove in for a third. "Seriously, though, if anything's going to stimulate my oxytocin, this'll do it."

Liam threw his hands over his ears in mock horror. "Whoa! I don't know where your oxytocin is, but save the naughty talk about stimulating it for your husband."

He barely had time to cover his face as a truffle was catapulted at him. It bounced off the back of his hands and tumbled down his chest, but he managed to catch it before it hit his crotch. Holding it out to her, he said, "Want this back?"

She took it with a chagrined look. "Sorry. Blame the hormones."

Spencer set the glasses on the table, handing the beer to his grandfather before sitting next to his wife. His hand seemed to automatically rest on the small of her back and rub in small circles as she snuggled closer. The simple intimacy of the gesture made the empty space next to Liam grow even more vacant.

Caitlyn reached for another chocolate, and Spencer said, "Do you want me to stop you?"

She whipped a glare at him and he held his hands up in surrender, laughing. "You've told me before to stop you from eating too much of the things that aren't good for the baby. Personally, I think you can eat what you want. None of it will do her any harm. It's not like you live off kebabs."

Not like Tess did. Or, like she used to before he'd started getting her to help him in the kitchen. Now she was determined to learn how to cook. For some reason it mattered to him that she didn't fill her body with junk. He didn't like to think about all the rubbish she ate shortening her life, like it had his father's.

Polishing off her fourth truffle, Caitlyn sighed, rested her hand on her belly and smiled at Liam. "So where've you been hiding yourself?"

"I don't know if you've noticed, but there's been something of a big tournament going on here. We call it the World Cup. Unlike you Yanks, when we host a world cup, we actually invite the world."

She waved away his teasing. "Yeah, yeah, I've been hearing lots of jokes about our World Series. I think I've been here long enough that I can say *sod off* and get away with it."

He laughed. "I'm not original? You wound me."

She rolled her eyes. "Right. Now, what's this I hear about a woman in your life?"

Spencer cleared his throat so loudly it sounded like he had a horse stuck back there. Liam hadn't told him about Tess, but he wasn't surprised Spence had figured out something was going on. "Woman? What woman?"

"Don't play dumb with me, Liam Callaghan. I hear she's not your usual type."

That piqued his interest. "And what, exactly, is my 'usual type'?"

An uncomfortable silence filled the room. He glanced from Caitlyn to Spencer to Philip, and each of them apparently had better things to look at than him. "What?"

Caitlyn opened her mouth to speak, but Spencer laid his hand on her thigh and said, "Don't."

Liam's shoulders tensed and he leaned forward. "Do, Caitlyn. What's my usual type?"

She grimaced. "Forget I said anything. Again—hormones."

He glanced at his best mate, who was no help at all, shoving a handful of chocolates into his mouth so it was too full for words. Philip took a long sip of his beer. Liam kept a steady gaze on him, waiting for him to come up for air, but he just kept guzzling until he'd drained it. Before Liam could press him, though, he set the glass down and chucked another chocolate in his gob.

Unwilling to give up, Liam focused on the one he figured would give in first. "Caitlyn…"

Spencer jumped up. "Caitlyn and Granddad just finished decorating the nursery. Come look."

Incredulous, Liam couldn't stop himself from bursting out, "You've got to be kidding me. Why the fuck would I want to do that?"

Spencer, who had several inches and at least a couple of stone on him, grabbed Liam by the shoulder and dragged him off the couch, saying through gritted teeth, "Because I think you'll like the shade of yellow they chose."

After being steered across the living room and shoved into the nursery—which was painted a shade of yellow that Liam would describe as *yellow*—he planted his feet and faced his best mate. "What's going on?"

"You're sleeping with our sponsor."

"No, I'm sleeping with his cousin."

"Whatever. All I told Caitlyn was that she seems nice."

That brought Liam up short. "Nice? She seems nice?"

"Yeah, she does."

"And *that's* why Caitlyn says she's not my usual type?"

Spencer grimaced and nodded.

"Fucking hell, I—" Liam mentally catalogued the other women he'd been with since Caitlyn had known him. Megan Grable, who had propositioned Spencer right in front of him and nearly managed to break up Caitlyn and Spencer. "All right, so Megan was a mistake."

"Huge mistake, mate. Huge."

"Fine, but after her there was Natália." The Brazilian supermodel so famous she only needed one name. They'd slept together for a few months, and he still didn't know her surname.

He knew what cut of diamonds she liked, though. "Okay, she was a little shallow."

"Shallow?" Spencer laughed. "The only time we met her, she completely blanked Caitlyn. Didn't even shake her hand. She left her hanging, Liam."

He cringed. "That might've been my fault. I was bragging about what Caitlyn does for a living before we met up with you. I don't think she understood that Cait hadn't actually built any sewerage systems that day. Her English wasn't great, you know."

Spencer's eyes narrowed. "So it's okay for her to ignore my wife because she thought she was dirty?"

"No! That's not what I mean. I just—" Liam conceded with a sigh. "No, it's not all right."

"How about Angie Sutter?"

Liam shifted uncomfortably, remembering the singer he'd been with at the beginning of the year, when everything turned to shit.

Spencer's voice softened. "Mate, she was in London when your mum died. She never phoned you, much less came to Cardiff to help you sort through your mum's things."

He swallowed hard, memories of that week still too raw to discuss without his throat swelling. "I wouldn't have wanted her to. I didn't ask her to."

Spencer said nothing, but he didn't have to. Liam hadn't asked him and Caitlyn to visit, either, but they'd turned up and done everything they could've—from making sure he ate when he was too shocked to look after himself, to figuring out how to sell his mum's house. Caitlyn had even helped him clean out his mum's things and had been by his side when he'd discovered his mum's backpack and a photo of her taken in front of the Taj Mahal, which he still kept in his wallet. Caitlyn's calm, steady presence had made it less awkward when he'd broken down and wept on her shoulder like a little...er, boy.

"Tess isn't like any of them," he said.

"Like I said, she seems nice."

It was more than that, though. He'd viewed his previous relationships as give-and-take from both sides. He got to be part of a flashy world of fame and fortune, and he'd always enjoyed buying gifts and taking care of his girlfriends however they needed him to, up to a point. He gave shallow and he got shallow.

Tess was the exact opposite. He wanted something more from her, but she didn't seem to want anything from him. She certainly never asked and, unless he was dense, she'd never hinted. The realization left him off balance. What did he have to offer if there was nothing she wanted?

Until tonight, he hadn't realized the reason why that made him uncomfortable. It was almost as if she didn't ask because she *expected* nothing.

Liam tried to push the brutal analysis of his love life from his mind. Too many other priorities competed for his attention. He needed to concentrate on other things. More important things. Winning things.

But the conversation gnawed at the back of his brain throughout dinner. Unsettled, he made his excuses early and texted Tess. He would've loved to surprise her by going over to hers instead—felt less like a cheap booty-call that way—but he was so shattered he knew he wouldn't make it all the way to Stoke Newington.

When she arrived with nothing but her handbag, his earlier worry about why she didn't want anything from him lurched inside him, and he snapped. "You know you're going to sleep over, Tess. Why not bring your clothes for tomorrow?"

Still standing in the doorway, she blinked at him. "Hello to you too. Tough day?"

He grunted.

She raised herself on her toes and kissed him softly, stroking his cheek. "I didn't bring my clothes because I don't want to make any assumptions. I don't want to push too hard for there to be an 'us.' If we get to the end of the night and we both want me to stay, then I'll stay. But if I decide I want to leave because you're being a big growly bear, then I'll leave. Simple as that."

It hadn't occurred to him that she might take the decision to leave herself. He was used to being the one who decided to ask a woman to stay over, and so far no one had refused. In fact, they sometimes brought several changes of clothing and tried to colonize his wardrobe before he was ready to see silky underpants folded next to his briefs. The thought of Tess deciding that she didn't want to fall asleep snuggled up with him left him hollow inside.

She must've read something of his thoughts because she wrapped her arms around his waist and hugged him. "I did bring something that might cheer you up."

"It'll have to be something really good," he grumbled.

She reached into her handbag and drew out a small bottle, which he took from her. One of his brows lifted. "Sensual body massage oil? You want me to give you a massage?"

Her smile turned to a frown. "No, I was going to massage you. I thought you might need a little help relaxing tonight."

The pressure that'd been growing inside him all evening finally started to break up and dissolve. Leaning his forehead against hers, he held her closer. Later he would have to examine why he'd be upset at the thought that the first thing she'd asked for from him was a sexual favor.

After that, the pattern of their weeks grew routine. He split his time between stadiums in England and Wales, and it was difficult to switch his mind off when he fell asleep in hotels unless he called her for a quick chat before bed.

Tess understood his frustrations better than any of his

previous partners, who'd known nothing about rugby. She listened to him grouse and shared his triumphs without him having to explain why a day had gone well or gone to shit. She seemed to learn how to deal with his moods—when he needed to silently stew before he could talk to her, when he needed the quick relief of hard, sweaty phone sex and when he needed his ego stroked.

Things shifted around inside him—things he'd never felt shifting before. She did all this for him, yet he still couldn't figure out what she needed so he could give it to her.

17

After an evening romancing the England team sponsors, Liam decided to drop by Tess's place. It was gone eleven, well past his bedtime, but he'd grown to hate crawling into bed alone. Besides, it was a Friday night, so she wouldn't have to wake up early the next morning and he didn't have to be at the training ground until the afternoon.

He knocked on her door and waited. And waited. After a full minute, he glanced at her living room window. Light shone through the curtains, so unless she left it on to fool burglars she was definitely home. He rapped his knuckles harder and was debating whether to call when he heard the tumble of the lock being released. She pulled open the door with a puzzled expression.

"Liam? What're you doing here? I thought you were busy tonight."

There went his fantasy of her throwing herself into his arms. "I—I just wanted to see you."

The confusion on her face softened, but she threw a glance over her shoulder at the same time a man's laugh came from the vicinity of the living room. His throat clenched in disbelief.

"I wasn't expecting you," she said.

"Yeah, I can see that." He fought to keep the shock from his voice. He'd never expected fidelity in his relationships before. He'd never even really seen them as relationships. So what was this sharp, hot-as-lightning pain arcing through his chest?

Her brow furrowed and her voice dropped even lower. "My family's here. We're having a birthday party for my dad. You'd better leave quickly because they'll get curious in a second."

Her family? Meet her family? It sounded equal amounts terrifying and appealing. Before he could make up his mind, a woman's voice called out, "Tessy! Where are you?"

Tess grimaced and whispered. "You've got about ten seconds to escape. I just happened to hear the door on my way down the stairs. They don't know anyone's here. If you're quick—"

He was quick. He pushed the door the rest of the way open, slowly enough that she could step out of the way, and closed it behind him. Leaning down, he captured her lips with his and murmured, "I'd like to meet your family...Countess."

She swatted his arm. "Don't call me that."

Smiling, he stroked her cheek with his thumb. "I've met your dad and he's already spilled embarrassing secrets about you. What else do you think I can find out from the people who gave their daughter such a ridiculous name?"

She grimaced. "As to that...there's a story behind that. But seriously, you need to go."

She tried to push him out the door but was interrupted by an Amazon of a young woman who teetered out of the living room, an unsteady wineglass held in her hand. "Tess—whoa!"

The woman spun back toward the living room, bracing her tipsy self against the doorjamb. "Dad! C'mere! You'll never guess who's here."

Tess briefly closed her eyes before giving him a pleading look. "We can work out a cover story."

A cover story? Okay, their relationship was supposed to be private—maybe even secret—but this was her family. Did she worry he wasn't ready for this step?

He probably wasn't, truth be told. But he wasn't prepared to lie, either.

The big man he'd met at the start of the season came out to the hallway, his perplexed face brightening when he saw Liam. Almost comically, he glanced between Liam and Tess, clearly trying to work out what was going on. Several other faces poked out of the living room door. A couple of people gasped and one woman whispered, "Who's that?" before being shushed.

Tess shifted uncomfortably next to him. "I asked Liam if he'd come over...as a birthday surprise for Dad," she finished lamely. "Happy birthday, Dad!"

Ben Chambers lowered a brow, making it obvious he knew she was full of shit. "Thanks, littl'un, but next time how about getting me a stripper?" he joked, grunting when the woman next to him elbowed him in the ribs.

"Why do think I'm here, mate?" Liam tried for levity, and it seemed to work for most of the crowd, but the fact that Tess was passing off their relationship as something else made him burn. He needed her to acknowledge him to this private group—fuck the consequences. He reached for her hand and forced his fingers through hers, wrapping his free hand around the outside so he cradled her fist in a gesture that made it clear they were intimate. And just in case anyone in his audience was an idiot, he said, "Actually, I wanted to see Tess. I didn't know she had guests over."

The group exchanged significant glances while Liam tried to figure out which of the women was Tess's mum. After meeting her dad, he'd figured Tess had to take after her mum. How could a man that big and blond breed a woman as petite as Tess unless he had a tiny wife? But the women of the group all looked built from the same genetic material as Ben and Charlie Chambers. This was a family descended from Viking warriors. The women could easily be named Hildegard or Brunhilda. Not a single one of them looked like Tess, and he began to suspect the funny story she'd mentioned about her name a few moments ago.

"Come in," Tess said to him. "They're not as rude as you might think, though they're doing a damn good impression, standing there staring at you."

A couple of people chuckled and disappeared back into the living room. Apparently the ones who hadn't recognized him were being schooled now because he heard a hissed whisper of "Liam Callaghan...rugby *legend*."

Tess let out a deep breath and led Liam toward the living room. Her father and two women still crowded the door. "Mum, Gwen, this is Liam."

Normally he'd have made a lame comment about seeing where Tess got her beauty from, but his niggling suspicion held him back. He shook their hands, noting with chagrin that they were both at least his height, maybe even six foot. And they were wearing flat shoes. The older one would probably have a good chance of kicking his arse—and the look she gave him said she'd enjoy it. "Liam, it's nice to meet you," she said. "Our daughter's told us nothing about you."

"Mum..."

The woman smiled, but it didn't quite reach her eyes. "So you're a very nice surprise. Come in. Can I get you anything to drink?"

For the first time in his life, he really felt he could use one. "Just some water would be great. Thank you." He glanced down at Tess. "Where's Charlie?"

"In Mauritius, checking out a couple of potential partners," she answered before muttering, "fortunately."

Tess's hand was squeezing the life out of his, so he carefully extricated himself and wrapped an arm around her shoulders, pulling her closer as he shook her dad's hand. "Happy birthday, sir. Sorry I didn't bring a gift."

"That's all right. It's...interesting to see you here."

The hot blush stealing over Tess's cheeks made it clear she really had been keeping their relationship secret, even from the people closest to her. Not only that, but they were clearly less than pleased with the surprise. He didn't know why it bothered him. He hadn't said anything to Spencer until it became clear his secret was out. But he knew Tess was close to her family, so the fact she hadn't let anything slip just seemed wrong. Not nearly as wrong as the way she'd tried to pass him off as being here for her dad, though. Was she ashamed of him? Did her family think he wasn't good enough?

The thought unsettled him, and he spent the rest of the evening watching Tess closely. She might've tried to hide their relationship, but she didn't do a very good job of hiding her discomfort at his presence. She sat next to him on the couch and let him rest his hand on her leg, but she didn't reciprocate. Her back stayed stiff as steel, even as she ensured he was included in the conversation and understood the private jokes her family made. But by the time they called cabs to take them home to various parts of London, Liam's face ached from keeping a false smile through gritted teeth.

He forced himself to try on her proverbial shoes. If his mum had been around, would he have introduced her to Tess already? He'd never brought any of his previous girlfriends home. Once, a girlfriend and his mum had ended up sitting near each other at the same match and his mum had introduced herself. He'd worried she would get the wrong impression and told her not to start picking out her mother-of-the-groom dress yet. "Thank God," she'd said. "That girl talked about nothing but herself for eighty minutes. I had to leave the stadium during the half to score some whiskey, otherwise I never would've made it to the end of the match without smacking her."

Mum would like Tess, though. Tess was forthright and strong enough to put him in his place, but she didn't put herself at the center of the universe. She listened to him and supported him, but she wasn't a pushover. She had a strong sense of family, like he did.

After tonight, though, a yawning emptiness gaped inside him. He feared he craved being part of her family far more than she craved having him there.

Tess let out a ragged sigh as the last family member finally left. She closed the door and fought the urge to sag against it, knowing Liam stood just behind her. His stare bored into the back of her head, and she gathered all her courage to face him and the confused disappointment he'd projected all night.

"Liam, I—"

She interrupted herself, not sure what to say.

He clearly wouldn't make it easy for her, either, raising a brow as if to say "Yes? I'm waiting."

"We agreed to keep everything private. I didn't know that you'd want me to say anything to my family."

She thought it was a good enough excuse, but he crossed his arms over his broad chest. "And when I made it clear that I wanted to stay and meet them? That wasn't a signal to you that I was okay with your family knowing about us?"

She hesitated. "It was."

"The real problem is that *you* didn't want your family to know about us, right?"

She winced. "I wasn't ready for that, no. I wasn't prepared."

"Why not? Do you think they'll betray our privacy?"

"No! No, never. They're not like that."

His jaw worked from side to side, as though he was chewing on the insides of his cheeks. "Tess...are you ashamed to be with me?"

She gasped, the notion so ludicrous it had never even crossed her mind. "Are you kidding? Why the hell would you think that?"

He shrugged one shoulder, but now his closed-off stance seemed to take on a different meaning. Not belligerent or holding himself back from lashing out, but protective, as if guarding himself from an expected blow.

"I *can't* get involved with someone from work. It's against my contract with Charlie, and I've had to ask my family not to say anything to him. Keeping secrets doesn't come naturally to my family, Liam. I could lose my job over this."

He didn't seem to believe her. She closed the distance between them and stroked his arms. When they didn't open, she tugged at his wrists until he let her move them. She leaned into him and gave him a hug. His arms looped around her loosely, as if he wasn't sure he wanted her this close.

"Liam, I'm not ashamed of you. Not in the least. If anything, I'm ashamed of myself."

His brows drew together, and for the first time since they started sleeping together she opened an emotional vein.

"I told you I was recalled to the stand at the inquiry, and that's why I had to leave Venezuela. I didn't tell you why I was recalled. I made a really stupid mistake at my last job. I...sort of slept with a colleague, and when I overheard him telling people about it, I got drunk and sent him an email that I'm really ashamed of. When everything kicked off, I had to testify about the nasty things my colleagues had said and done. The bank handed over my email to the legal team, and I had to go back to court to explain myself. To explain the nasty things *I* had said."

Her face felt like it was on fire, and nausea seized her. Liam watched her patiently, giving her his silent encouragement to continue. "It was humiliating. I had to tell the world about how I'd had sex with this man. The first time around, the panel asked me questions—awful questions—and I had to go over every detail of the degrading things I'd heard him say about me afterward. After Venezuela, I had to go back to explain why I'd said the stupid, juvenile things in the email I'd sent him. I'd been treated like scum and I acted like scum, and the worst part was knowing my family was sitting right behind me in the gallery while I went over every awful detail. I must've been such a disappointment to them, and I don't want them to think I'm making the same mistake all over, getting involved with someone I work with."

Tears stung her eyes at the memory and at the knowledge that she was doing it all over again, having to reveal her most private humiliations to someone whose opinion she cared so much about. Liam's big hand swept under her hair to press the back of her head forward until she buried her face in the comfort of his chest, giving her the privacy she needed. She took a deep breath to steady her emotions as he stroked her back, kissed the top of her head and held her close.

"Tess," he murmured, "what did the man say about you?"

She shook her head, refusing to share any more. "If you really have to know, you can search for it online. I don't want to talk about it anymore. I just want to move on. Please."

He squeezed her. "I won't search for it. If you ever want to tell me, you can. But that's up to you. I don't ever have to know."

She melted, making a funny little sound of relief. Every iota of energy drained from her, and the way he held her suddenly seemed significant—as if he was holding her up instead of just holding her close. When he tipped her head back and gave her a sweet kiss, she was putty.

"It's been a bitch of a long week," he said. "Come to bed with me?"

She nodded, too drained to do anything but whisper, "Thank you."

He kissed her again. "Anytime."

It was something people seemed to say automatically, but she got the impression he really meant it.

18

____

Tess woke up snuggled in a cave. A man cave. Liam's whole body surrounded her. For the first time since they'd started seeing each other, they'd slept together without having sex. Neither of them had had the energy. Figuring she might as well sleep comfortably, she'd worn an old Legends T-shirt to bed. Sometime in the night it had ridden up to her waist, and Liam's hand now rested on her naked tummy. They lay on their sides with Liam curled behind her, one of his legs nudged between hers. His deep breaths blew over her ear.

She could stay this way forever. The thought terrified her. The Liam Callaghan whose career she'd followed was not a forever man. He was a man attracted to a glitzy, glamorous world that she couldn't give him and didn't want to be part of.

But the Liam Callaghan she'd met in Venezuela and whom she'd been sleeping with for several weeks now? Yes, she could see him being a forever man. But did he see himself that way? Or was she a short blip in his life? An experiment in something different?

She couldn't lie around torturing herself with these ques-tions all morning. Carefully pulling her body away from his warm embrace, she rolled to the edge of the bed, pausing at his sleepy grumble of dissatisfaction. She allowed herself a few moments to watch him sleep. Her fingers itched to tug his unruly blond hair. He looked adorable all disheveled, with a day's growth of stubble that took on a reddish hue in the morning sunlight streaming through her shutters.

No matter what happened to them in the future, she would always have these moments when Liam Callaghan belonged only to her. Forget his legions of fans and scores of exes. This morning he was hers.

She slipped quietly downstairs and rooted through the fridge while coffee percolated and she tried to figure out what to give him to eat when he woke up. She'd always left his place before breakfast, not trusting herself to guard her heart if they shared everyday intimacies. But sometime in the night, she'd realized that guarding her heart was pointless. The way he'd listened to her, held her and let her talk about the inquiry's most humiliating moments had released something inside her. She'd always struggled to admit her own weaknesses, and asking for help was unthinkable. Yet Liam hadn't judged her, even though she'd obviously hurt him by trying to cover up their relationship to her family.

And when he'd held her and let her talk, he'd cracked her heart wide open.

Her fridge contained nothing but last night's Turkish take-away leftovers and some eggs she'd bought for a cake she'd tried —and spectacularly failed—to bake for her dad's party. Not wanting to serve Liam *taramasalata* and day-old Turkish *pide* for breakfast, she woke up her tablet and searched for how to cook eggs. She settled on a scrambled egg recipe, figuring anything she attempted would end up scrambled anyway.

When her eggs were nearly finished, her email popped up with a new message. Andre, the calendar photographer, had sent something with an attachment to her personal email account. She held her breath. It could only be one thing. Glancing over her shoulder even though her elderly stairs would've squeaked under Liam's weight, she took the eggs off the heat and bent over her tablet on the counter, opening the email attachment.

Holy mother of hotness...

LIAM'S HAND slipped across the sheet and told him he was waking up alone. Again. Blinking himself awake, he glanced around the unfamiliar room, momentarily confused by the fact that it looked so feminine and inviting compared to the nondescript hotels he usually stayed in. Then he identified it. Tess's room, but no Tess.

His gaze automatically wandered to the dresser and nightstands, checking for a note like the one she'd left him their first night together. When he found nothing but knickknacks, he heaved a sigh of relief and sank back into the pillows.

Huh. He'd grown used to her leaving early in the morning when she spent the night at his, but this was her bloody house. Where had she gone?

A creak provided his first clue. He glanced at the open bedroom door just in time to spot her coming up the stairs and rounding the corner, a tray in her hands.

He grinned. A tray with food.

"Morning," she said. "You look happy."

"Mmm...why wouldn't I be?" When she reached the bed, he took the tray and set it carefully on the nightstand closest to him. Then he grabbed Tess and tugged her into bed, growling against her neck as she squeaked in mock protest.

He couldn't get enough of her. He worked his hands up under the baggy old Legends shirt she'd worn to bed, and his pride spilled over. Seeing her in his colors, wearing his team's logo, released something primal in him. Something that made him want to growl and pound his chest and declare to anyone who asked that she was with him. He swept the shirt over her trim, naked hips until her belly was bare. She was so athletic he could see the play of muscles as she twisted away, laughing.

"Breakfast is getting cold," she protested.

"Don't care. I'm getting hot." He kissed her neck, rubbing his stubble against her soft skin while she went from laughing to moaning.

"Liam…"

"Mmm?" Mouth too busy tasting the skin of her shoulder to say anything else.

She didn't respond in words, so he glanced up and caught the way her eyes fluttered closed and her arms stretched over her head. "Oh, God, that feels good."

Yeah, it did. A lazy Saturday morning rolling around in bed with his nymph while their breakfast grew cold. He could make a habit of this.

By the time they started tucking in to their breakfast, the eggs had turned to Styrofoam. He didn't care, though. She'd cooked for him, and even admitted she'd had to look up a recipe…a scrambled-eggs recipe, for fuck's sake. "What do you usually have for breakfast?" he asked.

"Depends. On work days, I buy oatmeal at one of the sandwich shops near work. At weekends, I usually go to a cafe around the corner. But today—" she waggled her eyebrows suggestively, "—I had you."

"Please. No puns about me filling your belly."

She gasped and smacked his arm. "That's worse than anything I was thinking."

"Whoops," he said, biting back his grin, completely unrepentant. He took a bite of his toast, last night coming back to him quickly now that his lust and his hunger were both on their way to being sated. Tess sat cross-legged in front of him, Legends shirt covering her again, hair mussed up, mouth slowly chewing on breakfast. "Tess?"

"Mmm-hmm?"

"Who named you Countess?"

She paused her chewing momentarily, then swallowed, wiping some crumbs from her lips. "Um, my birth mum."

That was what he'd thought. "Tell me about it."

She took another bite, her gaze firmly focused on the tray on the bed between them as if rubbery scrambled eggs were the most fascinating things in the world. They'd been here before, him and Tess—the first night he'd come to her house and asked why she'd left him in Venezuela. She'd ignored him at first, and he'd wanted to reel the truth out of her like it was a stubborn fish fighting capture. But he'd learned that night that getting Tess to open up took time and patience. She had eventually, giving him morsels of a story that he'd been piecing together ever since.

He wanted her secrets, but more than that, he wanted her trust.

TESS SWALLOWED her bite and picked up her toast to take another, but a knot in her stomach had expanded, making the thought of food sickening. She put the toast down with a grimace. "I think she gave me that stupid name because she had high hopes I'd achieve more in my life than she did. God knows she was useless as a mother, by all accounts. I don't remember her. My parents adopted me when I was three, and I was in care for about a year before that."

"So you weren't adopted at birth?"

She shook her head. "I lived with my birth mum till I was two. Then...I was taken away from her."

Liam slipped his fingers between hers and gently squeezed. "What happened?"

She hesitated. After clearing the lump in her throat, she said, "My birth mum had had some drugs convictions, so when I was born she was put on a register with social services. I was tested at birth, and I was clean, but they still made sure to visit regularly. There were some things that concerned them. Nothing bad enough to justify removing me, until..." She chewed on her bottom lip, glancing briefly up at him through her lashes.

His nostrils flared and his eyes had gone wide, as if he was picturing all of the horrific possibilities. "Until what, love?"

"She met a man, apparently. And he wasn't too keen on having kids around. Neighbors told social services that she'd started leaving me at home alone at night, but no one did anything until she went away with this man for the Easter bank holiday."

His jaw unhinged. "Four days? She left you for four fucking days when you were two?"

Tess shrugged. "That was her plan, but apparently on day two I started crying. The neighbors got fed up with hearing it by day three so they called the police. They said it hadn't occurred to them that my mother wasn't around, or they'd have called sooner."

"Baby." He cupped her cheek and shoved the tray so it didn't come between them. "You could've starved."

"She wasn't that careless. She left dry Cheerios in a dog bowl for me, right next to a bowl of water." She was trying to be brave, but even she could hear a shudder of emotion under the steel in her voice.

"Fuck. Fuck fuck fuck." He wrapped his arms around her

and pulled her onto his lap. She held herself stiffly, not wanting to give in to his comfort. "I had no idea. I'm so sorry."

"Not like it's your fault. Shitty things happen, but honestly? That's probably one of the best things that ever happened to me."

"How?"

Her head pounded. He'd shared such a beautiful family story with her when they'd curled up together on his couch. She desperately wanted to be able to share the same with him. She dug deep to find it. "My family are amazing, Liam. They've stuck by me through so much. Not just the inquiry, which must've been so embarrassing for them, but even from the beginning. They started fostering me because they thought they couldn't have kids. Mum found out she was pregnant with Gwen before the adoption went through. They could've handed me back to social services, but they didn't."

Her throat ached as she recalled all the visits to child psychologists...the time she was kicked out of preschool after physically lashing out at a girl for reasons not even she under-stood... "I wasn't an easy child to love. I had a lot of emotional issues that must've been hell for them to deal with, especially when they had a newborn of their own."

His arms tightened around her, his chin sliding over the top of her head until she was forced to curl against his chest. Back in the man cave he'd created for her, only this time instead of the gentle, relaxed rhythm of his breath drifting over her, she felt his jaw tensing over her scalp, his heart thundering against hers.

"You really don't remember anything?"

It was what she told the few people who asked, but it wasn't quite the truth. Remembering the relief she'd felt when she confessed her humiliations to him last night, Tess gambled on letting him see a little more of herself than she'd ever shared with anyone else. "I can't picture what she looked like or bring to mind a specific memory. But whenever I think about her, I feel this bizarre mix of longing and loneliness, like I must've spent a lot of time craving attention I knew I wouldn't get."

The feeling still haunted her, creeping up whenever she least expected it. She'd never admitted that to anyone. Her family knew the circumstances surrounding her removal from her mother's care, but they'd never pried into her own memories. It was as if they were scared to know the answer. Maybe they worried that part of her wished she'd never been taken away from her birth mum. She didn't have even a shred of doubt about that. What terrified her was how it might still affect her twenty-five years later.

Reaching her capacity for gut-wrenching self-reflection, she shoved the memories down and kissed his cheek. "I have to get ready."

"For what?"

"There's a Legends home match today. I can't neglect my duties to the team by lazing around in bed with their captain."

"Fuck. I forgot." His arms tightened around her, as though he was unwilling to let her go so soon.

She hugged him back, whispering in his ear, "What're you doing today?"

"I've got the morning free and hoped we could watch Wales-Argentina together before I went to training this afternoon, but I guess not."

She brushed her fingertips through the hair at his temples, and the piercing look he gave her filled her with lusty shivers— lust for his body, his time, his attention, none of which she'd get for the rest of the day. "If you want, you can stay here to watch the match."

He perked up, as if thoughts of her home cinema eased some of his disappointment. "You wouldn't mind?"

"Nope. You can let yourself out when you leave. The door

locks automatically, but I have a spare set of keys so you can latch the deadbolt or get back in if you forget something."

He cocked a brow. "We're exchanging keys, are we?"

She eyed him silently for a minute. "I don't need a key to your place, and you can give me mine back later if you want."

Oddly, she didn't want. There was something comforting about the thought of him letting himself into her home, maybe surprising her with a kiss as she cooked a gourmet meal wearing nothing but her Rosie apron. Hey, if this was a fantasy, she might as well go all out.

She pushed herself off his lap and stood, purposely giving him a quick flash of her bum in the process. "Now, would you like me to give you a tour of my shower?"

SOONER THAN LIAM WANTED, she was dressed in jeans and her new Legends shirt, kissing him goodbye and pushing her bike out the front door. He felt oddly like a househusband, as if he were sending his wife off to work before he settled in for a morning of hard-core TV-watching. The feeling wasn't as uncomfortable as he would've imagined.

Her confessions last night and this morning weighed him down, making him realize that he hardly knew her even though they'd been sleeping together for weeks. He'd never pushed to discover more than a woman wanted to share. He rubbed his aching chest as he went over her story in his head.

She must've spent her early years terrified. While he'd known nothing but joy and love, she'd experienced abandonment from the one person who should've been her safe haven. No fucking wonder she never asked him for anything. If she didn't ask, she wouldn't face rejection. Problem was, her lack of trust hit him where he was most vulnerable. What was it about the women he most wanted to support having the least faith in him?

He pushed the unsettling thought aside and wandered into the kitchen for a glass of water. Spotting her tablet, he picked it up and carried it to the living room with him. He collapsed onto the couch and flipped on the TV, excitement buzzing through him when he saw the clarity of the picture and surround sound. Jesus, it was nearly as good as being on the pitch. He *definitely* wasn't giving her keys back.

As the commentators went over the usual pre-match bollocks, he woke up the tablet to connect her sports streaming service, but the website that popped onto the screen made his breath catch.

An appointment confirmation from a hospital on Harley Street. An expensive, private hospital—the kind of place people went to for treatment that wasn't covered on the NHS...or when they were too scared to wait.

The automated confirmation didn't say what the appointment was for or even give the name of a doctor. It just said the system had received Tess's request for an appointment and she would get an email on the next working day.

Liam's stomach heaved even as he tried to convince himself not to jump to conclusions. *She's fine. She's fine.*

That's what Mum said too.

Shite.

He went to the hospital's homepage, but none of the information helped. They specialized in everything from infertility treatment to cosmetic surgery to rare genetic disorders to cancer care.

Cancer care.

He shut the tablet's cover and lay back against the sofa, covering his throbbing eyes with his hand. She'd made the appointment this morning, while he'd still been asleep. And here he'd congratulated himself on getting her to open up about being adopted. Fucking hell, she probably wouldn't have told him anything if he hadn't pushed her to—and that was a pain she'd experienced decades ago. What would it take for her to trust him with her health information?

Your own mum *didn't trust you with the truth.*

Yeah, and he'd learned that lesson. No fucking way would he sit around waiting to know what was going on, blithely assuming like a complete dick that she was telling him the truth.

She was cycling to the stadium and was probably almost halfway there. If he called a cab, he might be able to catch her up.

He arrived at the stadium in time to see her pushing her bike toward the offices instead of locking it outside, where it was more likely to get nicked. He shoved a wad of dosh at the cabbie and followed her, keeping his head down in the hope he wouldn't be recognized by any supporters milling around outside the gates. By the time he reached the offices, she was already stepping into the lift with her bike. He sprinted for it, squeezing through the closing doors as if they were a couple of opposing defenders blocking him from the try line.

"Liam! Jesus! What're you—are you crazy?" she yelled. "You could've been killed!"

A slow grin spread over his face as she unconsciously echoed the first words she'd ever said to him. But her shocked little face reminded him of exactly why he was here, why he had to speak to her so badly, and his smile disappeared. "Yes, Tess. I'm crazy. Please tell me I'm crazy. I opened your computer this morning and saw something I probably shouldn't have."

Her eyes widened, her face paling. *Fuck!* This wasn't going to be good.

"I can't believe you looked at my email!"

"Email? It wasn't your email. It was a hospital appointment. Why? What's in your email?"

Blood rushed back to her face, staining her cheeks a furious red.

She turned away and pressed one of the buttons. "I can't talk to you about this. Not here, not now. I just...I don't have time. Ruth told me I could lock my bike up in her office, and I have to be in the stadium in ten minutes."

Pathetic. The lift started its slow ascent toward the management offices but came to a jarring halt when Liam slammed his hand against the emergency stop button. "Now you have plenty of time."

An alarm went off and Tess groaned, gently hitting the back of her head against the wall in a sign of frustration. "Why are you pushing this?"

"Because something's going on with you, and you won't tell me what it is. Because I feel—" What? How did he feel? Tess's curious face seemed to beg the same question. "I feel like I want to help you, but you're shutting me out."

"Because I don't need help, Liam. There's nothing wrong with me."

"Then tell me why you're going to that clinic."

"It's—it's a woman thing."

"For fuck's sake!" He slapped his hand against the lift wall. "Don't fob me off with that patronizing bullshit. That's how my mum explained her ovarian cancer to me, and she fucking *died* without even giving me a chance to say goodbye!"

He didn't realize what he'd said until he took in her shocked face. She laid a hand on his arm. "Liam..."

He tugged away from her, but the ghost was out there now. The specter of his fear and confusion floated between them, putrefying the air. "She lied to me, Tess. She told me she was fine—just a little tumor that could be taken care of with a minor procedure. I found out later that 'minor' procedure was a fucking *hysterectomy*. There were complications, and she was in hospital for two days before she must've realized it wasn't going to be okay." His voice broke before he could fix it. "She phoned, but I was at training. She left a fucking *voicemail* asking me to come to the hospital if I had time. *If I had time. Fuck.*"

"Oh, Liam." Tess backed him into the corner and wrapped herself around him.

He clasped her shoulders, not sure he whether he could stand the torture of her being so close as she realized that he'd let down the one person who would've done anything for him. "I didn't leave right away. I phoned her back, but she didn't answer. I dragged my feet, joked around with the lads before leaving the training ground. By the time I got there—"

He couldn't go on, but he didn't have to. Tess had lifted onto her toes, grabbed his head and pulled him down for a kiss. A long kiss full of contrition, comfort. He held her close until the shock and pain had ebbed some. He'd never told anyone that he'd arrived ten minutes too late. Not his sports psychologist. Not even Bailey.

"Liam," she whispered against his lips, "it's not your fault."

"The fuck it's not. She should've been able to count on me, but she knew she couldn't so she didn't even bother to tell me. And I proved her right."

"Did she ever *tell* you that she felt she couldn't count on you?"

He reached back in his memory and found nothing. "No," he admitted. "But I didn't visit her as much as I should've. I should've made her a bigger part of my life. If I'd known how little time I had with her..."

"Liam, you can't blame yourself for this. She was the one who made a choice—a bad choice, it turns out—but I doubt she did it for the reason you think."

"What other reason is there?"

"Maybe she thought she was protecting you. She was your mum. She probably didn't want you to worry about her. Or maybe she didn't want to admit her fears out loud because then they would become reality." She stroked his chest, and some of the ache loosened beneath her fingertips. "There are all kinds of reasons she would keep the truth from you, and none of them are because you failed her."

He squeezed her shoulders. "And why are *you* hiding the truth from me? You said it's a woman thing. Tess, I'm a grown man. Women's bits don't scare me or disgust me. Being kept in the dark? *That* scares me."

Her voice softened. "I'm sorry about your mum. I really am. This isn't the same situation at all, though. Please take my word for it."

He swiped a hand over his face, his eyes stinging and throbbing while every muscle in his body tightened. "I can't do that. I won't be able to let this go until you tell me what's going on. *Please.*"

The silence between them seethed, made infinitely worse by the screech of the alarm. Tension held him hostage as his brain imagined all of the worst scenarios, leaving him dumbfounded when she murmured, "I'm getting breast implants."

He slowly dropped his hand so he could see her. A blush had stolen across her face, and she stared at his shoes as if they were mesmerizing. "What?"

"I'm getting breast implants. Or, at least, I think I am. No—I plan to. Definitely. I think. God, I feel like such a dick admitting this after what you just told me about your mum."

Heart caught in the back of his throat, Liam collapsed back against the wall and slid down like a marionette with severed strings until his arse hit the floor. "That's it?"

She sliced him with her burning, angry gaze. "I told you I was fine. Why couldn't you just believe me?"

Relief washed over him in waves, but he'd lost so much energy through worrying about her that he couldn't stand. Not yet. He was down for the count. He reached up and took hold of her hand, tugging. "Sit with me."

"On the floor of the lift?"

"Yes."

Her breath whooshed out in a sound of capitulation, and she sat next to him, facing him. The outside of her thigh brushed against his. He drew her a little closer so he could skim his fingers over her jaw in gratitude. She wasn't dying. He'd wanted to believe it but hadn't been able to. "Look at me, Tess."

She did, her face grim.

"Why do you want implants?"

"Because I've heard they'll give me superpowers. Why do you think?"

His fingers trailed from her jaw down her soft neck to her shoulders, where they caught under the collar of the Legends shirt he'd given her. He pushed it as far down as it would go, then slipped his thumb under her bra strap, finding enough space that he could stroke her shoulder without the strap cutting off his circulation. The strap didn't cut into her skin, the way it sometimes did with big-breasted women. For Tess, wearing a bra wouldn't be about support but about coverage, or maybe modesty. She could probably go without and still be decent. "You're unhappy with the size of your breasts."

She raised her brows and tilted her head, giving him a look that said, "Well done, genius."

"I have some experience with breast implants, you know."

She smirked toward his pecs. "I knew those couldn't be real."

She might've intended to put him off with her barbed tongue, but he'd met far tougher opponents, and he understood that her sarcasm came from embarrassment. He tugged the hem of her shirt up to reveal her abs. "Did you know that some women lose sensation when they get implants?"

"I'm sure the doctor will explain all of the possible consequences to me."

"And that's a risk you're really willing to take?"

Her nostrils flared a little. "Liam, I just—"

"What, sweetheart?"

"I just want to be shaped like a woman, not a fourteen-year-old boy. Right now, I'm flat all over. I'm nipple on bone."

He kept up his gentle stroking across the top of her back, her shoulders, the sensitive skin behind her ear. "You might forget, but I haven't. I've seen you naked. You're not flat all over. Not by a long shot. And I happen to like your nipples. A hell of a lot."

"Why are you saying that to me?"

"Because it's true, and I think you should hear it. Take it from a man—you don't need implants."

She snorted. "I've taken it from plenty of men that I do."

"What do you mean?"

"Never mind. I don't want to go into it."

"Look, we're stuck here until they can get us out. You might as well tell me. Come on. Confess to Father Liam."

She propped her chin on her knees, hiding her chest from him. "I've seen how disappointed men look when I take off my top. It's not something they usually comment on, but a few of them have said really hurtful things, the kind of things that stick with you."

"Such as?" Blood already boiling, Liam was sure he didn't want to know.

"I lost my virginity at uni. I tried to before that, but the one boy I was interested in laughed and said sleeping with me would be like molesting a child."

She winced, and Liam realized his fingers had tightened

across her shoulder, squeezing her collarbone as if it was the boy's neck. "Sorry," he murmured, rubbing gentle circles over the area. "That was a really shit thing to say to someone."

"I can't blame him too much. I *was* still built like a child, even if I wasn't one. I just thought that seventeen-year-old boys were looking to get it wherever they could. He was hardly discriminating, but apparently I didn't inspire an erection in him."

"And since then?"

"Since then I've mostly been with men who had the nous not to say anything about it, but I can tell they're gutted that all my padding disappears when I take my bra off."

"Tess, you still have padding here." He brushed his fingertips across the tops of her breasts, and she sucked in a breath, her gaze flying to his. "See how sensitive you are? Did you see any disappointment on my face when you stripped for me at the waterfall? Or anytime since?"

"First of all, I stripped for myself, not you."

"Duly noted. And what was my reaction?"

She muttered something, forcing him to tilt her face up so he could hear her. "What was that?"

"I said, I wasn't watching you. I've learned not to look at men when I undress. It spoils the mood."

His chest ached with disappointment for her. She was beautiful. At first he hadn't realized how stunning she was—he'd mostly been dumbstruck by her pink hair—but her beauty had grown until he practically shook with longing whenever he saw her. "You want to know what I saw the first time you took your top off for me?"

"I didn't—"

"—take your top off *for me*. I get it. I'll try to be more accurate. Do you want to know what I saw the first time you took your top off *for yourself* when I happened to be in the general vicinity and watching with very close interest, deluding myself that you were doing it for me?"

"Not really." But the crack of her voice betrayed her.

"I saw these perfectly formed, perky tits that looked like the best fantasy I ever could've ordered. That water wasn't warm, Tess, but I went hard so fast I thought I'd pass out from the sudden rush of blood away from my brain. And don't even get me started on your nipples."

"Do. Start on my nipples."

He grinned. "So pretty and rosy. Like sweet strawberries just begging for my mouth. They're big and bold and so responsive I thought I'd taken a wrong turn and landed in heaven. I can't stay away from them."

He brushed her hair back from her face, tucking it behind her ear. "You do whatever you feel you need to, Tess. It's your body, and you need to be happy with it. I certainly wouldn't want advice on whether to surgically enhance my cock. I just hate the thought of you making this decision because a few arse-holes have made you feel you're not good enough, and I think it would be a shame if you lost sensation. Your tits obviously bring you a lot of pleasure. Fuck, I bet I could make you come just by playing with them."

Her brows shot up. "Is that a challenge?"

Now it was his turn to be surprised. "Is that an acceptance of my challenge?"

"Maaay-be."

He swept his hands down her back and grabbed the hem of her top before she stopped him. "Not here!"

"Why not?"

She glanced around, and he realized there could be cameras so he checked too. "I don't see anything even remotely looking like a camera. Do you?"

She shook her head slowly. "You really want to do it here?"

"Play with a nymph's breasts until she comes? I'd want to do it anywhere she lets me."

She hesitated a moment before reaching down and whipping off her top so quickly his head spun, leaving her in a plain white bra that shouldn't turn him on the way it did. But it wasn't the bra that had his bollocks tightening. It was the cute set of breasts inside, the fact that he knew them so well and would get to play with them again. The fact that he loved them.

"Okay," she said, "but you have to take your shirt off too. I'm not sitting here topless all by myself."

"Deal."

He leaned forward and stripped his shirt off much more slowly, teasing her with a hint of ab, a flash of pec before she groaned, "Come on, Cally. They could fix the lift any minute now."

Good point. He had no idea how long they had together, and he had to make every second count.

19

Off came his shirt, and dry went Tess's mouth.

Liam had the kind of body most men would kill for. And why shouldn't he? It was his career to strengthen his muscles, to see food as fuel and to burn that fuel with almost constant exercise. When he whipped the shirt clear of his head and leaned back, Tess's brain went numb. She'd always loved being active. Her career was far too sedentary, so she'd found ways of burning her energy and staying fit, like cycling to work through London traffic—which had the added benefit of making her feel like she'd run a gauntlet, leaving her exhilarated every morning and evening. She liked her thighs and her arms, but her breasts and bum lacked padding, and those were two areas she couldn't seem to build up.

How could a man who looked like this—a man who'd slept with some of the world's sexiest women—be interested in seeing her naked? Was it simply because he was a man and would want to see pretty much any woman naked? Or was it insulting to even think that about him?

He wrapped his hand around one of her legs and pulled her closer. She slid against the floor and dreaded to think what her dad would suspect when she showed up in the hospitality suite with dirt covering the bum of her jeans. But then Liam was draping her thigh over his lap and lifting her hips so she sat on him, and everything outside the lift faded away.

He sat on the floor with his knees bent and she straddled him, her back resting against his thighs. His eyelids had gone heavy as he stared at her chest, still decently covered by her padded bra. She'd expected him to yank it off her immediately or at least to ask her to take it off, but he seemed content to watch her as he let his big hands rove up and down her rib cage so slowly that she almost didn't notice the infinitesimal rise in her body temperature. The slower he was, the hotter she became, and she squirmed on his lap, making him groan.

"Christ. Just—" He couldn't seem to finish the sentence, but he grabbed her hips and repositioned her on his lap, and she felt his hard-on cushioned between the cheeks of her scrawny arse.

"Am I hurting you?"

His laugh sounded tortured. "Yes. It's the best pain in the world."

His fingers danced up each bone in her spine until he reached her bra strap. Why hadn't she worn a nicer one? Hadn't her mother always taught her to wear clean underwear in case she was hit by a car and doctors had to strip her? As if she would've worn dirty underwear. If she was ever a mother, she'd give her daughter much more useful advice: always wear sexy lingerie, because you never know when you might be stuck in a lift with a man you want to show it to.

The elastic band around her ribs loosened, and Tess held her breath as Liam drew the straps off her shoulders. Her chest barely moved, but already her nipples tightened painfully in anticipation. Their sensitivity usually embarrassed her. She could've got away with just wearing a tank top or camisole under her shirts, except for her damn hair-trigger nipples. Yet another reason for the padding.

She pulled her arms through the straps, and Liam flung the bra to the other side of the lift. His tongue came out to wet his lips. "Beautiful."

Only one word, but uttered with such reverence Tess couldn't doubt its sincerity. He thought she was beautiful? How? Why? She looked down at herself, but all she saw were the same breasts she'd had forever, the breasts other men thought it their right to comment on—no matter whether they were lovers or colleagues.

Given her warning that they could be discovered at any time, she thought he would dive right in, palming and pawing and suckling like an overeager bear going at a beehive until she was nothing but sore and covered in angry red marks. Yet again, Liam did the opposite of what she expected. He trailed two fingertips up and down the bone between her breasts, an area she had no idea until now was so sensitive. She sucked in a shaky breath and arched, unconsciously trying to get closer. The area he caressed was flat as flat could be, but still it seemed to have a direct connection to nerve endings between her legs. She grew wet just from this simple touch and the look of extreme concentration on his face, as though nothing in the world fascinated him more than her upper body.

"Tess, see how you react when I'm not even touching your breasts? Your nipples are so hard they look painful."

"They are a little painful."

He gave her a curious glance. "Really?"

"They're...achy."

His lips turned upward in a smile that made her inner muscles clench. "The good kind of painful, then."

"Yeah. Are you going to touch me?"

"In a minute. First I want to tell you what I see."

Oh God, enough of this talking. They'd talked for *ages*. Tess wanted action.

But Liam clearly wouldn't be rushed. "I see these incredibly tight, long nipples that I already know will fit between my lips perfectly. When I put my mouth on you, I'll really be able to feel you. I'll be able to suck your nipples deep enough that the tips will tickle the roof of my mouth, so my whole mouth can please you."

Oh. My. God. She grabbed his thighs and dug her nails in, his words turning her on so badly she could hardly keep her balance on his lap.

"And as for your breasts," he said, his voice as unsteady as she was, "they're perky and firm and so cute they make me want to play for hours."

"Do it. Please." She was so, so ready.

He stroked the faint lines her bra had left in her skin, first following the line beneath her breasts left by the completely unnecessary underwire and then the much fainter indentation from the tops of the cups. His fingers swirled around her nipples, not touching them but teasing just the same. Tess had never known the skin of her breasts could be so sensitive. She'd stroked herself here, getting herself in the mood whether she was with a partner or not, but the men she'd been with tended to approach her breasts far more aggressively, as though they could make them grow by squeezing and plucking them.

Liam took his precious time, and his simple touches made her heart pound. He could probably feel it thudding against her ribs. It might even be responsible for the way her breasts trembled beneath his fingertips.

He shifted her again on his lap, and she wriggled for him, wanting him to feel the same exquisite agony she did. He moaned and crunched his abs so he could bury his face in her breasts, latching on to one while he kept his swirling touch light around the other. His tongue flicked against the sensitive tip of her nipple while his lips suckled gently. Her pelvic floor seized, searching for something to grab onto, and she tilted her hips to try to put pressure on her clit. But Liam's free hand held her still, and he murmured against her breast, "No. Just your breasts. That was the deal."

She groaned and arched her back over his knees, giving him greater access if this was all the contact she would get. But damn if she wouldn't torture him a little for denying her the relief she craved. She wriggled her bum as much as she could against his erection, making him groan.

Her skin grew damp from his hot breath and tongue, and her clit tightened even though she could find nothing to rub against but the seam of her damp pants. Whimpers of need clutched her throat, and Liam increased the pressure of his mouth and fingertips, tugging harder, pinching until her pleasure bordered on pain.

"Come for me, nymph. Come for both of us."

The words, whispered with desperation against her nipple, made her body shatter with spasms. She sucked in air as if she'd just finished a sprint, one of her hands digging into Liam's rock-solid thigh while the other tugged at his hair, holding him close to her breast so he couldn't leave.

His mouth and fingers gentled as she came back down to herself. Her body trembled, and he pressed soft kisses against the flesh surrounding her nipples. His hands made big, sweeping motions down her arms and up her rib cage, avoiding the pleasure areas he'd just tortured into such exquisite pleasure.

Gradually she became aware that she was sprawled half-naked across his lap with her spine arched over his knees and her head thrown back at an awkward angle. He seemed to realize it was uncomfortable, because he cupped his big hands under her shoulders and drew her forward until she collapsed in a sticky, sated heap against his chest. His naked chest. Her naked flesh pressed against his, and she shivered and cuddled closer as he stroked her back.

"Liam—" What the hell could she say? This one part of her body had been a source of insecurity ever since her mum announced that Gwen needed her first bra and it became painfully obvious that Tess was still a long way off needing one, despite being three years older.

Liam stayed silent, seemingly content to snuggle even though the erection prodding her through their trousers told her he hadn't found any relief. After a few minutes, Tess pulled slowly back and grabbed the strap of her cycling pack, dragging it across the floor. She unzipped one of the pockets and pulled out her phone, tapping it until the email from Andre opened, showing the two of them wrapped in a passionate embrace, both wearing skimpy swimsuits. Turning it so Liam could see the screen, she said, "That's what I could look like."

His brows rose almost imperceptibly. Andre had turned her bra and underpants into a retro pink-polka-dotted bikini but, even better, he'd given her breasts that filled the bikini and spilled over the top like plump muffins.

She looked feminine. Buxom. Classic. So freaking hot she would've had sex with herself.

Liam took the phone and stared at it for a minute before meeting her gaze. "But why would you want to look like that when you could look like *you*." He slipped her phone back into her bag and skimmed her breasts with both palms, setting loose a series of delicious afterglow shivers. "Tess, you're beautiful. There isn't a single part of your body that disappoints me. Any man who tells you differently is a dick."

Anger pricked her eyes and she bit down hard on her back teeth. "That's not true. Men like women with curves, not women who can shop in the boys' section. It's nice of you to say these things, but you're already in my pants and I won't be kicking you out of them anytime soon, so it's really not necessary."

His sigh was ragged and punctuated by a *thud* as his head thwacked against the lift wall. "I swear to God, I'll never understand. Half the women I know starve themselves or get the fat sucked out of every curve, and the other half slice themselves open to insert bags of silicone. Why can't any of you just be happy?" He crunched forward, bringing his face level with hers. "Tess, you're fit. You have the legs of a cyclist, the abs of a yogi, and your arse is a thing of wonder. I worry about the god-awful state of your arteries, and mentally you're a bit fucked up, but on the outside you're lovely. If you want to worry about changing something, how about eating a piece of fresh fruit every now and then? One that doesn't come in a powder that you pollute your water with."

She opened her mouth to argue but clamped it shut again before any sound escaped. He was right. Sweet baby Jesus, he was right. Okay, so she would never describe her arse as being a thing of wonder, but she did like her legs and belly. A lot of women—her sister Gwen included—had told her how lucky she was to be so toned. Luck had little to do with it, since she literally cycled her arse off every day. But genes had to play a part too —probably the same genes responsible for her lack of a rack.

She'd wasted years listening to men who'd used her lack of curves to denigrate her. A stronger woman would've ignored them, would've owned her body instead of being wounded by the barbed insults. Damn it, why wasn't she a stronger woman?

"You're right," she murmured.

"About the fruit?"

"No. Well, that too. But no, about being happy. I've always found something to be miserable about—whether it's my boobs or my idiot former colleagues or my old job. And I obsess over them until I do something drastic that just seems to land me in a worse state than I started in. What's wrong with me?"

"Like I said, you're a little fucked up in the head. But that's all right. It's probably why you're sleeping with me, so I'm not going to complain too much."

Was that why she was sleeping with him? Obviously it wasn't the *whole* reason. The multiple toe-curling orgasms were right up there, as was the fact that she loved being around him.

But their relationship couldn't go anywhere. After the catastrophic way her last workplace fling ended, she couldn't risk being publicly involved with someone she worked with—especially not someone with such a high profile. Now that the inquiry was nearly wrapped up, the last thing she wanted was to swing the public's attention back to her love life.

And Liam was twenty-eight, a professional athlete and one of the world's sexiest men. He was with her now because their attraction was fresh and new, but how long would that last? How long until he went on tour and she was smacked in the face with newspaper photos of him cavorting with strippers in Cape Town or hooking up with a model in Sydney?

Pangs of distress seized her. She'd fallen for a man when they could only offer each other a few secret weeks. And she'd fallen hard. Who else would've taken the time to notice her most sensitive places or bothered to race after her today because he feared something was wrong?

How fucked up was it to decide—even knowing that it had to end eventually—that she would give him everything she could for as long as they had together?

She skimmed her fingertips down his stubble-roughened cheeks. He hadn't even taken time to shave before rushing after her. Leaning forward, she pressed her bare chest to his, her heart to his, letting her lips trace the wake of her fingers from the apple of his cheek to the corner of his mouth, down to caress his strong jaw until she reached his earlobe. Wrapping her arms around his neck when his closed around her, she settled into his warm embrace and whispered, "Thank you."

"For what?" His voice vibrated against the hollow between her shoulder and collarbone.

"For being kind to me."

He froze, and the wrongness of her statement stole her breath. She squeezed her eyes closed. Jesus, when had her expectations dropped so low? With Michael, she'd been shocked by his casual cruelty, but she hadn't expected much consideration in the first place. He hadn't been the first one to teach her that she didn't deserve common courtesy. He hadn't been the first to abandon her with a dog bowl full of Cheerios and expect her to make do.

"Tess—"

Bang! A knock on the lift's doors echoed off the walls, making them both jerk in surprise. "Anyone in there?"

"Shit!" Tess dove for her bra, fumbling as she tried to untwist the straps and hook it around her ribs.

"Tess—"

"Hello?" the voice from outside called, followed by more banging.

"Yeah, we're in here!" Liam yelled before lowering his voice again. "Tess..."

"Can you get us out of here?" she yelled.

"Engineer's here. Give us two minutes!"

She yanked her Legends shirt over her head and stood, avoiding looking at him still sitting on the floor with his hand stretched out toward her. "I really have to get going. The match must've already started. My dad'll be panicking." Checking her phone, she cursed. "No phone signal."

But Liam wouldn't be deterred. "Tess, talk to me."

Blood rushed to her cheeks. "About what? We've talked a lot today."

God, was there anything she *hadn't* told him? He knew about how her birth mother had abandoned her, that she'd been in a relationship that'd ended her previous career, and that she was humiliatingly self-conscious about her breasts to the point of thinking that she deserved something less than kindness from men she was intimate with.

How awful.

The lift doors opened and several concerned faces stared at them. Their gazes slid past her to land on Liam, still sitting on the floor. With a look of horror, one man said, "Mr. Callaghan! Are you all right?"

"Fine." Liam brushed his hands over the seat of his trousers, his voice tight and short.

"You certainly took your precious time," Tess snapped. The man who'd asked the question blinked and pulled his head back. A hot wave of shame flooded her at the tightening of Liam's lips. Swallowing her apology, she lowered her chin to her chest and rushed away, Liam's gaze burning a hole in the back of her head and his unspoken word echoing in her ears.

Coward.

20

Tess took the morning of the inquiry's closing statements off work. She dressed in her most sedate gray suit but, at the last minute, grabbed the long string of shells Liam had bought her during their magical last day in Venezuela. She looped them twice around her neck and considered herself in the mirror with a small smile. Putting on a suit had always made her feel stronger, more professional and confident. The shells were hardly professional, but they filled her with a sense of invincibility. The memory of stopping by the roadside stand and browsing through the selection of handmade tourist tat brought her smile out even more. Liam had been the first to spot these. He'd put them over her head and told her that every nymph needed shells.

He hadn't called her *nymph* all week. Not since he'd deliberately got them stuck in the lift together. They'd texted since then, but neither had mentioned the incident or anything related to it. She'd had her appointment at the clinic yesterday, but when he called her last night he hadn't asked about it and she hadn't told him.

She wasn't going through with the procedure. Her body was

her body, and she was good with that—especially now that she understood the power it possessed.

Didn't mean she was ready to surrender her push-up bras, though. With one last glance, she adjusted herself in the mirror.

Steeling herself to hear all of her work troubles dredged up again, Tess grabbed her handbag and left for the inquiry. After today, it would all be over. She would be able to concentrate on rebuilding her career and reputation while enjoying her remaining time with Liam. The World Cup semi-finals were tonight. England had triumphed over the odds and would face South Africa in about twelve hours. Come Monday, she and Liam would be colleagues again. The time they had to explore what was between them would be over.

But she needed to save those worries for Sunday. Today she had to shore up enough courage to step through the doors of the Royal Courts of Justice one last time.

When she arrived, Gwen was waiting for her outside the courtroom. Tess's heart swelled as she went up on her tiptoes and Gwen bent down so they could kiss each other's cheeks. "I didn't expect you to come today."

Shrugging, Gwen said, "I had the morning off. Dad and Mum both wanted to be here but Dad has a faculty meeting he couldn't reschedule and Mum threatened to go for Michael's throat if he showed up, so I convinced her I'd come in her place."

Tess took Gwen's hand and gave it a quick squeeze. "Cheers for that. The last thing I need is to have to hold her down."

Gwen snorted. "I know you're strong, Tessy, but I don't fancy your chances against her. I bet Mum's a biter."

They walked into the courtroom and found seats a few rows back from the lawyers. Tess was never so aware of her small stature as she was when she was with her sister. Six feet tall when she wore flats, Gwen towered over her. In fact, Tess had grown up feeling that Gwen bested her at most things. She'd been brilliant at school and perfect at all things domestic. Like their mother, she could spout off the periodic table of the elements and, like their father, she could name the dates of every battle the British army had engaged in since Hastings. She could whip up gorgeous cupcakes with professional-looking icing without consulting a recipe. If she hadn't cried herself to sleep most nights from the time she was ten and a boy had called her Freakzilla, Tess would probably have despised her.

Gwen was built like their parents: big. She'd hit a growth spurt that probably hadn't stopped yet, even though she was twenty-five. Her shoulders were broad and she had to special-order bras. As far as Tess knew, she'd never had a serious relationship. Only one boy had asked her out in school, and Gwen had returned home sobbing with a torn dress, saying the boy had thought she'd be grateful enough for his attention that she would at least give him a blow job. Tess had made the boy pay by passing out fliers with a picture of him getting out of the school pool with an erection. She'd been suspended from school.

In hindsight, she probably should've remembered that experience when she'd launched her blog. Lightning might not strike the same place twice, but Tess seemed cursed to remake her stupidest mistakes, only making them bigger and stupider each time.

Lord Justice Tarrington entered the courtroom with the experts who had quizzed her and other witnesses throughout the months of the inquiry. Tess's stomach knotted as she glanced across the aisle and found the man who had made her life hell: Michael, the scum dog she'd slept with.

Why was he here? Throughout the inquiry, none of her ex-colleagues had shown up unless they'd been called on to give testimony, and then they'd lied through their crooked teeth. She expected they were all at work now, trying to pretend it was a normal day.

It probably was. Nothing would change as a result of this inquiry. Filthy, shitty laundry had been aired, and the public had been titillated and outraged by some of the normal working practices they'd heard about, but nothing would really happen. The inquiry was not like a trial. People wouldn't be sentenced to jail time unless Lord Justice Tarrington recommended criminal proceedings. A month from now, he would simply publish a report listing his recommendations for how to improve working conditions in the financial services. He would probably apportion blame, which would be embarrassing for the people involved, since it would become a public document of historical record. But once his report was released, it would be up to the politicians to decide whether to implement his recommendations.

The lawyer representing the investment firms gave his closing argument, focusing on how the industry had been instrumental in advancing women throughout the last century and other bollocks. Tess's phone vibrated in her bag. Glancing around to check whether anyone had heard, she swiftly unzipped the bag and pulled the phone out to turn it off, but stopped when she saw the first few words of Liam's text on her screen: *That guy's a complete dick.*

The hairs on her neck stood up. She texted back. *What guy?*

The lawyer. Anyone with half a brain can tell he's a lying scumbag.

She sat up straighter. Trying not to draw any attention to herself, she pretended to stretch, twisting her back slowly to the right and left and glancing through the audience. Her phone vibrated in her hand. *Three rows behind you.*

Why?

There was an excruciatingly long pause, long enough for

Tess to regret asking the question. Finally, the answer came through. *Because I wanted to be your support team, even if I couldn't be right at your side.*

Joyful endorphins flooded Tess, and she touched the shells where they lay against her chest. *Thank you.*

A nudge from Gwen's sharp elbow brought her back to the courtroom. In a very soft whisper, Gwen said, "You're attracting attention."

She gestured subtly toward the other side of the courtroom, where Michael considered Tess with narrowed eyes. She raised her brows mockingly and battled her inner teenager, who desperately wanted to find a humiliating photo of the dickhead and spread it around.

"It'll be over soon," Gwen whispered.

Yes, it would. Perhaps then she could have a life again and start making plans for the future.

When the lawyers representing all of the parties involved had finished making their statements, Lord Justice Tarrington wrapped up the inquiry and promised to deliver his recommendations to Parliament in a timely manner. The inquiry was over. Tess released a deep sigh of relief as Gwen put her arm around her shoulders and squeezed her tightly.

"Done," Gwen said. "Now, my shift starts at one, but I'm famished. How about lunch?"

Tess stood and casually turned around. As promised, Liam sat a few rows behind her but, in his gold-rimmed spectacles and a perfectly tailored dark gray suit, he looked so much like just another lawyer or City boy. He'd slicked down his hair so it looked darker and straighter than it really was. Only his green tie—Legends green with a tiny embroidered rugby ball on it—gave a hint of his work. A casual observer would probably have passed him by.

A corner of his mouth flexed in a small smile, and he gave

her a subtle wink. She ran her fingers along the strand of shells, watching his smile grow as he noticed them.

"Tessy?"

"Hmm?" She faced her sister again. "Oh, lunch. That sounds great. Let me just see if—" but when she turned back, Liam was already out the door, striding away with his phone in his hand. Seconds later, her mobile buzzed. "Hold on a sec, Gwenny. That might be work."

The text made her flush all over. *Come over after the final on Sunday. Bring the shells. Bubbly's on me.*

Gwen cleared her throat loudly. "Nice of him to turn up."

"What? Who?" Tess flipped the cover over her phone to hide the text, too late apparently.

"Oh, please, Tessy. Who do you think? The same man who came over way too late for a social call last week. The one who got you to not only *eat* vegetables but *cook* them. The one, I suspect, who's responsible for that giddy smile on your face right now." Gwen hooked her arm through Tess's and the two maneuvered their way through the thinning crowd of lawyers, City workers and journalists until they reached the entry hall of the Royal Courts.

"Don't know what you're talking about," Tess demurred. "That smile's there courtesy of this torturous inquiry finally ending."

"Perhaps you should've thought of that before you launched your shitty little blog."

The biting voice behind her raised her hackles, and she stopped to face the man who'd inspired her to launch her shitty little blog in the first place. "Michael. Lovely to see you, as always."

"Oh, fuck off, Tess. None of us would've had to go through this if you'd just acted like a professional in the first place."

Tess gasped, head shaking slowly in utter disbelief. Her

temper rose from the depths of her gut, bringing with it a string of curses and insults that bubbled in her throat, desperate to escape and pummel him. But Gwen flexed her biceps around Tess's arm, a silent message of support that encouraged Tess to do the unnatural, to swallow her tit-for-tat instinct and take the high road.

Deep inside, she knew Michael was partly right. She shouldn't have slept with him. Shouldn't have written about him and her colleagues the way she had. Complaining through the company's formal HR channels would've got her nowhere, but as much as she'd wanted to inflict the same humiliation on him that he'd heaped on her, she knew she'd sacrificed the high ground when she'd told the world about his diminutive manhood.

She couldn't regret whatever good her blog had done, giving women who worked in the City a place where they could expose the everyday sexism they faced at work, but she could regret the immature way she'd written about Michael.

Squaring her shoulders, she stared him down with the blankest face she could manage. "I'm sorry for my part in this, Michael. If I could go back in time, I would've tried to find a different way to resolve our problems. I hope you can see that the way you treated me was despicable, but I didn't need to retaliate the way I did. Now I've met someone who's shown me what a real man is, so you can rest assured that I won't waste any more of my energy harassing you, or even thinking about you."

Okay, so maybe the high ground was too great an altitude for her to aspire to just yet. She'd settle for the middle ground today and work her way up.

Red stained Michael's cheeks and his nostrils flared as his gaze flicked to the side. Tess followed it to find an older man in a rumpled coat standing near them, his ear cocked toward them and his hand scribbling quickly over a reporter's notepad.

Fucking *hell.* She'd done it again, fueled a fire that the media wouldn't ignore.

"Tess, let's go," Gwen hissed.

Tess nodded tersely and exhaled a sharp breath. She spun on her heel, making Gwen stumble to keep up. "I can't believe I'm such an idiot," she muttered. "Why can't I learn to just walk away?"

"Because then you wouldn't be you, love." Gwen tugged her closer, shoring her up as self-recriminations burned her gut like acid. "You're our little hotheaded fireball, and we love you for it. You say the things the rest of us only dare think. Most people don't have half the guts you do."

"There's a reason for that. It's called evolution. My people get culled from the gene pool through our own utter stupidity."

They strode toward the exit, the end nearly in sight when the door to the men's loo opened and Liam stepped into the foyer in front of them. Tess drew herself and Gwen to a sharp halt, willing him to walk out ahead of them without seeing her, but today Lady Luck decided to crap all over her. He did a double take, his natural grin turning upside down as he took in her face. She didn't need a mirror to know what he saw. Shoulders so tense they nearly touched her ears. Moisture stinging her eyes. Lips pressed so tight her premature wrinkles were probably furrows around her mouth. Chest heaving as she struggled to get a grip.

He closed the distance between them and she tried to silently communicate something other than her distress. *Go away. Please. Turn around and let's talk about this later, away from the journalists. Away from Michael. Please.*

He didn't get the message. Worse, when he reached her, he clasped her arm in a tender grip he probably meant to be encouraging but which felt like a sharp-toothed snare. "Tess, what's wrong?"

"Go away," she whispered, unable to choke down the urgency that gripped her.

He blinked. "What—?"

"Please."

But it was too late. Michael strode toward them, the reporter a few steps behind. Giving Liam an assessing once-over, Michael said, "You must be Tess's *real man*."

Tess closed her eyes, but she couldn't block the confusion in Liam's voice. "Sorry?"

"Tess said she met—hang on. Don't I know you?" Michael snapped his fingers a couple times, as if the sound might prod his memory. Horror swept over Tess, and she opened her eyes just in time to catch comprehension dawn over Michael's face. "You *are*. You're Liam Callaghan."

Liam jerked his head in acknowledgment, a reserved smile tilting his lips but his normal effusive charm nowhere to be seen.

"I can't believe it," Michael laughed. "You're fucking a *rugby player*? I thought you had more sense than that, Tess."

"You're evidence I don't," Tess snapped before good sense had a chance to stop her.

Liam's face froze, shock giving him a grotesque mask, making a mockery of the polite interest he'd shown Michael moments before. "*This* is the guy?"

"What's wrong with that, mate?" Michael's fists clenched, as if he might actually have a chance in a fight with Liam.

"For starters, your head looks like a testicle."

Several people surrounding their group, including the reporter, turned to snicker at Michael, and if Tess hadn't seen her whole life crashing down she might've felt bad for him— especially since his shaved ginger hair and wrinkly forehead *did* make him resemble a bollock, one that was turning purple and veiny from lack of air.

Gwen, ever her champion, drew herself up to her full height and glared straight into Liam's eyes. "You don't have to shame her for it. Clearly it was a heinous mistake."

"Hey!" Michael protested.

The journalist's hand flew over his notepad, and several phone cameras clicked as their owners captured the debacle. Panic shot through her. A few minutes ago, the black cloud that'd hung over her for years had started to drift away. Now it returned with a sharp blast of thunder, a deluge of frigid rain and the chilling realization that her name and sex life would be all over the internet again within seconds—even more prominently this time, since she was sleeping with one of the world's greatest rugby players.

Worse, so much worse, Charlie's business would hit the papers for all the wrong reasons. He'd given her a chance to start over. All he'd asked was that she represent him with honor and avoid fucking around with anyone she worked with. And what had she done? She'd let her impetuous nature overrule her rational brain, yet again.

And that didn't seem to be about to change. Fighting panicky breaths, she tried to make things better by torpedoing everything. "I'm not sleeping with him. With Liam, I mean. I'm not."

Liam's brows inched upward. "Tess—"

But adrenaline gripped her now. She was in fight-or-flight mode, and she had to protect the people she loved.

TESS HAD GONE GHOSTLY pale except for the rosy stain working its way up her neck to her jaw. The white shells stood out in a contrast just as stark as the difference between the mouthy, self-assured Tess he'd fallen for in Venezuela and the panicky one who stood before him now.

Where had that woman gone? The woman who'd known who he was but still ripped the piss out of him. The one who'd felt insecure about her body but hadn't let that stop her from sharing the most erotic episode of his life.

The one he'd fallen in love with over the past six weeks.

Liam laid his hands on her shoulders, giving them a gentle squeeze. "Tess, it's all right."

He was ready. He'd come here today to be her support team, but sitting a few rows behind her had unnerved him, giving him a twitchy discomfort not unlike jock itch. When it spread to the rest of him, he'd realized there was nothing fungal about it. He'd been sitting in the wrong place. He'd needed to sit next to her—close enough to hold her hand, brush his shoulder against hers and whisper his support in her ear, not type it into a text message.

The deal that had allowed them to get to know each other over the past six weeks no longer satisfied him. He was ready to make their relationship public—but he wouldn't do it without her approval. Tess's brows drew together until they nearly touched, and her head shook in a jerky denial.

A voice recorder was shoved between them, and a glossy-haired woman asked, "Mr. Callaghan, what's the nature of your relationship with Ms. Chambers?"

He opened his mouth, but Tess drew in a quick breath and said, "It's strictly professional. We both do our jobs, and that's it."

It took several long seconds for Liam to hear the echo of the words he'd said on the pitch after the first match of the season, when he'd tried to convince them both that he was only talking to her because he had to. He'd done it partly to hurt her, and fucking hell did it ever burn being on the receiving end.

She couldn't mean it, not after everything they'd shared. He looked to her body to deny the truth of her words. The corners of her mouth tugged downward and her brow furrowed. The panic had left her face, replaced with an apology.

He understood, but fucking hell it hurt. A muscle in his jaw twitched and pinpricks of numbness shot through his fingers as the blood left them. Not only was she unwilling to make their relationship public, but she was publicly *denying* him? He let his hands drop from her shoulders, flexing and relaxing them to try to bring back feeling. Instead, a more intense coldness settled in.

"We had a deal," she whispered, as if the crowd hadn't drawn so close they could hear every breath.

The woman with the recorder shoved it closer to Tess's mouth. "What deal, Ms. Chambers? Does your deal have to do with the inquest? How long have you and Mr. Callaghan been involved?"

Another voice called out from the back of the crowd. "Did you give him any insider trading tips before you lost your job?"

Liam cursed and shot a furious glare toward whoever asked. "How dare you!"

"So you don't deny it?"

Tess exhaled so fiercely her fringe blew up from her forehead before fanning out and settling again. "Liam, I can't. I can't do this again. I'm sorry."

"Sorry?" He took in the sea of people drinking up every second of Tess's life imploding, and there was fuck-all he could do to help her. *She* was sorry? He'd convinced himself this time was different, this time he could fall for a woman without his celebrity getting in the way. But it still did—only this time, instead of being used for his famous face, his fame brought the wrong kind of attention to the woman he loved.

"You're not half as sorry as I am, Tess."

The red stain spilled over her cheeks, and her eyes went glossy and pink around the edges. Her teeth gouged her bottom lip, and he fought the urge to rescue it before she drew blood.

She'd just dumped him in front of a bunch of reporters who'd be desperate for a story now the inquiry was finished, and all he wanted to do was wrap her in his arms and shield her from the pain. She must have figured that out because she spun around and pushed through the throng of people, leaving him surrounded by strangers shouting questions at him.

She'd warned him that she was one bad news story away from losing her job again, along with all the pride and money that went with it. It killed him to realize that *he* was a bad news story.

21

Whistleblower Calls Penalty Against Rugby Legend.

Tess had only ducked into the newsagent's for an emergency chocolate bar, but a wall of tabloids and broadsheets confronted her. After a night when she'd consumed more wine than sleep, her eyeballs ached as if she'd scrubbed them with a scouring pad. She squeezed her lids shut, pressed her thumbs into the corners and released the pressure, hoping the headlines would magically disappear like the tiny black dots floating in her vision. Cautiously, she peeked again.

Callaghan Kicked Into Touch By City Siren.

Obviously she was an idiot to think her luck might've changed.

Her mobile trilled with the theme song she'd long ago picked out for Charlie—"This Land Is Your Land"—and she removed the phone from the pocket of her hoodie only long enough to reject the call, sending him to voice mail for the dozenth time since he'd received the first online alert linking the name of his beloved company with the brewing scandal.

Trying to ignore the full-color photos that captured Liam's shocked expression, Tess reached over the papers and grabbed as many chocolate bars as she could wrap her fist around. The memory of Liam's voice pushed through her thoughts. *Please sort your diet out. I hate to think of you having a heart attack at fifty.*

Her heart was killing her all right, but two decades earlier than he'd supposed. It had exploded for all the world to see yesterday, and a few hundred grams of saturated fat wouldn't matter one bit.

Still, she shelved the sweets and backed out of the tiny, cluttered store. Maybe she could grab some grapes from the organic shop around the corner on her way home. This time she'd stick to grapes of the unfermented variety.

Fifteen minutes later, carrying an old Legends tote bag full of fresh fruit, she trudged through the park to her house, not even bothering to pull her mobile out when it rang with Woody Guthrie's anthem again. Though she couldn't put Charlie off forever, hopefully she could shake off her hangover before she handed in her notice. But again, Lady Luck decided to crap all over her. As she rounded the last copse of trees, she saw a man sitting on her front steps, glowering and muttering at the phone in his hand like a complete nutter.

Swallowing as much of the guilt as she could get down her tight throat, she crossed the street and gave him a sad smile when he looked up and noticed her. "Hiya, Charlie."

He stayed silent as he stood, tugging his skinny jeans up to cover his ass crack before he slipped his phone into his man bag. Her eyes stung all over again as she took in his whisker-roughened chin and flat, product-less hair. He hadn't groomed himself today. She was in deep steaming shit.

"Come in." She unlocked the door and motioned for him to enter ahead of her. He made for the kitchen while she closed and locked the door, trying not to notice the tense set of his shoulders. By the time she stepped into the bright kitchen, he'd poured himself a glass of water and was pulling a packet of strawberry-flavored powder out of a cupboard for her.

"That's all right," she said. "I take my water neat now."

Both of his brows shot up. "Really? Any other news you'd like to tell me?"

She cringed. "I'm sorry?"

His nostrils flared as he shook his head in obvious frustration. "Is that a question?"

"No. It's not. I really am sorry."

He thrust a glass of water at her, and it sloshed over her hand. "I asked you to do one thing. One simple fucking thing."

"I know. I messed up."

"Royally."

She bit down hard on the corner of her bottom lip. "The thing is, I fell in love with him."

Charlie collapsed onto one of her barstools, his head dropping back like a flower on a broken stalk as he let out a gusty sigh. "Fucking hell, Tessy, that's even *worse*."

"Worse? Why worse?" If she was going to throw away the only job she was likely to get and compromise the reputation of her cousin's company, why not do it for love instead of lust?

"Because how can you work with him now? How can you go to matches to promote us if it means spending eighty minutes watching him play? How can you be part of the Christmas charity fundraiser we're sponsoring when he'll be a key part of it? How can you organize *any* promotional events when he'll likely show up with whatever cover model he's shagging at the time?"

Tess's gut churned, and her throat seized at the vision. For weeks, the one thing she'd tried to fight was the suspicion that she was nothing more than Liam's flavor of the month. Since yesterday afternoon, she'd had to confront the fear that maybe she'd been much more, and she'd thrown it away like foul-smelling rubbish. Work with him again? She couldn't even hear his name without feeling sick with regret. She choked out, "I can't. That's why I'm handing in my resignation."

Her grip tightened around the water glass until she feared it might shatter. "I'm so sorry I've disappointed you. I can't thank you enough for the opportunity you gave me, and I can't apologize enough for dragging Kijani into the mud with me."

Charlie drew in a deep breath and finally gave her his full, piercing attention. "What are you talking about?"

"I know you've been concerned about being linked with the notorious Titless Tess, Scourge of the City, Radical Feminist Freedom-Fighter, or whatever they're calling me this week. I tried to keep everything a secret so Kijani wouldn't be affected, but in the end I fucked up anyway. I'm so sorry."

His eyes rolled. "God, you're such a muppet. I haven't looked at the figures today, but I'd be willing to bet our web traffic and online bookings go *up* this weekend. If anything, you've given us the kind of publicity money can't buy. Now that people know you and Callaghan met in Venezuela, I'd be surprised if our solo backpacking trips don't fly off the virtual shelves. Thanks for that."

Tess blinked, her brows drawing together over her pounding headache. "And people know I met him in Venezuela how?"

One corner of Charlie's mouth quirked up. "I'm not a fool, Tessy. When life hands you a golden PR opportunity, you don't just grab it. You latch on and suck it for all it's worth."

Tess tried not to vomit at the mental image. "So, if you're not worried about Kijani, why do you forbid work relationships?"

"Because I don't want anyone to get their fucking heart ripped out! Mixing work with pleasure does nothing but ruin good solid business relationships. Do you have any idea how hard it is to work with someone when you get sick with longing every time you look at them?"

No. She didn't. "I know what it's like to work with someone when you get sick with revulsion every time you look at them."

"It's not the same. It's approximately five million times worse."

Yeah, that didn't surprise her. All night, the mental image of Liam's face had kept her from falling asleep. Every time she'd closed her eyes, she'd seen the flash of pain that he hadn't been able to hide from her or the photographers standing around. That expression had been a physical kick to her gut that she'd senselessly tried to drown in wine.

She collapsed onto a stool next to Charlie and dropped her face into her hands. "I hurt him. I can't believe I put my job and your idiotic contract above his feelings. No offense."

"None taken. And it's not idiotic. It makes perfect sense. I was just trying to protect the sponsorship agreement."

"And I was trying to protect you and me and him, and all I ended up doing was hurting everyone."

Charlie's arm wrapped around her shoulder, tugging her sideways against his chest. He pressed a quick kiss against her temple and held her close. "Don't worry about me, love. And don't hand in your resignation just yet. I'm certainly not ready to get rid of you, and I want you to decide what you're going to do next without the dole hanging over your head. If you decide you can't work with him anymore, I'll find something else for you. I promise."

Tess swallowed hard, but pride didn't go down easy. "I don't want a pity job."

"Fuck's sake, don't be daft. Cousin or not, I can't spare a salary on someone who's a waste of the office oxygen supply. You're clever and you've a ruthless business perspective few of my other staff do. You're good for us, whatever role you end up in. But you have more important things to think about now. What're you going to do about Liam?"

"I don't know. I hurt his pride."

Charlie snorted. "Hurt it? You fucking napalmed it. Have you seen the papers today?"

She scrunched up one side of her face in a "Sorta" expression, and he lifted his man bag from the floor, flipped open the flap and drew out a tabloid. Dropping it onto the counter in front of her, he said, "Look at the picture."

She forced herself to look. Only the headline—*Red Carded!*—and the top of Liam's head showed above the fold, so she flipped it open. The photographer had caught the expression that'd haunted her all night. Liam, with his brows drawn down and mouth slightly open, as if he couldn't believe the words he was hearing.

"I know that expression, Tessy. I've seen it in the mirror. That's the look of a man who's staring at his own heart and can't figure out why it's beating outside his body. Whatever happens, at least understand that he loved you."

She couldn't bear the look on Liam's face anymore, so her body conspired to hide him. Tears pricked Tess's eyes until he blurred and swam in her vision. "I love him, too. I can't believe how badly I messed this up."

An envelope dropped onto the newspaper, making Tess blink. "What's that?"

"Tickets. I already told your dad you have them, and he was so excited I think he just about pissed himself, so you can't back out."

Dread gurgled low in her belly. "Tickets to what?"

"The ballet," he said, irony dripping from his voice. "The World Cup final—what did you think?"

"I can't go to that! I've distracted him enough this week. My being there would totally throw him off."

"It's not like they're tickets to the changing room. He won't know you're there, but I think you need to go. You need to figure out how you can make it up to him. And don't worry about the fact that the producers will no doubt be looking for you in the crowd and make sure to show you on TV. Only millions of people will be watching. Including me."

Tess's brows shot up. "You? You're going to watch a rugby match?"

"You bet your sweet Fanny Adams I will be. You're going to look like a complete tit when you try to win him back, and—after the way you've been ignoring my calls—I can't wait to see it."

A few hours later, Tess and her dad stepped off the train with several hundred others and joined the swell of thousands making their way toward the stadium. Enterprising home-owners on either side of the main route had set up barbecues to sell burgers to hungry passersby, but even the tantalizing aroma of fatty grilled meat couldn't ease the knot making a mess of her stomach.

Her dad hadn't said anything about her current scandal since she'd met him at Waterloo. She'd gone there dreading his disappointment in her, but his silence on the matter was much, much worse. Instead, he chatted about the team selection and speculated on the referee's competence, two topics Tess would happily have joined him in if she could pay attention to anything other than manically scanning the crowd for camera phones pointed her way.

"I don't know about you, but I'm starving," her dad said as they reached the grounds.

"That bacon sandwich you had at Waterloo didn't last long, did it?"

He rolled his eyes. "Is that a hint of censure I hear, Tessy? Ooh, look! Kangaroo burgers." He grabbed her elbow and steered her to the side of the street, where a man was flipping several rows of huge burgers on a family-sized grill in his front garden. "Let's celebrate Australia's crushing defeat early."

She followed her dad with a resigned grimace and waited patiently in the queue next to him, trying to gently feel her way around a topic that had been brewing in her mind for a while. "Dad? Do you ever think about changing your diet?"

"What're you talking about? I *do* change it. I've never had kangaroo burgers before. That's a change."

"Not what I mean, and you know it."

He sighed. "Seriously? *You're* going to give *me* advice on how to make good choices?"

And there it was. The parental disappointment she'd expected. A bit delayed, but present nonetheless. Her fingers curled until the sharp clawing pain of her nails bit into her palms, a futile attempt to distract herself from the burning fear that had simmered just below her consciousness for as long as she could remember. *This will be the last straw.*

Except, forget straws. She'd been heaping great, heavy sycamores of disappointment on her parents since social services had first dropped her at their house. From raging temper tantrums that included flushing her grandmother's wedding ring down the toilet, to yanking a young Gwen's hair until her scalp bled, to being suspended from school for passing around that boy's unfortunate erection photo, to having a one-night stand that ended up publicly humiliating her parents. Where was the awards committee for Daughter of the Century when you needed them?

She trained her gaze on the kangaroo patties and let it go unfocused on the plumes of smoke drifting into the air. "I'm really sorry, Ben. For everything."

He reared back. "Ben? Who the fuck's Ben?" Grabbing her elbow, he tugged her out of the queue. Only once before could she remember her dad physically handling her, and—much like right now—he'd marched her down the street so he could lecture her in private instead of making a scene. She seemed to be the only one in the family who made scenes. And she did it well enough for all of them.

With his big hand wrapped around her arm, he gave her little choice but to stumble after him down a narrow road between two rows of houses. The hordes of rugby fans swarmed down the street they'd just stepped off, paying them no attention whatsoever. When they were far enough away to be out of earshot, her father stopped and spun to face her. "I'm Ben to your mum. I'm Ben to my colleagues. To *you*, young lady, I'm *Dad*. I always have been and I always will be. Got it?"

"I didn't mean any disrespect."

"'I didn't mean any disrespect, *Dad*,'" he repeated. "And respect isn't the issue here. You know I couldn't give a monkey's toss about that normally. No, this is about trust—or lack thereof. More specifically, it's about your distrust of me and your mother." His face flushed an unhealthy shade of rose all the way up to the roots of his pale hair, but he didn't give her a chance to react before his lecture continued. "What have we ever done to make you think we're not going to keep you?"

She gasped, her breath catching painfully in her chest. "Wh-what do you mean?"

"You know *exactly* what I mean. When you first came to us, we changed your nappies and cuddled you through nightmares. We taught you how to read and tried to protect you from everything and everyone who might hurt you. For almost thirty years, we've bragged on you to our friends and we've stayed up nights worrying about you. People just don't do that for kids they don't love."

His voice broke and he thumped his chest hard, as if to emphasize his point—or dislodge the emotion caught there.

"Tessy, you might not have come from our bodies, but you live in our hearts just as much as Gwen does. You are *ours*, little girl. And nothing you do will change that. *Nothing.*"

"I know...Dad," she finished quickly when one of his brows shot up.

"I know you *know* it, but it's not a matter of knowing. I wish to hell you'd finally believe it. You are no longer Countess Appleby and you never will be. Maybe we should've ignored social services when they warned us not to change your first name, but fucking hell, that is *not you.* You will never be abandoned by this family. We are *your* family, and you are ours. Now will you quit the hysterics and finally believe that?"

His hands gripped her shoulders, giving her a small shake as he bent forward to be as close to her eye level as he could get. If anyone was in hysterics, it was him...but she knew he wasn't referring to this moment in time. Like a near-death experience, her life flashed through her mind, playing a flickering film of rash decisions and thoughtless actions. She'd lived her life reacting hysterically to every conflict, and each time she'd expected her family to disappear on her. "Oh, God. You're right."

He rolled his eyes. "One would think you'd realize by now that I'm *always* right. It comes with the territory of being a father —like the annual Father's Day tie."

But his return to the sardonic father she knew and adored didn't make a dent in her moment of revelation. "All these years, I've been daring you to leave me."

His face softened into a gentle reprimand. "Not just me. And not just your mum and Gwen, either."

Liam too. She scrubbed a hand over her face and didn't fight it when her dad pulled her into a bear hug. "He must hate me."

Her dad took a moment to respond, and she thought her words might've been completely muffled by his chest. But then he pressed his cheek to the crown of her head and gave her the blunt fatherly insight she'd always underappreciated. "If he does, then what you did yesterday will make him more angry than hurt. But I suspect the opposite is true."

Hope blossomed in her chest. "Why?"

He hugged her tight. "Because I'm your father, and I can't imagine anyone *not* loving you."

When they finally made it to the stadium and found their seats, Tess discovered to her horror that their tickets were in the VIP section with players' families and friends. She recognized several of the men in attendance—all players who hadn't made it onto the England World Cup squad but who'd come out to cheer on their friends and compatriots.

Judging by the looks Tess was subjected to—ranging from disgust to loathing—they recognized her too.

She followed her father's lead as he ignored the judgment and introduced himself to the proud parents, wives and girlfriends sitting around them. Tess should've been one of those, wanted desperately to say, "I'm Liam Callaghan's..." but she didn't know how to end that sentence. What she didn't want to say was the truth that everyone knew anyway: *I used to be Liam Callaghan's secret lover, but now I've joined the ranks of women who've let him down.*

So she said, "I'm one of Legends' sponsors," and let them fill in their own gaps while she and her father pretended not to notice the frosty reception.

Thousands of people created tremendous noise, even though the teams hadn't run onto the pitch yet. The atmosphere brimmed with excitement and nervous tension. She wanted a win for Liam so badly a strange metallic tang spilled over her tongue, as if she could taste victory for him. Or maybe that was the flavor of her own defeat.

She tried to lose herself in the pre-match pageantry but was hit by a sudden longing. The players devoted their all to their sport, and their families sacrificed so much—especially time together and sometimes privacy. She wanted to support Liam, cheer louder for him than anyone else in the stands. She wanted to be able to stand up and claim him as hers. And she wanted to be worthy of him telling the world that she was his.

She wanted everything with him. To build a life with him at her side, sharing victories and helping each other along when life injured them.

She wanted Liam Callaghan—the man *and* the player. And if she had to risk rejection one more time to prove it to him, she would.

22

"It's time, men!"

The din of grunts, shouts and face slaps grew louder until everyone had gathered round to hear Liam's last-minute words of wisdom. "Lads, last time we faced Australia in the final, we lost in the closing seconds. That match was my first cap for England, and it made me puke to get so close to victory only to see it snatched from our hands in the final seconds. Make no mistake—*we* lost that match. It wasn't stolen from us. We let nerves get the better of us, and we gave them the win."

Somber, serious faces focused on him. They clearly hadn't expected him to bring the haunting defeat into the changing room. He wouldn't have, if Bailey-Boy had been in the changing room with them, since most of the country had blamed the team's loss on him. But Spencer wasn't here, and today Liam was speaking from the heart. This room, with these men, seemed to be the only place he could do so without being pitifully shot down.

"I don't know how many of you have been listening to the pundits for the last six weeks. They don't believe we're capable of it. They said we wouldn't make it out of the group stages, but we did. We'd get our arses handed to us in the quarter-finals, they said. Let's be honest—we had to fight hard to secure our victory. Lads, we've fought our way through every single match, and the prize is in sight. Do. Not. Blink."

None of them did. A sea of heads bobbed in agreement, every single man in the room gathering his thoughts into a single, determined line of focus.

"Concentrate, boys, and do your jobs better than you've ever done them before. Let's show those motherfuckers what it means to underestimate us."

The roar bounced off the walls and vibrated the floor. "Lean in! Lean in!" someone shouted, and they all gathered closer, arms thrown around each other's shoulders as they yelled together, "England!"

They walked silently through the tunnel, waiting at its mouth until the announcer called them onto the pitch. When they jogged on, it was to a hero's welcome and with the weight of the country's expectations on their shoulders. Oddly, that weight was lighter than any Liam had carried before. He was buoyant, floating on waves of anticipation as he lined up with his team and prepared to sing the national anthem.

Eighty minutes to prove himself. Eighty minutes to do the only thing he was good at, the only thing that gave his life meaning.

Eighty minutes to prove he was worthy of someone's faith, even if it was the faith of millions of strangers instead of the one person he'd given his stupid heart to.

This was the first minute of the most important eighty of his life.

. . .

SEVENTY-EIGHT MINUTES INTO THE MATCH, and Tess could hardly take her eyes off the game clock. England were down 14-16. They'd scored two tries, and Liam had converted them both. Unfortunately, they'd also given away a try and a few penalties, and the ball had been in Australian territory for the past ten minutes.

Tess had bitten her nails until one of them bled, and her dad grabbed her hand to keep her from doing more damage to herself. Or maybe he just needed someone to hold on to, since he was squeezing her so hard her bones might shatter any minute. He rocked back and forth, muttering, "Focus, lads, focus," every once in a while punctuating it with "Fucking hell, ref! Penalty!"

The ref never seemed to hear him.

Tess was beyond speech. Every fiber of her being swelled in hope for Liam, that someone on the team could gain possession —and keep it, for God's sake—and gain enough ground to be within Liam's kicking range. As the clock ticked far too quickly toward the eighty-minute mark, the three points a drop goal would give the team seemed the only chance for victory.

"Ball's loose!" Tess's dad screamed as an Aussie fumbled it. The whole crowd leaned forward, a collective gasp filling the stadium.

"Shit! Go! *Go!*" Her dad leaped up, taking her hand with him so Tess was forced to jump up too. The crowd around them surged to their feet, and Tess strained to see over the tall heads in front of her.

"What's happening?" Realizing she had no chance of seeing for herself, she stepped onto her plastic seat, ignoring the annoyed shouts of the people behind her.

"Penny's recovered the ball!" her dad shouted over the crowd just as she found the action again. The open-side flanker Eddie Penrose may have been only a few inches taller than Tess, but he was scrappy, fast and nasty as a hornet. He sprinted down the pitch, straight for a line of big-as-fuck Australians, as his team fell into formation behind him.

"Get it wide!" Tess yelled. Penny lobbed the ball backward to the number 8, who offloaded it seconds before one of the Australian backs flew into him.

"Late tackle!" she and her dad screamed. The ball flew from one pair of hands to the next, with the players gaining a few meters every time until they were in England's half and at the very edge of Liam's drop-kick range.

"Pass it to Liam!"

Her dad threw her a shocked look before turning back to the action and shouting, "Ignore her! Get it out to the wing!"

Tess nudged his shoulder against hers, and he grinned without looking away from the pitch. One by one the men evaded tackles until Liam finally had possession. Every muscle in Tess's body froze. She held her breath as he continued running a few strides, got within kicking range, faked out two—no, three—of the opposition, and ran for the try line. Ten meters, five meters, nearly—

Boom! A tackler at least five inches and two stone bigger slammed into him, both men flying through the air and landing with a sickening, bone-jarring thud.

The tackler rolled away, leaving Liam flat on the pitch just over the try line.

The stadium went mad, everyone cheering as they saw Liam's hand pressing the ball into the ground, giving England the victory. The crowd hushed, though, as the big screen focused on him, showing his arm ghoulishly twisted and his body completely still. Medics had rushed onto the pitch practically before Liam even hit the ground. Considering how many types of injuries they saw, their haste made Tess's breath seize.

"Get up. Get up," she whispered frantically.

Her dad's hand clamped harder around hers, squeezing the blood out, but she ignored the numbing tingles that came with the loss of feeling. She was suddenly too full of feelings—the sting of disbelieving tears, the cramp of a sick gut. The surge of adrenaline that forced her to leap away from the seat she'd been standing on, push past her dad and the two wives sitting next to the aisle and sprint down the stairs.

"Tessy! What the blazes do you think you're doing?"

Not for the first time, her dad's voice of reason made fuck-all dent in her impulse. She sped down several flights of stairs until she was at ground level and burst through the metal gate guarding the exit. When she and her dad had come for the London double header at the start of the season, Ruth had given them a stadium tour. She'd pointed out where injuries were treated and even let them poke their heads into the room. God, why hadn't she paid closer attention?

Head whipping from right to left, she jogged around the perimeter of the stadium, searching for anything familiar, anything that might help her—

There! A gate manned by a couple of beefy security guards instead of the average-looking ticket staff who'd all but abandoned other gates. Not wanting to look like a lunatic, Tess slowed down and forced herself to catch her breath. He would be all right. He *had* to be. Players were knocked out all the time. They almost always regained consciousness before walking off the pitch, groggy and concussed but still capable of walking.

Except when they couldn't.

She approached the guards. One stepped into her path. "Can I help you?"

Screwing her face into a politely beseeching mask, she apologized for nothing but politeness's sake. "I'm so sorry. I'm a team sponsor and I'm supposed to be part of the trophy ceremony on the pitch. Could you point me in the right direction?"

She had her ticket stub and pass out before he could ask and handed them to him. He examined them, then handed them back with a raised brow. "This is a hospitality pass for Legends Stadium, not Twickenham."

"I know. I'm one of Legends' official sponsors, but—"

He stepped aside. "Inside, then down the stairs. You'll come to a long hallway. Tunnel's at the end."

Shit, that was easier than she'd expected. Trying to keep the surprise from her face, she said, "Cheers," and walked through the gate he opened. Once she judged she'd cleared his line of sight, she ran again, down the stairs and along a corridor she vaguely recognized. She didn't have to worry about finding the medical room. A few men in England staff jackets were stepping out of a room close to the tunnel, and Tess tried to estimate the severity of Liam's injury by the way they moved or the looks on their faces. The darkened corridor threw shadows over them, though, and they were too far away for her to interpret their looks.

She gathered all her courage and forced herself to approach the room. Knocking on the door, she took a deep breath, held it...and was nearly blue by the time it cracked open with a stranger's face peeking through.

She blurted out the first thing that came to her head. "Is he okay?"

The man's forehead creased as he gazed at her with hard suspicion. "I don't just give out player information to anyone who asks. Who are you?"

"I'm Tess Chambers. I'm—"

A deep, rumbly murmur behind the man caught his attention, and he turned away momentarily. Was that Liam? Was he able to talk?

The man focused on her again. "I'm sorry but you'll need to leave."

"But I—"

"Now." The door closed, leaving Tess to fear something worse than rejection: that the murmured conversation had been about Liam's health, and that things had suddenly become much worse.

"He'll be okay," she whispered to herself. She was trying to figure out what to do next when a couple of shadowy figures stepped off the pitch and into the tunnel.

"He's just down here, Miss Hughes."

Tess stepped back as the two shapes became more distinct, morphing into a man dressed in official garb and a tall, busty woman with shampoo-commercial blond hair—exactly the kind of woman Tess had once accused Liam of going for.

"Thank you so much, Edward," the woman replied, her American accent carrying a worried undertone. Samantha Hughes, America's sweetheart.

Was she Liam's too? The man escorting the superstar seemed to think so. He rapped his knuckles against the door of the medical room. When it swung open, Liam stood in the doorway, and Tess's heart leaped to her throat. From this far away, Liam's features were indistinct, but a stark white bandage had been wrapped around his forehead, his left arm hung in a sling and he swayed a little as he grasped the doorjamb. But he was awake and standing on his own. *Thank you, God.*

"Special delivery," the security guard joked.

"Oh, baby! I was so worried!" Samantha Hughes threw her arms around Liam's neck and planted a big kiss on his lips. Liam roared with pain and pushed her back a little, his unbandaged arm wrapping protectively around the injured one.

Tess jerked forward to help him, but Samantha was already there, laying a gentle hand on his good arm and taking his weight when he swayed toward her. Tess shattered into a thousand million shards, each one an agonizing reminder of her own stupidity and loss. She thought she couldn't feel any worse than she had this morning. She'd been an idiot.

"Come in," Liam murmured. He tugged the actress's hand and pulled her into the room. The door clicked closed, leaving Tess alone. All alone with her stupid thoughts running wild—never a winning combination. She'd finally decided she wanted Liam and would give everything for a future where they fought in each other's corner. But maybe she was too late.

As she stared down the tunnel, she saw the light at the end. Literally. The organized chaos on the pitch beckoned her. The teams and stadium staff were preparing for the trophy ceremony. She could only hope everyone was focused on their own jobs without really paying attention to anything else going on around them.

Squaring her shoulders, she made her way toward the pitch. If anyone knew how to publicly humiliate themselves for the greater good, it was her. Of course, she'd never done it purposefully before, and she really only wanted one man's attention. But today she was a beggar, not a chooser. She had publicly rejected him. The only way to make things better was to proudly, publicly, share her feelings. She began formulating a plan to get Liam—and the rest of the world—to listen.

Bright light pierced her eyes as she stepped onto the pitch. She blinked it away and, when she could see again, scanned the field for ideas. And there it sat, unguarded and just begging for her to pick it up. The match ball.

Next to her, a cameraman fiddled with his equipment. She tapped his arm and said, "Hiya. I'm Tess, one of the PR people here. There's a slight change of plans to the ceremony schedule. Keep the camera pointed at me, and tell your producer to switch over to your feed when I get to the middle of the pitch, okay?"

She patted her pockets as if she was searching for something. "Damn. I forgot my mic upstairs. Do you have an extra in your kit?"

He nodded and bent to put together a microphone for her. She didn't waste another second with rational thought.

23

"Stop poking me. I'm fine."

Liam lied through clenched teeth as Dr. Bernard held one of his eyelids up and blinded him with a penlight. Doc Bernie leaned close enough to headbutt, and Liam's mood was so foul he was tempted to do it.

"You need to lie down, Liam. You're concussed."

He wasn't mentioning the shoulder. He didn't need to. Liam had dislocated it twice before, but he would never get used to the sickening feeling of his bone protruding under his skin and the agony of having it jarred back into its socket.

The concussion made him woozy. The shoulder would require surgery and leave him watching from the sidelines for weeks, maybe months.

The thrill of knowing he'd led his team to World Cup victory was severely tempered by the searing pain in his shoulder. All his life he'd pictured the moment when he would hoist the World Cup trophy above his head and lead his nation in celebrating their victory. Fucking trophy was huge. He wouldn't be able to lift it one-handed. Not without it toppling onto his head and finishing the job that tackle had started.

Doc Bernie stepped away to write something down, but his place was quickly taken by Samantha.

"You look awful, Liam."

"Thanks, Sam."

She grimaced, her face falling into a carefully practiced expression meant to strike a balance between showing concern and avoiding the need for Botox later in life. "I just meant that you look like you're in a lot of pain. Can't he give you something stronger?"

He shook his head. Truthfully, short of knocking him out, nothing the doctor could give him would help. The pain was soul-deep. "What are you doing here, anyway?"

"I flew in last night. I was going to surprise you after the match."

The room's overhead lights made his head throb. He closed his eyes, but it was no good. More pain waited for him when there was nothing to block images of Tess. He wanted her here. He wished like hell she was here.

Fingers brushed high against his thigh, and Tess's image wavered then disappeared as Liam thought, *Please be Tess.* He pried his eyelids open and found Samantha staring at him with what seemed to be genuine concern this time. Maybe it was the concussion, but he'd forgotten she was there as soon as he'd stopped looking at her.

"Liam?"

"Yeah?"

"Don't you want to get out there and celebrate with your team? I could help you lift the trophy, if you want."

Ah. The real reason she was here. He'd wondered, and he probably would've figured it out sooner if his brain hadn't ping-ponged against the inside of his skull a few minutes ago. What a photo op, being seen with the captain of the World Cup-winning team, especially when she had a movie to promote. Too bad for her he'd had enough of being a publicity whore. He tilted sideways so he could see Doc Bernie over Samantha's shoulder. "Sign me off, sharpish. I need to get back out there."

He might need someone to help him raise the trophy, and his shouts when he did it might be from agony rather than cele-bration, but nothing would stop him joining his team on the podium, goddamn it.

Doc Bernie kept his head down as he continued scribbling notes, his voice placid as he said, "Don't worry, son. They're delaying the ceremony a few minutes to give you a chance to unscramble your brains before you go out. I just need to make sure you can do it without taking a dive headfirst off the podium."

Liam exhaled a gust of frustration and tried to block out Samantha's chatter. Obviously he should've been clearer that he wasn't interested.

He tried to concentrate on bringing into focus the small TV across from the treatment bed. The volume had been turned down to a low buzz, but he could still make out the sound of commentators talking bollocks, clearly trying to kill time while everything was set up on the pitch. There were his mates, hugging and laughing. There were the Aussies, weeping. There was Tess, picking up a ball and walking to the center of the pitch.

Liam blinked. "Bernie, how badly did my brain get bruised?"

"Well, you're still conscious, but you'll need someone to keep an eye on you the next couple of days. Why?"

Because he was hallucinating. Surely he was hallucinating. He blinked again as he detected a change of tone in the commentators' voices. "Turn the volume up."

Samantha grabbed the remote and pushed a button until the commentators became more distinct.

"...hearing a rumor there's been a slight change in plans,

other than our brief delay while captain Liam Callaghan receives treatment, but we're not quite sure what that change is. Alan, do you have any idea who that young woman is?"

"Not a clue, but we're checking and...hold on. The security staff seem to be perking up."

Fucking hell. The camera caught several beefy guards standing on the sidelines pressing their earpieces deeper into their ears. They watched with hooded hawk eyes as Tess lined up twenty meters from the uprights and bent over to push a kicking tee into the grass.

"We're not sure, but this young lady doesn't seem to be an official part of the program."

Tess straightened up and raised a microphone to her mouth. It echoed as she tapped it a few times. "Can you hear me? Hello?"

She must've received a nod from the cameraman because she drew her shoulders back and looked directly at him through the TV. "I'd like to announce the Man of the Match—but he's much more than that. He's the best man I've ever met, a man I don't deserve but would gladly work hard to be worthy of. Liam Callaghan, I—"

As always happened when someone illegally invaded the pitch, the camera cut away to discourage other idiots from trying the same thing in the future. But before the picture changed to show England supporters singing "Swing Low, Sweet Chariot" in the stands, Liam caught a glimpse of guards leaving their posts and jogging toward the pitch. Toward Tess, who might be mouthy but couldn't back that mouth up with much brawn.

Liam leaped off the treatment bed and nearly collapsed as the room spun around him. Without waiting for his head to clear, he stumbled in the general direction of the door.

"Liam! Wait!"

He ignored Bernie and fumbled with the doorknob until he

jerked the door open. Pain ripped through his shoulder, and he clasped his good hand against it to keep it from jarring too badly as he ran through the tunnel and onto the pitch. The daylight nearly made his eyes explode and the movement in his shoulder made him want to puke, but he kept going, so familiar with the pitch that he didn't need to see well or even be fully conscious to know exactly where Tess stood, mimicking his stance as she glanced between the ball and the posts, judging the distance like she was about to kick a penalty. Even if he hadn't known right where she was, the blur of movement from the guards as they rushed toward her would have clued him in.

"Tess! Hit the deck!"

He ran as fast as he could, but he was too late. She took a couple of quick steps and booted the ball just before a guard twice her size tackled her, smashing her face-first into the grass. Fury-fueled adrenaline numbed Liam's pain, and he slammed into another guard before he could pile on top of Tess too. The man was out cold before he hit the ground.

Liam turned his attention to the guard trying to wrestle Tess's arms behind her back. He planted his foot into the guard's unprotected side, just below his ribs, and shoved him off Tess before dropping to his knees next to her. With his knee, he nudged her onto her side. Her eyes were closed, and mud covered most of her face. "Tessy..."

Her eyelids popped open and her brows drew down in confusion before she gave him a dreamy smile. "You saw me."

"*Saw* you? *Fuck.*" The adrenaline seeped out of him, and he collapsed onto his back, feeling like he'd bled out. "I'm dying here, Tess. You're killing me."

She propped herself on an elbow and leaned over him. Her suddenly serious face filled his vision. "Liam, I'm so sorry. That's all I wanted to tell you."

His nostrils flared. "That's it? That's all you wanted to tell me?"

"Um, well, there was one other thing, but judging by your crazy eyes I'm not sure you're ready to hear it."

"I swear to God, it'd better be *I love you* or we're going to have words, you and I."

A tentative smile touched her lips before they spread into a grin that eased his pain better than any cortisone jab. "Maybe you *are* ready to hear it."

She cradled his cheeks and laid her lips against his, kissing him long and luscious until the remainder of his pain journeyed south and he was in danger of embarrassing himself by sporting a very public erection under very short shorts. He pulled his head back as much as he could, considering he was flat-out in the muddy grass, and murmured against her lips, "Tessy."

"Hmm?"

"You still haven't said the words."

Her breath warmed him as she chuckled. "I love you, Liam."

"Good. I love you too, and you can stop pulling this crazy shit because nothing you do can scare me away. Not after this." He tried to lift his arms to pull her closer but ended up growling instead. "Fucking hell. Do you see a gray-haired bloke standing by the tunnel watching us, probably glowering?"

She lifted her head. "Yeah."

"Wave him over here. I think I dislocated my other shoulder hitting that security guard."

Tess gasped and rolled off him, motioning frantically toward Doc Bernie. Liam couldn't keep the stupid grin from his face, though, as the medics surrounded him for the second time and prepared to deliver another dose of torture. Bernie clasped his arm and said, "This is going to hurt, son."

Liam turned his head to find Tess kneeling next to him, muddy-faced and with a bloody scratched hand pressed to her mouth. "Kiss me, Chambers. I don't want anyone to hear me scream."

She wrapped her arms gently under his head and pressed her forehead against his. "I love you," she said again, and joy shot through him just in time to protect him from the wrenching jolt of agony.

EPILOGUE

ater slid over Tess's skin, cooling the pink burn she'd received during the paddleboarding lesson she and Liam had taken this afternoon. They'd been in Venezuela for two days—not long enough to get over jet lag, so she'd left Liam sleeping upstairs and wandered down to the beach where the sea had beckoned her. She scissored her arms and legs in a few breaststrokes before flipping onto her back and floating lazily. The midnight crescent moon shone down on her, painting her naked body with light and shadows.

Was Liam watching from their balcony? Probably. She'd deliberately closed the door with a loud click when she'd left ten minutes ago.

The past year had flown by. While Liam recovered from his shoulder surgery, Tess had looked after him. Gradually, more of his stuff had begun appearing at her house. Piece by piece, he'd colonized her drawers until he'd offered to buy her a bigger wardrobe to fit his clothes too. Soon, they would have to negotiate the possibility of selling one of their homes. But for now, Tess was content to snuggle with him every night he wasn't out of town for a match.

Water gurgled in Tess's ears and a current rushed underneath her, alerting her too late to the presence of a big creature. She twisted and kicked toward the shore, but two arms grabbed her around the waist and dragged her under. Salty water closed over her face and flooded her mouth as she gasped at the wrong time.

She kicked again, connecting with a hard, slick body, and suddenly she was free to shoot to the surface. She spat out the water and shook her head, pushing wet hair out of her eyes. Liam's head popped up in front of her, just in time for her to draw back her hand and slice it through the water, spraying him with a wave. "Liam! You scared the shit out of me!"

He wiped the water off his face and gave her the mischievous grin that never failed to jumpstart her heart. Good thing too, since her heart had frozen in fear for a second there. "Sneaking off in the middle of the night to swim in a lagoon by yourself? Chambers, you don't know *scared*—but you will, 'cuz I'm renting *Jaws* as soon as we get back upstairs, and I swear to God you'll never go in the water alone again."

He tugged her until her wet body slid against his. Not wanting to unman him, she stopped treading water and wrapped her legs around his waist, letting him put all those muscles to good use and keep both of them afloat. Nuzzling the sensitive skin behind his ear, she murmured, "*Jaws*, huh? You sure that's what you want to do when we get back up there?"

His stubble tickled her neck as he kissed his way up to her jaw. "Why wait till we get upstairs? That sand looks pretty soft."

She glanced over his shoulder at the moonlit beach. "It's too bright."

He lifted his head. "Tessy, there's hardly any light at all."

"What if someone's looking? I really don't want to have sex pictures of us plastered all over the internet. Seriously." She'd gone ten months without publicly embarrassing herself. She didn't need to tempt fate.

Seeming to understand, he gave in with a quick kiss on the cheek. "In that case, let's get back upstairs."

"You want me badly, huh?"

"Yeah. That and, unlike you, I *have* seen *Jaws,* and being out here gives me the willies."

"Let's go back upstairs and *you* can give *me* the will—" A wave of water hit her face, and she sputtered. "Maybe I won't let you give me the willy after all."

He gave her a loud smacking kiss before launching her out of his arms. She swam to the shore, enjoying the last few moments of water slipping over her bare skin before she got to the shallows and stood. Covering her bits with her hands, she bent over and rushed for her T-shirt and towel. Liam's laughter followed her, but she ignored him, getting dressed so quickly that she would hopefully be only a blur to anyone who might be pointing a camera in their direction.

Liam's bathing trunks were plastered to his body as he emerged from the water, and Tess wrapped her towel around her torso just in case they ran into anyone in the lobby. They walked hand-in-hand through the hotel to the lift where they'd first met.

The doors slid closed behind them, and Tess cuddled into Liam's side as the buttons lit up. First floor. Second floor. She glanced around. Still no security cameras.

Her hand shot out and jabbed the emergency stop button. The lift jerked to a halt, and Liam groaned. "I thought you wanted to avoid a scandal?"

Tess dropped her towel, pressed onto her tiptoes and whispered against his lips, "I can't seem to help myself."

Score! Want to see what happens next? Subscribe to Kat

Latham's newsletter, and you can read a super sexy bonus scene where Liam fulfills Tess's fantasy!

ALSO BY KAT LATHAM

London Legends series

Knowing the Score

Playing It Close

Tempting the Player

Unwrapping Her Perfect Match

Taming the Legend

Wild Montana Nights series

One Night with Her Bachelor

Two Nights with His Bride

Three Nights Before Christmas

Wild Montana Nights: The Complete Series boxset

Standalone books

Mine Under the Mistletoe

AFTERWORD

Dear Reader

I hope you enjoyed being part of Tess and Liam's happily ever after. If you did, there are a few ways you can spread the love:

- Leave a review at your favorite review site.
- Recommend or lend this book to your friends.
- Ask your local library or bookstore to include it in their collection.

Would you like to be the first to know about my upcoming books, plus get bonus scenes from your favorite characters? Sign up for my newsletter!

I'd also love to connect with you on my blog, Facebook and Twitter.

Thank you for reading *Playing It Close*. If you'd like to find out what happens with Tess's sister Gwen, turn the page to read the first chapter of *Unwrapping Her Perfect Match*. I hope you'll enjoy Gwen and John's story, too!

With very best wishes,

Kat Latham

Praise for *Knowing the Score:*

"The book is funny and real and the dialogue is fantastic...I want Spencer. I want to marry this man. Not only is he patient and a sweetie, he's sexy as hell. Spencer should be cloned and mass produced for export. Britain would have a trade surplus that would be the envy of the world."
    -Dear Author

"This is one of the best contemporary romances I've ever read! I had such a fantastic time watching these two characters fall in love..."
    -The Season for Romance

Latham keeps her debut fresh, with characters whose unique careers play a role in their relationship, and the romance runs at a strong pace. Readers will be eager for the next series offering, Playing It Close...
    -Library Journal

UNWRAPPING HER PERFECT MATCH
CHAPTER ONE

The goddess wore a rugby shirt with the wrong number on it.

John Sheldon watched the woman walk through the door of the stadium's hospitality suite, where he and his London Legends teammates would soon be auctioned off for charity. Outside, snow blanketed the rugby pitch while green and white Christmas lights strung around the stadium blazed with the team's colors. Inside, rich people were getting pissed on mulled wine and whisky he'd never be able to afford under normal circumstances. John had been trying not to yawn when the woman entered the room.

Her height drew his notice first. How could it not, when the next-tallest woman in the room came to her shoulders? She was the only woman here who wouldn't make him feel like a towering giant. Her face was angled away from him, and her wheat-blond locks of hair had been twisted and clamped behind her head in one of those casually elegant styles that begged to be undone, mussed up by big, clumsy fingers. Her neck was slender, her shoulders broad, and her rugby shirt had the number ten on it. His captain's number.

An elbow jabbed him between the ribs, jostling the tumbler of Islay whisky he held and splashing the amber liquid across his hand. "I count three for me, a dozen for the skipper and nil for you, Shelly. What do you make of that?"

John set his tumbler on a table, tempted to lick the alcohol off his hand so it didn't go to waste. Opting instead for a classiness he usually failed to achieve, he wiped his wet hand on a cloth serviette and looked down—a good eight inches down—at Matt Ogden, who'd recently become the team's starting fullback. "Nil what?"

"Bidders." Oggie raised his brows and nodded at the crowd gathered in the suite.

John scanned the people who'd paid five-hundred quid each to be here tonight. They'd come to raise money for several charities by bidding on a player to do pretty much whatever they wanted for a day. Last year John had been "won" to teach a kid rugby skills. That was a lot better than the year before, when he'd had to show up at a stockbroker's office and pretend to be his best mate. How he'd got through it without lamping the arsehole was a mystery.

And Oggie was right—not a single person wore his number. At the start of the evening, guests received a replica Legends rugby shirt, and they pinned on it the number of the player they intended to bid for. It was an ice-breaker that gave the players a chance to change people's minds before bidding started. A good dozen guests, including the goddess, wore the number ten—not surprising, since his captain Liam Callaghan was one of the best-known rugby players in the world. But why in God's green England would three people want to bid for Oggie when he'd barely played until last month, while John had started every match?

Okay, so Oggie was a little above average height, while John was six-nine. He could see how that might intimidate people.

And Oggie was apparently good looking—if you asked him—so that explained why all of his bidders were female.

"Fucking hell," John muttered, the potential for humiliation sinking in. "I'm not standing up there and having no one bid on me."

"Looks like that's *exactly* what you're doing. Meanwhile, I'll have to let those three ladies down gently," Oggie said, his voice betraying the fact that he might be here physically but mentally he was back home, shagging his best friend Libby.

The specter of a crushing defeat loomed over John, and his determination to come out on top finally kicked in. "I may not get as many bidders as you, mate, but I bet I can raise more money."

"Really?" Oggie laughed and stretched out his hand. "You're on. What does the winner get?"

"Pride. Bragging rights." He held up his tumbler. "And a bottle of this whisky."

"Done. Now go do what you do best. Knock some heads together."

John knew right where to start. The goddess might've started the evening wearing his captain's number, but by the end of the night she would be calling out his.

Buy *Unwrapping Her Perfect Match* now
Also available as an audiobook

ABOUT THE AUTHOR

Kat Latham is a California girl who moved to Europe the day after graduating from UCLA, ditching her tank tops for raincoats. She taught English in Prague and worked as an editor for a humanitarian organization in London before moving to the Netherlands, where she now lives with her husband and daughters.

Never miss a deal!

Sign up for Kat's newsletter
Follow Kat on BookBub

facebook.com/KatLathamRomance
twitter.com/KatrinaLatham
instagram.com/kat_latham_books
amazon.com/author/katlatham
bookbub.com/authors/kat-latham
goodreads.com/katlatham

www.ingramcontent.com/pod-product-compliance
Lightning Source LLC
LaVergne TN
LVHW031428170726
843492LV00010B/2908